PENG

The Set-Up

After studying Mental Philosophy at Edinburgh University, Felix began his career as a writer for radio and television. A change in direction took him into the City, where he worked for the major US brokerage Cantor Fitzgerald. Soon after, Felix launched his own company which he later sold to MF Global in 2008, just moments before the financial system imploded.

During this time, Felix was a regular contributor and commentator for Bloomberg, Reuters, *The Times* and the *Telegraph*.

Felix Riley lives with his wife and two daughters in Surrey, England.

The Set-Up

FELIX RILEY

PENGUIN BOOKS

PENGUIN BOOKS

Published by the Penguin Group
Penguin Books Ltd, 80 Strand, London WC2R ORL, England
Penguin Group (USA), Inc., 375 Hudson Street, New York, New York 10014, USA
Penguin Group (Canada), 90 Eglinton Avenue East, Suite 700, Toronto, Ontario, Canada M4P 2Y3
(a division of Pearson Penguin Canada Inc.)
Penguin Ireland, 25 St Stephen's Green, Dublin 2, Ireland (a division of Penguin Books Ltd)
Penguin Group (Australia), 250 Camberwell Road, Camberwell, Victoria 3124, Australia
(a division of Pearson Australia Group Pty Ltd)
Penguin Books India Pvt Ltd, 11 Community Centre,
Panchsheel Park, New Delhi – 110 017, India
Penguin Group (NZ), 67 Apollo Drive, Rosedale, Auckland 0632, New Zealand
(a division of Pearson New Zealand Ltd)
Penguin Books (South Africa) (Pty) Ltd, 24 Sturdee Avenue,
Rosebank, Johannesburg 2196, South Africa

Penguin Books Ltd, Registered Offices: 80 Strand, London WC2R ORL, England

www.penguin.com

First published 2011

1

Copyright © Felix Riley, 2011

The moral right of the author has been asserted

Set in 12.5/14.75pt Garamond MT Std
Typeset by Jouve (UK), Milton Keynes
Printed in England by Clays Ltd, St Ives plc

ISBN: 978-0-241-95166-8

www.greenpenguin.co.uk

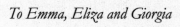

To Emma, Eliza and Giorgia

'I believe that banking institutions are more dangerous to our liberties than standing armies'

– Thomas Jefferson, third president of the United States of America

Things were looking up.

First Bank of America had gone from stonewalling me to setting up a meeting. And not just any meeting. A meeting with four of its most senior executives on a Monday evening. Why the big turnout for me? It wasn't the magnitude of my family's custom, that was for sure. I was forced to conclude that it was the perk of my job. Financial investigators were a bit like journalists – companies assume we can kick up a stink that could get noticed. Frankly I wasn't so sure, but you take your breaks where you can. Still . . . four senior executives? They were looking to settle this or kill the problem dead. Either way I figured they were about to show their hand, which was fine by me.

The setting was a plush boardroom high up in Manhattan's newest skyscraper. Commissioned in the boom days it felt somehow out of place – inappropriate – now the world had gone bust. Everything about it was expensive and pristine, virgin almost. From the warroom-length veneered walnut conference table to the Hamptonesque tea and coffee trolley, it felt like everything being used was being used for the first time. Like the wrapping had just come off.

When I entered the room I had been informed that the chief executive officer 'himself' had promised to try and join us on the video-conference screen that virtually covered the top half of the wall at one end. But for now the large hi-tech television showed an empty chair behind a desk in an executive office. If I knew the city correctly, the downtown view behind the CEO's empty chair suggested his office was somewhere above the current location. God forbid that he should ride the elevator down and join us.

Everybody in the room read the summary document I had prepared. Me on one side of the conference table, the four bank execs on the other. Me in smart leather jacket and jeans, them in tailored pinstripe two-pieces, the men with ties.

An owlish banker nodded sympathetically and took off his thick round tortoiseshell glasses with a sigh. 'Ah, another victim of Bernard Madoff.'

I gestured at the four people across from me. 'Actually, another victim of First Bank of America.'

'Sorry?'

'I don't quite follow you, Mr Byrne.' It was the unnecessarily attractive blonde. I assumed she'd been inserted into the meeting to make the client go all soft and gooey. They were trying to push the client's buttons. This client hated having his buttons pushed.

I waved at the improbably long conference table we were sitting round. 'My father didn't bank with Bernard Madoff – he banked with First Bank of America.'

'You're not seriously blaming us for the actions of Bernard Madoff are you, Mr Byrne?' said the Owl.

'Not the actions, no. But I am blaming you for the outcome. My father trusted you, and you put his money with Madoff.'

A likeable middle-aged male lawyer spoke next. 'Mr Byrne, you're not the only one less than happy with some of the things the banks – this bank included – have done of late, I assure you.' The group of bankers shared raised eyebrows and discreet rueful shakes of their heads. 'But, if I may correct you, it wasn't First Bank of America that put your father's money with Madoff – it was your father himself. We merely informed him of some investment opportunities then facilitated the subsequent investment decision made by him and him alone.'

I was OK with their feints – I'd been expecting this kind of beginning to the meeting. At the very least they were going to go through the legal motions. But they didn't have a monopoly on that game. I tried to keep the irony out of my voice when I spoke.

'Let's just be clear. Are you saying that my father called First Bank out of the blue to enquire about investing with Madoff?'

The Lawyer knew where this led. 'No, but –'

'Are you saying that he ever called this bank with any intention of investing my mother's money anywhere other than the long-term bond it had been sitting in? That *he* called *you*? That *he* initiated *any* phone calls? Any calls *whatsoever*?'

The Lawyer allowed me my run. 'No.'

'In fact, when he had little or no money – as was the case for the first sixty-five years of his life – did you ever call him?'

'No.'

'No.' I spoke very evenly, deliberately. I wanted them to understand how this looked outside of the cocoon they lived in. 'You called him for the first time when one of your salesmen saw the money that had appeared in my parents' joint account. He called my father – not my mother, mind, my father – and told him of the great returns Madoff was making and persuaded my father to cash out a safe, conservative, boring bond and move the money into the nice and exciting Madoff fund. Client monies which I believe Bernie Madoff paid your bank an unrivalled commission for.' I looked at each of them in turn. 'But, hey, why should that set off any alarm bells?'

The Lawyer winced at my departure from the clubby feel to the meeting. Then he put on his best empathetic look. 'Mr Byrne, we have reviewed the tape of that conversation and your father was made fully aware of the risks involved.'

They were stalling. They had come mob-handed to either cut a deal or close me down. Nobody was suggesting a deal, so . . .

'Are you seriously suggesting that every retired blue-collar worker knows the true nature of their investments?'

The granite-faced chief operating officer stepped in. 'Your father signed paperwork that told us he did.'

I took the measure of the COO and knew it would be dumb to underestimate him. My experience was that in any good corporation it was the COO – not the CEO – who was often the son of a bitch, the nuts-and-bolts guy, the drill sergeant beating the best out of the troops. This one was no exception. He pushed on.

'What Bernard Madoff did, Mr Byrne, was terrible but, legally speaking, your father doesn't have a case. To be perfectly blunt, nobody at this bank forced your father to invest with Madoff. Furthermore, Madoff's misappropriated funds are being handled by a court-appointed trustee. You're speaking to the wrong people.'

'No, Mr Oliver, you're just speaking to me the wrong way. You – like all the other feeder funds into the Madoff scam – have had the good fortune to see the spotlight land on Madoff himself to date. You're sitting there thinking you've dodged a bullet. I'm here to tell you that you haven't.'

The COO gave me an enquiring look. 'A bullet? Is that a threat, Mr Byrne?'

I smiled in a friendly but firm way. 'No. It's a figure of speech. But I also do literal threats. How about: I will launch a law suit against this bank for performing insufficient due diligence on Madoff and thereby putting its customers' money at risk?'

I placed both my hands flat on the table in front of me. The Lawyer seemed briefly distracted by something about them. Maybe because they were almost twice the size of his. Maybe because of the nicks and scars from a hundred different incidents. Either way, when he did look at me, he spoke sympathetically, trying to steer the room towards a more conciliatory outcome. 'The entire Madoff . . . thing . . . is a matter for review by Congress, the SEC and no end of regulatory bodies. Your case would be pending each and every review, and in the meantime we'd kill it. I'm sorry but it's true.'

'Fine. I'll launch a class action. I'm sure I could attract, oh, I don't know, a few thousand aggrieved First Bank investors.'

The Lawyer spoke again, but I didn't think his heart was in it. 'Class actions can be expensive.'

I gave the tiniest of shrugs. 'We'll fund it by shorting your stock.'

The Owl coughed pointedly. 'Are you threatening to manipulate our share price, Mr Byrne?'

I gave the executives across from me a sceptical look. 'You bankers, you see threats everywhere. I'm saying you have a duty of care towards your customers. And when I stick you four on the stand and explain to the twelve members of the jury that you sat there skimming commission off every Madoff investment, throwing your customers to the dogs, the verdict's only going to go one way. You know it and I know it.'

The COO was bottling up a brutal mood. 'As we have repeatedly said, Mr Byrne, we don't recommend investments here – we merely advise our clients of the existence of certain opportunities. After that it is their decision and their decision alone. In this case it was your father's decision. We have all the paperwork to prove it.'

I couldn't resist a small sardonic laugh. 'Oh please. We all know how these so-called investment opportunities are put together – it's about commission to the bank. The welfare of the client comes a distant second. Who does the due diligence round here, the interns? A jury is going to conclude that this bank is run by either idiots or charlatans and we'll get our pay out.'

Blondie interjected. 'Michael, you're making some very serious allegations here. Is it possible that the personal element in this has influenced your judgement in this matter?'

I fixed her with my best Shut The Fuck Up stare. 'Compliance, right?'

'Head of Compliance,' she replied with a smile that was pure Fuck You back at me.

I was momentarily thrown that somebody so young would be head of Compliance at one of the country's biggest investment banks. Maybe she was more ambitious – or able – than I'd first guessed. Either way I found her over-familiar manner grating in the extreme.

'Well, Head of Compliance, I'd worry a little less about my emotional state and a little bit more about why you felt Bernard Madoff's activities complied with your bank's investment criteria.'

The Chief Operating Officer was keen to nail myself and a meeting he clearly resented. 'Mr Byrne, we both know how this is going to play out. It's not going to reach court . . .'

That was a bold statement. Perhaps they were going to cut a deal, after all. I went to speak but he lifted a hand, requesting I hear him out.

'. . . It's not going to go to court because the SEC and First Bank believe that the public interest would be ill-served by spending the next decade in litigation with each other. That is why we'll agree to pay a fine and in return the SEC will agree to waive our liability for our involvement with Madoff. And that will be an end to the matter. Justice will have been seen to have been done. The politicians will be happy, the regulators will be happy, the press will be happy. And not one cent of that fine will ever come to you.

Ever. That's the way it's going to be.' He took a small pleasure in one final remark. 'You know it and I know it.'

I spoke calmly, matter-of-factly, but I wanted them to be in no doubt that I meant what I was about to say. 'Mr Oliver, you lost my mother's money and I will make this bank pay.'

He wore the kind of smile a man with a multibillion-dollar institution standing behind him wears. 'You want to take on this bank – let's see who wins.'

We stared at each other, the COO and myself, our positions on the table, our positions understood. A deal with the SEC? First Bank of America must already be in talks. They must know or be very confident of the outcome. They must have known they could tell me to go take a running jump into the Hudson. OK, fine – but now I was confused.

'If you're so confident you won't need to pay out on this, then why bother seeing me?'

There was a pause in the room, a pause I couldn't read. Everybody looked to the COO – for guidance.

'Consider it a professional courtesy, Mr Byrne.' He looked at me with an air of finality, like the conversation was over.

That collective pause bothered me . . . but perhaps it was academic.

'Well, for the record, I didn't come here for professional courtesies – I came here for my mom's money.'

9

I stood up and took my leather satchel from the chair next to me. Like anybody I wanted to deliver a great exit line, but '*Fuck you and the whore you rode in on*' wasn't going to help my cause any. I cast a glance at them. There was nothing left to say.

I left the room.

The four bank executives relaxed and grimaced in their own ways. The COO checked his watch and inwardly cursed every minute of the meeting. 'Why did Jerry ask us to see that guy this evening?'

The Lawyer was nonplussed. 'Said he was some sort of financial investigator. "Trouble" was Jerry's exact word. Said he could make things difficult for us. Said we should sit on him. Let's face it, what if he started digging around a bit more . . . ?'

A stillness fell over the room as they swapped slow nervous looks.

The Lawyer broke the silence. 'Mind you, that aside, poor guy. Taking it up the ass like the rest of them. Madoff . . . What were we thinking?'

The Owl spoke for all of them. 'We were thinking of the money.'

The COO's head was already filling with the landslide of corporate actions sitting in his in-tray. 'The quicker we cut a deal with the SEC the better. I don't want any more meetings like this, even if the customer is a financial investigator.'

The Compliance Officer had already moved on and was swiping an arm across the well-polished table before her. 'How about these new offices. That elevator was like something out of *Star Trek*.'

The Owl almost shuddered. 'I'll prefer it when we've moved in. There is nothing scarier in the world than an empty skyscraper.'

The COO couldn't hide his contempt. 'Correction. There is nothing scarier in the world than the *bill* for a skyscraper.' He shook his head then smiled with resignation at some kind of blackly humorous thought.

The Lawyer added some morbidity of his own. 'Like it will matter by Friday.'

They all exchanged sharp looks and their smiles faded away.

Then the door opened.

They all looked up. With bemusement.

It was me.

Pointing an automatic revolver at them.

Before anybody could do anything more than register horror and pathetically try to protect themselves by raising their hands I emptied the gun into them.

Calmly going from one to the other in turn.

Bodies freezing.

Bodies twitching.

Then bodies motionless. Except for the bullets ripping into them.

Smoke drifting out of the barrel of the gun.

The job was done. Then I left. Still without that great exit line.

The entire scenario at the First Bank of America offices had just been played back to me on a film shot from the point of view of the boardroom's video-conference camera. I had had to watch the very encounter I'd experienced for real the night before on an NYPD laptop. The camera set up to include the absent CEO had caught the entire meeting, from its officious beginning to its bloody end.

I was sitting in a police interview room in downtown Manhattan. Detective Ashby had paused the laptop we'd been watching the film on, sat back in his chair and grinned. He looked at the attractive Latino woman detective to his right like he wanted to say something, like he was fit to burst.

The detective grabbed the computer mouse and rewound the film to the moment where I had fired the first bullet. The frame he froze it on had a blurry flame coming out of the barrel of the gun. He pointed at me on the screen, he pointed at me in the interview room, he pointed at the interview room table. He'd just won the lottery and he *was* fit to burst.

'Mike – can I call you Mike?' He had a strong voice. The voice of a man who had survived the Bronx projects and made his African American parents swell with pride as he passed out of the New York Police Department.

'Detective, you're calling the shots, so I guess you can call me anything you want.'

'Mike, you're gonna have more prison visitors than any convict in history.' He imagined my name up in lights with his hands. 'The Madoff Murderer. When the networks play this you're gonna be the poster boy for every person who ever got screwed by their bank. And everybody's been screwed by their bank, right?' He looked at his partner for confirmation of his humour.

Detective Martinez was leaning against the wall, arms crossed over her chest, a cat-like smile playing around her lips. 'Is it even illegal to shoot a banker?'

This tickled Detective Ashby even more, who leaned back in his chair now. 'Not if you got one of them banker hunting licences, but they only give them out to Treasury Secretaries.'

'Shit. Did we ask him if he was the Treasury Secretary?'

Detective Ashby slapped the desk at that one. 'I was so busy reading him his Mirandas I just plain forgot. Sir, are you by any chance the Secretary of the Treasury?'

'Detective, I know that film doesn't look good but, you see, there's a problem.'

13

Detective Ashby grew mock serious. 'Oh, and what sort of a problem would that be, *Mike*?' Emphasizing my name, emphasizing whose party this was.

I spread my hands out on the desk before me, almost apologetically. 'I didn't do it.'

2

The two detectives went deadly quiet. They looked at each other to confirm that they had just heard what they had just heard. Then they both looked at me blankly. Then they burst into laughter. The pair of them. Ashby even had to leap up and pace off some of his excitement.

'You're good. Ain't he good?'

His partner gave me a smile that under any other circumstance would have been delicious. 'The best.'

Ashby was almost dancing with amusement. They were *loving* this.

I could understand why. The life of a detective is the life of somebody confronted by violent crime after violent crime, way too many of which don't get solved for lack of resources, lack of community support or lack of morale. To get an open and shut case that takes a bad guy off the street and helps the department get closer to some half-assed mayoral performance target is cause for celebration. Why not? If I was them, I'd be doing the same.

Detective Ashby wasn't going to let me spoil his

fun. He showed me a large evidence bag containing a visitor's badge with my face and name on it.

'Just which bit wasn't you, Mike? The bit where you signed in and had your visitor's picture taken in the lobby?'

'No, I'm not . . .'

'You mean, that's not you meeting with the four victims at the First Bank offices on the film we just watched?'

'No, I'm not saying that . . .'

'That wasn't you talking about dodged bullets and bullets they *weren't* going to dodge?' The light tone evaporating quickly now.

'The bullet was a figure of speech.'

Ashby looked to his partner for help in his mock confusion.

'What you think, Martinez – the Madoff Murderer or the Figure-Of-Speech Murderer?'

She played along, played like she was trying out both the nicknames in her head. 'Nah, I'm still going with the Madoff Murderer. It's got more of a feel-good factor about it.'

Ashby looked back at me. Smiling but not friendly. 'That wasn't you making the threat about making First Bank *pay*?'

'That wasn't meant to be a threat . . .'

The detective dropped his smile. Gave me a stare intended to remind me that beneath the rollicking good humour on their side of the flimsy table my ass was theirs.

'Really? Cos that sounded like a threat to me. That sound like a threat to you, Detective Martinez?'

She wasn't lacking in steel herself right now. 'Sounded like a big helping of threat, drizzled in hate with a side order of menace to me.'

'And she'll have that to go. She can eat it while we drag your ass over to the courtroom to complete this slam dunk of a case.'

Ashby adopted a basketball shot-making pose. 'Boom. Three seconds to go, the crowd are on their feet, can Detective Ashby put it in the hoop? He has the suspect, he passes the suspect, Ashby dodges the bullshit defence, the DA passes the suspect back, Ashby leaps into the air and – *slam* – game over, case closed.'

Still leaning coolly against the wall, Detective Martinez quietly mimicked an imaginary baseball crowd clapping and roaring.

Quite the pair.

I sat there thinking about my options. The film did not leave me a lot of wriggle room. And things were not going to improve when they found out who I was.

I straightened up in my chair. 'Look, Detectives, I know it looks bad, I really do, but I didn't come back into the room, I didn't have a gun and I didn't kill those people.'

Detective Ashby dropped his head into his hands.

'Don't do this, Byrne. Please. I got a wife and family to see occasionally. Just occasionally.' He looked at me through splayed fingers. 'Don't do the insanity defence. *Please*. Have some dignity. Think of your children. Do you have children?'

'No.'

'OK, think of somebody else's children. But please just let us wrap this up nice and quick. Could we . . . ?'

Detective Martinez crossed the room to join us, leaned in next to her partner and levelled an earnest look at me through her long Latin eyelashes. 'You cooperate with us, Byrne, and we'll make sure the judge is told all about it. You play ball with us and, who knows, you could be out in . . . ?' She looked to her co-conspirator for help.

He gave it some thought. 'Sixty . . . ?'

She wasn't buying that. 'Nah, fifty years tops.'

They both sat back and beamed.

They had me where they wanted me and they were going to have their fun. Fine, but that film was filling my head with questions. Questions that would be the difference between jail and freedom, life and death.

For some there's no end of reasons to kill people – hell, people got killed for staring these days. But it's not often that this much effort was taken to do it. Somebody had played a high-risk strategy for a reason. I had to find out who and why. And fast.

As I saw it, there were two ways this situation could

play out. On the one hand there was escape. But the detectives were unarmed. A pity. I could have done with stealing a gun right now. Also, I didn't want to hurt them long-term, which restricted my options. Either way I'd have to risk breaking something to disable them long enough to get out. Ashby would be fine but Martinez had a nose that rounded off a stunning face. Still, if I timed it right I could be out the door and out of the station before their fellow officers even knew what the alarm was being raised for. On the other hand, well, there was the case against me. Would forensics clear me by picking apart the film footage? Somehow I wasn't so sure. Certainly not quickly. Somebody had gone to a lot of trouble to fake my involvement, which meant they had probably gone to a lot of trouble to make sure it was top quality. Either way, waiting to be cleared by forensics was going to mean time – wasted time. And my gut told me that time was the one thing I didn't have much of here.

I sat up straight in my chair. *It was moving time.*

'OK, Detectives. Let's assume for a moment that I'm telling the truth and that the person who walked back into that room wasn't me and that I didn't do it.'

Ashby pulled a long amused face. 'Ah, the John Wilkes Booth Defence. "You see me with the gun pointed at the president. You see me using the gun on the president. You see the body of the president . . . But it wasn't me." Come on, Byrne, let's not do this.'

I brushed aside his scepticism. 'Somebody went to great lengths to kill some senior bank executives and to frame me for their murders. Not only that, the film shows a calm methodical killer, which suggests a very professional hit.'

Detective Ashby couldn't disguise the fact that he was suddenly seeing a more assured suspect in front of him and was suddenly not so sure how to handle me.

'Very good, my dear Watson. Use it when you no doubt represent yourself in court. Hey, Martinez, who did you say he used his call on?'

His colleague was watching me thoughtfully. 'His stockbroker.'

'Shit. You're up for multiple homicide and you're calling your stockbroker? Well, if you were looking for bail money, forget it – no judge is gonna let you loose on the streets before this goes to trial.'

Despite Ashby's disbelief I could see I'd tapped a little way into Detective Martinez, who reprimanded Ashby with a rap on the arm. 'Let him say his piece.'

I pulled my chair in slightly, getting into my stride now. 'OK, this wasn't a random drive-by shooting by some drugged-up gang member. This was as professional a hit as you get. It poses the following questions: why had the four people in that room been killed? Did the killer want to kill all four or, because they were all together, did he have to take out some unlucky bystanders? How long had they prepared to make it look like I did it? And why did they want it to look like *I* did it? Why me of all people?'

Ashby was eyeing me suspiciously, but I had Martinez's interest and she was willing to pursue it, if just out of curiosity.

'OK, let's say you didn't do it – let's say you were set up . . .'

Ashby didn't like the direction this was taking. 'No, Martinez. Let's bag it and tag it and give it to the DA's office. Every fruitcake theory we start to entertain now is paperwork I'm going to have to fill out. You know how slow I type . . .'

The Latino officer pushed on. 'If it was such a professional hit, then it doesn't make sense that they were "innocent" bystanders.'

This was better. I was leaning across the table myself now. 'Exactly. Which begs the next question: what did four Wall Street bankers know, or what had they *done*, to get themselves killed? Or, if it was purely to set me up, what do I know or what have I done to deserve getting set up like this? And let me tell you right now – in all honesty – I can't answer the questions about myself.'

Ashby was becoming impatient with the direction the interview had taken – and unsettled by my logic and calm.

'Martinez, before we start entertaining Walter

Mitty's pet theories on how the US government was behind the bombing of the Twin Towers, let's go with the evidence. We've got motive, we've got opportunity, we've got it on film and for all we know his jacket is going to come back from ballistics with more gunshot residue on it than a gangster at the Valentine's Day Massacre.'

I decided to put them out of their misery.

'As a matter of fact you will find gunshot residue on my jacket.'

'Are you jerking my chain? Martinez, is he –? Scratch that – he's given you a chain and he's jerking that as well.'

Martinez was filled with the irritation of somebody just made a fool of.

'Your jacket's going to show GSR but you didn't kill those four people yesterday?'

'That's right.'

She was pissed now. 'Then who the hell did you kill?'

'I killed four *other* people.'

3

The interview room was silent for some time. Ashby went to speak then changed his mind.

Martinez rubbed her eyes. 'Either we're going to solve eight murders today or the captain's going to re-assign us to Traffic.'

But Detective Ashby was already on his feet. 'Fuck this, Martinez, I'm getting the psych. He may be a cool customer but right now he's making the Son of Sam look like a model fucking citizen.'

'Maybe he's telling the truth . . .'

'Jesus, Martinez, not again!' He slammed the back of his chair, causing it to crash over. 'How many bad people you gotta meet before you stop giving people the benefit of the doubt? How many?'

Martinez was a strong character, but this got her blushing. I could see there was a history here. A history of him covering her back for her backing the wrong people.

'OK.' She stood and joined him. 'Back to the cell for you, buddy.'

'Where a nice doctor is going to fit you for a fucking Napoleon costume. Fucking fruitcake.' Ashby was seething. Fair enough. Every cop gets to the point where he's sick of every last suspect. Or just plain tired. Or both.

I hadn't moved from my place at the table. They were almost out the door when I spoke. And what I had to say stopped them in their tracks. *Froze* them in their tracks.

'Four bodies. Eastern Europeans. Tribeca. Third floor. I didn't get the exact address, but give me a map and I can point it out.'

Ashby and Martinez swapped a stunned look then slowly stepped back into the room. She took her hand off the door. Ashby strode towards me and leaned close into my face, close enough to let me know he'd been living on coffee and tacos for the last eighteen hours. His demeanour told me that if I fucked with him now he was going to forget for one second that he was a cop.

'Three, there were *three* in the apartment.'

'Did you check the dumpster down below?'

I didn't know if Ashby was going to punch me or scream with delight. He raced to the door and yanked it open. 'Johansson – get the captain. Now!'

I opened the door to my apartment. It was dark and the only light I was looking for was the one in my refrigerator showing me the way to the six-pack of Bud I had carelessly failed to finish the night before. However, I quickly realized the beer was going to have to wait.

I heard a heavy click and the unmistakeable feel of an automatic pistol on the side of my head. I stood still so as not to startle my intruder. The gun was pointed slightly up. Whoever he was, he was slightly smaller than me, five foot ten or eleven. Useful to know if it went that way.

A heavy Eastern European accent kicked in. 'Do exactly as we say and nobody has to get hurt.'

The only illumination was from the corridor behind me. I tried to count how many were present but everybody was keeping very still. Like they knew what they were doing.

The ringleader stepped into view, smiled, showing me a row of dirty teeth. 'Now, Mr Byrne, we can do this the nice and easy way or the not so nice and easy way.'

I spoke quietly and reassuringly, not wanting to cause any alarm or set off any jittery trigger fingers. 'Look, if this is about the rent . . .'

I heard three more heavy clicks and the glint of guns in the room.

Tough crowd.

The interview room was filling up. Along with Detectives Ashby and Martinez were Captain Novak and some kind of male desk jockey assistant. The captain had Hollywood good looks that seemed better placed on a salesman than a jaded departmental head, which is what he was.

The four of them stood over me as if I wasn't there.

Captain Novak spoke to his team. 'OK, Detectives,

good work. I want a full statement and this report completed and on my desk by end of play. As of tomorrow we are on a skeleton service until the weekend. If we can't hand him over to the DA by tonight then stick him in a cell for the rest of the week. If there wasn't such a body count I wouldn't even entertain this right now.'

In the presence of their glorious leader Ashby and Martinez were transformed into upstanding members of the NYPD, with a decided lack of levity from Ashby.

'The suspect is proving very cooperative, sir. We should be able to expedite this relatively swiftly.'

The captain looked at him dispassionately then looked at me with the Authority of Office. He reviewed some information contained on the clipboard before him.

Behind the captain, Martinez mouthed to her partner. '*Expedite?*'

Ashby mouthed back at her, 'Kiss my black ass.'

The captain looked up. 'Have we spoken to Organized Crime yet?'

Ashby was revealing the other side to his joker persona – the hard-nosed cop. A good one at that. 'I've apprised Organized Crime, the Marshals Service as well as the FBI of the apprehension of the suspect. They are running over his prints as we speak and I've promised to share all and any case notes as we collate them.'

The captain nodded approvingly. He eyed me, assessed me. Then, as if he had reached some conclusion in his mind, he took off his jacket without fuss, placed it on the back of a chair and sat down across the interview table from me. He took his time because it was his time, and once he was comfortable he spoke.

'Now, how about you tell me all about Monday night, Mr Byrne? How about you tell me what you were doing in a particular apartment in Tribeca?'

The blacked-out SUV idled to a stop down a back alley between two redbrick apartment blocks. A gun in each side, I had chosen to cooperate with their request that I go with them as their guest.

Once out of the SUV a small barrel-chested conscript type shoved me towards a dark doorway. I was marched at gunpoint up several flights of stairs in silence, using the time to take in my surroundings. They were grim. Very grim.

My hosts had not said much but enough to tell me they were Russian. I'd been to Moscow a few times on business, a long time ago, in a different life. On one occasion, as I was leaving, there'd been a snarl-up on the roads and the airport taxi had taken me the scenic route through some of their projects on the outskirts of the capital. This place was luxury by comparison. Maybe these guys were living the American dream here. Maybe they just wanted to show somebody what they'd done with the place. Or maybe they thought it was a good place to put a bullet in my head. I was leaning towards the latter.

We reached a third-floor landing where the ringleader

unlocked an apartment door. At the same time another door in the corridor opened and a tall young woman — looking like a down-at-heel early-era Madonna — stepped out. Her clothes looked like somebody had ransacked a wedding dress to make a disco outfit. But with the strikingly platinum-blonde hair and high cheekbones of what I guessed was an eastern Russian background, she pulled it off and then some. Not that I was in the mood to appreciate it. She greeted the guys with a disparaging grunt and took as much interest in the guns on display as she might somebody's shopping.

The Russians made no attempt to hide their weapons or step out of her path, forcing her to elbow her way to the landing. A couple of the guys tossed lewd remarks after her in their native tongue, which she answered with her middle fingers raised behind her as she walked down the stairs.

I was ushered by the flick of a revolver into a dimly lit room that had nothing to do with living quarters and everything to do with hiding out. The furniture was minimal and the décor decades old. I was invited by the same gun to sit on one of the living room's two battered couches whilst somebody turned on an equally battered television in the corner.

The barrel-chested Conscript settled himself into the far end of my couch, gun pointed at me. He stared at me almost unblinkingly. I could see he was overly alert. I guessed he was the newest member of whatever their association was, and therefore keen to earn his stripes with a display of vigilance. In other words, he was bad news.

The Ringleader calmly lit himself a cigarette. In fact, I'd

*noticed that everything he did was calm. This wasn't an extraor-
dinary day for him, this was business as usual. They hadn't
shouted, they hadn't made B-movie threats, they hadn't roughed
me up. They were very cool, very calm and very collected. They
were very bad news.*

Everybody in the interview room was waiting for my
answer to the captain's question. I had to suppress a
sigh, viewing this, as I did, as a slightly hopeless cause.
'I was taken there at gunpoint by four Eastern European individuals. I believe they were Russian.'

Across the room Ashby nudged Martinez and whispered into her ear. 'I told you he was good.'

She rolled her eyes.

The captain smiled at me as if to say, 'OK, I'll play
your game.' 'That must have been very distressing for
you, Mr Byrne.'

I overlooked the insincerity for the moment. 'It's
not my preferred method of spending an evening.'

The captain continued his performance. 'And did
they make their intentions clear? I mean, are we talking
ransom demands here?'

*Food had been sent out for and everybody was settling in before
the television. I knew enough to realize we were going to be here
for a while. Now I needed to know why. I didn't doubt I'd made
some enemies in the past – OK, plenty of enemies – but the
Russians?*

'Is there a reason you've brought me here?'

The Ringleader was sitting on the couch between a bear-like bearded Russian and another sporting a 1980s blond mullet. He turned his head to me, drew deeply on his cigarette and exhaled in his own time. 'There's a reason for everything, Mr Byrne. Maybe you were bad in a former life. Maybe you were bad in this life . . . ?'

He lifted an enquiring eyebrow at me. I was meant to get that remark. I was meant to understand what I had done, but what? What was it?

'I don't mean to sound slow here, but is this personal? Have I done something wrong to you?'

The Ringleader cursed in Russian for comic effect. It elicited a big laugh from his cohorts. He spoke with his thick Russian accent, but he spoke with charm.

'It's not personal to me, no. Let's just say you're here as the guest of a mutual friend.'

'Mutual? Will I be meeting this mutual friend?'

He played with smoke which rolled out of his mouth. 'No.'

One of those *mutual friends* . . . I looked around the room at a bit of a loss. I needed information, something, anything. 'Can I ask how long I should expect to be here?'

The Ringleader smiled at me. Everybody smiled at me. 'Check out is four p.m. on Friday.'

I went through the motions of trying to tell my story to the assembled officers. 'They said they were going to hold me until the end of Friday afternoon. Four p.m. to be exact.'

The captain looked at me curiously then back at his detectives. They all exchanged concerned but confused looks. He returned to me.

'Four p.m. on Friday?'

'That's what they said.'

'And you're sure of that?'

'Not much else was happening. I'm sure.'

'And when they told you this you just killed them all on the spot, is that it? . . . Or have I skipped a bit?'

I got cold stares from around the room.

Empty delivery boxes with half-eaten pizzas lay strewn about the floor. It was late and the television was blaring out some kind of World's Scariest Police Chases. *It had ignited a small amount of banter amongst the group who were rooting for the escaping drivers and cheering every collision with every innocent bystander. Even the Conscript had managed to take one of his eyes off me.*

'Could I use the bathroom?' I asked politely.

The Ringleader didn't even look up, but waved myself and the Conscript away down the hall. The Conscript was quite hooked on the show and left the room grudgingly, looking back at the television, pointing his gun after me.

I went down a hallway with wallpaper peeling on all sides to a shabby bathroom at the end. The Conscript stood guard outside. He muttered something to me in a dialect I couldn't follow, but which by its tone suggested he wanted me to hurry up so he could return to his show.

My escort hadn't performed a security sweep of the room before I entered so I was not surprised to see that the small, neglected bathroom had bars on the window. I half closed the door and took a leak for appearances' sake whilst checking all around me. No razor blades, no toiletries, no nothing. Just a naked bulb hanging from a wire that had been stapled along the damp ceiling.

I took the last sip of water from my styrofoam cup before me. 'It wasn't quite that straightforward.'

The captain clasped his hands together and smiled his best disbelieving smile. 'And just how straightforward was it, Mr Byrne? Because in my experience, and my experience is considerable, there is nothing straightforward about killing four men in cold blood.' His eyes were hard now, at odds with his smiling face.

I said nothing, didn't feel like playing Ginger to his Fred.

The captain read my mood and broke the silence. 'What do you know about the Odessa Mafia, Mr Byrne?'

Answering a call from the living room the Conscript shouted something to his gang down the hall then impatiently banged on the bathroom door.

'Come, come.'

'Sorry.'

I turned the light out and stood in the doorway, one hand behind my back as I tucked my shirt in. The Conscript checked me before a roar erupted from the others. He momentarily glanced up at the commotion. A moment was all I needed.

I swung my other hand out, smashing the light bulb into the front of his neck and twisting it. Instant astonishment. Instant laceration. Instant desperation. He briefly waved his pistol hand about, but knew he needed all his efforts to release my grip from round his neck and the jagged bulb-end I had rammed into his throat, the ceiling wire still attached.

I answered the captain as patiently as I could. 'Russian crowd operating out of Brighton Beach in the seventies before moving into the city, Los Angeles and San Francisco. But these weren't Odessa. This was some kind of new Russian outfit. Different.'

The captain's interest was piqued by my take on it, but he responded with an amused air, retaining his condescension. He believed that his line of questioning had one unavoidable result for me, and wanted to get to it, with a little bit of a show for the troops thrown in. 'Care to tell us why you were associating with this new and "different" Russian outfit, Mr Byrne?'

'Same reason I'm associating with New York's finest today, Captain. They turned up. Unexpectedly.'

Martinez smiled at that.

The Conscript dropped to his knees. Choking, he lurched into the bathroom. The hand holding the broken bulb crashed into the toilet itself. For good measure I flicked on the light switch.

His body arched briefly before falling between the toilet and the bath.

I knelt and took his revolver. A 0.50 Action Express Desert Eagle. Not so much a gun as a cannon. I checked the cartridge for bullets. Plenty. I punched it back into the gun. Perfect.

The captain took his glasses off with the air of a man who considered dealing with suspects like myself akin to swatting flies. 'And tell me, Mr Byrne. Do you always kill people who turn up . . . unexpectedly?'

'Depends on their line of work.'

The captain squeezed his lips together like he was fighting a smile. 'And what is your line of work, Mr Byrne?'

I took one step into the living room, directly opposite the three gangsters on the couch, the Ringleader in the middle. Each looked up slightly, then each flinched to see me standing with the gun pointed at them. Each tried to act in their own surprised way. But surprise meant chaos. Surprise gave me the edge.

'I'm a financial investigator at W. P. Johnson and Partners.'

The captain gave it some thought, like he understood some profundity in my answer that was missed by the others. He had the management thing down pat. 'Financial investigator? Audits, forensic accounts, that kind of thing?'

*

The blond Russian had his gun off the arm of the couch in a second so I fired a single bullet into his forehead. He crashed back into the couch like he'd been thrown there from across the room. The cannon in my hand decorated the wall behind him with most of his brains, leaving a hole in his forehead a fat man could stick his finger in.

I nodded at the interview-room table as the banality of my job left everyone nonplussed. The captain was enjoying his leadership display.

'Financial investigator? Real James Bond stuff.' He looked around as everybody smiled at his joke. 'And before that?'

The bearded Russian didn't have his gun to hand so leapt up from the couch to grab me. However, his first footstep was on an open pizza box that skidded from under him. He fell sideways between me and the Ringleader, taking the bullet meant for me.

As the bearded Russian dropped to the floor I blew a hole in the Ringleader's shoulder. His gun got thrown involuntarily across the room, leaving him consumed by the scorching pain spreading across his chest.

'Who sent you?'

He took a moment to collect himself. 'Fuck you.'

These were people who put the mafia above their own families. Answers weren't going to pour out. I stuck the barrel of the gun onto one of his kneecaps.

'Every wrong answer gets a bullet. Who sent you?'

*

I waited a moment before speaking to the assembled officers. 'I worked for the Treasury.'

'Who sent you?'

The pain was making the Ringleader struggle for breath.

'Fu-fu . . . Fuck y–'

Behind him I saw a reflected movement in the window. I leapt to one side as the Conscript, clutching his throat with a blood-soaked hand, threw a hunting knife where I had just been standing. Into the chest of the Ringleader.

I swung my gun at them both. But they had nothing left. The Ringleader was busy bleeding to death. The Conscript stood tee-tering in the doorway. Teetering then charging – charging at me, the last charge of a dying bull.

I sidestepped his attack, leaving him to hit a large open win-dow at full steam, where he rolled out, helpless to stop himself. After two seconds there was the deep metallic banging of a body landing on a dumpster down below.

I looked back at the Ringleader sliding down in the couch, fighting death, losing the fight.

Then it hit me like a freight train.

'I know you.'

He stared at me with a perverse pleasure.

'I know you. I've seen you. When have I seen you?' I was pointlessly grabbing him by the shoulders. 'Where? When?'

He tried another smile, but couldn't muster the energy. 'Fffff . . .'

Then he expired.

Damn it. I took in the carnage around me. One dead Russian on the floor, two on the couch and one somewhere in the alley down below. Four dead Russians . . . Four dead Russians and no answers.

The captain placed his clipboard on the table. 'The Treasury? How interesting. Any particular part of the Treasury?'

I had to get out of here. Eight people were dead and whatever I'd been drawn into was taking place as we spoke. It was moving time.

I looked the captain square in the face. 'The United States Secret Service.'

4

Think Byrne, think. What the hell was going on?

Why were people dropping like flies and why was I connected to all eight of them – if it was still only eight?

My reward for telling the captain about my CV was to be transferred to a holding cell. It was standard procedure to call in the Secret Service to investigate its own and I had to hope I'd get a better ride from them. In the meantime I had to figure out what or who had dragged me into this sorry mess.

For some reason my mind wandered back to the early days of my training, the quirks of history that had me ending up in the United States Secret Service. When people hear 'Secret Service' they normally think of men and women in dark-glasses, wires running into their ears, as they move in front of and behind the president. In other words, they think of Protection. I know I did when they approached me at college. I was quickly to learn that it was just a bit more than that.

The Secret Service was created by the Treasury in 1865 to investigate the rise of the counterfeiting of the relatively new US dollar. That was the whole point of it, to protect the fledgling currency. It took the assassination of President Abraham Lincoln and a few other attacks besides for Congress to formally request that the USSS take responsibility for protecting the president as well. Not until 1901, in fact – Congress snapping into action as ever.

The Secret Service was the United States' first domestic intelligence and counter-intelligence body but a lot of these powers were given over to the Federal Bureau of Investigation when it was formed in 1908. Protection grew, however, sped up by the various attempts on the presidents' lives, successful or otherwise, so that eventually the Secret Service was looking after the president, the vice-president, their wives, their children, presidential candidates, visiting VIPs, diplomatic missions, the whole of the White House itself – essentially all the people within the sphere of the president.

Meanwhile the Secret Service's financial investigation remit was being expanded. By the beginning of the twenty-first century its mission encompassed fraudulent credit cards, telemarketing, identification theft, cyber crimes, transnational crimes by organized crime or terrorists and any crime involving a federally insured financial institution – which these days seemed like just about every financial institution. My life in the Service was far from dull. But my life in the Service was over. A long time ago. Yet if I thought leaving the

United States Secret Service had put all my problems behind me I was clearly mistaken.

But that was almost ten years ago. How could there be a connection?

Think, Byrne, think.

At W. P. Johnson I was currently investigating a children's hospice where the boss, a priest, was concerned the financial director might have embezzled as much as $20,000 from the charity. It had taken a lot for the priest to approach us as he had enjoyed a twenty-year relationship with the finance director and was godfather to both of his children. Well, I was going to put the priest's mind at ease: not only was the finance director embezzling – he had been doing it to support his long-term and now-pregnant mistress. And the amount he'd stolen? Try $285,000 plus loose change.

Percentage chance of the finance director knowing this and/or calling in the Russian mafia? Zero. He was small time and would be enjoying the company of the NYPD blue before the month was out. The only question unanswered by my hospice investigation was whether the prison authorities would allow my finance director to wear his toupee on the inside. Personally, I'd ditch it. Why look more womanly than you had to.

Think.

Life as a financial investigator at W. P. Johnson was tolerable for one reason and one reason only – I could come and go as I pleased. Nobody questioned my results so nobody questioned my methods, and because I did most of my work on the web it didn't matter where I was based. My days were fairly standard. I invariably worked from my loft apartment in Brooklyn, followed by a possible trip to the office in Lower Manhattan, a little checking up on subjects of investigations, followed by a gym trip and your typical book, music and food shopping.

At 5.45 a.m. Tuesday I'd woken up in my apartment in a foul mood. The night before I'd attended a meeting at First Bank of America only to discover that they were cutting a deal with the regulators that would, effectively, see them escape liability for their involvement with Bernard Madoff – and any requirement to compensate investors, specifically my parents. Then I'd been kidnapped by Russian gangsters. Not your average New York day.

Think.

Today was Wednesday, what time I wasn't sure. One thing I was sure of was that time was slipping away. What had I missed? What had happened?

I lay down on the bunk bed in the cell.

Think.

Yesterday. By six a.m. I was showered and enjoying my first cup of coffee of the day. That was my ritual. That was my life. Except today I wasn't going to look at a W. P. Johnson case file, today I was going to start a new case file labelled 'Mike Byrne'. Who was sending Russian heavies after him? Who wanted him out of the way till Friday? What was the significance of Friday? Why me?

When a crime has just been committed the evidence is as fresh as possible. The trail of whoever was behind my kidnapping was the hottest it would be. But I couldn't go back to the Russians' apartment to look for clues until the police were out of the way – if they even knew about it by now. That made my investigation ten times harder. Still, I wasn't without the wherewithal to get started. I still had access to my former employer's database.

There is a common misconception about 'back doors' into IT systems. People often think that they are built by a maverick geek on the software team who dreams of striking gold with a clever spot of blackmailing or by selling on their employer's secrets. But back doors into systems typically exist for two other reasons. The first is that IT guys use them as the quick way in when they're actually building the system – rather than biometrically testing themselves every time they want to change the colour of a font. The other reason is that IT guys like an emergency entrance when a fault in the preferred way in locks everybody out. The only thing is, when the system is finally signed off, IT guys either forget about the back door or keep it as their preferred way in. And if you know the right IT guy it's not long before you know his way into the system. And I always made sure I knew the right IT guy. Gotta love a geek.

So I hit the Secret Service database – only to hit a brick wall. Six hours of referencing and cross-referencing every criminal emanating out of Russia yielded nothing, *nada – nichego*. There was no shortage of States-side suspects being monitored by the various agencies but nobody matched the profile I was running through the system. Nobody was shaking down the banks, nobody was kidnapping to order – nobody was doing what had just been done to me. I studied the notepad where I had written down a list of Eastern Europeans on the various agencies' Watch Lists. It didn't feel like much. What to do? Call it in . . . ? Yet my instincts told me that if I called it in to the police, or even the Secret Service, that bureaucracy would steal the very time I needed to find the Russians before they got the hell away. I wasn't awash with ideas.

But doorstepping suspects would have to wait for now. I was off to Greenwich Village. I was meeting my old boss, Diane, for lunch and I didn't want to be late because . . .

'Time is tight,' she said as she slipped into the chair opposite me.

'Not as tight as those pants. I don't know what it is, Diane, but you've got *it*.'

She pulled a face that was a mix of pleasure and embarrassment. Diane Mason, twenty-five years in the Service with ebony good looks that women of forty would kill their plastic surgeons for. After a particularly drunken lunch a few years back I had made a complimentary crack about her large breasts. She had groaned, explaining that they were the first and last reason too many men were interested in her. I had cringed at my own lack of thoughtfulness then. But it had broken the ice and I was able to drop the 'boss thing' that had overshadowed our annual lunches since I'd left the agency.

'Yeah, well, I don't see *Vogue* smashing down my door, do you? Can we just say that they weren't this tight on the store mannequin – but then I guess she wasn't living on a diet of doughnuts and adrenaline.'

'Hmm, yeah, I'd heard Krispy Kreme had introduced that combo.'

She smiled.

'Diane, you're all woman. There's nothing sexy about anorexic chicks. They look good in magazines but you wouldn't want to hug one at night.'

She picked up the menu to push proceedings on. 'Well, I wish somebody would hug me at night.'

I went to say something then got tongue-tied

remembering that I'd always wondered about her private life. No mention of men, even casual dates. Nothing. I knew it was the Secret Service, but *that* secret? Was she a lesbian? If she was, there were some lucky ladies out there. *Careful, Byrne, or you'll be daydreaming through lunch* . . .

'So, why the pant-tight schedule?'

She raised a warning eyebrow at me. 'I'm heading up the Advance Party for the president's visit to New York this week.'

'UN?'

'No, a ground-breaking with the Chinese premier. They're building a new skyscraper to house the Bank of China's American HQ in – of all places – Wall Street.'

'Ouch. The Leader of the Free World *and* the Leader of the Not-So Free World at the same time.'

'Tell me about it. It's bad enough liaising with our people let alone with an army of Chinese bureaucrats.'

'Do you speak Cantonese?'

'Mandarin, dah-ling.'

'I sit corrected. Do you speak Mandarin?'

'*Da jia hao.*'

'What does that mean?'

'It means, "I've learnt one phrase to show I have nothing but respect for your peoples and culture, now can we speak English and agree on how *not* to have either of our guys killed." ' She looked over the menu. 'Shall I order for both of us? I'm going to share yours anyway.'

Diane ordered some Italian food to go with our espressos and tap water. No drunken faux pas this year.

'So how come you're heading up the Advance Party? Why haven't they given that to somebody in Protection?'

She gave me a not-so-humble smile. 'What can I say, Michael – they wanted the best.'

I let her enjoy the moment, but just for a moment. 'And the real reason?'

She shrugged. 'Since they created the Department of Homeland Security we've been playing Musical Restructuring Chairs. The New York field office is now merged with New Jersey. We're now the – wait for it – NYECTF.'

'Let me guess . . . New York Electronic Cyber . . .'

She recoiled in jest. 'Nooo.'

'Crimes – The New York Electronic *Crimes* Task Force.'

'You do pass Go, you do get $200.'

I smiled at her quip. We started on our food. In the pause I found the events of the night before, my surprise party thrown by the Russians, tugging at my reason. Should I say something? How would she react? Who would I get, Diane the friend or Mason the agent? I was uncertain how to proceed so I put it to one side. For the moment. Because, for the moment, there was something else I wanted to broach.

'Seriously, though, Diane – and no offence – but why you? This is a Protection gig?'

She sipped on her water. 'What Carlton wants Carlton gets.'

Incredulity overcame me. '*Carlton* chose you?'

'The man himself.'

I looked around the cafe with its bohemian diners, shaking my head ruefully.

'You know he's a prick, don't you.'

'I am aware of his shortcomings, Michael.'

'His shortcomings are that he is a prick.'

'You have made me cognizant of this opinion on numerous occasions.'

'It's not opinion, Diane, it's fact. Newton's Fourth Law. Plus – he hates you.'

'Correction, Michael. He hates *you* and I stood up for you. I was merely in the line of fire. Collateral damage.' Understatement of the century – and for a fleeting moment there was a motherly look, but the arrival of the food knocked it away.

I bit into a buffalo mozzarella and sundried tomato sandwich, taking the time to think. I wanted to be delicate about the next thing I was going to say. 'Diane.'

'Hmm?' spoken through a three-cheese omelette.

'You're not Protection, Diane – you're Investigations.

And you're heading up *protecting* the president and his Chinese counterpart. Has the department been *that* restructured?'

She was keen to allay my suspicions. 'No, Carlton just wants to bring me on. There's nothing more to it, really. We discussed it – at length. Listen, he's up in Washington now, deputy director of the Service. Mark my words, in two years he'll be deputy director of Homeland Security. You can be a prick and still need to develop the team beneath you.'

I toyed with my sandwich.

'Michael, what?'

'Nothing.' But I didn't want to look at her.

She sat back in her chair exasperated. 'What are you saying? That Carlton wants me to drop the ball? That he wants the president whacked on my watch? Have you lost the plot . . . ?'

'Diane, I'm not saying that . . .'

'Then what are you saying?'

'I'm *saying* that you should be careful. He's wanted your scalp since before you started taking bullets for agents like me. Somebody could attempt a botched attack on the president or Chinese premier and it'll be your neck on the line.'

'That's generally the idea with Protection, Michael. If I don't protect, I carry the can. There's a better model I haven't heard about?'

'I mean –'

She was giving me that 'And?' look that drove me so mad. Because it was generally correct.

'I mean, be careful, that's all.'

She let the tension go out of her and returned to her meal. Well, my meal, since she had swapped plates with me. 'Michael, don't let your hate of Carlton blind you. He may be an egotistical power-crazed careerist but he loves his job.'

I sighed. 'I'm sorry, Diane. I'm off my game today. I saw First Bank of America last night . . .'

'Your father's money –'

'My *mom's* money, my *dad's* decision.'

'Sorry, I forgot. How did it go?'

I could feel my shoulders sag. 'They're cutting a deal with the SEC.'

'Will your mother be compensated?'

'I'm not sure. No. I don't know. It just got a lot harder, that's for sure. Impossible maybe.' I shook my head. 'Just gets me so angry.'

'The banks getting away with it every time?'

'No, my dad.'

'Your father?'

'Yeah, I mean, the whole thing with Mom, first and second time around. Blowing *Mom's* retirement pot. I mean, he just fucks up everything he touches.'

'He didn't fuck you up.'

I looked up to read her face and saw a broad and way-too-innocent grin. We burst out laughing.

'Parents, Michael.'

'Madoff.'

'Bankers!'

'Is there anybody decent left?'

'Just you, me and the US Secret Service.'

We raised our tap water and chinked the glasses.

'To the good ole Secret Service.' I looked up. Diane was staring intently at me. 'Oh, don't give me that look.'

She was all innocence. 'What look?'

'That look. That look you give me at this lunch every year.'

'It's not a look, Michael, it's a reality. The Service needs people like you. Come back. You're good, Byrne – you're really good.'

'No.'

'Please –'

'Not whilst it's got people like Carlton in it.'

'Carlton is not the Secret Service, Michael. Look –'

'No . . .'

'Hear me out. I'm setting up a Markets Abuse Task Force and I want you to head it. You'd be reporting directly to me – I'd keep you away from everybody.'

I gave her my best sceptical look. 'Don't write cheques you can't cash, Diane. Anyway, the Service only investigates financial crimes against the government, what's that got to do with market abuse?'

'Michael, the markets almost brought down the

government. Next time somebody puts us in that position we're going to make it their problem not ours.'

I pulled an uncomfortable face. 'I like my new life.'

'Investigating small-time embezzlers? "Ooh – ooh – somebody tell the commander-in-chief that the head of sales at the photocopy store has bought himself a new suit out of – heavens above! – petty cash!" Oh, come on, Michael, give me a break.'

I chuckled. She had me there and she knew it. 'Look, Diane, I've got an easy life and – and I can't be hassled with all the training, the firearm drills . . .'

It was Diane's turn to chuckle. 'Training? I've never seen you looking so buff. And don't feed me a line about having *any* kind of a problem with guns – there's nobody I'd rather have covering my back.'

I was about to demur but was touched by her last remark. It was just about the nicest thing one law enforcement officer could say to another. She was pulling my levers and pulling them well. But then my mood swung back to reality, the dark reality.

'Diane, I used to think that we did just about the most important job in the world. You know I did. And going after the financiers who were tearing the ass out of the system, Jesus, it was a holy mission to me. But after 9/11 . . .'

'We've never needed people like you more.'

'No, Diane. When we flew Osama Bin Laden's

family out the next day . . . ? Christ, we betrayed America. We betrayed every person who died down here –'

'Michael . . .'

'Our field office was the first on the scene. It was a fucking war zone down there, dust everywhere, people injured and dying, and us with nothing, but doing everything we could. America was under attack, Diane, and we had one lead in the whole world: the Bin Ladens. And did we detain them? Did we question them? Did we find out who did this to America . . . ?'

'I . . .'

'No, we flew them back to Saudi Arabia. As our guests. First class. The only civilian flight on September 12. The government asked us to solve the goddamn crime and then flew the evidence out of the country. It was like asking the Yankees to win the World Series without baseball bats. We sold the American people down the goddamn river, Diane. It was a joke. A charade. And if what we're doing is a charade then what's the goddamn point in doing it? I mean, really?'

She waited. Let the air calm between us.

'Michael, I don't disagree with anything you've said. I even started writing a resignation letter myself . . .'

'Did you?' I was taken aback. I couldn't imagine a world where Diane Mason wasn't in the Service.

She tilted her head towards me with a wry smile. 'Didn't you hear? There's other ways of resigning apart from punching Carlton in the face.'

There was a pause – then we burst out laughing at the memory.

I shook my head. 'God, that felt good.'

'You were the envy of every single agent. We still can't talk about that without busting a gut. And the blood –' She mimed it spraying everywhere.

I smiled with mild disbelief, recalling the moment. 'I've never seen a nose bleed like that.'

'I thought he was gonna faint!'

We laughed some more and Diane wiped away a tear. We relaxed and looked at each other. She signalled a waitress for the bill.

'Michael, that was one administration. They change. The Service is, well – forever.' We smiled at the hokiness of that. But she grew serious. 'I know you get tired of me saying it, but you know my mantra: "All that evil needs to prosper . . ."'

'". . . Is for a few good men to do nothing." And I agree.'

'Then agree to come back.' I shook my head. 'Imagine, if you'd been working for the Service you might have caught Madoff.'

'Oh, you mean it's *my* fault?'

'Yeah, him and the credit crunch have got your fingerprints all over them.' I tried to take the bill from Diane's hand but she wouldn't let go. We held the bill between us. She gave me a soft but a deeply meaningful look. 'And you're sure this isn't about Nicole?'

Everything went very still. There was a long pause between us. I pulled the bill from her hand.

'I'm sure.'

'Because . . .'

'I'm sure.'

'You can never be sure.'

I gave her that with a shrug. Then she frowned at my hand, and the grazes across the knuckles.

'Bar-room brawl?'

I did the stupid thing of withdrawing my hands – guiltily. 'Something like that.'

She was troubled all over again. 'Michael, is everything OK?'

For a moment I was tempted to tell her. For a moment I reasoned that if she knew she could make some calls, give me the heads up on what she was hearing in the Agency. Then I remembered all the rules, the procedures, the right way to do things – and Diana did things the right way. So I finessed. 'Yeah, fine, yeah. When it isn't I'll tell you.'

'Be sure to do that.'

She was looking at me, worried – too worried. I stood to break up the serious mood and put some bills on the table. We kissed each other's cheeks, which still felt weird after all this time. She gave me that look of concern that would always make me want to fold into her arms. 'You take care now.'

'I will, Diane. And good luck with the presidents. Cover them – and cover your ass.'

'My big ass.'

We laughed. She gave me a lop-sided grin and I walked off.

I drummed my fingers on the cell bunk where I was now sitting up. Nothing. I'd gone from the cafe back to my apartment where the NYPD knocked on my door two minutes later . . .

Think Byrne, think.

Special Agent Diane Mason watched her former colleague walk out of the cafe and pass by the window as he sauntered up the street. Satisfied he was not coming back she pulled out her phone and redialled the last number.

'OK, he's leaving . . . No, nothing . . . I can't explain that either . . . Keep the tail on him and see where he goes for the rest of the day . . . Let's not call the Tribeca incident into the police until we see what his next moves are.'

She killed the call and cradled the phone in her hands. Her department had been tracking the Russians since their illegal entry into the United States a little over a month earlier. She had wanted to know what they were up to. After today she wanted to know what Byrne was up to. She was no longer the friend or maternal figure. She was now the special agent in charge of the Advance Party for a presidential visit to New York. There was a very dangerous murderer loose in the city. A murderer she prayed to god was not Michael Byrne.

5

Jeremiah Rankin was that rare thing, a man who struck fear into his employees. Real fear. The fear that made their palms sweat before meetings. The fear that made their mouths dry when explaining themselves before him. The bank CEO's features did nothing to put anyone at ease, his face resembling something between a horse and a hawk. Long and equine yet with a brow and nose that hooked forward and that, when he was angry – which was often – animated his features into the most grotesque of masks.

Jeremiah Rankin seemed to hold everybody and everything in contempt. His equals he greeted with curtness, his bank directors he treated as underlings, his employees he treated as if they were invisible. To the point that new employees were told never to make eye contact with him and only ever to speak when spoken to. Stories – which were true – circulated of minor employees being fired for breaching this code. If his private elevator was out of action and he had to enter yours, you got out. He didn't ride up with anybody below executive level.

Jeremiah Rankin was obnoxious, brutish and cruel. It was not enough to succeed, but others – all others – had to be seen to fail. He arrived early and left late and expected no less of any aspiring employee. He stalked his offices with a permanently bad smell in his nostrils. In all respects he was a man consumed with an almost feral hate, a permanent tangible anger. In any other walk of life he would not have been tolerated. He would have been removed, sued or both. But in Wall Street, the financial capital of the world, he was lauded.

Because he made money.

The most unpalatable boss in the US received the most CVs of any financial institution in the country. Because he made his employees *rich*. Richer than any other financial institution. Richer than any other bank. The best trading teams from his competitors queued round the block to jump ship to First Bank of America because nobody would stuff their mouths with more gold. Fully twenty-five per cent of the bank's shares were held by the staff. They were the best rewarded in corporate America, but, more than any other competitor, their fortunes were tied to the fortunes of their bank.

Of the remuneration, the other banks complained. The liberal media complained. Grandstanding Democrat politicians complained. But there it ended. Because Rankin made money. For his shareholders, for his employees, but mostly for himself. And in Wall Street money is the first and last word. It was there in the beginning and so shall it be in the end.

Up until recently Rankin's stock – realizable over the next five years – was worth $700 million. Every commentator expected him to become the first Wall Street bank CEO to pull a full billion out in remuneration from his bank. His thirty-two years of service at First Bank of America, his decade plus at the top, his three marriages, his gruelling eighty-hour weeks – they were all paying off.

So everybody believed. So Jeremiah Rankin believed.

Everybody seemed to believe it.

Except the market.

Because First Bank's share price had halved in two days.

The gym of the New York Racquet and Tennis Club was housed in an unassuming Manhattan brownstone building which sat between two low-rise offices in the financial district. Membership was strictly by invitation only. The members – the elder statesmen of America's mightiest financial companies – were never overly pleased to see Rankin present, but today they were amazed. The news of the slaughter of four of his closest executives, lieutenants no less, had broken just before the close of markets Tuesday and had rocked the whole of Wall Street, causing the Dow Jones to come off over one hundred points.

But to see Rankin amongst them the very following day unsettled even his hardiest enemy. He entered the oak-panelled changing room and walked to his locker fresh from a game of squash that had seen him dispense his coach three-two. The club coach hadn't obsequiously buckled – Rankin was as razor sharp on the squash court as he was in the board room, if a little more gracious in victory.

The two other members present in the locker room, elderly gentlemen, exchanged rather disapproving looks followed by expressions of non-understanding. The eldest of the two saluted his friend and mumbled Rankin's name as he left. Rankin gave him a serious nod before returning to dressing.

'Terrible news about your colleagues, Jeremiah.' The speaker was Thomas Carpenter III, a white-haired bank chairman of one of the country's biggest mutuals.

Rankin turned, buttoning his shirt. 'Yeah, we're all still in shock.' His accent was Queens and even at his most civil he struggled to hide the pugilist within. 'They were good people. It was ... unexpected.' Rankin pulled a face that said he didn't know what to say.

The chairman picked his words with care. 'Do the police know who did it?'

'Yeah, they got some nut-job on video. Came in complaining about his dad losing some money then before you know it he's going crazy with a gun.' Rankin's face shrouded in disgust and sadness as he pictured the scene.

'Well, I'm sorry. We're all sorry. Terrible thing.'

'Thank you, Thomas, thank you.'

Rankin returned to his locker, keen to not continue the conversation.

'And how goes it otherwise, you know, with business?'

Rankin turned as he worked on his gold Hermes tie. He gave the old man a dead-eyed look, pointedly impassive in the face of the aged bank chairman's probing. 'What can I say, it just gets better.'

'Really?' The gentleman was no bruiser, but he was a fire-tested banker who had seen every kind of operator and wasn't easily intimidated by the worst of them. 'You seem rather sanguine about a fifty per cent drop in your share price.'

'That's the sea we swim in, Thomas, full of sharks thinking they can scent blood everywhere.'

'So, no gaping wounds then?'

Rankin fixed him with a smile that was all Fuck You. 'Just a couple of paper cuts. Otherwise, business is great. How about yourselves? I hear you're having trouble paying back the government bail-out? You struggling, Thomas?'

The chairman allowed himself a smile at Rankin's pugnacious stance. 'No, no. We're heading in the right direction, paying it off nice and steady.'

'We were the first bank to pay it back.'

'I read, yes.'

'We didn't want it in the first place. Treasury forced

it on us to cover the backs of those boy scouts at Goldman's and Morgan.'

The chairman smiled genially at Rankin, patiently allowing the Young Turk's spite to drift off. 'We seem to have a different understanding of events. I understood Goldman's and Morgan have had a very good credit crunch.'

Rankin turned his back to him to reach for his jacket off the locker hanger and spoke dismissively. 'Believe what you want. I wouldn't want their balance sheets, I know that much.'

In his locker mirror Rankin could see the chairman quietly waiting. Self-conditioned to never run from a fight he turned to face his elder. 'What?'

'Oh, it's probably nothing.'

The elderly CEO picked uncomfortably at a piece of imaginary fluff on his cashmere jacket.

'If it's nothing, then we have nothing to talk about.'

'Just that the tittle-tattle round here is that it's First Bank's balance sheet that's the cause for concern.'

'Is that so? And who told you that?'

'Just a little birdie.'

Rankin sniffed hatefully, drawing his face into a cloak of scornful distaste. 'Well, I'd like to meet this "little birdie" so I could wring its little birdie neck. If there's a problem with our balance sheet, then why did the SEC just give us a clean bill of health?'

'For the same reason they didn't stop Bernard

Madoff or the credit crunch – they are understaffed, underfunded, underqualified, as well as too in thrall to the pushier elements of the Street.'

'Or maybe they couldn't find their pricks in the shower.' Unconsciously Rankin had edged towards Carpenter.

'Well, if that's true, then perhaps that might explain how they missed your toxic assets.' The chairman flashed a small smile.

Rankin wanted to pummel his face in, but decorum denied it. 'Or *perhaps* they liked what they saw.'

Carpenter, not a little uncomfortable, took off his glasses and polished them to keep himself busy, keep a bit of space between them. 'Perhaps they couldn't get past the smoke and mirrors that your army of off-shore experts bounces your portfolio off.'

'That's a fairly outrageous thing to say, Carpenter.' The politeness of the words contradicted by the venomous tone they were spoken in.

'Well, you're not the only one with experts and ours think your time's up. In fact, I do believe there are a lot of contracts settling this Friday and it will be most interesting to see what happens then.'

Rankin was now standing over the bank chairman, itching to shove him into the locker opposite, aching. 'I wouldn't be so sure, Carpenter.'

'On the contrary, we've spent a long time looking at your books and the numbers don't add up, Jeremiah.'

'Really?'

Thomas Carpenter could feel Rankin's breath on him now as he replaced his spectacles on his face.

'Really. I happen to believe that when you announce your results on Monday they're going to make for pretty dire reading. In fact, I'd bet the farm.'

'Be my guest.'

The chairman smiled and made his way to the door. He turned to confront the daggers staring at him from Rankin. 'I'm glad you said as much because our bank did just that.'

Thomas Carpenter III left the room whilst Rankin filled with fury. The banker slammed his locker door closed, but it banged back to where it had sat open, only now the mirror was broken, cutting up Rankin's reflection as he considered himself and his bank's prospects. He settled his nerves and focused on the job at hand.

Let them short my stock. Let them bet the farm. I don't do bets. I do certainties. I am not the victim of events – I am the master of them. I am not a participant in the game – I am the game. And when the markets open on Monday my bank will have the best balance sheet in Wall Street.

I just need two days. I just need to get to Friday . . .

6

I opened my eyes and for that brief moment between sleeping and waking, between alert and dreaming, I was anywhere. I was in a luxury hotel, I was in a villa by the beach, I was in a house in the country – and she looked beautiful. For a fraction of a second she was a Latino vision swaddled in light. A curvy woman of endless possibilities, of friendship and sex and shared experiences. For a fraction of a second.

Then she was Detective Martinez. Staring at me with her head cocked to one side. In a poorly lit holding cell in a police station in Lower Manhattan.

'Wakey wakey, Special Agent Byrne.'

I struggled sleepily up on the bunk. '*Former* Special Agent Byrne.'

'Hey, they can take the boy out of the Service but they can't take the Service out of the boy, am I right? Why didn't you tell us?'

I swung my legs to the floor and looked at her, standing there as she was, relaxed in my company. Odd behaviour given the charges against me. 'I didn't think it was relevant.'

'Bull*shit*. This some undercover thing?' She grinned playfully. 'Let me in on it, I won't tell.'

'Did the Secret Service tell you to release me?'

That got her brain working – and concerned. 'No.'

I remembered it was Wednesday and stole a look at her watch. Just gone noon. I gave her a considered look. 'Then do you think this all happened with the Service's blessing?'

She stopped leaning against the cell door and took an understated but more ready position. 'You're going round killing people *without* their blessing? Shiiit. You gonna try and whack me?'

She was a tough cookie and had said it half in jest, half probing. I gave it the wry smile it deserved.

'Depends what you mean by whack.'

I let the remark hang in the air till she saw some of the double entendre in it.

'Did you flirt with the Russians before you *whacked* them?'

'Yeah, told them I loved what they'd done with their hair.' I yawned. I felt very peaceful. I had always noticed this, that, despite circumstances, people have a strong capacity for feeling quite at ease in what were, in reality, uneasy situations. For now, my mojo was working just fine.

'Well, time to come upstairs. Your Secret Service nanny has come to pick you up from school.'

'Special Agent Mason?'

66

'The very same.' The detective dangled a pair of handcuffs from a single finger. 'And the captain has given me the honour of handing you into her custody.'

I got up slowly. 'Look, Martinez, I don't normally do this kind of thing on a first date.'

A smile crept round one side of her face. Jesus, under different circumstances . . . I held out my hands, wrists together. Her smile turned apologetic.

'Round the back, sorry.'

I frowned and turned round. 'I should have listened to my momma when she said stay away from fast women.' Unseen by Martinez I dipped my fingers into the small right-hand pocket at the front of my jeans as I turned. I passed my closed hands behind me and she cuffed me.

'There, signed, sealed and soon to be delivered.' She walked me out of the cell and up through the station. At one point a wall-mounted television was silently showing the midday news on CNN. There were pictures of four bank executives that I recognized, with the strapline 'Police Arrest Madoff Murderer'.

I gave the impression of a man taking in his surroundings, but really my mind was running over my predicament – running over it and getting nowhere.

What I needed was to find out who had set me up for the First Bank murders and who had had me kidnapped . . . Were the two connected? . . . Are bears Catholic? Two events in two days, they had to be. But neither of them run of the mill. Somebody was going to a lot of bother to nail me and I had to find out why. And, somehow, Friday was the deadline. Somehow.

Being in custody was bad. Nobody else was going to go looking for the truth and being stuck in a Secret Service holding cell, no less, was the worst possible way to solve all this.

However, getting handed over to Diane was not a terrible development. Maybe I could persuade her to look the other way whilst I slipped off . . . ? Yeah, great, make her an accomplice to a suspected murderer. Or maybe she would believe me and help me find out who was behind this . . . ? And maybe Dick Cheney would win the Noble Peace Prize. *Byrne – wake up and smell the cappuccino.*

Still, it was going to be a relief to see a friendly face.

We arrived at a frosted-glass door labelled 'Captain Novak'. I could see there was something of a crowd inside. Martinez swung the door open to reveal the captain behind his desk, Detective Ashby beside him. Standing across the desk were Diane – and four Service agents.

I took in the unpromising scene. 'Diane.'

I gave her a small, slightly awkward smile. I got an arctic glare in return.

'Michael Byrne, you are charged with the murder of eight people.'

I blinked in surprise at her hard tone. Gone was

Diane the friend and old boss and in her place was the Head of the New York Secret Service field office, Special Agent Diane Mason. I didn't like this one bit.

Captain Novak handed one of the special agents a clear evidence bag in which I recognized articles relating to me. This was his room in his station and he was underplaying what was a major feather in his police cap – the handing over of a suspected multiple murderer.

'Detective Martinez, if you could uncuff the prisoner and hand him into the custody of the Secret Service, thank you.'

The fastest I'd ever seen somebody pick the lock on a set of handcuffs was six seconds. Using a hair pin. We're not talking safe-cracking here. I wasn't quite that fast, and my hands being behind my back didn't help, but the long walk through the precinct headquarters had provided ample time. As a result, I was still able to save the Latino officer some trouble by bringing my hands round, free of the handcuffs which I dangled on one finger for her.

'I told you, not on first dates.'

Everybody in the room recoiled with various degrees of alarm as they saw the prisoner had broken free. All except Diane. Almost instantly four .357 Secret Service-issue guns were pointed at me along with Detective Ashby's own pistol. To my surprise I noticed that Ashby had been the quickest on the draw.

A beefy, crew-cut Caucasian agent yelled at me. 'Put your hands up, now!'

I obliged, moving very calmly. No need to cause any trigger-happy fingers to twitch more than they needed to. This situation was becoming a habit. But I'd also gotten what I wanted: the measure of my new Secret Service friends. Agents on active protection duty train two weeks out of every eight. Two weeks of assault courses, two weeks on the range, two weeks practising being ambushed, being shot at, being bombed, being attacked. Twenty-five per cent of their lives spent training to handle the onset of any threatening situation not with their cognitive processes but with their instincts. Which makes you good. And these agents were good. Very good. Which was bad, very bad, for me.

Captain Novak had recovered himself enough to aim his ire at the young female officer. 'Martinez, what in god's name were you thinking bringing the prisoner up from the cells unrestrained?'

Martinez was at a complete loss. How could she have possibly known that escaping police-issue handcuffs was one of my specialities, easily done with the paper clip I had retrieved from my pocket and dropped in the corridor outside. However, I was now regretting my stunt a little as I saw the hole I had dropped Martinez into.

'Sir, I swear he was handcuffed – I did it myself, in

the cell.' She looked at me with a mixture of disbelief and a sense of betrayal. I felt terrible for her. Nice one, Byrne.

Novak was in no mood for excuses. 'Well, allow me to give you plenty of time to work on your handcuffing skills by suspending you until further notice.'

Martinez was aghast. 'Sir . . . !'

Simmering with anger the captain held out his hand. 'Your badge and gun.'

Detective Ashby lurched to her defence. 'Sir, if I might –'

'Be quiet unless you want to join your partner on suspension?'

Ashby backed down, threw Martinez an apologetic look, then me a threatening one.

The room waited. Four agents with their guns pointed at me, the rest watching Martinez struggle to keep a lid on it before reaching the inevitable conclusion and tossing her badge and gun onto her superior's desk. Diane did nothing to interfere, respecting the jurisdiction of the captain.

Novak, determined to reassert his control over his domain, barely looked at Martinez. 'That will be all, Detective.'

I had a rising feeling of remorse but had the wit not to offer useless words of apology. The Latino officer swapped looks with her partner and left the room – but not without flicking a vengeful look at me.

Diane held up her hand to her agents and motioned for them to lower their guns. 'Gentlemen, I believe that is the last we'll be seeing of any Harry Houdini impersonations for today. Isn't that right, Mr Byrne?'

I stood impassively, trying to understand where Diane was coming from.

'Let's get our prisoner back to the office. Deputy Director Carlton wants to see him immediately.'

Oh. Carlton. That's where she was coming from.

Shit.

There went my mojo.

7

Diane, myself and the four agents travelled down in an elevator in silence. Once again I was handcuffed behind my back – only this time they were plastic handcuffs with the added measure of Crew-cut Agent keeping a firm grip on my wrists throughout. If Diane was intent on me not counting on any favours or familiarity from her, I had got the message loud and clear. You didn't rise up the Secret Service ranks without being a cold, hard, ruthless professional, and right now Diane was ticking all of those boxes. The only look I did manage to catch from her was the sort you would give a multiple murderer in your custody. Something had changed and not for the better. I hadn't banked on this and I certainly hadn't planned for it.

The elevator opened on the stationhouse's basement car park level where a large, heavily armoured unmarked prisoner transport wagon was waiting for me. One of the agents opened the back door and Crew-cut guided me by my elbow up the stairs and into the rear box compartment where all four agents stepped in with me. Diane went up front with the waiting driver.

I looked around the cabin. I looked at the men about me.

Crew-cut snorted. 'You looking for a way out? You ain't got a hope.'

Which was a pretty accurate reading of my thoughts. We fell into silence. And that's how it was all the way to the New York field office in Brooklyn.

I sat in yet another interview room behind yet another interview table high up in a building in Adams Street, Brooklyn, only this time rubbing the circulation back into my wrists. Diane was sitting opposite, a sizeable envelope before her. At the door stood an agent watching me with the same warmth a cobra exudes before plunging its fangs into a small marsupial.

Diane looked up at her colleague. 'Quinn, could we have a moment, please.'

The agent stepped outside leaving Diane and myself alone, and me confused. What she did next only made me more disorientated.

Diane opened the large envelope and poured the contents onto the table between us. A dozen photographs spread out. Poorly lit photographs of me with the four Russians. Leaving my house. Getting into their SUV. Getting out of their SUV. Entering their apartment block. Three grainy pictures taken from an apartment block or stairwell *opposite where I was being held* – showing me holding a gun, showing me firing the gun, showing one Russian crashing out through the window, towards the photographer.

'We've been tracking these subjects for almost six weeks. Care to explain why you are associating with Russian criminals?'

'Jesus, Diane. I was being held at gunpoint and your reaction was to take *photographs*? If they'd killed me, what would you have done, burst in and taken a group portrait?'

'Michael, what the hell have you gotten yourself into?'

'Diane – what are you talking about? Look at the photographs – they had me at gunpoint.'

'That tends to happen when a deal goes sour.'

'What deal?'

'You tell me. You tell me why you killed four bank executives and why that soured your relationship with the Russians.'

'There was no relationship and I didn't do the bank . . . That wasn't me. Check the film.'

'We did.'

'And?'

'It was you, Michael.'

'No. No way.'

She didn't even comment, condemning me with silence.

'Who the hell checked it, Diane? A fifth-grader?'

'Forensics.'

'Who the hell have you got in Forensics these days?'

'Park.'

'Park? But he's good.'

'Exactly.'

'No, Diane, I mean, he's *good*. There's no way he wouldn't see through that film – it's a fake. Fake. What did he say? That it *could* be me? That he needed to look at it *again*? What?'

'He said, "That's a keeper."'

No, no, this couldn't be happening.

What the Secret Service did, it did well. Not only did it train its staff almost fanatically, it only hired the best and then gave the best the best possible equipment to work with. The technology at their fingertips is at least two generations ahead of anything in the civilian domain. The closed-circuit footage of a bank job is too pixelated? Forensics will turn it into an HD spectacular. The picture of a suspect too blurry? Forensics will make it something Annie Liebowitz would hang on her wall. They were the best working with the best. And the best of the best of was their Chief Video Analyst, Park Yong-Ho.

Then there was the added problem. Park didn't like me. Park held a grudge against me. And Park was never going to do me any favours until he had delivered payback. To see me on film killing some bank executives must have been like all his Christmases rolled into one and then coming early. But – and this was the bit I didn't understand – Park only delivered the most professional results. So if he said it was me that killed those four bank executives even I was starting to doubt myself. I rubbed the sides of my head – it was spinning.

'Diane, I'm sorry I don't have an explanation . . . If that was me, then nothing makes sense.'

'You're right, Michael, you're not making sense. But I'll tell you what does make sense. You know every last way to play the system. The very things you learnt in the Service when you were investigating the fraudsters – the things you taught *us* – makes you the best placed person to commit a fraud.'

I couldn't believe what I was hearing. 'What are you saying, Diane . . . ?'

'I'm saying you know how to make money appear and you know how to make money disappear. You know how to move it with a trail and you know how to move it without a trail.'

'But I wouldn't do that –'

'In the right circumstance anybody will do anything. You know that.'

She was doing more than pointing the finger – she was kicking me in the gut. A woman I had worked for, for ten years. A woman I'd stood shoulder to shoulder with in bust after bust, arrests that involved shooting and being shot at. A woman I had taken a bullet for – literally – telling me she had *me* pegged as a murderer and a fraudster. Everything I'd fought against for ten years was now being heaped on my head. *My* head.

'I would *never* do that.'

'Then what did you do?'

'I – I don't know. The bank, I was getting my mom's money back . . .'

'Motive – you were angry about your mother's money.'

'How is killing four bank executives going to get me her money back?'

She paused. Somewhere deep inside her I could see a conflict at work but she quickly conquered it, conquered herself. 'Crime of passion.'

'Don't be ridiculous, Diane. If I wanted to hurt First Bank, I would have hit them where it hurt, on the bottom line.'

She held my look for a moment. She was about to say something she wasn't comfortable saying. 'Michael, when those Colombians murdered Benedict, did you walk in and arrest them or did you make it look like the Texas Chainsaw Massacre?'

I stared at her.

Seething.

I was speaking through gritted teeth. 'Our job was to break up a counterfeiting operation. I broke it up.'

'You didn't just break it up – you obliterated it.'

'I'd do the same for you.'

'Do me a favour, Michael. Don't. Don't ever think

78

I want anybody to transgress the law to enforce the law. It's what separates us from the bad guys.'

'It's what weakens us against the bad guys.'

'There's that maverick streak in you, Michael. There's the part of you that could be so enraged that First Bank would receive a nice fat commission from Madoff whilst frittering your mother's money away that you would want to tear the heads off every last person involved in that deal.'

'Diane, you've got this all wrong –'

'No, Michael – I've got this on film. And unless you give me something to work with I can't help you.'

She stared at me. Challenged me. Dared me.

I threw up my hands weakly. 'I don't know what to say.'

'Tell me you were being blackmailed by the Russians, tell me you were on prescription drugs, tell me you were hypnotized – tell me anything but "I didn't do it".'

'Oh, but he did do it . . .'

We both spun our heads round to see Deputy Director George Carlton standing in the doorway. Carlton. One of those people who wasn't tall but nobody stood taller. Shocking thick white hair that would have made a weak man look old, but made Carlton just more distinctive. Perfect white teeth that betrayed his vanity. Perfectly tailored suit that betrayed his ambition. He was a man who was 'On' 24/7, a man who was always impatient to get to the next meeting, a man for whom nothing was ever enough. A man driven to drive everybody about him. A man perfect for the Service.

He smiled wolfishly, maliciously, at me. '. . . And we have it on film and we have it on photo and we have it from witnesses. But, most of all, we have a former agent bringing *this Service* into *dis-re-pute*. And when you did that, Byrne, you got my full, undivided promise of utter crucifixion.'

I looked from Carlton to Diane for some clues. Nothing.

'You chose the worst possible time to pull your little act of revenge on First Bank of America and I can't help but believe that you were aiming for maximum embarrassment for the Service.'

I was losing his thread now. Diane was impassive, offering no clues as to where she stood in all this. Which was unfortunate, because right now I needed an ally.

I shook my head, confused. 'I'm sorry, Carlton. I'm not sure if it's your nasal sound but I'm not following you.'

Carlton controlled a moment of anger which had flared up in him at the memory of me flooring him when I resigned the Service. 'Never mind, follow your trial instead. Because as well as being charged with the murder of eight innocent citizens you will be charged with being a threat to national security, charges the special prosecutors are drawing up as we speak.'

I looked at Diane for some guidance on this – because I was in freefall here.

'Michael, you shot four bankers in a building' – I went to protest but she silenced me with a not-to-be-argued-with look – 'not five hundred yards from where the president and the Chinese premier are performing their ground-breaking ceremony on Friday. If there is any chance of a link –'

A light of understanding suddenly flooded my mind, overwhelmed me, and I had to restrain myself from grabbing her. 'Did you say Friday?'

'Friday, yes.'

'Diane, that's when the Russians said they were holding me till.'

Diane's eyes locked onto mine like lasers – but Carlton had ideas of his own.

'Are you saying there is a connection between what you were involved in and the president's visit?'

I ignored him. 'Diane, what time is the ground-breaking?'

'Mid-afternoon. Three till four.'

'*That's it.* They were holding me until the end of the Friday afternoon. That's it. That's what they were . . .' This was about to sound inexplicable even to me. '. . . keeping me away from.'

I was at a loss, a complete loss.

Carlton clapped his hands together. In victory. 'You admit the connection. Excellent. Now, let's see if we can't find a reason why Michael Byrne would want to kill the President of the United States of America?'

'Fuck you, Carlton.'

'Oh, that's right. Did Special Agent Byrne go off the rails after 9/11? Did the grown-ups who actually have to run this country and deal with every despot and shady regime around the world fly out the estranged members of the Bin Laden family? Did Special Agent Byrne – like thousands of others – lose a loved one that day? Did Special Agent Byrne also lose a little piece of his mind that day? Did he turn from loving his country to hating his country? Did he feel betrayed? Did he burn and fester and plot to hurt the very people he had sworn to protect? Did he? . . . Did he?'

I clenched my fists on the table before me. 'When this is over, Carlton, I'm gonna fuck you up.'

Carlton laughed. Laughed in the way a man who has waited a long time to get his own back and then gets it back in spades laughs. Real, savoured laughter. Delicious Michelin-starred laughter. Then he brought his face close up to mine and spoke very clearly and very carefully. 'No, Byrne. When this is over you're going to be eating through a straw and calling a seven-foot tattooed redneck from Alabama "Daddy".'

8

It was moving time.

The forehead bone is one of the strongest in the body. The nose bone one of the weakest. Hell, it's just cartilage. That is why when my forehead connected with Carlton's nose there was only going to be one outcome.

A crunch, a lot of blood, and one man down.

My next move was to get to the doorway in one stride. Before the burly Agent Quinn could register the commotion within, I delivered a blow to his windpipe, dropping him to all fours where he struggled for air.

I reached down and took his FN Five-seven semi-automatic pistol and swung round just in time to halt Diane in her tracks.

'I will *not* hesitate to use this, Diane.'

She took a step towards me. 'You wouldn't shoot me. I don't know what you're into, Michael – shit, I don't even think *you* know – but there is no way on god's emerald earth that you would shoot me.'

I took a step back. 'Diane, I do not know what the fuck is going down here but something tells me that if I don't try to stop this nobody will. And I will be damned if I'm wearing an orange jumpsuit for something I didn't do.'

Diane took another step towards me. 'Then what did you do, Michael, tell me? Please.'

I took another step back. 'Diane, I *swear* I didn't do this. Please, you have to believe me.'

We hovered in the corridor for what was a dangerously long moment. Diane looked about her. There was one agent gasping for air, Carlton moaning in the room behind her. She looked at me, opened the door to another interview room and with a flick of her head indicated that we should go in.

I followed her carefully as she hit the light switch and took her position in the middle of the room. I was nonplussed.

'What?'

'You can't hurt any of the agents on your way out.' She spoke like she was cutting me a deal – which she was.

'Of course not.'

'And you're going to have to hit me.'

'*What?*'

'Michael, I can't just let you walk out of here without doing something about it. Hit me.'

'I don't want to hurt you . . .'

'Michael, we haven't got time for this.'

We were both breathing heavily. Both electric with tension. I couldn't do it and she knew it.

So she swung a punch at me.

I blocked it and slapped her – hard – around the face. The force hurled her into a table which she spun round onto and lay upon.

I waited. Panting. Looking at her bent over the table. Waiting for what happened next – whatever that was.

She righted herself and turned to me. 'Harder.'

I went to object – then slapped her. Harder.

She spun round, both her and the table crashing over. I leapt on her where she lay and slapped her again. I raised my hand to deliver another blow but I had done enough. When she took down her hands I could see tears streaming down her face.

I didn't have any time. I stood up.

'Diane . . .'

But she rolled away from me to hide her face.

I opened the door and almost leapt back to see Carlton standing there awash with blood. What a trouper. I grabbed him by his shoulders and tossed him into the room behind me. He had nothing in the tank and careened off the wall to the ground.

I held my revolver up and stepped out, checking both routes. The partially asphyxiated agent was dialling a number into his cellphone. I warned him with a 'Sorry' before kicking his phone from his hand into the room beyond.

I got to the door at the far end and pulled it open to see an empty stairwell. But I knew that was about to change.

I knew from experience that the route down involved a locked door. It might take a second to break through, but it might take a minute. That only left one option.

On the thirty-second floor of the New York field office two dozen special agents had burst into action. The alarm had been called and each was reaching for their weapon. Most took up their Service-issue revolvers but a core group broke off into a gunnery room where they were swiftly donning body armour and grabbing MP5 submachine guns.

The escape of a prisoner was unexpected – but not unplanned for. Every possible eventuality was considered and drilled for and this was no exception.

The Counter Assault Team made its way across the large open-plan office towards the stairwell whilst ten agents peeled off to seal the building. This meant halting all elevators as well as fanning out and blocking the exits onto the street below.

The Counter Assault Team reached the exit to the stairwell when their team leader, Commander Becker, stopped. Becker was a mountain of a man who wouldn't have looked out of place chasing the Taliban across the Kandahar mountains. Which is exactly what he had been doing covertly for a full year before the Allied invasion of Afghanistan. He had the dead, black eyes of a soldier who had killed too many men to feel anything in the taking of a life. A man to be terrified of. A man perfect for the dark ruthless tasks assigned and denied by his government. Becker was a hulking German American whose idea of hell was nothing to do. Chasing an escaped prisoner certainly didn't fall under that category.

He turned to a female intelligence officer sitting before a bank of screens in the middle of the large open-plan room and barked at her.

'Have we got visuals on the target yet?'

The intelligence officer was frantically rewinding recorded closed-circuit film of the areas surrounding the interview rooms when one clip showed a running figure. The figure of Byrne.

'Got him!'

She jabbed a button that synchronized all the recordings by time-code, and following Byrne's movements was suddenly straightforward. The footage kept changing angle as the audio-visual software automatically jumped from one ceiling-positioned camera to another, tracking the escapee running below. After watching the sequence for a few seconds the intelligence officer turned to Commander Becker.

'He's making his way to the –'

I kicked the door to the rooftop open. I quickly scouted around for something to wedge it closed with, but nothing presented itself amongst the service vents and massive air-conditioning engines.

My mind raced through possible options including

hiding inside one of the building's service ducts or even escaping through them. I swiftly discounted these ideas and decided to stick with the reason I had come up here in the first place.

I returned to the stairwell and saw an agent in body armour straining to look up at me. I fired a couple of rounds into the wall near him. The barked commands between the agents below told me I had made them more cautious – and bought myself some time.

I slammed the door shut and ran to the edge of the roof and looked over. There was a drop to the wider rooftop below which I leapt down onto. I rolled to my feet and ran to a far railing and looked over – nothing but a thirty-five storey drop. I ran to another side of the rooftop and looked over – more of nothing.

The Counter Assault Team snaked its way up the final flight of stairs and looked to its commander. Wordlessly but with jabbing fingers, Becker signalled for the formation he wished the team to take on exit. Assured by the team's nods that everything was understood he turned and kicked the door open himself. After a pause he charged out, rolling into position where he scoured the rooftop for Byrne with his M5 submachine gun. Behind him five other agents burst out and covered various angles of the roof.

Nothing.

The commander signalled for the team to push out

in every direction, which they did speedily and stealthily, the only sound the scuttling of feet racing across the grit of the rooftop towards the target.

As I ran to a third railing and looked over, I heard the rooftop door above explode open and the group of agents rush out. I looked down over the side but there was nothing but a hell of a long drop to Brooklyn. One side to go and no time to do it.

I put my back up against the wall and slid along, checking above me. It was only a matter of time before somebody took a shot . . .

'He's over here!'

Behind me the helmet of an agent was visible high up at the far end. I took aim and shot, forcing him to duck out of sight. I ran in a crouch along my wall to the last railing, but heavy footfall above told me agents were on the move.

I stole a look over the edge and saw what I was looking for. I glanced up at the roof above and sprinted further along. When the attack came it was going to be coordinated and shooting warning shots at them wasn't going to work.

They had me pinned in to the left, to the right and above. I'd run out of roof.

The Counter Assault Team had split into three pairs, Commander Becker and another on the upper roof, two others on each side of the lower main roof – all squeezing Byrne like a tube of toothpaste. Each agent was in position, each agent slid a finger over the trigger of his submachine gun.

Radio silence was about to become an irrelevance as Becker pushed a button on the communication device at his lapel.

'On my command . . . One, two, go!'

On each side of the lower roof a pair of CAT agents leapt out whilst simultaneously the two above swung their weapons over the edge and down at the roof below. All six guns zeroed in . . . on dead air.

'What the hell?'

Momentarily the agents looked about them for some inexplicable emergence of Byrne before one pointed a finger over the edge of the lower roof.

'Commander, he's gone over the side.'

All four agents on the lower roof leaned over to look – to see a figure sliding down the thick steel wires of a window-cleaning platform, ten, eleven, twelve storeys below.

Up above Becker gripped the rail in front of him. 'Can you get a clear shot?'

All four agents below took aim.

In room 1617 of the Marriot Brooklyn a middle-aged Hispanic couple clenched each other in a state of lustful half dress. He was escaping the boredom of midlife, she was escaping the fear of never being an object of desire again, both were escaping the office under the pretence of a sales meeting that had never existed.

As he half kissed, half sucked her neck she pulled his tie from round his collar, almost dizzy with pleasure.

The man spoke into her neck. 'Are you sure your husband doesn't suspect?'

She was almost purring. 'Rufus? Even if he did he wouldn't have the balls to do anything about i –'

That was when the sixteenth-floor window exploded in a hail of bullets, sending glass and the terrified couple falling to the floor.

The Hispanic couple's terror was complete when I swung in through the window, landing, rolling then standing.

The couple stopped screaming as they attempted to compute my presence.

I considered them for a moment, knowing a daytime tryst when I saw one. 'Were you the couple that complained about the room service?'

They cried, 'No,' emphatically, in unison, before continuing their screaming.

Twenty or so special agents were meeting on the thirty-second floor of the New York field office building, including the six members of the Counter Assault Team. Diane had an ice-pack to the side of her head and Deputy Director George Carlton was alternating between yelling at people and trying to halt a nose-bleed that wouldn't stop despite the pressure from the towel he was applying.

'Will somebody tell me where the hell the target is?'

The attendant agents were working on the problem furiously when one young female operative covered the desk phone she had cradled in her neck. 'Sir, the hotel is reporting an intruder entering a room on the sixteenth floor – via an external window.'

Carlton took the towel away from his face to speak. 'Get down there and seal him in. Don't involve the hotel guests because chaos is exactly the cover he's looking for. Locate him and close in on him.' He pressed the towel to his nose for a moment. 'Do not – I repeat – do not allow the hotel to evacuate the guests unless we have absolutely no other choice.'

A fire alarm began to ring.

Everybody shared looks of confusion that were swiftly replaced by agonized looks of understanding.

Despite herself Diane almost had to contain a smile of relief. But she kept up the coldly efficient demeanour. 'I do believe that's the hotel's fire alarm. So much for not evacuating the guests.'

Carlton took the towel off his face and addressed the Counter Assault Team. 'Listen up and listen carefully.' He had everybody's attention. 'I want the target stopped.'

As the agents made their ways out in various directions, Carlton stared at Diane with a snarl of suspicion.

I had to get out of this building.

One of the financial realities of funding a huge government agency like the Secret Service was that, often, offices were located in other people's buildings. In the case of the USSS New York field office they had rented the space above the Brooklyn Marriot. I had always figured it would come in handy for a lunchtime liaison à la the couple I had just burst in on. What could be sweeter than brushing past your colleague's desk and both of you making your separate way down to a suite two minutes away for fifty-six minutes of secret servicing before both getting back behind your desks for the end of lunch? Nothing. Unfortunately, whilst the bedroom gymnastics were to die for, no agent could live with the bill. I couldn't keep doing that every month on my pay grade. Not when Karen from accounts was going for Olympic gold. So I did the only sensible thing. Rented a former artist's studio in Williamsburg, two blocks from the office. However, the lunchtime practice had left this hotel familiar to me – I'd rented half its rooms at one time or another. But, fond memories or no fond memories, I had to get out of this place.

Every corridor was filled with a soft but determined fire alarm, which was bringing a ragtag of guests out of their rooms. Most were hoping it would pass and were complying with the evacuation procedure reluctantly, others were marching towards the stairwells without pause. I had already made the decision not to follow any line of people down as it was a certainty that Secret Service agents were filtering them as they left the building. In fact, I had to assume they were covering all the public exits. Which only left the private.

I strode down the corridor looking for a door that guests were not meant to see but which was clear enough for the cleaning staff to spot. I found it, almost just another wall panel but a door nonetheless. I stuck my borrowed revolver into the back of my jeans, lifted a stack of towels off a nearby trolley and stepped inside to a long space, which was occupied by a Philippino maid about to enter a service elevator. I joined her. She chose the lower car park, presumably the staff assembly point, which was fine by me.

'Manager say it OK to leave hotel things during fire alarm.'

I smiled reassuringly. 'It's my first day – I'm being thorough.'

We rode the elevator down to its bumpy halt below the hotel. The door opened and I saw a large number of hotel staff milling about in the centre of the car park attended by a Secret Service agent and a hotel manager with a clipboard.

The maid and I approached the manager who was checking off staff. The manager looked at me behind my pile of towels without recognition and spoke quietly to the agent next to him.

The agent held his gun towards the floor and put a hand up to me. 'Sir, I am going to have to ask you to put the towels down.'

I was six feet from him when he spoke. 'Sure.' I dropped the towels to reveal my revolver pointed straight at him. It was too late for him to lift his gun towards me.

The maid jumped away from me – the manager almost leapt backwards. 'Jesus!'

The agent was stressed but keeping his cool. His gun was pointed towards the ground and before he could raise it I'd be able to get off at least two shots. He tried negotiation. 'The building is surrounded by over thirty Secret Service agents . . . why don't you put the gun down.'

'What a coincidence – I killed thirty agents on the way down here. Shall we stand around bluffing all day or are you going to put that gun down without my help?' We stood staring at each other but I couldn't drag this out. 'What's your name, Special Agent?'

'Kaminski.'

'Tell me, you got kids?'

He wasn't going to have a problem humanizing the situation. 'A boy. Six years old.'

I pointed my gun at his pistol shoulder. 'Well, if you want to play catch with him ever again put the gun down.' I slipped my finger over the trigger. The agent's training told him what that meant.

Wordlessly and with great care Special Agent Kaminski put the gun down. He moved just a little too slowly and I could see he was wondering whether he could get the jump on me, whether he could flip the gun up and fire off a shot. But he saw me watching, not moving a muscle, not missing a thing. Not realizing that my mind was racing as to how to neutralize him without breaking my promise or desire to shoot at any Secret Service agents. Thankfully – for both of us – he made the right call and laid the gun on the floor. I waved them back with my own weapon. The manager scuttled back, the agent calmly stepped away. I kicked his gun across the car park where it disappeared underneath a pick-up truck.

I pointed my gun from the agent to the elevator. 'Go back upstairs.' He stood, thinking. 'Now.'

The agent paused momentarily and then walked to the elevator resignedly. I waited until its doors had closed, then swung my gun at the staff who all wisely huddled together and took a further step back.

I scanned the car park and found what I was looking for. A motorcycle. In fact, better than that. A yellow Ducati GT1000.

'I want the keys to the bike.'

I got baleful stares in return. And one mutter from my Philippino maid.

'I want the keys to the bike or I will kill you one by one.'

There was a collective gasp that turned to muffled cries when I pointed the gun at the maid. She in turn very nearly punched the manager's arm.

'OK, OK.' The manager pulled out a key. 'It was a fortieth birthday present. Please be careful.'

I smiled a smile that told him I would be anything but.

In the elevator the agent was almost shouting into his sleeve. 'I said, "The target is in the lower car park. Possible hostage situation."'

On the thirty-second floor Deputy Director Carlton stood before a bank of large computer screens showing different views of the hotel whilst buttoning up a new non-bloodstained shirt. All eyes were on the frustratingly unclear video relayed from the basement car park, of the target mounting a motorcycle near a crowd of hotel staff.

Carlton squeezed a microphone, alarmed and angry at how events were unfolding. 'Are we getting this, Commander?'

In the hotel lobby the Counter Assault Team was

sprinting towards the exit, Commander Becker speaking urgently as he ran.

'Sir, we are already on our way.'

The Counter Assault Team burst out of the building onto Adams Street and ran round the front of the Marriot Hotel towards the side alley at full pelt, giving no thought to group formation.

They heard the roar before they turned the corner.

Stopping haphazardly they were met by the howling of the thunderously loud yellow Ducati as their prey raced by them and joined the Adams Street traffic at a furious pace. The CAT agents trained their weapons on the rider but he was weaving in and out of the surrounding vehicles before a clear shot could be taken.

And all that was left was the disappearing roar.

'Goddammit!' Carlton slammed the microphone against the desk, smashing it in the process, making his support staff freeze. 'Mason, in my office.'

Diane took a deep breath and followed him out.

9

Nobody hated like Jeremiah Rankin. Nobody brooded and plotted and schemed with such black bile. Nobody applied such brilliance of mind, such excess of talent, such force of will to the task. Hate and a complete determination to get away from the crummy kids in his crummy street had won Jeremiah Rankin a scholarship to Archbishop Fitzsimons, a Catholic elementary high school in his native Queens, New York. Once there he didn't have to dig too deep to hate the Jesuits who ran the place. It was here that he discovered the strength of purpose that hate can fuel and used this when dealing with a priest who took too great an interest in him. Quickly these men that struck fear into every other boy in the school learnt not to take an interest in the boy Jeremiah. And no punishment went beyond the cleaning of the Brethren's shoes with the threat of the birch for failure. But the birch was never required as every shoe was parade-ground brilliant, the act of shoe-shining quickly becoming Jeremiah's preferred method of securing time alone.

Time spent cleaning shoes was time spent plotting. Plotting ways to make money. Jeremiah was good at shining shoes but he got his fill of that at school. Instead he turned to delivering newspapers. But whereas other boys might have had just one paper-round, Jeremiah had three. And years of rising at 4.30 a.m. every day saw him rewarded with the best rounds in the richest neighbourhood. Where the Christmas tips were the best.

Leaving his parents' tiny apartment in Flushing before dawn each morning, Jeremiah would point his bicycle south towards the affluent Queens suburb of Forest Hills, where he would pick up his sack of newspapers and deliver them to the premier houses in the premier roads of Forest Hills Gardens itself. Except perhaps in the worst of the snow – and the newsprint on his fingers – it never felt like work to the young schoolboy. He never tired of the housings' architecture, emulating, as it did, an architect's ideal of an English 'Garden City'. The buildings were in the neo-Tudor and Georgian tradition, but what captivated the young Jeremiah was their size, their comfort. These people in their leafy streets had money. And a lot of them read the *Wall Street Journal*. And so Jeremiah read the *Wall Street Journal*. One article per house, so that by the end of each morning he had read the newspaper cover to cover. Month in, month out. And because Jeremiah had street smarts in spades he managed to see past the equities and commodities and currencies and tips and commentaries and predictions and analysis and CEO profiles and the government this and the regulators that. He saw what the markets were really about. He saw that they were about Risk.

Risk, the secret ingredient of success, was no secret to Rankin. As a boy he was a voracious reader, but not of boy's own fiction – or any fiction. He read biographies. He did not care for the where, when or why but only the how. The *how* they did it. And so he read – consumed – the lives of J. D. Rockefeller, Sam Walton, Henry Ford, Andrew Carnegie, J. P. Morgan, Marcus Goldman, Vanderbilt, and every other great financier down the ages. These careers digested he turned to the great men of history, Napoleon, Alexander the Great, George Washington, Abraham Lincoln, Thomas Jefferson, Gandhi, Marconi, Edison, Bell, Columbus, Polo, Magellan, Churchill, Stalin, Hitler . . . From the good to the bad he saw the one key ingredient, the secret of their success. And that ingredient was Risk.

Each of these great men had taken great personal risks with either their person or their money. Of course, it was the money risk that Jeremiah was most interested in. And when he saw that the markets also were about risk he saw with crystal clarity that *risk was everything*. That each of these heroes and villains had taken great risks that had led to greatness and that success in commerce required taking these same risks too.

And the young Jeremiah Rankin thought, *What idiots*.

Because Jeremiah saw an even simpler truth. A truth that rolled out a yellow brick road, a destiny, ahead of him. A truth that was achingly simple. And he asked himself a question that would define his life:

'Why take risks with your own money when you can take risks with other people's?'

And thus he chose banking.

In 1969, at the age of sixteen, Jeremiah Rankin was impatient for Wall Street. However, the feeling was not reciprocated. He could not get beyond the door of any bank or brokerage as institution after institution shook their head at his lack of qualifications and experience. He begged, pleaded, even demanded, but to no avail. Until finally he reached the conclusion that he was not going to get into a bank through the front door, not at this time. Which he hated.

So at the age of seventeen Jeremiah decided to roll the dice, take a risk. He arrived at the offices of Wall Street's oldest investment bank, First Bank of America. He knew enough about the institution to know who he wanted to speak to. He asked the lady at the front desk for Charlie Castle. When the lady struggled to get through he did little to hide his irritation, letting her know he was already late for his appointment. Flustered, she let him through. Once upstairs he repeated his story to another young lady who, after initial scepticism, buckled at the young man's firm manner and insistence that Mr Castle would be most unhappy about her delaying their meeting.

He was shown into a side room with no view to

speak of. So he waited and paced. He hadn't worn the carpet out much before the door opened and a man, smaller than Jeremiah but twice the age and instantly recognizable as no-nonsense, entered.

'Jeremiah Rankin?'

'Yes, sir.'

Charlie Castle was all impatience. 'My secretary tells me that you told her that we have an appointment.'

Jeremiah's bravado was on the wane. 'Yes, sir.'

'But we don't, do we.'

The young man felt very small in his borrowed suit. 'No, sir.'

Charlie Castle, his position understood, allowed Jeremiah's nerves to fray as he looked him up and down. 'What is it that you want?'

Jeremiah looked him in the eye for the first time since the meeting had started. 'I'd like a job, sir.'

Charlie Castle scratched the side of his bulbous nose and pondered this for a moment. 'You've contacted this bank about this before, haven't you.'

'Yes, sir. A few times, actually. But they never let me through to you.'

The banker smiled humourlessly. Jeremiah's heart sank at the expression then fell to his exquisitely polished shoes as the older man reached for the door handle. Then the banker surprised him.

'Be here Monday and be here smart.'

*

He was and he was. Charlie Castle took the young man under his wing and made him his personal trading assistant – his runner on the floor of the New York Stock Exchange. A runner runs. Runs with trade tickets, runs with corrections to the trade tickets, runs with disputes about the trade tickets, runs with messages, runs with coffee, runs with his trader's orders ringing in one ear, runs with other traders' abuse ringing in the other. And nobody ran like Jeremiah Rankin. He ran for his life. Ran everywhere, but never ran out of steam.

They called him Monkey Boy. And he smiled. And he hated them.

For two years Jeremiah ran, ate shit and ran. Then one day Castle took him for a beer after work. Which he had never done before. He told Jeremiah he had good news and the young man's face broke into an unforced, genuine smile.

'I'm going to get my shot at trading?' Jeremiah was almost out of his chair, ready to shake the hand of his saviour opposite.

'No, better than that.'

The young man was confused. There was nothing better than that. Nothing.

'I've got you an interview at the University of Texas.'

This didn't make sense, any sense at all. This was irrelevant. Castle might as well have offered him two tickets to *Swan Lake* at the New York Met.

'Why would I want an interview at the University of Texas?'

'Because, buddy boy, education is the future. The days of climbing the greasy pole with nothing more than a quick wit and winning smile are coming to an end. They're talking about trading on computers one day. You think they're going to let some runner, some glorified gofer use those?'

Jeremiah protested in every which way, insisting he could sneak in under the wire before the old ways changed but Castle was having none of it.

A senior trader from First Bank walked by and Castle buttonholed him. 'Hey, Stevie, the boy thinks he's got a future in banking without a degree.'

Stevie didn't take his eyes off the game on the TV above the bar. 'Don't be a prick, son, we're fucking dinosaurs. Get yerself a degree or get yerself another job. I hear they're always looking for postmen.'

That was that. And with the promise of as much assistance as he could offer in the future Castle packed Jeremiah off to Houston where he graduated with a Bachelor of Science three years later.

And he had hated every waking minute of it.

Before the ink was dry on his university diploma Jeremiah Rankin presented himself at First Bank of America's headquarters on Wall Street where he found that Charlie Castle had been 'kicked upstairs' to Head of Bond Trading.

Rankin stood in the massive open-plan office with its rows of desks after desks, each laden with heavy telephone equipment and a seemingly NASA-like panel of buttons which he would learn connected each trader to every other trader they would ever need to speak to around the world. The young graduate gawped at the reality of the trading room, the shouting, the yelling – the *noise*.

'Well, don't just do something – stand there.'

Rankin looked with slight confusion at his boss.

'Sit next to me and don't say a word for a month. Shut up and listen and learn.' Then to the room, 'I'm offering twelve at thirty . . . twelve at thirty and a quarter – done!'

Rankin sat down, in awe, in terror and in heaven. He didn't interrupt his boss for a month except to ask Charlie Castle what he wanted for breakfast, brunch, lunch and afternoon sandwiches. He was a runner all over again, but a runner *in a trading room*. Before long he would be taught to trade and not long after that he would become a trader himself.

Rankin proved to be a good, but not a great, bond trader. He hated it when trades went against him and he hated that he never made enough from his winning trades. He hated that getting in before everybody else on his desk didn't help him trade better and he hated that shouting at his analysts didn't mean that he got better information with which to beat the markets. He hated bonus time, hated that his bonus was never big enough and hated Merryweather – the Global Head of Trading – for his annual suggestion that he could always go work somewhere else.

Rankin hated his time as a bond trader and lobbied to manage the traders themselves. Eventually Castle – feeling the strain of his years on the Street – capitulated, giving him the run of the fixed-income business. To the surprise of everybody but Rankin himself he excelled. Not at people management, at team-building or esprit de corps, but at squeezing every last cent from his traders' trades. Profits were up and so were Rankin's prospects with them. By the early 1980s Rankin had grabbed control of both fixed income and equities and was soon responsible for a department that generated two thirds of First Bank's profits.

Eventually, after years of being the first in and last out, of ever-greater black circles round the eyes, of sweating others, of tearing into others, of managing directorships in departments that were nothing more than stepping stones, Rankin reached the peak of the mountain. In 1997 First Bank merged with American Credit. Castle, with differing ambitions to his protégé and with 'too many miles on the clock' took the role of chairman of the company and elevated Rankin – *finally* – to the position of CEO.

Rankin looked out of his window, out onto Madison Avenue, looked about his new room and noted that Castle's office had the better view, the larger executive toilet, the private conference room. He hated it.

Rankin's first act as CEO was to fire his old boss Merryweather.

His second act was to demand and get Castle's office.

His third act was to finally put his plan into action. The plan that had haunted and obsessed him since he first stood outside the New York Stock Exchange at the age of twelve. Watching the men striding to and fro with purpose, importance and expensive shoes. The plan that defined him.

The plan wasn't to make First Bank of America more profitable. Profit was a necessary evil of the plan. The plan wasn't to be bigger than Bear Stearns, Lehman Brothers, Merrill Lynch, Morgan Stanley or Goldman Sachs. Again, leapfrogging them was a result of a well-executed plan. The plan, as Rankin sat in his corner office looking down on Lower Manhattan, in 1990, was to be a member of the most exclusive club in the world. Not a club like Augusta National or Wimbledon. Kiss the right behinds, work the right circuit, glad the right hands and they could be gotten into. Hell, you could even marry into royalty these days if you wanted to. But a green jacket, tie and tiara did nothing for Rankin. He wanted to be – *was going to be* – a member of the club for which there are no invitations and yet exists as the most exclusive in the world. A club which anybody could enter but only a handful ever did. A club that nobody questioned, that everybody respected, that everybody envied.

The billionaires' club.

And this was 1997, when a billion was real money.

For Rankin a billion was the magic number. A man can win the lottery, buy and sell property, back the right stock and that man can make a million, ten million even. But you cannot luck into a billion. A billion has to be *made*. It has to be earned, created, *fought for*. And at that moment it is more than money. It is a fact about the person, a fact that precedes them, that announces more about their person than any character reference ever could. There can be fifty opinions of that person but at the end everybody would have to admit, concede, that *he had made a billion*. He was a financial war hero and to question his stature would be downright indecent. He was a member of the elite.

Rankin was going to make a billion. And then he would be a player, the biggest player on the Street. The vehicle for this plan was First Bank of America. The route was Risk.

10

Suspended Detective Martinez. This did not have the same ring as 'Detective Martinez' or even, for that matter, 'Patrol Officer Martinez'. In fact, to Jenni Martinez, it had the ring of doom. With the mayor's office circling the police department to make cutbacks, no police officer wanted to give their boss a good reason to 'let them go'. Martinez couldn't help feeling she had given Captain Novak a very good reason to let her go.

As for Ashby, it had taken all of Martinez's powers of persuasion to get him to not offer his resignation to the captain there and then. It took charm plus remonstrations to get him to not head down to the USSS field office to 'smack Byrne around whichever cracker-jack interview room he's talking shit in right now'. It was a crap end to what had looked briefly like a successful day. The Madoff Murderer delivered courtesy of themselves but taken away by the Secret Service, along with any hope of credit or involvement.

Martinez walked up the three flights to her one-bed apartment in South Harlem, or SoHa as her landlord had advertised it. Signing up to $2,000 a month rent on her shoebox-sized accommodation hadn't felt so reckless a year ago. Now it seemed like the biggest of a long list of things she soon might have to give up. Like the gym membership she had made full use of that afternoon in a vain attempt to lower her stress levels from Defcon 1 to something approaching Defcon 2.

As Martinez reached her floor she struggled with her gym holdall and a large brown paper shopping bag with its cheaper-than-usual supply of ingredients. Her mood turned worse still when she smelled a mouth-watering Italian sauce wafting along the corridor. Old Man Morello's daughter-in-law must be rustling him something up. Something tastier than she'd be having for a while.

Resting her bags on one raised knee against the wall, Martinez cursed her jumbo-sized key collection and put her key in the door. Then stopped.

The smell of hot food was stronger. She had the sudden realization that whatever was cooking was cooking inside her apartment. Had Ashby told her mother? The idiot. He'd promised not to say a word but he would have gotten home and Mila would have put him up to it. 'It's only Queens . . . She'll need company . . . Of course she said not to but she doesn't *mean* it . . .' No, no, no, Ashby. She goddamn well *did* mean it. She pushed the door open with the vigour of irritation.

'Mom, how many times do I have to tell you . . . ?'

Then she screamed and dropped her shopping, the

bag's contents spilling and bouncing and exploding across the living-room floor.

I looked up from the kitchenette counter that stood between us. I raised my inadequate chopping knife from the garlic I'd been slicing and pointed it at the shopping.

'I hope there's some basil in there otherwise one of us is going back to the store.'

Martinez's face registered a dozen different thoughts and emotions including incomprehension, outrage, confusion, caution and defiance. But mainly outrage. With an indignant finger she took in me, me cooking, *anything* cooking, her dropped shopping, the intrusion, the me-in-the-apartment-at-all, the everythingness of it. Then she got mad and slammed the door behind her.

'I don't know what you think you're . . .'

Then she had another thought. Self-preservation. Wearing a startled look, she dashed out of the room and into her bedroom. Within seconds she was back pointing a Kahr K9 semi-automatic 9mm pistol at me.

'OK, put the knife down and spread your hands on the counter.'

I looked at her in her slummy mismatched gym clothes, grey old-school sweat pants and boxer's hoodie over a T-shirt advertising an ancient community policing initiative. This was a woman who went down to the gym to train and didn't give two hoots who watched her on the running machine. They broke the mould.

'Are you listening to me? Knife down, hands spread.'

I made no sudden movements. 'Or what?'

She didn't need to reposition herself to fire off a round because her stance was already commanding and prepared. 'Or so help me I will take you down.'

'With what?'

'With this, asshole.'

I stuck the knife in the chopping board. 'What you gonna do, club me to death?'

Her face betrayed a nanosecond of doubt but she rallied herself quickly enough. 'Nice try, Byrne.'

I tipped over my hand and dropped seven bullets onto the counter.

Martinez weighed up the situation and swiftly came to a doubtful conclusion. She lowered the gun and put her hands on her hips. 'If you were going to attack me, you would have done it by now, wouldn't you?'

'I never attack an off-duty police officer until after we've eaten.'

'I'm not off-duty, Byrne, I'm suspended – because of you.'

'For which I apologize.'

She rocked her lower jaw from side to side to help her think. 'You didn't come here to apologize.'

'No, I didn't.'

'So why are you here?'

I recalled Ashby's remark to her in the interview room. That she was too trusting. Well, right now I was banking on a big slice of that. 'I need a laptop and somewhere to sleep: you need your badge and your gun back.'

She stared at me, lips pursed. Waggled the revolver at her hip, to remind me she wasn't short of a gun.

I nodded at the thing on her hip. 'Your police-issue gun.'

She kept up the stare.

'As opposed to that *Sex in the City* fashion accessory you've got there.'

She waved a finger at me. 'Oh no, don't you go criticizing the gun. This baby packs a bigger punch than a Walther PPK. It's light and slimline, which makes it one of the most discreet 9mm guns in the world. Killing people and looking good doing it.'

'Yeah, if you don't mind snagging the slide arm on your panties in a crisis.'

'I don't keep it in my panties.'

'Oh. Must have been the way your clothes were hanging when you came in.'

She gave me an Is That All You Got look. 'Don't tell me, a .45 Magnum man yourself? Dirty Harry with the big penis, I mean gun, in his hand?'

We stood in silence. Then I laughed a little and she smiled despite herself.

'Has the Secret Service released you?'

'Yeah.'

'Really?'

'No.'

'Oh Jesus.' She threw her hands up, exasperated, her light mood deserting her. 'Have you killed anybody?'

'Since when?'

'Since – did you kill anybody today during your escape or whatever it was? What *has* happened?'

I took a brief moment to find the right words. 'I left without their permission. But no. It was nothing like that. I promise you, nobody got hurt, really.'

She gave me a deeply sceptical look.

'OK, one guy, broken nose' – I mimed a nose erupting with a splay of my hand – 'but . . . he was a prick. I mean, he was a prick before I, you know . . . his nose.'

She exhaled with what seemed like an air of defeat. 'If I have a lie down, will this all have been a dream?'

'If you have a lie down, you'll miss dinner.' I reached down and brought up two bottles, one red, one white. 'I brought wine, look, one of each.'

'Why one of each?'

'I didn't like to assume.'

Her hands were back on her hips and she struck a pose. 'You break into my apartment, but you don't like to assume?' She shook her head disbelievingly and walked towards her bedroom. 'I'm taking a shower. I will not be offended if you are outta here when I come back.'

11

Jeremiah Rankin looked at his reflection, concave and dark. Smeared. He was resting the offending shoe on the seat of his office chair. He buffed it with a cloth. The wax worked its way into the leather leaving a flawless sheen. Perfection. Except now his fingers had a hint of polish about them. He hated it when his hands were dirty, which they had a tendency to get. Try as he might his nails were forever blackening underneath. Had been ever since his days as a paper boy. He opened a drawer and swapped the shoe cloth for some hand cleanser and a towellette.

'Jerry, we're toast.'

'Charlie, if we can survive Bear Stearns and Lehman's we can sure as hell survive this.'

Charlie Castle squirmed in his chair. 'We only survived those because we ran and hid. Jerry, there's only so long we can keep these losses off the balance sheet. There's only so long we can hide. The share price has tanked this week – the market's on to us.'

Rankin gripped the cloth in his hand and pointed a finger of barely controlled anger at Castle. His former mentor, now greyer and slower, fighting a third bout of cancer, had never reconciled himself to Rankin's constant threat of smouldering violence.

'The quarter's not over yet.'

'It is on Friday, Jerry. And when we – *finally* – admit massive write downs on Monday we're going to make Lehman's look like Bank of the Fucking Year. We have personally signed the accounts since Sarbanes-Oxley, Jerry. We're on the hook for every penny of this.' Castle dropped his head into his hands. 'Christ, we're going to jail, aren't we.'

'Nobody's going to jail, Charlie. Are you forgetting that our own in-house legal counsel approved every vehicle we created out in Bermuda? Approved them, Charlie. To the best of our knowledge we have done nothing wrong.'

Charlie levelled a challenging stare at his CEO. 'Our in-house counsel was telling quite a few people that he was going to reverse that advice, that he had delivered it under duress.'

Rankin shrugged. 'Just as well he can't then.'

'Jerry!' Castle leapt out of his chair. 'How the fuck can you say that?'

'Oh fuck you, Charlie. You know I was as shocked as anybody about that Secret Service nut killing our people. I'm just saying that, well, it's better this way.'

'Jerry . . .' Castle was shocked almost to the point of nausea.

'Not the deaths. Fuck me, Charlie, how long we

known each other? Those people were like family to me, how dare you – how very fucking dare you. I mean, if our own legal counsel was going to blow us all up, then it's better this way. It's better . . . better we can manage the situation. Better all round. Think about it, be practical.'

Castle considered Rankin for a moment then blew his red bulbous nose into a handkerchief. 'Dead or alive this Monday we're still going to have to tell the SEC, the Fed – the whole goddamn world – that we've got a $20 billion hole in our finances.'

Rankin calmed his posture, inviting, by example, the bank's chairman to do the same. They both took a moment, a deep breath then sat down together.

'Charlie, there isn't going to be a $20 billion hole in our finances on Monday.'

Almost defeated Castle slumped back in his chair. 'No, no, no. Please. Have you lost your mind? Do you genuinely believe you're going to move $20 billion off-balance by end of play on Friday? That's two days away Jerry.'

Jerry smiled a killer's smile. 'Charlie, don't give up one yard from the touchline. This is what we do. This is where the money is made. When things turn around, we'll rebalance the books. It's not illegal, it's just complicated.'

Castle felt sick. He waited to collect himself. 'The ratings agencies are going to downgrade us, Jerry.'

'Nobody believes the ratings agencies any more.'

'Jerry, everybody's short First Bank, everybody.'

'Good, let 'em short us. I've told the boys on the floor to take the other side of every trade.'

Castle blinked at him. 'Seriously?'

'Fuck it. It's hero or zero on Friday, isn't it.'

The First Bank chairman sagged, the fight almost out of him. Right at this very moment he regretted ever letting Rankin talk him into staying on at the bank, when his doctor, wife and mistress had all begged him to retire. Damn it, he regretted maybe ever meeting him at all. He leaned his head back, easing the ache that had developed in his neck, the ache that had been there for weeks. Unseen, Rankin watched him with spitting contempt, a quitter, the worst of the worst.

Castle didn't take his eyes off the ceiling. 'You should have been at the executives meeting today, Jerry.'

'Why, what were the maggots whining about this time?'

'Capital requirements, have we got enough money. They're worried we're over-exposed. They're worried the market is right to call our shares down. Worried we're days not weeks from collapse.'

Rankin considered this intelligence. 'How bad was the mood?'

'The *Titanic* metaphor was in use.'

'Don't tell me, let me guess – the "rearranging the

deckchairs" one or the "heading towards an iceberg" one?'

Castle looked at the CEO and sighed at the lack of progress he was making. 'Both.'

'Little pricks. They should be using the "women and children fucking first" one, those rat fucks.'

'Jerry . . .' But Castle didn't want to say it.

'What? Charlie, what?'

'You should show your face.'

'Where?'

'On the floor.'

'Charlie, don't . . .'

'Everybody is on edge – they're terrified. All their money's tied up in this company. The trading room is like a goddamn morgue.'

'Because they're fucking cowards, Charlie, zombies.'

'Jerry, they have a point. They're worried about our book and they don't even know the half of it. If this bank goes down, their money goes with it. Christ, if they knew the truth they really would be heading for the lifeboats.'

'You too with the metaphors?'

'Jerry, everybody on the Street is demanding more collateral . . .'

'Stall them.'

Castle leaned forward earnestly in his seat. 'I *have* stalled them. If I stall them any more, it will set off every alarm bell in Lower Manhattan – and if any of them actually does the math and asks for the collateral we should really be putting up? We'll be screwed, Jerry. Why the hell did you insist on paying the Fed back so quick? Really, I mean, goddammit, Jerry, what were you thinking?'

'Hey, if Goldman Sachs can pay back the TARP then so the fuck can we. You know what message it sends out needing the government's money?'

'That was the best money we ever borrowed, Jerry. Virtually interest free from the tax payer. What sort of message will it send out when we don't have enough collateral to cover our trading? I mean, it hasn't hurt Citibank.'

'Fuck Citi, Charlie!' Rankin slammed the desk three times with his right hand then turned and kicked his chair against the window. 'Fuck, fuck, fuck, fuck everybody else.'

Castle flinched with every blow. But he felt compelled to speak. 'Jerry, calm down.'

'I am calm. It's you and that fucking TARP.'

Rankin dropped into his chair almost sulkily. They sat across from each other, quiet over the need for money, smarting for totally different reasons. Jerry collected himself and tried to take the tension out of the encounter.

'So, how much have we raised?'

'It's hard, Jerry. If we let people know we're trying to raise money because we *need* it – urgently – the game will be up.'

'How much?'

'I've had to be discreet.'

'How much?'

'Five hundred million.'

Jerry reeled in his chair, the number almost like a body blow. 'Half a billion? That won't pay the interest. Have you tried the Arabs?'

'Of course I've tried the Arabs. We've just turned down a loan to Dubai and the rest are balls deep with Citi and Barclays. And, before you ask, the Chinese are thinking about it.'

'*Thinking* about it? Their president, or premier or whatever the commie fuck is, is over here this week – it'd be the perfect piece of public relations. What the fuck does thinking the fuck about it fucking mean?'

'It means they know we are shitting ourselves about capital requirements but when we get to the point where we're about to pimp our own children they'll get a better price.'

'What's a better price?'

Castle went to speak then didn't. Didn't want to say it. But the look of rising anger in his CEO made this futile. 'The whole bank.'

'The *what*, Charlie? I asked you to raise fucking capital not sell the fucking store.'

'Don't shoot the messenger, Jerry.'

'Don't shoot him? I'm ready to torture him to death. How fucking hard can it be to raise $4 billion? We're First Bank of America. Have you tried Warren?'

'He passed.'

'Passed? What do you mean he passed? That cocksucker didn't pass on lending Goldman's $4 billion. Why the fuck did Buffet pass?'

'Maybe he can read a balance sheet.'

But Rankin wasn't in the mood for flippancy.

'Jerry, he said he had some concerns. Said he wasn't comfortable with our numbers.'

'But we gave him the same numbers we gave the SEC.'

'He used his own numbers.'

That stumped and worried Rankin. He had to think quick. 'Maybe we can persuade him . . .'

'Jerry . . .'

'I'll get him on the line, we've met a dozen times, he likes me.'

'Jerry, he said he was "going to pass at this time". His exact words.'

A silence hung between them.

'We need to feed the beast, Charlie.'

'I don't think the appetite is out there, Jerry. The share price is tanking, they know, they know . . .'

'Don't you dare, Charlie. We are two days from rising like a fucking phoenix. We are two days from sticking it up the rear end of every smug smiling fuck on Wall Street. We are two days from victory. The money's out there, Charlie — you're just asking the wrong people. We need greedy people, people who aren't going to ask too many questions.'

'Like who, Jerry?'

'Like investment bankers.'

12

Martinez's apartment was compact, to say the least, but the touches she had put about the place made it a nice place to be. The furniture, what there was of it, was as much yard sale as IKEA. Small bookshelves, small armchairs, a sofa that doubtless doubled as a bed. And the colours, bright without being loud. All in all, attractive. Just like its tenant.

A red dusk over Manhattan dimly lit the dining portion of the small living room. Isaac Hayes played softly in the background. The detective eyed the large bowl of fresh pasta in front of her. Conflicted. Then as the steam carried the blend of Italian flavours up to her face she drew them in through her nose. Quite unselfconsciously she paused to savour the moment that comes before savouring the food.

'OK, we'll eat then you really are outta here.'

I poured her a glass of dark crimson wine to match my own. Without any hurry she took a forkful of spaghetti and Bolognese sauce to her lips and slowly began to eat. She made a faint noise I had last heard a woman make in bed when I had been in a particularly thoughtful frame of mind.

'Oh Jesus, oh fuck that's good.'

Which by coincidence is pretty much what the woman in question had said. I half raised my glass to her.

'No, that's better than – fuck. Fuck, Byrne, this is – Did you –? Where did you –?'

'Took a year off after the Service. Went travelling. Tried different things. Worked in some kitchens and stuff.'

'Jesus, Mary . . . Why did you have to be a felon?'

'I'm only a suspect.'

She reached for her glass. 'You escaped custody. I'd say that was slightly more than – what the fuck?' She slowly pulled away from the wine glass and looked at its contents with bewilderment.

'The 2004 Barolo. Just goes great, doesn't it.'

Martinez laughed.

'What?'

She shook her head and smiled, bleakly I thought.

'Come on, what?'

She put her glass down with a whisper of regret in her face. 'This would be . . . nice if it wasn't so . . .' She trailed off and looked up at me.

'Fucked up?'

'Mm. Yeah. That.'

We both ate. Pleasing food occasionally broke into her gloomy thinking but a cloud had descended.

'Let's assume you didn't come here to cook me a

meal as an apology. Though, if meals could act as apologies this would come pretty near the top. You mentioned a laptop and my badge.'

'I did.'

'How does you getting access to a laptop and a place to crash get me tight with my captain?'

'OK, Jenni, if I can be allowed to –'

'How did you know my name was Jenni?'

'Um, came across some mail when I was looking for the gun.'

Her hand went up to her mouth. 'Did you find –?'

I spoke quickly. Too quickly. 'I didn't find anything else.'

'I've never used it.'

'Fine. I mean, whatever.'

'It was a present, a joke, from an ex. A very ex.'

'OK. Doesn't matter.'

'Oh, because now you think I'm a –' Defensive now, emphasizing every remark with a jab of her fork.

'Martinez, I don't think anything. If anything . . .'

'What?' Her embarrassment was now fuelling a righteous anger.

'Well, if anything, given how useless the gun was to you . . . I was just pleased . . .'

'Go on, Byrne, I'm listening.' Which was Woman for 'There is nothing in Shakespeare's language that you can say to dig yourself out of this planet-sized hole that you have dug yourself into, but give it your best shot anyhow.'

She was glaring at me – daring me.

'Well . . . I was just pleased there was another weapon in the apartment.'

She looked at me askance, wrong-footed. Then she laughed. I waited. She laughed some more and reached for the wine. 'Jesus, Byrne. I guess this is so fubar there's no point worrying over minor details. What's your plan?'

'Simple. To find out who killed those bankers and why they put me, specifically, in the frame.'

She sipped her wine. 'Go on.'

'What do you mean?'

'I mean, elaborate.'

I sat back in my chair. 'That's as far as I got.'

She raised her eyebrows mockingly at me. 'Oh, well, that's that case sewn up.' She battled with a roll of spaghetti that was refusing to stay wrapped round her fork then took in a scent in the food, tried but failed to identify it. 'What is that . . . ?'

'Celery.'

She chided herself with a tut. 'Of course.' Then she shook her head as if enjoying a meal so much bordered on nonsense before pulling herself back to the matter at hand. 'So, let's get this clear. You were going to get a good night's sleep and then first thing in the morning Google "Who set Mike Byrne up for the murder of four First Bank of America executives?" Great plan. How can that not fail?'

I gave her as tight a smile as I thought her remark

deserved. 'The Russians. They went to the trouble of kidnapping me. The first thing I need to do is to find out who was behind that.'

'Yeah, maybe the Russians were bragging about it in an internet chat room.'

'Did the police get any leads on the bodies?'

'No. DNA will take a while but fingerprints showed nothing.'

'Nothing?'

'Not a thing. They're ghosts.'

'Nothing. That means they were smuggled into the country to do specialist work.' This troubled me. I looked at Martinez. 'You know this isn't Odessa, don't you. This is way too big.'

'Then who is it? Russian mafia?'

'Maybe. It's something – somebody . . . new. Maybe not from here, maybe the mafia out of Russia itself.'

'What about your job as financial investigator? Make any enemies?'

'Plenty. But just white-collar petties, nobody with this kind of pull.'

'What about First Bank of America? Could they be behind it?'

'First Bank?' I looked into my wine glass like an answer might pop out. 'I wouldn't assume that. For all we know, they might be on the receiving end of this themselves. It's their executives getting bumped off, after all.'

Martinez's face lit up. 'Blackmail fits.'

She'd got there. I wasn't worried about her drawing the same conclusion, she was whip smart, but I needed her buy-in desperately. 'Blackmail. Absolutely.'

She was getting excited now, the detective in her detecting a thread to cling to. 'Dig a little deeper we might find First Bank being threatened with extortion, blackmail, all kinds of shit. This is bread and butter to the Russian gangs, Byrne, and who knows what new schemes they're dreaming up these days. All the victims worked for the bank – I wouldn't be at all surprised if the answer to this is in there somewhere.'

We both thought on its implications for a moment.

I looked up at her. 'What did the other security cameras show?'

'Where?'

'In the First Bank building?'

Martinez shrugged. 'Nothing. They were all wiped by y– whoever did it.'

I acknowledged her slip with a wry smile. 'What about the security guard?'

'What about the security guard?'

'Who else did he sign in on Monday night?'

'We don't know.'

'What do you mean you don't know? You mean you haven't interviewed him?' I couldn't believe it.

'Byrne, we never found him. We assumed that . . . whoever perpetrated the crime disposed of the guard, as the only material witness.'

'What about other people in the building? Didn't anybody see anything?'

'There were no other people, Byrne. Nobody is due to move into that building till the weekend. It's their new offices or something.'

This didn't add up. 'Then why hold the meeting there?' I felt a sudden surge of excitement as I seized on a lead. 'Who arranged the meeting?'

'Already checked. Oliver, the chief operating officer.'

My rush of enthusiasm slammed into a wall, battering my spirits. 'Well, what about Rankin?'

Martinez shook her head. 'Who's Rankin?'

'Jeremiah Rankin, the First Bank CEO. He had promised to make the meeting but didn't show.'

'Oh, yeah, I was going to ask him – but then you got me suspended, remember?'

It was only half in jest. Martinez collected the plates and headed towards the kitchenette.

'We'll need to speak to Rankin. He might even know who had it in for his bank staff.'

Martinez's movements around the kitchenette had the sharp edge of dredged-up anger. I could see her mood was swinging between interest in my theories and bitterness at the mess I'd gotten her into. I couldn't depend on her support. Not yet.

'Did your AV guys say anything about the film of the shooting?'

'No, we didn't get that far.' Talking slightly sullen now, preoccupied. 'And as far as I know we handed the investigation over to the Secret Service.' As Martinez put an espresso pot on the stove I could see her mind whirring. 'What about the Service? Can't anybody there help? Give you a heads-up?'

'I don't know. There is one person but she wasn't very forthcoming. I don't know what to make of her.' 'Heartbreaking' was the word that kept coming to me when I thought of Diane. I found her lack of faith in me harder to bear than the fix I was in.

'So why did the Service take you into custody? Was it one of those "We clean up our own shit" things?'

'Oh god no.'

'Then why?'

'They think I want to kill the president.'

'Fuck.' I turned at Martinez's sudden movement. She had poured coffee over herself in surprise. 'Why the fuck didn't you say? What the fuck aren't you telling me, Byrne?'

'Nothing. I mean, I'm telling you everything.'

'Then why the hell did they make that connection?'

'They didn't, really. I did.'

'Sorry, you're going to have to explain.'

'The Russians said they were holding me till the end of Friday afternoon, just after the end of the ground-breaking visit to Wall Street by the Chinese premier and Potus, I mean, the president.'

'I know who Potus is – I've seen *24*. Why the connection?'

'The kidnapping deadline was four p.m. The ground-breaking visit is three p.m. to four p.m. It seems reasonable to assume a link.'

Martinez headed over with the coffees. 'So the Secret Service concluded that somebody's planning to attack the president?'

'No. *I* concluded that – or something like it.'

She sat down with the coffees.

'Really?'

'Definitely.'

'But what's it got to do with you?'

'I've no idea. Either they want me as the fall guy – again – or . . .' I shrugged.

'Or what?'

'They're worried I can stop it.'

She looked at me with curiosity, trying to size me up. She added two sugars to her tiny espresso cup and stirred thoughtfully.

'Where you gonna start with all this, I mean, apart from Google?'

'Go back to the apartment in Tribeca, find out what I can find out.'

She sipped her coffee.

'Helping you could be dangerous.' She was watching me carefully over her steaming coffee cup.

'Helping me *could* be dangerous.'

She contemplated me. Contemplated me like she needed one more thing to pull her over the line.

'And what's in this for me?'

At last. 'Simple, Martinez. Help me and hopefully by Friday you'll have solved the murders of the First Bank executives and discovered why Russians are driving around New York kidnapping people.'

She eyed me carefully. 'Or if we don't I at least get to take in the Madoff Murderer.'

I took a moment to take on board her terms. 'Of course.'

A little smile creased her eyes. 'I like that.'

The horn of a cab carried through the Harlem night. She sipped her coffee and took a slow long look at me through her long dark eyelashes.

'And if I don't help you?'

'Simple.' I finished my coffee and put the cup on the table. 'I think somebody will kill Potus.'

13

Where the president moves, the United States Secret Service Protection detail moves too. They move ahead, alongside and behind. They have to strike the balance between the president's desire to 'meet the people' and their desire that the bed the commander-in-chief sleeps in that night is his own and not a hospital one. In a world where everybody wishes their job was more interesting, a good day in the Secret Service is a day where nothing happens.

For Special Agent Diane Mason today was the opposite of a good day.

She was beginning to doubt the wisdom of her career ambitions within the Service. What she didn't doubt was that she regretted mentioning to Deputy Director Carlton in her annual review that she felt her natural next step was to HQ in Washington. Carlton had called her on it pretty damn quick. Challenged her to prove her abilities outside the running of a financial investigations team, personally recommended her to head up Protection for the upcoming state visit to New York by Potus and the Chinese premier. The words of Michael Byrne floated back to her from her vain attempt to talk him out of quitting the agency all those years ago. 'Be careful what you wish for, Diane.' After the logistical boot camp of the last few weeks, she'd be a lot more careful in future.

Sitting at her desk in the New York field office in Brooklyn, Mason considered a parcel in front of her. With a passing moment of guilt she looked out of her small glass-walled box of a room to the large open-plan office beyond. Nobody was watching. The parcel had been couriered over this evening and whilst she hadn't seen his handwriting in a long time she instinctively felt it had been sent by Byrne. She pulled a set of scissors out of a desk tidy and cut the tape at one end. Inside was a shoebox which she carefully pulled out. Something almost childish inside her wanted to guess its contents before lifting the lid. Knowing Byrne it could be anything from vital case evidence to cupcakes from Magnolia Bakery. Right now she found herself wishing it was the latter. Tentatively she lifted the lid of the box. For a moment could not comprehend its contents but then as she pulled the broken-down parts of the gun out the penny dropped. Byrne had returned the FN Five-seven service revolver stolen from Agent Quinn during his escape earlier that same day. Stolen by Byrne, used by Byrne, dismantled by Byrne and sent back by Byrne. She shook her head. *Only Byrne.* Diane considered the parts of the gun in her hand unhappily, and thought the same thing she had been thinking since lunch with Michael the day before. *Oh god, Diane, what have you done? What have you started? What have you gotten Michael into?*

But as bad as things were there wasn't time for this. She placed the parts of the gun back in the box and locked them in her bottom drawer. Another problem for another time. She touched the side of her face, wanted to check the swelling brought on by Byrne's attack earlier that day, wanted to see if it was noticeable or nothing more than a dull ache. But that too could wait. Because right now she had a Class A problem waiting for her in a conference room down the hall.

As Special Agent Mason walked briskly through the large open-plan office her mind raced with the preparations for the presidential visit to the groundbreaking site in Lower Manhattan in two days' time. The site had been inspected every week for the last six weeks, now it was being inspected daily. She had coordinated each and every team assessing and preparing for all perceived threats to the president's security and well-being, as well as Chinese security with their concerns for their premier. Advance Teams from DC had travelled ahead of the trip to plan the minutiae of manpower, equipment, the preparedness of hospitals – including the readiness of supplies of the president's blood-type – and evacuation plans from all and any points along the route during the visit.

Such preparations had involved Mason liaising with the military, federal, state, county and local law enforcement bodies, fire departments, port and civil aviation authorities. Ultimately Mason's security plan involved what every presidential visit includes: an air plan, a waterway plan and a transportation plan. She ran through the checklist, which had become akin to an internal mantra for her. She breathed a little easier, believing every aspect accounted for, everything mapped out.

Every eventuality has been planned for, thought Special Agent Mason. *Every eventuality except this.*

She put her hand on the outside of the briefing room door, took a deep breath and entered. Inside were seated two dozen Counter Assault Team agents, with Deputy Director Carlton standing off to one side. She strode unflinchingly to the head of the room where a fifty-inch television on a stand was displaying the United States Secret Service symbol of a five-point gold star.

'Good evening, Agents.' She was acting natural, professional, in command. The opposite of how she felt or how she would be viewed after letting a suspect flee from the room in which she was interviewing him. 'I am Special Agent Diane Mason and I am the lead agent on this presidential visit. We will not be covering the details of Potus's visit but reviewing what we believe to be a highlighted danger.' She looked up and caught Deputy Director Carlton staring intensely at her. 'A clear and . . . present danger to Potus.

'As I am sure you are all aware there was a severe security breach at this field office earlier today when an individual wanted in connection with two multiple homicides escaped during questioning.' She looked squarely at the team of trained counter-terrorist experts. 'I am sorry to say that this suspect was formally a special agent working in this building.'

Something approaching a collective gasp filled the room. The news had rocked the hardened group of men with many putting their hands up to pose questions.

'Gentlemen, please, my briefing should cover most of the questions that you will – naturally – want answered.'

'Who is he?' A murmur of support endorsed the last enquiry.

Mason stood her ground until the room had settled. She didn't doubt their discipline – their iron discipline – but the events of the day deserved an explanation if her credibility was to remain intact. The men stilled, she clicked a small remote control in her hand. The large widescreen television showed a Secret Service identity card from a decade previous.

'His name is Michael Byrne, no middle name. Caucasian, six foot one, dark hair, grey-blue eyes. He worked for the Service from 1992 to 2001. He left the

Service in what – it is fair to say – was a state of disillusionment over the administration's strategic direction.'

Deputy Director Carlton stepped in. 'We should also add that psychologically he was traumatized by the loss of his fiancée in the 9/11 attacks.'

Special Agent Mason wore a sceptical look that went no way to endorsing her boss's contribution.

A hand went up. Mason accepted the interjection with a nod.

'Ma'am, are you saying the suspect in question has gone rogue? Is he targeting the Service?'

'Well . . .'

Carlton moved further into the men's field of vision. 'I think we should adopt that as a working assumption, yes.'

Mason was determined to be straight about Byrne, if only for the benefit of the Counter Assault Team members. 'It should be noted that former Special Agent Byrne had worked with a private financial investigations company for the last few years without any complaints from his employers or any reports of any untoward behaviour. If he has "snapped" it is sudden and currently unexplained.'

Another hand. 'Ma'am, his ID card says he was a financial investigator with the Service.'

'Yes?'

'With all due respect, ma'am, how much trouble can a Fin be?'

Mason gave nothing away but instead clicked her remote control. A new slide showed Byrne's employment record. There was another bout of surprise from the men – but a respectful surprise, with more than one impressed whistle rising and falling. The record showed no less than two or three outstanding achievements in every one of Byrne's years with the Service. Byrne had passed top of his class at the Federal Law Enforcement Training Centre in Glynco, Georgia, at the subsequent Criminal Investigator Training Programme, as well as the main Secret Service training centre in Beltsville, Maryland.

But the respect of these men was mainly reserved for the citations accrued by his annual victory in the Service's Marksmanship, Unarmed Combat competitions and, finally, the presentation of the Secretary of the Treasury Award, the highest investigative achievement award attainable within the Department of the Treasury.

An agent rubbed a hand across his shaved head and turned to Commander Becker next to him. 'Handy mother.'

Becker lifted a finger. 'Ma'am, may I ask why an agent like Byrne wasn't in Protection or Counter Assault?'

Mason handed out two piles of documents for passing along. 'He liked financial investigating, believed the money world was full of bad guys who just needed catching. Couldn't be convinced to move. And, as you will see in the profile being handed out, he took a pretty hands-on approach to arresting offenders. I attended a number of arrests with him in this country and Central and South America, involving everything from drug cartels to human trafficking. I can assure you, he got his fill of action.'

Mason could see from the nodding heads of the CAT members that a few of them had read down his resume to the description of the facts surrounding the apprehension of targets. The situations were hostile – Byrne's actions had been uncompromising.

'Plus, whilst it's not on his record, I can tell you, anecdotally, that he felt his mindset was better suited to what he termed "proactive work" over "reactive work".'

There was a grumble of hurt pride. Commander Becker spoke for the room, for his troops. 'Let's see how proactive he gets when he's got the CAT on his ass.'

Mason let the alpha-male nodding subside. She didn't disapprove. A room full of tree-huggers wasn't any good to her.

'Gentlemen, as you are aware, Potus is here in a little over forty hours. The Advance Party has completed a comprehensive security plan that is being actioned as we speak. However, it is our belief that – regardless of whatever security measures are put into place – whilst former Special Agent Byrne is in New York Potus's security is compromised. We have shared our concerns with the White House's chief of staff but, at her request, we have decided to proceed with the visit by Potus and the Chinese premier. Our job is to apprehend Byrne before he finds an opportunity to breach our security. We have forty hours to track him and bring him in.'

Commander Becker raised a finger and earned a nod from Mason. 'Do we have a location on the suspect?'

'The Police and Transportation departments are scanning their security-camera footage in and out of the city and have been unable to locate him beyond entering Manhattan via the Brooklyn Bridge on motorcycle. After that . . .' She gave a small apologetic shrug. 'Our best course of action at present is vigilance coupled with the hope that he shows his hand. I don't need to remind you, gentlemen, that Michael Byrne is a highly able individual who should be approached with caution. Extreme caution.'

Deputy Director Carlton stepped forward. 'By which Lead Agent Mason means – for the avoidance of doubt – that the use of all necessary force is sanctioned.'

Mason needed to clarify this. 'In truth, whilst an escapee, he is at this stage no more than a suspect in an investigation.'

Carlton turned and glanced at her. None of the

Counter Assault Team saw what she saw. A flash of menace. A look that said, 'Don't you *dare* fuck with me.' He turned calmly to the assembled agents.

'Agents, be in no doubt: if you get a shot at Michael Byrne – take it.'

14

Tribeca, Wednesday night. The red-stone apartment block. The scene of my kidnapping two nights before. Perhaps the only building in the area not yet redeveloped by Robert de Niro. I wondered what he'd do with this one? Maybe a little boutique hotel sprinkled with a touch of 'hostage chic'. Fur-lined manacles on the radiators, velvet-covered designer bars on the windows, that kind of thing.

'What are you thinking?' It was Martinez behind me on the Ducati. We were parked in an alley opposite the offending building, looking for signs of activity. But despite a coming and a going, Russian criminals were noticeable by their absence. What we had seen for the last fifteen minutes were people leaving to party when most people would be hunkering down to sleep. Creatures of the night.

'Guess I'd better go take a look.'

I kicked down the stand on the motorcycle and stepped off. Martinez remained seated but pulled the helmet off her head and shook her hair down onto her shoulders. A streetlight reflected in her eyes, just in case I'd forgotten how pretty they were.

'Want me to come with you?'

'No, you stay here with the bike. Be ready to walk away from it if you think it's been spotted.'

I hung my helmet on the handlebar and made to leave when she reached inside her leather jacket and pulled out her 9mm semi-automatic. She spoke hesitantly.

'Here, take it.'

I considered the gun for a moment, considered the two minds she was in about offering it to me. Regretted fleetingly having sent Agent Quinn's pistol back, a gun I lived and breathed with back in my Service days, a gun I could use in my sleep.

'Thanks but no thanks. I'd hate to ruin any designer clothes by putting a pin-prick in them.'

'How about I put a pin prick in your leg?'

We smiled kind of seriously at each other.

'Look, you're already out on a limb here, Martinez. I don't want to give you another cause for concern. Keep it and if you suddenly come to your senses you can "take me down".'

'Fuck you, Byrne.' But it was said with just the right kind of smile.

I climbed onto a dumpster below a fire escape and made the modest leap up to the bottom landing. I pulled myself up and over the railings and paused to listen. There was a TV playing in the apartment next to me but the outside stairwell was virtually pitch black. I wouldn't be seen. I climbed the two floors to the third. The window was closed but if memory served it would be a small matter to force it open.

Diane had always scoffed at my insistence on leaving cash with trusted equipment suppliers around the city. The Service's unofficial motto is 'Hope for the best but plan for the worst'. Given the sleazebags I was dealing with – rich sleazebags at that – I had always calculated that one day I might get compromised during an investigation, that some money-is-no-problem crook would go all out and set the dogs on me, that I would have to go to ground without Service back up, however briefly. Being able to get my hands on some cash and supplies in a crisis could be the difference between a long and happy retirement and an unclaimed corpse in the morgue. What I hadn't planned for was that it would be the Service itself hunting me down. Perhaps it was true what they say: even the paranoid have enemies.

I reached into my pocket and pulled out a Leatherman multipurpose tool. I flipped out the sturdiest-looking flat screwdriver head and jammed it in between the window frame and the sill. I tested the weight then leaned down on it. I could see a near-useless catch on the other side ride out of its fitting until it popped and the frame rose up an inch. I looked about me and listened for a reaction to my break-in.

Nothing revealed itself and I slid the window up, slipped into the living room and guided the window back to closed. I reconfigured the Leatherman and had a tight-beamed flashlight at my disposal. Streetlights washed the rooms but no amount of light was going to illuminate this crime scene for me. There were body-outlines showing where my kidnappers had fallen. One on the floor and, rather surreally, two marked out where they had been sitting on the couch. Behind the head of one was a large dull patch where they had cleaned his brains off the wall.

Guided by flashlight, I moved carefully from room to room, diligently looking for a scrap of writing, the butt of a foreign brand cigarette, a rail ticket – anything. I didn't expect to find much. This was, I conceded, a temporary location. The living room, mattress-only bedroom and bathroom offered nothing. I soon concluded that between the probable carefulness of the Russians and police forensics there wasn't enough here to bother an obsessive compulsive housemaid.

Still, the visit didn't have to be a complete waste.

I made my way to the bathroom. Naturally, nobody had repaired the ad-hoc ceiling light I had used two nights before on my guard, so the room was in darkness. Allowing for its age, I carefully stood on the toilet seat, the flashlight in my mouth shining on the high-up cistern lid I had raised by one hand. With the free hand I pulled a plastic bag dripping with water out of the tank. My last act before leaving the apartment two nights before was to hide this here . . . planning for the worst. I replaced the lid and stepped down. I unrolled the bag and let it float to the floor as I held its contents. The Mark XIX Desert Eagle 0.50 pistol.

All 10.75 inches of it.

What diet of straight-to-DVD sub-Hollywood action flicks and R-rated shoot-'em-up computer games leads an immigrant gangster to buy one of these was beyond me. The Desert Eagle Magnum was twice as heavy as it needed to be, twice as long as it needed to be, twice as loud as it needed to be. Hold it incorrectly and the recoil could snap your wrist. And as for stopping people? This thing could stop a maternally outraged grizzly bear. There was no arguing with militia nut jobs that it looked the part, but until shoot-outs were won with 'My gun's bigger than your gun', I was yet to be convinced.

Still, beggars, choosers and that kind of thing.

I shoved the pistol half down the front of my pants and hoped the bagginess of my jacket would cover it. It was when I was about to make my way back to the living room that I heard a noise in the communal hallway outside.

I stood stock still and gripped the handle of the gun.

Motionless, I watched under the door, listening for any untoward movements. A shadow broke the beam of light that filtered in underneath, its owner dropped

149

something heavy just beyond the door, then returned past and down the corridor. The walker wasn't being careful and, I guessed, wasn't interested in this apartment.

I crept to the door, pulled on the latch and ever so slowly opened it a crack. The view was impeded by a zigzag of police crime-scene tape across the doorway. Thirty foot away the platinum blonde from the previous night was heaving a large, cheap suitcase out of her front door. Only now she didn't look like a vampiric night-clubber but more like a college student in sweater and jeans. She seemed in a hurry but she didn't seem scared. Late for a plane? Putting distance between herself and the Russians?

The Eastern European woman tugged without success at her front door. Then she thought better of it, pushed the door open, tossed in the keys and slammed the door closed as much as she could. Clearly what was behind that door was no longer her problem.

She turned and leapt back. Only a quick hand to her mouth muffled the cry.

I was one long stride away from her. She collected herself and quickly feigned indifference. The shakiness of her hand was soon cured by the lighting of a cigarette that she pulled out of a packet inside the open handbag that hung sloppily from her shoulder. Sloppy like the rest of her get-up. Her rather pleasing get-up. When she spoke her Russian accent was as thick as an exchange student's on her first day in the country. 'You shouldn't do that. You could scare somebody.'

I nodded at the cigarette in her hand. 'You shouldn't do that. You could kill somebody.'

She looked at the cancer stick she had just lit and gave me a slanted smile. 'We've all got to die of something.'

I took a step towards her. She fought the urge to back off but tightened all the same. I reached down and lifted up her suitcase. She relaxed an iota and gave me a queer look, knowing she recognized me but not being able to place me. She couldn't gauge the situation and – quite rightly – it was bothering her.

'You don't remember me, do you.' I wasn't posing a question.

I turned and headed for the top of the stairs where I collected her other suitcase. She followed me – or, at least, her bags – down, unsure of me and what might be about to happen.

'Should I? I meet a lot of . . . men.' Somehow I felt that the word 'customers' would have slotted in there without too much trouble.

I made my way down the stairs with the girl in tow.

'Maybe you don't recognize me. I was outside your neighbour's door.'

'Excuse me, no, nothing.'

'Monday night?'

'Again, sorry, no.'

'Oh, Mike, by the way.' I lifted up the suitcases to show I was helpless to shake hands.

'Oh, Nadia. A pleasure.'

We continued down the building.

'Erm, let me think. I was wearing this.' I indicated my dark leather jacket like it might ring some bells.

She looked lost. 'No.'

'There must be something . . .'

We reached the building's main entrance and stepped out onto the sidewalk where I put the suitcases down.

'Oh, I know . . .'

'Yes, please to tell me.'

'I had four Russians pointing guns at me.'

We looked at each other, me with an air of expectation, her with the cigarette glued to her lips to cover her ratcheted nerves.

'Know anything you want to tell me?'

She shook her head and adopted a defensive attitude that involved crossing one arm across her stomach to prop her other elbow up, the cigarette to her lips. 'I'm sorry about what happened, very bad. But I don't know who they were. Really. I tell the police all this.'

We stood. Me waiting, her stressing.

She lit another cigarette off the first. 'I saw them about, you know, now and then, but it's not like we exchanged business cards.'

'Do you have any business cards?'

'Hmm. I'm more, how you say, word of mouth.'

That crooked smile again, but less confident. I stared at her.

'I'm sorry I can't help, really. I don't choose my neighbours. You think I like man like that where I have to live?' She looked up and down the street, waiting for someone.

'Doesn't seem like you live there any more.'

Her response was to smile. 'No, no. After the bang bang killing, my boyfriend insist I move somewhere more, hmm, respectable.'

'Oh, so my kidnapping wasn't all bad.'

'Exactly.' She looked me up and down with more than a modicum of interest. 'Let's just say I owe you one.' She smiled the kind of smile that other women hate and every man loves.

Careful not to give the impression that I wasn't getting her attention, Nadia covertly resumed her checking of the street both ways and showed palpable relief when a yellow cab slowed to a halt towards the kerbside. 'OK, well, nice to meet you, Mike. Sorry I couldn't help you more. Really I am.'

I didn't believe her, not completely, but investigations are about getting a result and I didn't think there was much left in this line of questioning. She shifted her weight from one foot to the other awkwardly.

I nodded a goodbye. 'Hope it works out for you in the new apartment.'

She brushed her expensive platinum hair from her eyes, looked up into my face and smiled a smile that told me it already had.

15

'What was that?'

'What was what?'

Martinez was speaking in an urgent whisper so as not to attract attention to ourselves down our alleyway. We were watching Nadia get into her taxi in a hurry, struggling to give the driver instructions to her destination, her haste probably making her attempts all the worse.

'That was me talking to Nadia.'

'Nadia?' She emphasized the familiarity, critically I thought. I suspected she was glaring at me from her position behind me on the motorcycle. 'On a street where we know Russian criminals are active? What if a vanload of Russian goons turned up? What the hell would have happened then?'

'Is this your way of saying I was flirting with the witness?'

'Do you know any other way? I mean, for somebody with a Secret Service background you don't know much about "secret", do you.'

The yellow cab pulled away and I booted up the Ducati. I revved the engine back into life and enjoyed the Jurassic roar that filled the alleyway behind.

'Martinez, time is not our friend here. If standing in the middle of the street will flush out the people behind the First Bank murders any quicker, then all the better.'

She started to say something else but I was already on the move and unable to hear. I got a smack on the back for that.

Nadia's cab headed east across Broadway before turning north up Lafayette Street. Nothing dramatic was happening up ahead and I was more interested in who might be following her – or us. But despite falling back and drifting to different sides of the road, no other cars warranted attention. At East 14th the cab turned right for two blocks before heading north up Third Avenue. I was half expecting the taxi to take the tunnel towards Queens but it kept on up past 34th, 42nd and eventually 59th. This was the Upper East Side, Central Park way, a nice part of town and, from the way she was leaning into the screen behind her driver, one I felt she might be expecting to move to.

Her car stopped between 68th and 69th and we pulled over a hundred feet further behind. Trump Condominium territory. Somebody had some money.

A doorman walked towards the rear of the cab and opened the door. Nadia stepped out and gave him a little wave in passing, not breaking from the animated conversation she was engaged in on her cellphone as she ducked into the building with an air of familiarity. She had been here before. My guess was that whatever had been their love nest had now become her home. I let the bike creep forward until we were level with the entrance to her building. Inside she was off the phone and waiting for the elevator.

'What does this tell us, Byrne?'

I wasn't awash with answers – or optimism. 'It tells us she's probably going up in the world.'

'Are you certain she's linked to the kidnapping? Living next to criminals doesn't guarantee an association. A stakeout feels like a bit of a long shot right now.'

'I know.' We watched Nadia and her bags disappear into the elevator.

'What do you want to do, Byrne?'

I quickly did the math then came to a decision. 'Let's do some investigating instead.' I checked the traffic and made my way north towards Harlem.

One minute later half a million dollars' worth of Maybach limousine pulled up outside Nadia's building. The same doorman opened a rear passenger door, delighted by the unparalleled quality of the door's mechanism, its smooth operation. Out stepped Jeremiah Rankin.

The First Bank CEO did nothing to acknowledge anybody's presence but, phone glued to his ear, strode past the saluting doorman and into the building.

'No, no, listen, listen, listen to *me*. Once a deal is

agreed upon there is no going back, that's how it works. I placed a trade and I want delivery . . .'

He was in the plush elevator, an exercise in gold-leaf kitsch. An elderly woman pushed her button and looked at Rankin. He pointed at the eleventh floor and smiled curtly. She was slow to pick up on his signal so he reached across her and stabbed his floor, the conversation continuing his ear.

'No . . . No . . . How many times – if you accept my trade, that's it. That's how it works . . . I know there are not many brokers who can handle a trade like this, I don't dispute that, but we worked our balls off –' He gave a small apologetic nod to the momentarily offended woman in his elevator and turned half away from her. 'I need you to work this trade for me – everything is riding on it, *everything*. We agreed it was up to you to put the deal together. If you have mispriced part of the trade, I am prepared to look at that – but the trade *must* go ahead.'

The doors opened and he strode out of the elevator and up the floral-decorated corridor, clenching his fists, furious that this was the one person in the world he could not get furious with. At least, not right now.

'Good, good, that's all I'm asking. There's enough upside here for us to both take a little hit . . . Good, good. Well, goodnight.'

He arrived at a door and stopped. He looked at his phone and punched it off for the night. The door opened. His scowl melted away and his face broke into a greedy smile.

Before him stood Nadia.

Dressed like a schoolgirl. Platinum hair in bunches.

'Please, sir, I forgot to do homework.'

16

Martinez dropped her keys on the kitchenette counter as I dropped into a chair by the small dining table. It had been a long day and it wasn't anywhere near over for me. My eye fell on a line of CDs on a nearby bookshelf. Not a lot but what there was was good.

'So?' She waited by the sink, wanting an answer.

I looked at her enquiringly as I pulled a CD out from her collection. 'I need a bit more . . . Maybe a noun, an adjective, a verb . . . ?'

'This whole run-in with First Bank and you *not* shooting those four executives because of your parents' lost savings?' She was rinsing out the wine glasses in the kitchenette. 'Didn't you know Madoff was a crook, being a financial investigator and everything?'

I leaned over and slid Marvin Gaye's *What's Goin' On?* into her music system. 'I only ever looked at him once, back in 02 when I was investigating some wealth manager. He had the lion's share of his clients' money with Madoff. A quick look at Madoff's returns told me something was wrong.'

Martinez came over with glasses and the bottle of

white and sat opposite as she did the honours. 'How was it so obvious?'

'His returns were too high and too consistent. Nobody's perfect and if you tell people that you are, that you win day in day out, then you're a liar. God couldn't beat the markets every day.'

'Wow. Really?'

'Well . . . maybe, if he worked for Goldman Sachs.'

'So why didn't you turn Madoff in?'

'He wasn't the subject of my investigation. I dropped a friend at the SEC a line, told them they might want to take a look.'

'What did he say, your friend at the SEC?'

'*She* said' – I took a moment to lay my gender correction on thick, which earned me a look that was more Fuck You than Thank You – 'she said they were swamped with a big case involving mutual funds and she'd have to get back to it.'

'OK, so she passes, but when your dad sticks his money with Madoff that must have set alarm bells ringing with you?'

I sipped on my wine. Sicilian. As close as I ever wanted to get to the mob. 'If I had known my dad was putting my mom's money with Madoff, I would have had a lot to say, but . . .'

Martinez pulled a sympathetic face. 'Not close?'

'Not overly.'

'The short version?'

'Boy meets girl, girl gets pregnant, girl and boy wed, boy walks out one day with all the money, girl devastated and brings son up the hard way, on her own. Fast forward thirty years, now retired girl inherits some money, boy – now a widower – comes back, flowers, apologies, changed man, all that bullshit, girl takes him back. Boy goes bragging to his buddy at First Bank of America, buddy sets up sales meeting, boy hands *girl's* money over to First Bank, First Bank hands money over to Madoff, Madoff makes off with girl's money, First Bank say, "Nothing to do with us." The end.'

She whistled in appreciation of the scale of the rip-off. 'No wonder you *didn't* shoot them.' She raised her drink and an eyebrow. 'So much for me having a monopoly on asshole fathers.' She put her glass down with some purpose. 'Now, I've followed the Bernie Madoff thing and here's what I don't understand: He was robbing Pedro to pay Paulo, right?'

'Using new investors' money to pay the fabricated returns on existing investors' money, yeah.'

'Well, how did all those investors and bankers and analysts and all those other people with their smarts not see what he was doing?' She sat back with her glass.

'Simple. Greed.'

'But it didn't add up.'

'Collectively, no, but as long as a Ponzi scheme is paying out to the individuals, the individuals don't question it. People's capacity for greed, stupidity and laziness are fairly limitless. Con artists bank on it and they are rarely disappointed. People are too lazy to do the leg work involved in careful investments.'

She wagged that finger at me. 'Bullshit. People don't just put their money with any old person.'

'Really? Who do you bank with?'

'Me? Wachovia.'

'They solvent?'

'Yeah, I guess.'

'Are they about to run out of money?'

'No. Well, I . . . don't know.'

'Did you look at their books before you put your money with them?'

She took the bait. 'But I don't need to – the SEC approves them. Ah . . .' She raised her glass touché-style.

'And that's how Ponzi schemes flourish. People trust the regulators, you have to. But the regulators have a comically small budget to police the financial world with and as long as the Wizard's paying out you don't look behind the curtain.'

Martinez sipped on her wine pensively. 'Ponzi. Italian, right?'

'Yeah.'

'As in Italian for "pyramid", as in "pyramid scheme"?'

'No, as in Italian for Ponzi, Charles Ponzi.' I topped us up. 'He's not the guy who invented them but he's the first one the press really seized on. Let's just say he had a better PR agent than most crooks.'

'And was he trading like Madoff?'

'First of all, Madoff wasn't doing any trading, he just said he was. But, no, the thing Charles Ponzi *wasn't* doing was a kind of arbitrage.' She gave me a knitted brow look. 'It's where you can buy something over here and sell it over there immediately at a profit. After the First World War, Ponzi claimed that it was possible to arbitrage – make a quick profit – on a thing called International Reply Coupons. They were like pre-paid post from overseas. Well, he discovered that it was often cheaper to buy the stamps abroad, say, in Italy, than they cost over here. So, you buy them in Italy for a dollar, sell them here for two dollars, instant profit, arbitrage.'

'But he was lying, right?'

'No. You really could make a great profit on this trade – *before* costs.'

'But nobody looks behind the curtain, nobody checked the costs . . .'

I lifted my glass to her. 'Right. The story sounded good, enough of the facts added up and the good citizens of Boston piled in.'

'But when he failed to make a profit surely it all unravelled . . . ?'

'He did make a profit – for his early investors. He gave them their fifty per cent return. Then a combination of advertising by Ponzi and bragging by his early customers required him to go out and buy the biggest and shittiest stick in the state of Massachusetts to keep new investors away.'

'Like Madoff with investors begging him to let them in.'

'Exactly.'

'People *begging* to be ripped off.'

'Exactly.'

'That would be the greed, stupidity and laziness you mentioned.' She shook her head in disbelief at her fellow citizen.

'The holy trinity of personality traits in every sucker, Martinez. Anyhow, then Ponzi hires a bunch of agents and pays them over-the-top commission to put their friends and family and clients and fellow country club members into his scheme –'

'Like Madoff.'

'Just like Madoff and the feeder funds, the fund of funds, and so on.'

'So how did Ponzi get found out?'

'Well, a freelance financial analyst did the math and when two plus two equalled minus a half, he said as much.'

She pulled the wine glass she was drinking from away from her lips, excited to get a point in as the jigsaw started to take shape. 'Like that guy did with Madoff, the one who tipped off the SEC.'

'Harry Markopolos. Told anyone at the SEC who would listen.'

'Which was . . . ?'

I took a sip of wine myself. 'Nobody.'

'So, this Numbers Guy, was he listened to?'

'Yep. By Ponzi, who promptly sued him, for libel.'

'And lost . . . ?' She was sceptical. She was a fast learner.

'And won. Half a million dollars – in the 1920s.'

'So it was the authorities that got him?'

'Try the local Boston newspaper. They got another analyst, Clarence Barron, to look at Ponzi's scheme. He quickly concluded that for it to work Charles Ponzi's company would have to be buying and selling 160 million of these International Reply Coupons he said he was arbitraging.'

She looked at me, waiting for the other shoe to drop. 'The catch?'

'There were only 27,000 in existence. There was an immediate run on the scheme as investors wanted their money back.'

'And that's when it all came crashing down?'

'Oh no. He had so much money he just paid off the sceptics until the storm passed.'

'Didn't Madoff –?'

'. . . Do that occasionally? Yep. And Ponzi did exactly the same thing again when the financial regulators finally took an interest.'

166

'So how did it end?'

'The *Boston Post* finally dug up Ponzi's past as a convicted fraudster with his two stretches inside. At that point the authorities stepped in.'

Martinez emptied the last of the bottle of wine into our glasses with assiduous fairness. 'At least the regulators have improved if they didn't have to wait for the press to out Madoff.'

'Madoff wasn't caught by the regulators.'

She put down her wine glass in amazement like she didn't trust herself not to drop it. 'But the SEC . . . ?'

'Went in when he fessed up. Madoff was caught because the credit crunch caused his customers to need cash in a hurry. He paid out billions but was suddenly on the hook for $7 billion which even he couldn't rustle up.'

'You mean if it wasn't for the credit crunch Madoff could still be . . . ?'

'Could still be raking it in.'

Martinez whistled, somewhat dumbstruck. Almost nervous about the world she lived in.

I drained my glass to match Martinez's now-empty one.

She was impressed by the scale of it, mulling over the ramifications of it all. 'And there's the average robber using shotguns to hold up liquor stores. They should learn to think bigger. If you want to commit a robbery, just wear a suit and tie and people will queue round the block to give you their money.'

I nodded in agreement.

We sat in silence, the room lit by a soft light from across Central Park. Manhattan lay sleeping but not sleeping, like it does. Marvin Gaye riding high in the midnight sky.

Then I felt it.

Our legs resting against each other under the table. Not on purpose, but now that they were neither of us was making any move to separate them, both of us enjoying the unfamiliar touch.

We looked across into each other's eyes. For one second too long.

The Latino woman's fulsome lips parted. She was either about to say something or knew just how plain crazy parting her lips like that would send me.

This could go either way.

Which is why I hated to do what I had to do next.

'Martinez?'

'Yes, Byrne.'

'Could I borrow that laptop?' It took a moment for my request to filter through all the other possible comments she was evidently expecting. 'I need to take a closer look at First Bank.'

It took her a further moment to suppress the conflicted feelings that had risen up in her. 'Sure, yeah.'

Martinez rose slightly sluggishly, tired from the events of the day, the late hour, the wine. She disappeared into her bedroom and was back a minute later with a large laptop, its cable piled on top. I could see she'd had a talking with herself back there and that she was in a different frame of mind now. More steadfast, maybe even a little bit angry.

'Don't look at my stuff.'

'No, no, of course not.'

I set the laptop on the table. Martinez made another journey, this time returning with a duvet and pillow which she dropped onto the small couch.

I yawned for both of us. 'Thanks.'

'Byrne, nothing personal, but taking everything into account . . .' I waited. '. . . I'm gonna put a chair up against the door.'

'The apartment door?'

'My bedroom door.' She flashed her eyes knowing I'd turned the screw of her discomfort.

'OK. Very sensible. That way any intruders will only get as far as me.'

She rolled her eyes and walked away. 'You *are* the intruder.'

I booted up the PC and prepared to do what I do. Investigate.

Martinez was lying on her side, dull strips of sunlight creeping in around her curtains. She opened her eyes slowly and checked her alarm clock radio. Just after seven. She'd slept in on what she still called a 'school day'. She'd slept in when all her colleagues on her shift were dragging themselves to the station. She'd slept in. And it felt awful.

She looked at the door beyond her crumpled bed-covers, her small ineffectual faux-rustic chair wedged under the handle. She was under no illusion about its purpose. One more self-imposed obstacle telling her not to do anything stupid. It had worked. Regretfully.

Her senses picked up something else. There was a smell, a lovely smell. They were becoming a habit with Byrne. Coffee. Fresh coffee. Fresh coffee –

– in her bedroom.

Martinez sat up alert, unconsciously sweeping her gun up in her hand from under the near-side of her bed. Ready. Ready for something, anything. Still waking up, she looked around, pointing her gun about her. Nothing making sense. The chair still in place. The window closed. But there it was, a hot mug of coffee next to her bed. A Post-it note attached.

Alarm was replaced by curiosity. She pulled off the Post-it note. The top line of writing, underlined, read: 'Morning, Princess: To Do List'.

And the New York Police detective placed the fully loaded Kahr K9 semi-automatic 9mm pistol on the duvet before her, smiled and thought, *He called me Princess.*

17

Rankin took his place.

Every day at the appointed hour before the markets opened he was welcomed with the practised and enchanted smile of the maître d' in the restaurant of The Carlyle hotel on East 76th and Madison Avenue. It was genteel and luxurious and the right side of chintzy. It was a little piece of England on the Upper East Side, equidistant between the penthouse Rankin shared with his wife on Park Avenue and the condominium he shared with his lover on Third. Framed prints of aristocratic fox hunting and silverware on the finely laid tables banished any thoughts of the busy New York streets beyond as patrons were transported for the duration of their visit to Piccadilly, London.

The First Bank CEO knew that here he would not be bothered by the bratty commotions of Z-list celebrities or the chic-addicted A-listers. The clientele was typically politicians, socialites, fashion and media magnates. But even this look-at-me crowd would not be stirring at this hour and breakfast would be as it always had been – in silence. The rest of the day would be non-stop meetings, organized mayhem with black coffee. But the start of the working day allowed for a pot of English Breakfast Tea, served in silver pewter with a Wedgwood bone-china cup. The fare was typically something off the Reduced Calorie carte, unless a mood lifter was required, when something more indulgent was allowed an outing. Today was such a day.

The discreet European waiter paused whilst Rankin lifted his *Wall Street Journal* and *Financial Times* from the table. An exquisite white plate of eggs Benedict was delicately placed before the banker. This might well prove the highlight of his day and he was determined to enjoy it. Which made the arrival of an uninvited guest doubly unwelcome.

I slid into the bench seat perpendicular to Rankin's own. The banker did not recognize me and took a moment to assess the intrusion before realizing it was wholly unacceptable.

'Do you mind? I'm about to eat.'

'I do not mind that you are about to eat. Mike Byrne, concerned activist investor.' I put out a hand by way of a greeting.

Rankin's immediate reaction was heightened irritation and a contemptuous look at the proffered hand. He had to retrieve my name, but once he had he froze and clearly felt dread in his stomach. Guilt was writ large across his face and even if I hadn't sat down with my suspicions I had them now. This was a guy who would not only deny chopping down the cherry tree but would sue for damages anybody who suggested otherwise. In my mind, that one-hand-caught-in-the-cookie-jar look changed Rankin from walk-on part to leading actor.

'What is it, what is it you want, Mr Byrne?'

I put away my unwanted hand. 'I want two things.'

I looked down at the poached eggs on ham and toasted muffin, the thick luscious hollandaise sauce drooping off the side, perfect, untouched. 'Do you mind if I order the same? Starved.'

Rankin was eyeing me across the table the same no-sudden-movements way he might eye a rabid 150lb Rottweiler. He gave the plate a gentle, slow shove towards me. 'Here, I've lost my appetite.'

I looked at the plate like the gesture had melted my heart. 'Aw, shucks, and there's the press giving you bankers such a hard time.' I pulled the plate towards me and added some salt and pepper.

Rankin kept his movements to a minimum. I could see he had no inclination to tackle me on a physical level, which suited me just fine, as I was about to eat. He spoke with caution, wanting to do nothing to provoke what he saw as the mad dog now eating next to him. Rankin was confused that a man who ought to have the hunted look of a convict was instead tucking into breakfast like we did this every Thursday morning.

The food was delicious. Showdown or no showdown

I was determined to enjoy it – who knew how many prison meals I had coming? 'Mmm, you know, Jerry, whenever I'm in London I try to eat breakfast at the Wolseley, next door to the Ritz. You ever been there?'

Rankin spoke like he was waiting for a trap. 'Can't say as I have.'

'Oh, you should. They do this thing called Eggs Arlington Royale, at least they did last time I was there. It's basically your eggs Benedict, but instead of the eggs being served on ham they serve them on Scottish salmon with – get this – a teaspoonful of sevruga caviar. Mmm.' I shook my head at the memory. A preposterous but undeniably great meal.

'You said there were two things, Mr Byrne.'

Rankin sat motionless, watching, calculating, hoping. He braved glances at the waiters but none caught his furtive looks.

I noticed the bank CEO's distress and stopped eating for a moment. 'I'm sorry, am I keeping you from your day?'

'Obviously, yes, I guess.'

I used the last piece of muffin to clean up the golden yellow egg yolk from my plate. I could see he was trying to read my mood, read where I wanted to take this. 'What was I thinking.' I shook my head, reprimanding myself. 'Your bank loses all of my mother's money and I have the audacity to keep you from your day. Where are my manners?'

I chewed on the last of my/his food and looked at Rankin, without emotion, blank.

Rankin gave a small uncomfortable cough then made the smallest open-handed gesture. 'I apologize, you take as long as you want . . . need.'

I beamed a smile at him. 'So, number one. My parents' Madoff investment went south.'

'I can . . . assure you that those monies can be refunded.' Rankin waited to see the effect of his words.

'Shall I pop by this afternoon, pick up a cheque?'

The CEO retained his studied air of calm, but I could see his mind racing. 'I can't see that being a problem.'

I thought about it in a way that told Rankin I was balancing the options in my mind. 'You know, just mail it to my mom.'

'OK, not a problem.'

'That's agreed, is it?'

Rankin stiffened slightly and looked back at me with resolve. After decades on the Street, I could see that the agreement, the contract, the bond ran through him. 'You have my word.'

Did I believe him? No. Did I want to get into it now? No.

'OK. Number two . . . Who wants to hurt First Bank so much that they would gun down four of your top executives?'

Rankin wet his mouth where I guess it had gone dry. He chose his next words carefully, wanting to tread carefully. He didn't want to anger me by dancing around what ought to be said but didn't want to anger me by not saying it either.

I gave the hint of a smile. 'Apart from me, that is.'

'I . . . really don't know who would want to murder members of my staff. Everybody and nobody.'

'No angry customers, no bitter rivals, no ripped off counterparties . . . ?'

Rankin was on more comfortable ground. 'It's Wall Street – everything's love-hate. We all love the game, love beating the other guy, and we all hate anybody who's doing better than us.'

'And who is doing better than you, Jerry?'

Rankin stopped to choose his words. 'What do you mean, "better"?'

'What else would I mean? I mean money. Who's making money right now?'

'Some.'

'Some rivals?'

'Us, some rivals . . .'

'Really? First Bank's doing well?'

'Sure. Who says otherwise?'

'Well, apart from your stock price looking like the dying days of Enron, I've been looking at your filings with the SEC. They don't add up.'

'Maybe you can't add up.'

I really smiled now. 'I read that about you, Jerry. Two speeds. Attack and Kill.'

Rankin was careful to talk with authority but without antagonism. 'Our CFO went through all the numbers with the SEC this summer. The numbers add up.'

'You see, Jeremiah, I own shares in every bank you've ever heard of and a few you haven't. Not a lot. Where possible, just a single share. But you know what that single share gets me, don't you.'

Rankin wasn't thrilled about the direction this was taking. 'It gets you their annual report.'

I pointed at him approvingly with the napkin I'd just wiped my mouth with. 'Gets me their annual report. Just sits there on my computer. Gathering virtual dust in its virtual world. Until I need to look at it.'

'So you looked at it. This year's numbers add up.'

'They do. They do, Jeremiah, of that you are correct. So did last year's. And the year's before.'

'So the numbers in our annual reports add up – what's your point?'

'Sorry, keep forgetting about your busy agenda.' I smiled until I was sure that that was the last time Rankin was going to demonstrate impatience. 'Well, since you ask, Jerry . . . The thing is, try as I might I just can't get the numbers to add up when I run a few years through the system all at once.'

There was a flicker of unease in the CEO's eyes. 'I don't follow.'

'Exactly. I couldn't follow one year to the next, couldn't see where all those great sub-prime derivatives you had on the books before the credit crunch had gone once the proverbial had hit the fan.'

From Rankin nothing, just thinking. Thinking how to manage the situation.

'Almost, Jerry, like somebody somewhere picked up a large rug the size of, say, a small Caribbean island, and swept all those bank-crippling losses underneath. Away from prying eyes. Prying eyes like mine.'

Nothing from Rankin.

'If I was a betting man, Jerry, I'd be taking a big fat short on your stock right now. Because from where I'm sitting you look like a very little boy with a very little finger in a very big dyke full of shit. Am I wrong?'

That's when Rankin's entire being rebelled against the direction the conversation had taken. Because either First Bank's balance sheet was his little baby – or I'd just found his very sorest point. His teeth gritted, his face contorted. 'You listen here, Mr Byrne In Hell, there is nothing wrong with First Bank's balance sheet and not only are you welcome to short our stock, I'll lend you the money to do it – with pleasure.'

I watched him. Asking myself what that response told me. One thing was for sure – I didn't believe a word he was saying.

On the table his smartphone started to ring. It was sitting between us, vibrating, the ring a tiny chirrup, no louder lest it offend the other restaurant guests. I peered at the screen.

'Peterson? The Treasury Secretary at this time of day? Must be important.'

Rankin looked at the phone, uneasy, unsure, not knowing what to say or do.

I put on a genial demeanour. 'Go on, pick it up. Maybe he'll be calling to congratulate you on your balance sheet. Maybe you've won Creative Accounting of the Month.'

Rankin looked at the phone. He almost licked his lips.

'Pick it up. I insist.'

Rankin believed me, took the call and put the phone to his ear. 'Richard? . . . Yes, would it be possible to have this . . . ? . . . Today? I . . . Oh, I didn't realize you were in town . . . Great, see you there at noon . . . Perfect. OK.'

I watched him. Watched him try to hide his consternation about the call. 'Lunch? With the Treasury Secretary? Today? Why the rush?'

Rankin was keen to underplay the call. 'No rush, we just meet up periodically, that's all. He likes to hear the word on the Street, as it were.'

Rankin began to put his phone into his inside jacket pocket when I held out my hand.

'What do you want my phone for?'

'Gadget freak.'

I kept my hand out. Insistent.

Hesitantly, Rankin handed over his phone the way

most people would hand over their life savings to a mugger. I held the phone up to my face, inspected it, wiped the screen with my napkin.

'Nice. Has it got any games?'

'I don't have time for games, Mr Byrne.'

I looked at him with a squint of amusement. 'Very good, Jerry.' Unnoticed by the CEO, I had slipped a phone-jack into his phone and began to upload some software. 'I see your phone's wallpaper is a picture of King Kong.'

Rankin shifted, uncomfortable, but knew enough about selling to build on small talk. 'Oh, that was Zoe, my PA. King Kong is the nickname I got as a bond trader. Of course, they were talking about the original, not the, er, remake by that, erm, *Lord of the Rings* guy.'

I smiled, two buddies talking shit to each other. 'Peter Jackson.'

Rankin pulled a slightly helpless face. 'I wouldn't know.'

'Slave to the markets? No time for going out to the movies?'

'Pretty much.'

Unseen, I pulled out the phone-jack as the phone buzzed again and a caller name blinked into life.

I wore a look of surprise at the name flashing up. 'Charlie Castle calling? What, no nickname for your chairman?'

'Like what?'

'Oh, Bitch. Patsy. Fall Guy.' I handed Rankin the phone back. 'Go ahead, he's calling to tell you the stock's fallen out of bed again.'

The CEO eyed me warily but, despite himself, wondered why I was saying it. 'Charlie, what's up?' Rankin's head jerked back and he could not help but look at me, angry and suspicious. 'Rumour? What fucking rumour? . . . But I just got off the – did the leak come from Treasury? Those fucking pricks have fucking mouthed off for the last – . . . How the hell could anybody know? . . . What SEC inspection? . . . No, no, I can't exactly, not right now . . .'

I waved away Rankin's concerns. 'No, no. This meeting's over.'

The bank CEO spoke with caution to his chairman but was in reality posing a question to me. 'I'll be there in ten minutes.'

I nodded easily.

'See you then.' Rankin carefully put away his phone. 'That everything?'

'That's everything.' I dropped my napkin on the plate in front of me. 'You know, Mr Rankin, the newspaper profiles . . . They tell us where you eat but they don't go anywhere near enough in telling us what great company you are.'

Rankin waited.

'You go, Jerry, losses don't hide themselves you know. I'll get this. I ate it.'

Rankin wiped his hands on his napkin and slid out of his bench seat. 'I'll get that cheque sent to your mother.'

I lied for both of us. 'I know.'

Rankin wore an expression that told me nobody had talked like that to him for a very long time, but he swallowed his pride and walked away.

I watched him leave. Knowing the bank CEO would be damned if he was going to hand over the money.

Then I made a mistake.

I looked down.

I looked down when I should have been looking around me.

I pulled out my own smartphone to access a website, wanting to check the software I'd just uploaded to Rankin's phone.

I looked down and didn't see the Russians walk in.

Didn't see a thing until two Russians slipped into the long seats either side of me, four of them, penning me into the crook of the bench.

I instinctively went for the gun inside my jacket, but large vice-like hands on each of my arms stayed my movement. The one on my right snaked his hand down my arm, closed his fingers round the Desert Eagle and took it out and into his lap before dropping a napkin onto it.

I checked out the gorillas sitting immediately next

to me. Heavyset, like Russian T-90 tanks. Next to one of the tanks sat a small wiry blond who looked like he survived on a diet of hamburgers and coke, only the wrong kind of coke. On the other side, next to the other tank, was a familiar-looking face, but a face that was confusing me.

'Do you recognize me, Mr Byrne?' His accent thick, his accent familiar. Not just Russian but a Russian I'd heard recently.

It was my turn to be caught off-guard. 'I'm not sure. Have we had the pleasure . . . ?'

I recognized him and I didn't recognize him. I was trying to place him but I couldn't. He was angry at me, livid. Why . . . ?

He smiled a smile of dirty teeth. 'Fuck you, Michael Byrne.'

And that was when I knew who he was. My stomach turned. This wasn't making an awful lot of sense. It was the Ringleader from my kidnapping.

'Didn't I . . . kill you the other night?'

He waited again. 'You killed a part of me.'

It was my turn to wait. I was out of answers.

'I believe you met my brother, Vladimir.'

I studied his face. 'Twin brother.' Half question, half guess.

'Bingo.'

I nodded in a way that let him know I was suitably impressed. 'Well, Mr Bingo, a pleasure.'

His eye twitched, but he checked himself with a cold smile. 'I will tell you my name just before we have finished with you.'

I wasn't exactly awash with ideas and buying time was the best I could think of. 'Would you mind if I had a coffee before we go?'

The Russian was half amused, the prerogative of the confident. 'Sure, why not.'

He caught the maître d's attention and mouthed the word 'coffee' and gestured a circle to indicate a round of drinks. Across the room the maître d' nodded with practised grace.

'Am I allowed to ask what this is about? I mean, apart from the obvious revenge element?'

Mr Bingo gave me a long, languorous stare. 'You kill me, Mr Byrne.'

His look was dead eyed but his colleagues chuckled gamely.

The Wiry Blond smiled at me but spoke in Russian to his boss. 'You want me to slice him right here?'

Mr Bingo seemed to dismiss his subordinate's suggestion. Instead he spoke in English. 'Mr Byrne, we have car outside. After coffee we take you for ride. We tell you what we think of you hurting our operation, our start-up. America love start-up – you being a bad American.'

Mr Bingo nodded at the hotel restaurant exit. I followed his gaze. Guarding the way to the lobby were two serious-looking men who I didn't doubt were part of my current group. From the bulges in their long black coats I also didn't doubt they were packing metal, either.

I sat back in my bench seat. 'OK, I'll bite – what's so important that your boss keeps sending people to pick me up?'

'All in good time, Mr Byrne.'

'Go on. Tell me here.'

A waiter moving with a complete lack of fuss approached us with a silver jug of coffee on a tray, which he hovered over our table. He smoothly rotated the jug so the handle faced us.

Mr Bingo allowed himself a small grin. 'Why so impatient, Mr Byrne?'

'Because I'll be fucked if I'm going anywhere with you.'

If you know where to pinch a person, you can cause them to faint. If you know where to hit a person, you can cause them to faint or experience pain out of all proportion to the effort involved.

I stamped a foot onto the top of one foot of each of the gorillas sitting immediately next to me, grabbed the coffee jug's handle, slammed it into Mr Bingo's face, then turned and threw the pot at the Wiry Blond whilst I uplifted the table towards the rapidly retreating waiter.

The gorillas had doubled over at the shock and

injury to their smashed feet, Mr Bingo was grabbing his scalded face, but the Wiry Blond was up and after me almost immediately. He flailed out a hand which I grabbed and twisted, snapping back enough fingers to send him to his knees in paroxysms of agony.

A table being upturned plus four people yelling in pain had brought the genteel room and its pampered clientele to a shocked standstill and I wasted no time in sprinting off towards the kitchen, the two Russian guards by the hotel restaurant entrance – pulling out their guns – immediately on my tail.

I burst through the swing door and found myself in a long, sizeable kitchen with a central cooking island down the length of the room, people working both sides. I ran down the left aisle as the door exploded open behind me. I dodged chefs big and small, surprised and irritated, each panicked and wrong-footed by the fast-moving trespasser. That's when the bullets started.

Indignation in the kitchen turned to terror as the two Russian door guards paused to pour automatic gunfire after me. I ducked as I ran, pulling a shelf of pans down behind me, hearing the bullets pound into them, the shelving blocking one aisle, forcing one of the overweight gunmen to double back.

I stopped to get my bearings and realized I had run down the wrong side, the exit door being across the island from me. *I had to get through that exit.*

I scooped up three chef's knives from the counter, gripped the blade of one and whipped it towards the Russian charging down the opposite aisle, waving his gun at me. The knife driving into his throat caused him to shoot wildly, his automatic revolver spraying machine-gun-like into the ceiling. The Russian stumbled then dropped gasping to the floor, his aimless gunfire finding the leg of a young Vietnamese dishwasher. The dishwasher fell to the ground screaming. One of the scattering chefs paused to grab her and dragged her through the door I so wanted to reach.

I looked up and down the island and spotted that a large pan of oil had been abandoned on a stove, but there was no getting to it. The second Russian was now barrelling down the other side of the island, gun raised, as the gorillas and Mr Bingo charged through the kitchen entrance. I threw both remaining knives at the foremost Russian, one missing, one embedding in his arm. He staggered against the wall and reached for the knife to pull it out. By now the three extra Russians were pointing their guns in my direction.

I pushed over two large boiling pots of soup into their aisle and sprinted away at a crouch. The three Russians skidded in the thick liquid which had covered the floor before them, half falling on top of each other in the confusion.

I had to get through that exit.

I swung my body over the island as they attempted

to get to their feet. Around me were knives and pans and appliances, and I relentlessly delivered each one as if it were a throwing knife into the Russians in turn. Way more chaotic than I wanted but momentarily effective in slowing them. Buying me a split second to think. *Trying to get to that exit, but not making enough progress . . .*

The gorilla nearest to me was righting himself under my blows. I grabbed a rolling pin and smashed it fiercely into the side of his head, breaking his skull and the wooden cylinder in my hand, dropping the gorilla like a sack of potatoes.

But the knifed Russian was suddenly on me, throwing punches and kicks at me that revealed a martial arts training more advanced than any conscript's. This felt like Spetsnaz training, the mongrel martial arts they taught their elite Russian forces, their Seals, their SAS. This guy not angry that he'd just had to pull a knife out of his arm, but steadfastly forcing me back with a series of calm, controlled strikes, taking up all my focus. We exchanged blows, the Russian raining punches and kicks down on me, softening me up for the inevitable grab. I stepped away to disrupt his rhythm. He swiped a large carving knife from the counter. I did the same and we stood opposite each other, blades flashing. He lunged at me, round and towards my neck. I caught the blade with my own and swooped his arm down and between us. I grabbed the forearm of his armed-hand but he slapped it away and brought his knife across me. I slapped him away with my forearm, my blade pointing at him, but he punched it away, bringing his knife round. I blocked with my knife, forced his arm down, round, up – he punched my knife-hand away, came at me, got punched away. I plunged, he parried, my blade snapped –

He swung his knife arm round, I blocked, grabbed his wrist, twisted it. He arched backwards, I punched his stabbed arm – a yell – another punch – a cry, the Russian forced to cover the wound with a hand, me reaching for the nearest thing – a long carving fork, bringing it round, swinging it up under his chin, the Russian staggering backwards, clutching at the handle of the fork embedded in his brain, the two tongs appearing out of the top of his head, blocking one gorilla and Mr Bingo – *everybody between me and the exit* – levelling their guns at me . . .

I dropped to the deck as automatic bullets ripped around me. Moving fast, I rolled myself over a large shelf underneath the island, pans and crockery showering around me as bullets tore through them.

I scrambled along the floor, looked back down my aisle, saw the gorilla lifting and throwing my improvised barricade of shelving out of his way towards the entrance. I jumped to my feet, he aimed and fired. I dragged a nearby fridge door open, shielding myself, watching the bullets thump shapes into its industrial-strength plating.

I grabbed a jug of milk, *anything*, from the shelf, stepped out and threw it towards the gorilla.

The huge Russian ducked instinctively but even he could tell immediately that it had been a harmless missile. Until he saw where it had landed. Into the pan of boiling oil next to him. Which woofed a flame up and about itself, spraying that portion of the room and the gorilla with oil and fire. Instantaneous roaring, raging flames – engulfing him. Consumed by the fire, he lunged away from the blazing pan, toppling backwards towards me, a staggering inferno.

Now Mr Bingo was at the far end of my aisle, gun raised.

Gorilla and flames at the other end.

Gorilla turning, pulling his revolver madly, enraged, enraged that this should happen to *him*. Roaring, screaming, charging tank-like towards me but blinded by the oil burning his face, firing his gun, firing at the world. Mr Bingo ducking these wild attacks on me, on the room – me dodging the charging Russian, stepping behind him as Mr Bingo emptied his gun into his associate's massive frame.

And in that chaotic moment I rolled over the island and dived through the exit, pursued by bullets.

I watched Mr Bingo through the door's tiny window. He was looking at the chaos around him, the out-of-control fire spewing into the ceiling, the smoke rumbling along and above, the out-of-control scene that had left his comrades dead. Furious, he came in my direction. Evidently expecting me long gone, he pushed through the door unguardedly. And received a two gallon oil can in the face which sent him flying back into the burning kitchen.

I tossed aside the large can of olive oil as I stepped in after him. I reached down to Mr Bingo's concussed body and pulled a heavily modified revolver from his hand, all gangster bling – unnecessary sights and an Uzi-style magazine. Boys and their toys.

The Russian was not quite out of it and hazily, groggily, was attempting to come round.

'Mr Bingo, who sent you?'

He looked at me, coming round, making sense of it. 'Who sent you?'

Then I heard it, police sirens. And if I could hear them in here they must be close.

'Who – sent – you?'

Weak, he smiled an evil smile, blood pouring from his gums, covering the teeth that weren't broken by the olive oil can, shattered crimson tiles.

I stuck the gun in his face, under the cheek to deliberately hurt a nerve. But he was beyond that kind of pain. 'Who ordered my kidnapping? Who set me up? Who wants me dead . . . ?'

He spluttered a single laugh. 'Fuck you.'

I looked down the length of the room, through the porthole of the kitchen entrance. Police officers were entering the restaurant beyond at speed, looking around, trying to get their bearings.

Mr Bingo was smiling at me. Beyond pain, beyond caring.

I let go of his shirt, let his head smack off the floor.

The police were approaching.

It was moving time.

18

Martinez leaned against the small nondescript rental car she had acquired for the trip. She looked at the map. Scarsdale, Westchester County, New York. She'd heard about it but never had cause to come here. Had first noticed it in an article about Beyoncé, how her and her man had set up home here. Shit, if New York royalty chose to live here, what did that tell you about the price of real estate?

Martinez looked through the gates and up the driveway at the address she had sought out. Mock Tudor. A mock Tudor mansion. Except calling this a mansion was like calling the Sahara Desert quite sandy. It was a very big mansion with exactly too many rooms and too much square footage. Martinez couldn't figure who would buy such a thing or why they would think it was a nice idea. The size of a country hotel. She groaned inwardly when she thought of her rabbit-hutch of a pad back in Harlem. Evidently, making New York a safe place to live in wasn't where the money was at.

For the fifth time that day she rang a Florida number. Standing in the crisp air, surprisingly biting for such a bright September day, the Latino hit the speakerphone button, tired of holding the device to her aching ear.

It rang and it rang and then it got picked up. Martinez wasn't ready for that.

'Yes?' It was a middle-aged woman's voice, guarded, firm.

Martinez was fumbling, forgetting the sequence of buttons required to un-speakerphone it.

'Yes?'

'Mrs Stewart? Mrs Stewart?'

'I can't hear you. Try calling ba —'

'Mrs Stewart? I'm sorry for the speakerphone, I'm, erm, driving.'

'Yes?'

'This is Detective Martinez of the New York Police Department.' It distressed her to be using her title off-duty, suspended as she was.

'I've gone through all this with the Boca Raton police department.'

Martinez was struck by the impatient tone of the recently widowed lady. 'I do apologize for taking up your time . . .'

'Look, is this strictly necessary?'

'Well, we're investigating the murder of your husband, Mrs Stewart, and I just had a few questions.'

'No, no, now can I stop you there? What could you possibly want that I haven't already told the local police?'

'It's just that this is an ongoing investigation, Mrs Stewart . . .'

'Well, have you got any new information?'

'No, that wasn't the purpose of the call.'

'Then what is the purpose of the call?'

Martinez had gotten past her initial awkwardness and was now finding her temper tested by the woman. But what could she do? She was abusing the privileges of her position and felt awful about it. 'The purpose of the call, ma'am, was to ascertain a few more facts about your husband, facts that might help us to construct a better understanding of how he might have been caught up in this terrible crime.'

'No, no, I don't believe there is anything I can add that I haven't already told the Florida police.'

'Sometimes it's the most incidental –'

'Look, this is a very difficult time for myself and my children. We didn't see their father for weeks at a time, especially recently. The last thing I need is to be asked the same fifty questions by fifty different people.'

Martinez was finding the woman hard to deal with. Rich bankers' wives – could they all really be this unpleasant? Was there some other race of people, some Great Gatsbyesque banking world where the women really believed they were better than the mere mortals around them?

'Then could I give you a number, in case you change your mind . . . ?'

'It's not about changing my mind – it's about wanting to grieve with my children and about getting back to a normal life. Now, if there's nothing else, I believe the local police and our family law firm can deal with any further questions you may have. Do you have our law firm's details?'

Martinez didn't speak. She didn't trust herself.

'Do you? . . . Hello? Are you there? Oh, really . . .'

And Mrs Stewart hung up.

Martinez stared at her phone, nonplussed by the widow's behaviour. She wanted to kick something. Wanted her job back so that she could nail that woman for failing to cooperate with a police enquiry. Then thought, *Oh crap, it's not the widow's fault, it's this . . . it's this feeling of impotence.*

She sighed. Shook her head, read the 'Morning, Princess' note again, with its To Do list. The things to do being to visit widows or next of kin, to look for clues, however small, that might explain all of this. Byrne had provided exhaustive contact details for relatives of each of the victims. Martinez had gone over the list to decide how best to move the investigation forward. The young female compliance officer had been single, her parents in Alaska, not the best starting place. The lawyer, Avey, had lost his wife to cancer a year earlier. No obvious person to speak to there. The financial controller's wife had just proved herself to be unhelpful *and* shitty. Which just left the chief operating officer's wife, in her palatial mansion in New York's richest suburb. Martinez felt she knew how this was going to go.

With a pessimistic heart, Martinez pushed the buzzer on the gate's intercom. She leaned into it, waiting for the inevitable straining of the poor-quality speaker. But instead the gate clicked open and swung away from her in a slow, wide sweep. Martinez hadn't expected that. She then made the long trek up the herringbone-bricked driveway, preparing the question to put to the protective housemaid, or perhaps butler, wanting a phrasing that would give the lady of the house no choice but to speak to her, running through so many variations that she wasn't ready for what happened.

What happened was that the oversized door was opened by a small, sixty-year-old woman with chestnut hair, if you ignored the grey roots. To Martinez, she had the unassuming looks and dress of a librarian perhaps. A neat, unfussy cardigan, shoes round-toed and practical. However, the red, sleep-deprived eyes told Martinez she was not a librarian.

'Mrs Oliver?' Martinez spoke gently.

The woman went to reply cautiously, but was distracted by the appearance of a large leopard-patterned cat stroking up against her leg. The woman was pleased to see the animal and picked it up in her arms, needing to hug it, needing to be shielded by something.

Martinez was struck by the animal, forgetting herself. 'What a beautiful cat. I don't think I've ever seen a cat like that. Can I ask, what is it?'

The woman regarded the animal in her arms with a grateful affection. 'It's an Ashera. They're related to Asian leopards, you know. They don't produce the glycoprotein that makes you sneeze. Very good for people with allergies.'

'Oh, are you allergic yourself?'

'Thankfully, no, but my . . . Well, I had to justify the expense somehow.'

The woman realized she was talking about money to a stranger and suddenly felt like she had exposed herself in a way that she had not meant to. She held the cat tight. Martinez saw all this and continued with her soft tone.

'Mrs Oliver?'

'Yes.'

'Detective Martinez, New York Police Department.'

She looked at the Latino, out of uniform as she was, picking her words with care more out of habit than concern. 'I spoke with your colleagues yesterday. But not you.'

'No, I wasn't around yesterday and . . .'

Martinez could feel herself trusting this woman and decided to take a risk, the kind of risk that always drove her partner Detective Ashby so mad. 'Mrs Oliver, the truth is, I'm worried the man we're hunting isn't the man involved in the . . . death of your husband.'

Mrs Oliver's eyes widened. Then she thought about this. She looked beyond Martinez.

'You can park the car on the driveway if you like.'

Martinez smiled, relieved.

'What a wonderful garden.'

Martinez meant it. In fact, unfettered by social niceties she would probably have opened with a jealous expletive. The garden was enormous. A trick of the landscaping made the high-level plot seem to travel uninterrupted down into the countryside beyond. The reality was almost two acres. Two expensively manicured acres. Then something curious came into focus.

'Mrs Oliver, is that a . . . ?'

Mrs Oliver was approaching with two mugs of filtered coffee. 'A golf green? Yes, complete with four bunkers. Just what I always dreamt of looking out on when we were courting, my husband swinging furiously at the sand every evening after work.' She raised her eyebrows to leave Martinez in no doubt that the obsession was her husband's and her husband's alone.

Martinez had smiled at the word 'courting', such a lovely bygone word, romantic somehow. The detective turned and saw that Mrs Oliver had placed the mugs by the couch, on the same side of the coffee table.

Inviting, accepting. She moved to join the widow and the cat that had now hopped onto its owner's lap.

'Now, Detective Martinez . . .'

'You can call me Jenni, if you'd prefer.'

'Jenni, that's a nice name.' Mrs Oliver tugged her burgundy cardigan about her front to keep out a chill. 'A friend of mine has a daughter called Jenny, just qualified as a doctor.' A shadow passed over her face, which she tried not to burden Martinez with. The Olivers were childless. It was rare that Martinez met an older woman who hadn't at least tried – very hard – to have kids. With her husband so ambitious in Wall Street Martinez was in no doubt that this woman would have wanted to build her own world, her own family, with or without her husband's daily input. 'Well, if we're going to be on first-name terms, then you must call me Samantha. So, Jenni, can I ask something?'

'Yes, ma'am – Samantha – of course.'

'You're not doing this with your superior's blessing, are you?'

Martinez's heart was in her mouth. She instantly regretted ever turning up, ever teaming up with Byrne. She wanted to run. Suddenly helping Byrne was about to blow up in her face. She took a deep breath. 'No, Samantha, no I'm not.'

'And why is that?'

Martinez didn't know why, but she felt this woman

could see through her like other people see through windows. 'I'm, I mean, I've been suspended.'

Mrs Oliver waited.

'I made a procedural error and embarrassed my boss in front of some important company, company from another agency, the Secret Service actually. I'm on unpaid leave.' Martinez had expected a bossy rich banker's wife, not a perceptive mind reader.

'Well . . . I'm glad we cleared that up. Thirty years of listening to children making up tall stories about which domestic pet ate which assignment teaches you a thing or two about people.'

Martinez laughed despite herself. 'We could do with you at the stationhouse when we're interviewing teenagers, I can tell you that.'

'Oh, don't start me on young tearaways or you'll have to listen to a rant about the breakdown of the traditional family unit and the lack of father figures in the modern urban family.'

Martinez sipped her coffee. 'Well, don't wait for me to disagree. We don't know if we're police detectives or family therapists these days.'

Mrs Oliver smiled a smile that stopped at her sad eyes. She had remembered herself. And that involved getting down to business. 'So, Jenni, what does your unauthorized investigation require of me?'

Martinez responded to Mrs Oliver's practical manner by putting her own mug down. 'Well, Samantha, we –' She looked up, caught a stare and wilted under the gaze of the retired teacher opposite. 'That is, *I* suspect that the man we had apprehended was set up by the person or persons who really did this.'

'You said "had" apprehended. Has anything changed?'

Martinez had to stop herself from cussing at her mistake. Then she thought, *I've come this far.* 'If you repeat what I'm about to say, I will get in a whole world of trouble.'

Mrs Oliver sipped her coffee placidly. 'I thought we reached that point when you knocked on my door today?'

Martinez pulled a face that told her she couldn't argue with that. 'We handed the man we apprehended over to the Secret Service and he escaped.'

'When?'

'Yesterday afternoon.'

'Does the Secret Service know his whereabouts?'

'No, I don't believe they do.'

'Do the police?'

'I don't think so.'

Mrs Oliver took a moment. 'Do you?'

'Samantha, if we don't catch the right person there is a real danger that this situation could escalate into something even more serious.' Mrs Oliver waited for more. 'Also, I don't want the wrong man to go down for this.'

Mrs Oliver considered the young detective for a moment. 'But not necessarily in that order?'

Martinez knew she was betraying neediness and guilt, not the strongest hand. 'If there is anything you think could help the – my – investigation, anything at all?'

'Jenni, can you guarantee my safety?'

Martinez had a rush of excitement, wanted this news, went to trot out the standard reassuring line then checked herself. Brought herself down to earth with a bump. Because this nice lady, so removed from the ball-breaker of a husband that Byrne had described, deserved that little thing called respect. 'No, Samantha, I cannot.' Mrs Oliver nodded slowly, comprehending. 'What I can do is my best to catch the people who did this to your husband and hopefully stop them before they strike again. Nothing more.'

Mrs Oliver gave her a knowing look. The look that perhaps only a teacher of long-standing, faced with thousands of stories, can give. Wanting to believe, yet experience demanding caution. She took her time weighing up a decision, going through a kind of calculation in her head, the pros and the cons, the sense and senselessness of trusting this young heart-on-her-sleeve woman, honest and yet not altogether forthcoming. Whatever the process, she seemed to come down in one very definite direction.

'My husband was scared.'

Martinez felt achingly close now. 'Did you mention this to the police?'

'No.'

'Why not?'

'They said I was perfectly safe. What's the point in trusting people who lie to you?'

'Did you mean that to sound loaded or is that just my guilty conscience talking?'

The widow smiled maternally. 'That's the better part of you speaking.' She thought about which words to use. 'He was scared twice. Once when the share price collapsed a few years back, back in early 2008, when Bear Stearns fell to pieces. I mean, he was angry that First Bank was suffering in the marketplace. But he was scared about his share options – our share options. This house isn't completely paid for, you see.'

'Will you be forced to sell it?'

'Well . . . his life cover will pay off the mortgage.'

'Oh, so you'll stay.'

'You must be kidding. I can't sell it quick enough. How big a pod does a pea need to rattle around in? I've got family near Boston – that's where I'll go. Terrible time to sell, though, not that it matters.'

'What's a million here or there?' Martinez winced inside, hoped she hadn't been too familiar.

The widow smiled philosophically. 'Precisely. He was dreadfully overpaid.'

They drank their coffee.

'When was he scared, the second time?'

'Recently.'

'How recently?'

Mrs Oliver thought, tried to locate the precise moment in her memory. 'After they went to the regulators, after they went to the SEC.'

Martinez didn't realize it, but she was sitting further forward in her seat. 'After who went to the SEC?'

'The four . . . people who were murdered at First Bank. They went to the SEC just over two weeks ago.'

Martinez was leaning forward now. 'What about?'

'Oh, "the balance sheet" was all he would say. Well, "the fucking balance sheet", if you want the exact quote. But he didn't want to say more, said it was dangerous to know more. Dangerous for me.'

'And who did know about the trip?'

'As far as I know, nobody. Just John, Stephen, Chris, that compliance girl, whatshername –'

'Sharon.'

'Sharon, that's it. I . . .'

There was a pause. Martinez prompted her hostess with a look. 'What, Mrs Oliver?'

The widow was wrestling with something then appeared to acquiesce. 'I feel a bit bad about saying this but it might be relevant.'

'Go on.'

'Sharon was rumoured – rather unequivocally, I should say – to be . . . having an affair with Jeremiah Rankin, the CEO.'

'I wouldn't call it irrelevant. Thank you. Go on, you

trip?'

Mrs Oliver had to remember where she'd gotten up to. 'Well, it was the four I mentioned and whoever they met at the SEC. As far as I know.'

'Did they mention these concerns to the CEO? To Rankin?'

Mrs Oliver shook her head slowly, trying to recollect. 'No, not to the best of my knowledge. He isn't what one would call approachable.'

'But wouldn't he have wanted to know about problems with the bank's book?'

The widow finished her coffee. 'He knew all about the balance sheet. But wouldn't act. John clearly felt things were so serious he had to go behind his boss's back. They all did.' She looked directly at Martinez. 'Do you think it cost them their lives or do you think it was a random act of violence?'

'I don't know. I really don't, Samantha. But I promise to try my hardest to find out.'

'I know you will. And I'm glad I told you, really I am. I feel better already.'

Martinez stroked the cat's head, thinking, *Whoever did this, it wasn't Mike Byrne.*

And she realized that was the biggest relief of all.

19

Lower Manhattan lay resplendent down below in the bright blue of the September mid-morning. But the view of billions of dollars' worth of the world's finest real estate, this financial Vatican City, with the added vista of Governor's and Ellis Island out beyond, was doing nothing to lift the mood in the room.

'What the fuck is he doing here?'

By 'what' Rankin meant what possible reason, by 'here' Rankin meant his massive Citizen Kane-proportioned executive office on Madison Avenue, by 'fuck' Rankin meant fuck.

The tired First Bank chairman bobbed gently, his body language torn between appeasement and a certain necessary resolve. But he was missing his weekly appointment with his oncologist to be here this morning and the indignation that such a sacrifice created in him gave him a little more backbone than he'd felt for a while. 'Jerry, don't.'

'Jerry don't? *Jerry* don't? Charlie, you're the one who needs to be told *don't. Don't* bring him here, and *don't* let the whole fucking world know that the lunatic Chairman of First Bank has lost his *fucking mind* and started to put the whole *fucking enterprise* into Chapter 11 when it's on the cusp of its greatest *ever* reporting season. What – the – fuck – is – *he* – doing – *here*?'

'He' stepped in. 'He' was Harvey Rosenbaum, the oldest, most experienced, most expensive, most respected, and, by the distance of a country club waiting list, best insolvency lawyer on the Street. Silver-haired with jet-black streaks along the side of his head, a bespoke suit so crisp you could be forgiven for thinking he had just dressed in the elevator. 'Jerry, nobody's suggesting Chapter 11. Charlie just wants me to walk you through what we might need to prepare for.'

Chapter 11, the term that could make the grown men and women of Wall Street break out in a cold sweat. It was a hair's breadth from full bankruptcy. The corporate entity got a stay of execution from creditors whilst it reorganized its finances, hopefully coming out the other side leaner and fitter. It was a popular, if drastic, measure in corporate America. But on Wall Street? Such an action was the kiss of death for a bank's credibility. It was tantamount to suicide. The very notion was nothing short of appalling to Rankin.

The bank CEO stood behind his desk, pacing, the two others standing across from him. 'Walk me through?'

'That's right.'

'But not walk Charlie through?'

Charlie smiled, unsure. 'That's right.'

'Because . . . you've already walked Charlie through what we need to prepare for because he's gone behind my motherfucking back and tried to organize a coup against me, is that it?'

Charlie, exasperated and fearful, almost clasped his hands together, as if in prayer, to reassure his CEO. 'Jerry, nothing could be further from —'

'And don't tell me, Harvey, you came here to praise me not to bury me?'

The insolvency lawyer was rabbi-like in his calmness, a manner not unlike a doctor practised in the art of breaking the news of a terminal illness, skilled in handling the denial, the anger, the bargaining, the depression – the acceptance. Every CEO, no matter what the size of the company, went through the same routine, factory or bank, conglomerate or mom-and-pop store. It was predictable almost to the minute. The refusal to accept that the balance sheet told the whole story, that success lay just round the corner, always insisting the bigger picture was better than this moment in time suggested. Then the finger-pointing, the naming of the names that let the company down, that let *you* down. This followed by negotiation, desperate attempts to stave off the inevitable by ring-fencing the best bits of the corporation, as if you could ring-fence the best bits of a dying patient. Then the unfathomable depression, the tragic sadness as the irreversible scale of the situation was understood.

Then peace, acquiescence, resignation to the truth. Except those stages took time, and . . .

'Jerry, we don't have time for this.'

Rankin shot a fierce look at the aged lawyer. 'I certainly don't, you're right about that.'

'Jerry, in a perfect world I would want to explore the different scenarios facing your company . . .'

'Bank, Harvey, bank. The oldest goddamn investment bank on Wall Street.'

'Bank, forgive me. But we can't pretend that we can explore every avenue here.'

'Because we don't have time?'

Rosenbaum waited a beat, giving Rankin a moment to prepare himself. 'There are no other avenues. It's the end of the road.'

'You said nobody was talking about Chapter 11, you said we weren't looking at bankruptcy.'

'I'm not talking about Chapter 11, Jerry.'

The bank CEO was bemused. This wasn't adding up in his mind, wasn't making any sense. If Rosenbaum wasn't talking Chapter 11, then what the hell was he . . . Jesus H. Christ. Because now – *now* – Rankin was astonished. Then he was staggered. Staggered beyond belief, beyond reason. Staggered in the true sense of needing to hold on to something to stop from falling. Because suddenly he understood, *really* understood. Understood how First Bank must be looking to outsiders, understood how little oxygen was left, how perilous the bank's position must be, must look. For a long moment he had to fight the possibility that he was so divorced from reality that his secret plans were borderline insane. But they weren't, were they? Were they . . . ? His whole being screamed against it.

'Chapter 7, Harvey?' whispered Rankin.

'Jerry . . .'

'Liquidation?' The strength in his voice returning now. 'You come into my office and tell me you think my bank needs liquidating? Oh, Harvey, fuck you.'

Castle was all waving hands now, appeasing hands. 'Jerry, you have to listen.'

'Jerry, the regulators are coming to examine the books tomorrow, the press are scenting blood and the competition is moving in for the kill.'

Rankin pounded the desk with his hand, half speaking, half hectoring. 'The SEC will find nothing untoward in those books –'

Rosenbaum raised a hand in objection. 'Jerry, they're coming in heavy. A full-scale emergency review of the books – overseen by the Federal Reserve – with a view to a sale at the weekend. You know that's what they have to be planning. Less than two days away.'

'They will find *nothing* untoward in those books and on Saturday they will be praising the healthiest balance sheet in North America.'

Rosenbaum raised an eyebrow at Castle. Rankin

was blending the denial and anger stage into one – this might save time. 'Jerry, the only story in the press right now is First Bank as the next Bear Stearns, the next Lehman's.'

'And what the fuck do you think the press will make of you visiting First Bank? They will have a field day.' The bank CEO turned towards – turned *on* – his chairman. 'Charlie, you've fucked the bank. You cunt. Harvey is the fucking grim reaper, and now that he's put his hand on our shoulder it's a self-fulfilling prophecy. We're dead, dead, DEAD.' The last word shouted, the last word verbally punched into Charlie's being.

Castle was moving round the table now, imploring. 'Jerry, I brought him in the back way. You think I would have taken Harvey through the front door? With the press watching? Who do you think I am?'

'Who, Charlie? Good fucking question. I don't know. I don't know who you are any more. You're dead to me, you understand? Dead to me.'

Castle was scared, sad, welling up. 'Jerry, I'm doing this for the bank – I'm doing this for you.'

Rosenbaum had to press on. 'Jerry, your share price is off eighty-five per cent from the end of last week. Sixty dollars down to nine dollars in a little over three days. When the markets discover the regulators are tearing up the floorboards looking for bodies they'll be pricing your shares in cents.'

'Let 'em!' Rankin pounded the desk. 'Let 'em! Let 'em! Let 'em! I'll kill them all, I'll fucking kill them all.'

Rankin and Castle were standing by the breathtaking and enormous wraparound window, Manhattan laid out beneath. Castle reached out to Rankin, went to take his shoulders, to console him, soothe him. Rankin felt disorientated, enraged, betrayed. He grabbed Castle. Castle was petrified, paralysed into inaction, limp like a doll. Rankin slammed him into the window.

Rosenbaum screamed. 'Jerry, for god's sake!'

But the red mist had descended over Rankin and he slammed Castle into the window again, willing it to smash, Castle pathetic in his lack of defiance, the window shuddering. 'You bastard, you stupid fucking bastard . . . !'

Rosenbaum was moving as quickly as he could round the table, pulling at Rankin, careful to stay away from a window that might shatter, failing to stop the CEO from ramming Castle haphazardly into the full-length window once more –

'Mr Rankin!'

The words cut through the melee, through the room, the guilty caught in the act.

They stopped.

Rankin looking into Castle's face with an all-consuming hate.

'Mr Rankin, the phone.'

All three men looked round. It was Rankin's thirty-something personal assistant at the door, fifty feet away. The ex-model, in an outfit lifted from the latest edition of *Vogue*, was watching in fear, unable to fathom the scene.

'It's the chief executive of JPMorgan. He said it's urgent.'

Rankin, breathing heavily, the blood lust subsiding, let Castle go. The bank chairman stepping back, no drama, almost embarrassed by the PA's appearance. Rankin didn't want to look at her. 'Tell him I'm busy.'

She stood her ground, but her tone told them she didn't take responsibility for her words. 'He said that you would say that. He said either you or the Treasury Secretary were going to talk to him about First Bank. I-I'm sorry.'

Rankin gave her a sharp look. Her heart raced with anxiety, terrified by the possibilities in these moments. Rankin's face began to contort, but he remembered that Harvey Rosenbaum was watching this display. He checked himself, controlled himself. 'Put him . . . put him through.'

She nodded briefly and slipped away behind the art deco door.

The men remained as they were, too tense from the melee to unwind. Rankin didn't move, stuck between a myriad of thoughts and feelings. Castle brushed himself down, sadness turning to bitterness. Rosenbaum watched the scene, questioning whether he needed this kind of a ball-ache assignment at his age. Then the insolvency lawyer who had seen – almost – everything tried to right the mood.

'Jerry, the wolves are at the door. If we act now, there is a chance – a slim chance – that we can take control of this situation. *But* we need to deal with the reality of the bank's book. We need to know the math, the truth, once all the off-balance items are taken into account.'

Jerry was regaining his composure. When he spoke it was with the numbness of grief, a man spent of emotion. 'We just need till tomorrow. A lot of contracts settle tomorrow – if the markets are kind to us I believe we'll be in good shape. We just need till the close of business – what's that? – thirty hours, that's all.'

They waited in silence.

The phone rang softly.

Rankin stood staring at it. Doing nothing until after a few rings Castle leaned over and hit the speakerphone.

'Jerry?'

First Bank's CEO, beyond anger, spoke almost softly. 'What can I do for you, Bob?'

'Jerry, we need another $8 billion in collateral – and we need it by this time tomorrow.'

Rankin's whole face seemed to hook forward like a

murderous bird of prey. 'Is this some kind of a sick joke? Bob, I am in no mood to deal with this.'

Castle tried to avert the inevitable explosion. 'Bob, you're holding $47 billion worth of First Bank's assets.'

'Charlie?'

'Yeah, sorry, Bob.'

'Charlie, the banking sector's coming off so fast we can't get a value on half of these contracts.'

Rankin was leaning on the desk now, wishing he could bite the head off the JPMorgan banker. 'Bob, excuse my French, but how the fuck can you be happy with those contracts a fortnight ago and suddenly wake up and decide they ain't worth shit?'

The disembodied voice of the JPMorgan CEO was unemotional, all business. 'Because, Jerry, two weeks ago your share price wasn't trading at nine dollars and you didn't have Harvey Rosenbaum standing in your office.'

Rankin reared back appalled, Castle looked up startled, Rosenbaum dropped his forehead into his hand. Rankin emitted a small strangled sound, pointed an accusatory finger at his chairman, stuffed his fist into his own mouth – stopping an outburst he didn't trust, in the grip of the nightmarishness of events. Then he turned away, squeezed his eyes. Had to stay calm. Had to. Because a panicking CEO panics the markets.

Rankin turned back to the phone. 'Bob, with all due respect, those assets are still worth $47 billion.'

'Our head of Risk begs to differ, Jerry. And I've got twenty-four hours to put an $8 billion smile back on his face.'

'Well, you tell him to check his math because our Risk guys say the value of those assets hasn't changed.'

'Even the mortgage and security-backed derivatives?'

'Even that little bundle of derivatives, Bob, still worth the same.'

'Mmm, I'll tell you what, Jerry. We go back a long way . . .' Rankin's shoulders relaxed at the improved tone, the respite. 'Why don't I sell a few of these contracts in the market place and see what the market thinks they're worth? How about that? Then I won't have to tell my Risk guys what they're worth because they'll know for sure. Sound fair to you?'

The most honest and therefore cruellest thing you could do on Wall Street. Find out the true value of a contract being held as collateral. Elevate an arrangement above the mutual backslapping winks of the quietly agreed price of a thing and instead lift the lid on it, expose it to daylight – see if it shrivels and screams at the touch of the sun's rays.

Rankin was incensed, his eyes betraying the momentary madness within. He grabbed the phone, lifted it, tore the cables out and hurled it down the length of the room, fifty feet of clattering telephony.

The other two looked on. Mortified more at the

lack of diplomacy than the physical vandalism. This was Wall Street, after all.

A moment later the door opened, where the catwalk secretary only half stepped into the room. 'Mr Chiklis says he was cut off . . .'

Rankin tapped a finger on the table, exhausted. 'Tell him he will get his money. Within twenty-four hours.'

She disappeared.

Rankin regained some of his composure. He straightened his tie, shrugged his jacket back into place, then lowered himself gently into his seat behind his enormous desk. He looked up at the septuagenarian lawyer across from him.

'Harvey?'

'Yes, Jerry.'

'Fuck off.'

20

'Been waiting long?'

'No, just got here.'

I looked down at Martinez sitting on a bench set into the striking stone wall that curved its way round one end of the beautifully maintained garden within. To add to the serenity of the setting, the whole curved walkway was topped by a grand wrought-iron pergola that carried an ancient Chinese wisteria on its frame. But fall was the wrong season to enjoy the vine's spectacular bloom. I'd come back in the spring, May. If I could.

The detective looked around at the grounds. 'I grew up in Queens, I live in South Harlem, I work in Manhattan and I didn't even know this place existed – let alone visited it.'

I smiled in appreciation of the surroundings. The Italian Gardens within the Conservatory of Central Park. A six-acre oasis within the bustling metropolis. The result of generations of gardeners and their passionate dedication. 'Yeah, well, you need to be raised by a garden nut for a mother, then you too can be an expert on the Municipal Gardens of the United States of America.'

'You think we've got less chance of being spotted here?' She looked around again.

'No, I think there's a better chance of seeing some nice flowers.'

She screwed up her eyes against the sun, looked at me, checking to see if I was being serious or not. She shuffled herself and her motorcycle helmet along the bench and I sat beside her.

'Nice morning, Byrne?'

I sensed a slight irritation in her voice. 'Slightly more eventful than I would have liked.'

'Eventful? I've just got off the phone to Ashby.'

'I've been meaning to ask: what does happen when a detective's partner is suspended? Do they solve half as many cases or solve the same amount of cases only half as well?'

She gave me a briefly mystified look then wiggled her head with an attitude of annoyance. 'Tells me somebody fitting your description shot The Carlyle hotel up this morning.'

'He should check his sources – I was shot *at*. And they only really trashed the kitchen. I once dated this Italian girl – she used to make more mess cooking dinner.'

'This your idea of going undercover?' Eyeing me humourlessly. 'What happened, the Secret Service fire your ass for taking out adverts in *The New York Times* or something? "Undercover Agent Seeks Money Launderer. Please send photo?" You're a one-man demolition derby, aren't you, Byrne. Thanks to you they've got two Eastern European badasses under police guard over at Bellevue and two more in the morgue.'

'Four. Only four?' I didn't like that. Mr Bingo must have gotten away. Knew me, hated me. I wasn't sure if that was a good thing. He was gunning for me, but it did give me someone to track.

'Jesus, Byrne, you sound disappointed it wasn't more. I thought you wanted me to help you find who set you up, not aid and abet a killing spree.'

'Martinez, they started it . . .'

'But you finished it, is that it?'

'Something like that, yeah.'

She gave me a sideways look, a sceptical sideways look. 'You gonna take down any police officers or Secret Service agents on this little crusade of yours?'

'I wouldn't do that.'

She narrowed her eyes. 'They got you cornered . . . Gun on you . . . You're facing custody . . . Life . . . You're facing death . . . Their fingers are on the triggers . . . They got orders to kill . . . You telling me you get the drop, you wouldn't take it?'

'I swear.' And I meant it, just as I had meant it when I said it to Diane back at the New York field office. And I hated the position it put me in. Because these people were soon going to be protecting the president, which made for a very Shoot To Kill policy.

She was looking at me, mulling something over. She looked out across the fountain to the peaceful square of lawn beyond the wisteria pergola we were sitting beneath.

'I lied to my partner . . . Lied to Ashby. Lied to him.' She was looking at the gardens, not at me. 'Almost seven years with the NYPD, five with him, godmother to his daughter . . . Shit, I'm only sitting here because of him. I used to tease Ashby. We'd be in the locker room at the station and he was always practising yanking that thing out of his shoulder holster. "You never know when, Martinez," he used to say. I used to stick pictures from the newspapers and magazines in his locker door. Deputy Dawg, Gary Cooper from *High Noon*, Clint Eastwood in those spaghetti westerns, Yosemite Sam . . . And he'd wag his finger at me, "You never know when, Martinez." "Yeah, whatever, Ashby." Then one night this smacked-up punk pulls a Saturday-night special on me. I'd been all community officer, doing my Oprah routine, feeling his pain, that kind of shit. Jesus, my guard's down, no chance of getting to my piece. Ashby . . . he did what he had to do. That dumb kid . . . Never seen a gun drawn so quickly in all my life. Never. And that's the man I just lied to.'

I waited. Waited to let her say more. The gentle

rhythm of the fountain's spray the only sound between us. 'Look, Martinez, you don't have to do this.'

She looked directly at me. 'You hurt a law enforcement officer getting to the bottom of this shit and I will put so many bullets in you they won't know if you died from gunshot wounds or lead poisoning.' She stared at me. Wanted to know it had sunk in. 'We good?'

I allowed a small affirming smile to shape my mouth. We were more than good.

Martinez looked down at the bench between us. There was an 'In Loving Memory' plaque screwed to it. We considered it together until she looked back at me.

'Do you think there'll be a seat with your name on it one day, Byrne?'

I smiled a conciliatory smile. 'Maybe.'

She looked at me, thinking a mischievous thought. 'Yeah, when they put plaques on electric chairs.'

Now I had to fight the smile splitting my face. Somehow getting that one over on me made her feel better about herself, at least in her mood.

The detective spoke softly. 'So far only one relative has spoken to me, Mrs Oliver.'

'The chief operating officer's wife?'

'Yeah. Nice lady. Oh, but you should have seen her cat, markings like you never seen. If somebody had told me it was a, oh, what's the term, cryogenic, no, that's not it, er, genetically modified, that's it, genetically modified to look like a leopard I swear I would believe them.'

She saw that I was watching her.

She tucked a stray hair behind her ear and smiled self-consciously. 'What?'

I grinned a little. 'Are all your police reports this concise?'

She smacked that away with a look. 'Anyhows, this widow, she says that her husband was scared.'

'Scared? Scared of what?'

'She didn't say.'

'Didn't say or wouldn't say?'

'No, I don't think she knew. But she said her husband was preoccupied with the bank's balance sheet, worried about it.'

'He should have been – the bank's in the toilet. I can't get their books to add up – and I don't put it down to human error. What about the other executives? Anything on them?'

'I was just getting to that. All four of them went behind Rankin's back and spoke to the SEC about the bank's book.'

A picture was emerging and there were enough brushstrokes to place Rankin at the centre of it. 'The Russians turned up at The Carlyle just after I'd had breakfast with Rankin.'

Martinez unconsciously placed a protective hand

on my arm. 'Jesus – do you think Rankin set them on you?'

'Actually, no. I've played it over in my mind and, no, it didn't feel that way. He didn't have the confidence of a man who could call in air support if he got cornered. I think they were following him and stumbled upon me.'

'Following him or guarding him?'

I looked at her with slightly raised eyebrows. She couldn't suppress the smile of the A-grade student.

'Did Ashby say if those Russians had spoken yet?'

She pulled an upside-down smile. 'Both refusing and he doesn't believe they're gonna crack. Got that crazy loyalty thing we keep seeing in the Eastern European gangsters. Give me an American criminal any day. Hey, but Mrs Oliver did tell me one thing – you know the compliance officer?'

'The blonde?'

'Yeah. Rankin was sleeping with her. Think that's got any bearing on the case?'

I pulled a face. 'No, but I think it has on her rapid promotion in the company.'

I retrieved my smartphone from my jacket pocket and started tapping away.

'What you doing there?'

'I want to know who else Rankin is screwing.'

I hit a couple more buttons and an audio-player application popped up on my smartphone's screen.

I tapped the PLAY symbol and we were both listening to a phone call on its speaker.

> *Rankin: Charlie, what's up?*
> *Castle: Jerry, have you heard the rumour about First Bank?*

I paused the file. 'Jeremiah Rankin and Charlie Castle, First Bank Chairman. Rankin took this whilst I was with him at breakfast at The Carlyle hotel this morning.' I hit PLAY again.

> *Rankin: Rumour? What fucking rumour?*
> *Castle: Apparently, you've been called to the Treasury for a crisis meeting.*
> *Rankin: But I just got off the — did the leak come from Treasury? Those fucking pricks have fucking mouthed off for the last —*
> *Castle: There's no word on the source.*
> *Rankin: How the hell could anybody know?*
> *Castle: Jerry, it gets worse. Have you been contacted about an SEC inspection?*
> *Rankin: What SEC inspection?*
> *Castle: They've told us to expect them tomorrow morning. Jerry, can you get back here? There's somebody I think you ought to meet.*
> *Rankin: No, no, I can't exactly, not right now . . . [mumbled voice] I'll be there in ten minutes.*

Castle: OK, see ya.
Rankin: See you then.

Martinez looked at my phone like it was a ray gun from outer space. 'What the hell . . . ? How did you do that?'

'Slipped some tracking software onto Rankin's phone. Every call he makes and receives – phone numbers, the lot – gets copied to a website and sent to me as a file. Gotta love the internet.'

On my smartphone's screen I had a list of files with times against them: 8.47, 8.51, 8.56 and so on. I clicked the next one.

Chiklis: Hi, Jerry, it's Bob here, JPMorgan. Jerry, we need to talk about collateral. I want to work with you on this but my hands are tied by Risk. Call me as soon as you get this message. Please.

I opened the next file.

Woman: Chief executive's office?
Rankin: Zoe, Jerry.
Woman: Hi, Jerry.
Rankin: Zoe, hold all my meetings till Monday, OK?
Woman: I've already done that, Jerry. Has Mr Castle told you about the SEC?
Rankin: Yeah, he's mentioned it.

Woman: Your personal bank manager chased again. What should I say?

Rankin: Ah, tell him . . . tell him I'll get back to him just as soon as I can.

Woman: OK. And you've got messages from The Journal, The New York Times, *the* Financial Times, CNBC . . .

Rankin: Yeah, yeah, yeah. Zoe, I'll get back to them.

Woman: OK, sorry. Jerry?

Rankin: What, baby?

Woman: Is . . . is everything OK, Jerry? Are you OK?

Rankin: Thanks sweetheart. Everything's fine. We haven't explained ourselves as well as we should have. With everything that's happened nobody knows where anything is. You gotta remember, the people who looked after our books are, well, you know. In fact, what's the latest on the funerals?

Woman: The first one is not till Monday.

Rankin: Thank god for that.

Woman: It's in Florida.

Rankin: Florida? Christ, that frigid bitch, Vanessa Stewart? Fuck, I don't know if I can face flying all that way just to commiserate with that ice maiden.

Woman: I'll have one of the company jets on standby either way. You've had messages from three of the families thanking you for the flowers you sent them.

Rankin: Zoe, you're an angel.

Woman: Your angel.

Rankin: What you got on today?
Woman: That grey tweed number we saw in Vogue. *We might need to talk about my wardrobe allowance, though.*

I shared a rather interested look with Martinez.

Rankin: Why, what's up?
Woman: Well, I spent so much on the outfit and shoes that I had nothing left for underwear.
Rankin: And?
Woman: And so I came in without any on. I just feel so . . . slutty. Did I do bad?
Rankin: You did good, baby, real good.
BEEP BEEP
Rankin: Oh, I gotta take this call, babe.

Martinez shook her head, as much bewildered as antagonized. 'Do you think he's banging all the women at the bank?'

'Only the ones with pulses.' I hit another file.

Rankin: Rankin.
Russian: We have another problem with the trade.

Martinez and I both stiffened. We'd hit pay dirt.

Rankin: Wha −? How? How can there be another problem?

Russian: Six of my traders went to close their accounts this morning — at the hotel.

Rankin: And?

Russian: The, er, banker, how you say, was not cooperative. In fact, has meant suspending trading on two accounts and closing down two others altogether. I am very unhappy.

Rankin: For . . . How? How can this have happened again?

Russian: I must be compensated for loss of earnings, da?

Rankin: We had a trade. You deliver on your side, I deliver on mine.

Russian: We were never told what sort of banker we were dealing with. I mean, I've met some cutthroat bankers in my time but this guy . . . Belad.

They were talking about me. Martinez tried to pull a face that told me not to get above myself, but she couldn't hide her concern over the heat I'd attracted.

Rankin: Look, we need that banker put out of business. Otherwise it puts the whole deal in jeopardy. We're still OK with the other trade, tomorrow, right?

Russian: Da. *This is not problem. Two separate trades.*

Rankin: Do I need to know any of the details of the second trade? Meet up?

Russian: Nyet. *The less you know the better all round. Even I don't know — I just know it will be done. But will I get compensated for my loss of earnings?*

Rankin: [sighs] Yes.

Russian: And you still want this banker from the first trade . . . ?

Rankin: Yes. Definitely. I want him out of business. Permanently.

Martinez didn't know it but she was staring intently at the phone. Worried and angry.

Russian: Let me see what I can do. We might have been lucky this morning. He might not be in the market after what happened.

Rankin: Oh he will. And when I find out I'll tell you where.

Russian: Good. Till then.

Rankin: OK. Till then.

We sat in silence, thinking about the call. There was a lot to take in.

'They spoke very carefully. Do you think they know they're being listened to?'

I shook my head. 'No, I don't think so. Your word is your bond in the markets. Trades are done verbally over the phone. That makes you very careful, the habits of a lifetime. They're assuming the worst, that these calls could be dragged over by the security agencies one day. That's why they didn't say anything that would stand up in court.'

'Rankin wants you dead.'

'I know. I wish I'd known that at breakfast – I wouldn't have offered to pay.'

Martinez rolled her eyes. 'Do you think he was behind the murder of the four executives?'

'It's certainly starting to look that way.'

'We get enough evidence I could call it in to Ashby, get Rankin arrested.'

I shook my head again. 'No, not yet.'

'Why not?'

'Because it's that other trade they mentioned, the second one, that I'm worried about. The one tomorrow.'

Martinez was incredulous, annoyed. 'Rankin's got a contract out on you and you're worried about whatever else he's up to – why?'

I spoke in measured tones, not wanting to upset her. 'Martinez, what's happening tomorrow?'

She ran her mind through the city's diary, a Friday, the usual events, the end of the working week – then . . . The realization was appalling to her. 'The president and Chinese premier are in town. Oh my god – they really are planning an attack on the two presidents. It's really happening. What should we – what are we going to do?'

I held up the screen of my smartphone.

'Find the Russian – and find out what the hell that second trade is.'

21

There is a Florentine palace in the middle of New York City. Just as the Medicis demanded buildings whose grandeur matched their own banking achievements in sixteenth-century Florence, so it was decreed that the rising financial principality of Manhattan should have its own rusticated palazzo to announce to the world, and to those who entered its hallowed portals, that the United States of America had arrived as a monetary powerhouse. That was 1924. Five years before the first Wall Street crash brought the country to its knees. The palace is the Federal Reserve of New York.

The lime and sandstone fortress sits in Lower Manhattan, its vaults fifty feet below street level. The vaults contain around $160 billion of gold bullion – more than Fort Knox – the vaults so deep they rest on the bedrock of Manhattan Island itself. On the ground floor its corridors are, appropriately enough, palatial. Magnificently high, arched and wide, they were designed to inspire a reverential shock and awe in those that tread their hallowed hallways, and they succeed completely. The perfect setting in which to steer the greatest economy in the world, to set its interest rates, oversee its immense financial institutions, to govern. And one of the few places on earth which would bring an ounce – just an ounce – of humility to the players of Wall Street.

'Jeremiah Rankin to see Richard Peterson.'

The smart middle-aged receptionist tapped in his details then looked up at the First Bank CEO with a curt, professional smile. 'He's expecting you.'

Two high-backed leather chairs sat askew from each other beneath a huge arched window in a first floor library of the Federal Reserve. Between the occupants was a small table with a tidy silver tray of coffee. They were to serve themselves as nobody else was present, which meant that nobody else was privy to the meeting. Which was the point.

Treasury Secretary Richard Peterson was pouring the coffee for both. 'The markets didn't like that hotel shooting this morning. Everybody's on edge.'

Rankin wasn't sure how to play it but was wary of a fishing expedition by the Treasury Secretary. 'I'd had breakfast in there just before it all kicked off.'

Peterson flinched in surprise. 'My god, were you caught up in it?'

'No, no. I was long gone. Just . . . life. It's so random, isn't it.'

The Treasury Secretary wore a crooked smile as he

passed across a coffee. 'Attracting trouble like a bad penny these days, aren't we.'

Rankin was keen to take the conversation away from this. 'I hadn't realized you were in town? Glad-handing the Chinese?'

'An opportunity for our economies to join together to better our commercial harmony.' The sun winked off the Treasury Secretary's bald pate, saving his eye the trouble.

'Is it true the Chinese are going to cram more floors into their Wall Street skyscraper by only having five-foot-high ceilings? That's one way to get us to bow to them, eh?'

Peterson didn't react to Rankin's attempt at humour, but instead allowed Rankin's smile to leave his face with a noncommittal look of his own. 'Jerry, there is a state dinner at the White House this weekend and I would like to be able to announce, beforehand, the purchase by the Chinese of First Bank of America.'

Rankin shot bolt upright as if hit by an electric shock. 'You must be fucking kidding.'

'That's right, I brought you here to swap jokes.'

'First Bank is *not* for sale.'

Peterson sat back in his chair and slowly stirred in the one sugar he allowed himself as a pep-me-up around noon each day. 'Jerry, we both know that every-thing is for sale – at the right price.'

Rankin, leaning forward. 'And what would be the right price?'

'I don't think you're going to like it.'

'Then don't bother to say it. Hey, why the Chinese? Why not sell us to JPMorgan for a cent in the dollar? Hell, we'll pay them.' Rankin sank back in his chair, knowing that anger would be self-defeating.

Peterson let Rankin simmer down. 'You doubtless know that the SEC has insisted on examining your books tomorrow.'

'I need to talk about them.'

'You need to cooperate with them. They would have done it sooner but we chose a Friday to limit the damage to your share price and the markets.'

'Which just happens to kick our share price in the balls just as you want us to negotiate with those Chinks.'

'Your share price has been collapsing without any help from us, Jerry.'

'Richard, this is market manipulation. I will not be the next Dick Fuld, I will not stand idly by whilst my bank is chopped into little bits of chop-fucking-suey and sold to the lowest bidder.'

'It's not your bank, Jerry. It's your shareholders'.'

'Oh, you know what I mean.'

'But do you know what I mean? If your books are to be believed —'

'They are.'

'— then come Monday you will personally have taken

almost two per cent of First Bank as remuneration for being its CEO.'

Rankin fidgeted slightly in his chair. 'I don't really watch my share options that closely.'

The Treasury Secretary could not contain a surprised laugh. 'Ha!'

'Well, I don't.'

'Jerry, I could pick up the phone to any CEO on the Street and he could tell me exactly how many shares he owns and how much he is worth right now to the nearest dollar.'

The First Bank CEO looked at the floor like he'd found an interesting spot on the carpet. 'Yeah, well, that two per cent ain't worth so much right now.'

Peterson sipped his coffee and placed the cup down between them. 'The question is, Jerry, is the two per cent worth *anything?*'

Rankin looked him dead in the eye. 'There is nothing wrong with our balance sheet.'

'You're the only one saying that, Jerry.'

'With all due respect, Richard, that is bullshit. My entire team stands by that book.'

'What's left of your team.'

Rankin recoiled, scandalized. 'Richard, that is thoroughly inappropriate.'

'It is thoroughly appropriate. Were you aware that your four deceased colleagues had approached the SEC about their concerns over the balance sheet?'

Rankin's eyes sprang open. 'They did *what*? You're shitting . . . That's impossible, Richard, it's impossible.'

'Why? Why is it impossible for four banking executives to walk down Madison and tell the SEC they think their CEO is juggling the books?'

Rankin's face was the picture of sincerity, hurt even. 'Because they did the books. Richard, they did the books and brought them to me to sign. That's how it's always been at First Bank.'

The Treasury Secretary had not expected such an innocent response, but could not allow himself to waver. 'Jerry, they said there was a vast amount of offshore special purpose vehicles whose – in their words – "incredibly flattering" contribution to the balance sheet they couldn't begin to understand.'

'But I agreed with them. I agree with you. I want them all accounted for. There was just no way to get them into these September's figures, that's all. It was just too insanely late in the day to run all the numbers again. We'd have botched it for sure. I assured them – I'm assuring you – that every item in the First Bank balance sheet will be transparently laid out in the December figures.'

Peterson was less sure of himself, wrong-footed by Rankin's seemingly sensible approach, but the course was set. 'Whatever the truth, Jerry, you're the only person who believes your version of it. The market is generally correct, Jerry, that's our doctrine, our credo.

And right now you're being shorted by every bank, hedge fund and trader who can get hold of your stock.'

Rankin thought of all those people shorting his bank's stock, betting that it would go down, down, down. In the old days you couldn't bet against a company's share price unless you physically held the stock. It put a cap on the amount of downward bets. But these days – with all the derivatives and mechanisms and instruments – there was theoretically no limit to the amount of people who could bet against you, short you, if there were others willing to take the other side. It infuriated Rankin, gnawed at his nerves, that sons of bitches were rolling the dice against him.

'You're right, Richard, we are being shorted by everybody who can get their hands on the stock. But we're also being shorted by a lot more who can't. We need to stop these naked shorts, Richard. Have we learnt nothing from Lehman's?'

The Treasury Secretary didn't know whether to laugh or explode. 'I believe the most successful desk at First Bank this past twelve months trades using virtually nothing but naked shorts, Jerry?'

Rankin was stumped momentarily. 'Well, I wouldn't know the exact percentage. I'd have to check.'

'I can get the figures brought up if you like?'

Rankin looked up at Peterson and his blood ran cold as he began to understand the scale of the ambush, of the Treasury's real intentions. 'No, that won't be necessary. But I want to take this opportunity to protest that this move by the SEC and the Fed is both premature and unnecessary.'

'Protest noted, Jerry, but we didn't want to leave it to the eleventh hour like Lehman's.'

'But making your move against us has made our falling share price self-fulfilling.'

'I believe this would have happened either way eventually.' It was the Treasury Secretary's turn to fidget in his chair. 'However, Jerry, let's face the facts: you're holding more mortgage-backed contracts than any other bank on the Street, I know at least three banks who are unhappy about the value of the collateral they have from you, and your stock's dragging down the whole banking sector and the markets with it. Furthermore, an entire team here at the Fed has spent four weeks trying to unravel your web of companies and they say they are nowhere near to understanding your accounts . . .'

'We'll have a sit down.'

'. . . And to top it all you have the dubious honour of earning more fees from Bernard Madoff than any other company in the United States.'

'So, what you gonna do, send in the Fed to whack us all like that psycho Byrne did to my four executives? Is that how it's gonna be, is it?'

The Treasury Secretary did not react immediately. Wanted to remind Rankin who was running the meeting. 'That's not how we do it at the Treasury, Jerry. Tomorrow I'm informing the heads of all the major banks that they are to report to this building this weekend to discuss a bail-out of First Bank.'

Rankin was almost out of his chair. 'Gang-banged by those fucks? I'd rather be raped by the Chinks.'

'A team from the Bank of China will also be present.'

Rankin was beside himself with disgust and disbelief. He realized he was feeling slightly light-headed and had to control himself, calm himself. 'This isn't happening . . .'

'You should have sold this bank when you could have, Jerry – not when you had to.'

'Just give me till Monday.'

'Just give you till –? What's that supposed to mean? Have you got a buyer in the wings, Jerry? Is there anything you can tell me to help you here because this is your last chance to say anything that might affect the course of events.'

'Tomorrow's triple witching, Richard.'

'And?'

'It's when a hell of a lot of futures and options expire.'

'I know what it is, Jerry. Are you telling me you've got a big position in the market? Because nobody can find that in the books. What exactly are you saying?'

Rankin hesitated, realizing he was damned if he did,

damned if he didn't. 'There is a certain scenario whereby we could see some serious upside. I think it only right that we take that into account.'

But Peterson was on the money, literally. 'If there's upside, there's downside, Jerry. What's the downside of these trades?'

'Nothing, we took these deep out of the money, way back.'

'What's the downside?'

'It's nothing . . .'

The hard stare from the Treasury Secretary.

'A hundred mill, maybe a bit more.'

Peterson felt a certain creeping dread. 'A hundred million dollar potential loss? Tomorrow? That's not coming up in your books, Jerry. Where is that in your books?'

'I can't just . . . I don't do the accounts myself, do I? And the people who did are not here to assist – they're not here any more.'

Peterson had come to a very definite decision. He finished the last of his coffee and put the cup down on the table between them with an air of finality. 'The bail-out process begins here at the Fed, 0800 Saturday.'

'That's less than two days, Richard.'

'I know. Don't make me regret giving you that long.'

Rankin swallowed his fury and took a deep breath. 'Fine. But on Saturday I think you'll find that I will make the case for First Bank in the most strident terms and will convince my banking peers of the premature and unnecessary nature of this development.'

The Treasury Secretary levelled a very hard and very unequivocal stare at the First Bank CEO. 'I think you'll find, Jerry, that come Saturday you're not invited.'

The colour drained from Rankin's face.

22

The tiny store in Little Italy had a slim single window beside the door. The window was completely taken up with a poster advertising 'Alternative Medicine' that the sun had bleached to almost nothing years ago. I jammed a finger against the decrepit buzzer for a prolonged period, knowing that anything less wouldn't get her attention. Martinez looked at me, puzzled.

'We're going to save the president with homeopathy?'

I raised a less than impressed eyebrow at her.

'Who is it?' The female Hungarian voice coming through tinny from the small speaker.

'Byrne.'

'I'm kind of busy – can it wait?'

'Yeah, I'm here because it can wait.'

'All right, all right, but you'll have to give me a minute.'

There was a loud buzz which signalled for me to thump the door with the heel of my hand. It swung open and I waved Martinez in.

Once inside she took in her surroundings with the usual suspicion that the room provoked. Apart from the counter at the end of the very narrow store there was nothing but shelves down both sides sparsely filled with alternative medicine products no less than a decade old. At the end, blocking off the rear of the store, was a counter with a flat-screen television on it. Sitting before it on a stool behind the counter was the store's owner, Gabriella Hudec, playing a Second World War shoot 'em up on a flat-screen TV on the right hand wall.

I made my way through the gloom of the neglected store to the counter and leaned against it, watching Gabriella play her game. Her tidy boyish looks, cropped hair and black, thick-rimmed glasses were somehow contra to the slovenly clothes she wore, a T-shirt dragged over a long-sleeve top, like she had dressed efficiently rather than smart, all function over form. The Hungarian made no attempt to look up or indulge in pleasantries. On the screen her computer-generated American G.I. character was negotiating its way through a bombed-out town slaughtering German soldiers at a rate General Patton would have been proud of.

Martinez's face told me she was getting increasingly bewildered – and frustrated – that we were taking in what seemed like a diversion. On the screen I watched the game's American G.I. machine-gun his way through half a dozen Germans.

'That's a lot of Nazis you're killing there.'

Gabriella didn't waver from her game play. 'It's cheaper than therapy. Bastards raped my grandmother.'

Martinez was outraged. 'They did that in the game?'

The Hungarian looked at her for the first time, doubting what she'd just heard. 'No, in real life.' She tossed her gamepad onto the counter, casting a doubtful look at me, questioning my taste in friends.

I pulled out my smartphone and held it towards her. 'I need to trace a call urgently.'

Gabriella spoke matter-of-factly. 'Why didn't you say it was urgent?' She whipped the phone from my hand, lifted up a portion of the counter to let us through then walked away through a curtain towards the back.

Martinez lingered a moment, uncertain, so I followed behind the store-owner before she followed on behind. We walked down a poorly lit narrow flight of stairs to a concrete landing blocked by a grey-blue steel door. It was old and battered but, even to the untrained eye, clearly very strong. Gabriella pulled out a key from a chain round her neck then paused, looking from Martinez to me enquiringly.

'You can trust her.'

She stared at the detective for a moment longer, sceptical, unphased by the social niceties she was trampling on. I tried to put her at ease.

'You can't trust me, but you can trust her.'

She shook her head and unlocked the door with the key. The handle took some effort to turn, not from poor machinery but from the number of bolts it discreetly controlled. There are not a lot of bullet-proof nine-bolt doors in Manhattan. She pushed through the door with us behind. I'd never known Gabriella to allow anyone else down here before and had no idea how many people were allowed, but I figured Martinez was about to work that out for herself.

Beyond the door was another flight of concrete stairs that led down to yet another landing. This next door was shiny to the point of reflective. A slightly hazy impression of our small group stared back at us. Martinez was about to comment on this fact when she saw Gabriella place her hand into a hole in the wall next to it. A red light glowed inside as a device scanned the inserted hand.

Martinez clucked with intrigue. 'I thought those biometric door systems went out of fashion after the Colombians kept cutting people's fingers off to break into places?'

'You're right. Gabriella used to have one of those at first. Now she's upgraded to a metabolic version. No blood-flow no entry.'

There was a heavy *thunk* behind the door. Gabriella pulled her hand out of the hole in the wall and held it up for the detective to see. All four digits of it.

'I may owe Mike my life but he owes me a pinkie.' The Hungarian's demeanour told her that she meant it.

Martinez looked from Gabriella to me, baffled, studying our faces for the truth of this remark. Then she believed it. She went to speak, but the door began to slowly and smoothly slide to one side. It was only then, when it left its fittings, that the door's sheer depth, its thickness, was revealed.

'Christ, Byrne, that door must be . . .'

'Blast proof.'

'What the hell's she got in there?'

The space emerging behind was pitch black, giving no clues to what lay in wait for us.

'What's your favourite store in all New York, Martinez?'

She fired it back so quickly I thought she'd been wanting to say it all morning. 'Christian Louboutin, Madison Avenue. I almost licked the window once.'

That stumped me and the look on my face told her as much.

'It was during the sales.'

'Well, this is mine.'

The door had slid fully open. Gabriella walked in and a motion sensor responded by switching on the strip lighting above. The room revealed had the exact same effect on Martinez as it had had on me all those years ago. I wanted to hear her thoughts, hear her reaction.

She surveyed the room left to right, up and down, then spoke.

'Is that it?'

'Yeah.'

'I was expecting . . .'

'More?'

'Well, yeah.'

I walked into the white space the size of a large double garage. In the middle of the room was a clean workbench with a few tools sitting beside a small opened-up electrical device. Down three walls were floor-to-ceiling shelves filled with tightly packed boxes. At the far end corner was a computer station with half a dozen large screens. It was here that Gabriella had already positioned herself, plugging my phone into a USB lead and synchronizing the information.

'Which one, Mike?' Gabriella referring to the log of calls on my phone.

'Nine fifty-six, a Russian and an American.'

Gabriella slipped on some large padded headphones and one of her screens showed green sound waves expanding and retracting scratchily as she listened to Rankin's phone call with the Russian.

Martinez tentatively stepped into the room. 'What is it?'

I gestured expansively like I was letting her into a show-home. 'A gadget store.'

'A what store?'

'A gadget store. Look.' I pointed at the myriad boxes jamming the shelves. 'Bugging devices, tracking devices, surveillance, *counter*-surveillance, transmitters, cameras, lock-picking equipment, spy software, the works.'

She looked about herself, the underwhelmedness staying with her. 'So, it's just a spy-equipment store?'

'Yeah.'

'Like all the other spy-equipment stores?'

'Not quite.'

'How d'you mean?'

'They haven't got Gabriella.'

'What's special about Gabriella?'

'She's got Asperger's.'

'Is that good?'

'I'm not sure you'd choose it, but in her case what she lacks in social skills she makes up with a spot of high-functioning autism. I found her when I was in the Service. She has a genius for taking good covert equipment and turning it into great covert equipment, bespoke stuff, you know.'

Martinez dropped her voice. 'So, what you're saying is, she's a geek?'

'More like a super geek.'

As if on cue – or as if she'd been listening – Gabriella popped the headphones back down off her head and round her neck. In a dark mood.

'I can't trace the number.'

Martinez bit down on a smile. 'She's good.'

Gabriella's face clouded over, her mind struggling with not getting a result. 'It's not my fault – it's the phone he used.' Petulantly pointing at an inactive sound wave on a monitor.

I tried to soothe her, stop her from beating herself up. 'It's OK, Gabriella. What's he done, blocked his number?'

She shook her head, bothered by this technology she didn't have a handle on. 'No, it's more than that. Even then the caller should leave some kind of fingerprint, the phone carrier's ID at least. This phone is a ghost, like it never existed. That's high-end stuff, Byrne.'

Gabriella stared at her screen, the problem growing into a demon that would haunt her until she had cracked it. Her face threatened to turn into a mask of self-loathing. I put a hand on her shoulder, not wanting this to eat at her – but secretly knowing it would be her sole focus for as long as it took to defeat it once we had gone.

'Don't worry, we knew it was a long shot. Let me pick a few things up and we'll be out of your way.' Despite my reassuring words my spirits began to sink a little.

'I didn't say I didn't have anything.'

She swivelled round on her chair, still tormented by the challenge.

'I think I know which part of New York he made the call from.'

The Hungarian hit a key on her keyboard and the green audio waves on the monitor began to flicker. The phone conversation was relayed over the computer's powerful speakers.

> Rankin: *Look, we need that banker put out of business.*
> *Otherwise it puts the whole deal in jeopardy. We're still*
> *OK with the other trade, tomorrow, right?*
> Russian: Da. *This is not problem. Two separate trades.*
> Rankin: *Do I need to know any of the details of the*
> *second trade? Meet up?*

She hit the keyboard and the track stopped. Martinez and I both waited for something that we weren't sure was coming.

Gabriella was showing off a little, but I had to give her that – her mood needed a bit of a lift. She skipped back to the clip and turned the volume up, way up.

> Rankin: ... *We're still OK with the other trade,*
> *tomorrow, right?*
> Russian: Da. *This is not problem. Two separate trades.*

The sound of a horn could be faintly discerned. Gabriella struck the keyboard with a slight air of accomplishment.

Martinez wasn't sure what we should be concluding from this. 'A horn?'

Gabriella shook her head. 'A *ferry* horn.'

23

The bright yellow IKEA river taxi pulled away from Pier 11 on the southern tip of Manhattan. Most of the passengers headed upstairs to enjoy the picture-postcard view of Manhattan and Brooklyn that the bright blue day afforded. Up top the craft's open aspect allowed unobstructed views of these two opposing flavours of New York, and soon every camera and camcorder was working sixty to the dozen. Down below it was seen-it-all-before types, people with their faces buried in reading materials, or their heads filled with music or phone calls, and often a combination of all of these things. Perfect for two people who needed to meet but who didn't want people to be interested in them.

Rankin sank onto a seat at the front of the lower deck, totally demoralized. His companion gave him a sideways glance.

'Hell, what happened to you? Did the door knocker at the Fed turn into Marley's ghost?'

Rankin didn't answer. Just sat, downcast, his stomach in knots, his world falling apart. He tried to muster a brave smile, but couldn't do it. Next to him Deputy

Director George Carlton of the United States Secret Service was considering the banker gravely.

'What's up, the Treasury Secretary break the news about the fire sale?'

Rankin's head snapped up to look at him, but the words wouldn't come at first. 'You . . . you knew? You knew and you didn't say?' Incomprehension stoking anger.

'It's my job to know these things.'

'Well, you have to – you have to stop it, George. You *have* to.'

The Secret Service chief pinched his lips together. 'I don't have to do anything, Jerry, remember.'

Rankin checked himself, calibrating his attitude to the deputy director's role here – but pushed on nonetheless. 'Look, you have to stop this . . . this – this decapitation, George.'

The deputy director held his hands up. 'Let's be realistic, Jerry. There's only so much I can do. I am eyes and ears. Beyond that I have to work within the law.'

Rankin motioned his hands about them, indicating their meeting here, their meeting at all. 'This . . . ? This is within the law?'

Carlton's expression turned acrid, like Rankin had cracked a tasteless joke at a funeral. '*This* is about the greater good, Jerry. Don't go there, please.'

'The Treasury is going to break up First Bank at the weekend. We had plans, George – we had a vision.'

'Are they right, Jerry?'

'About what?'

'Did I back the wrong horse? Is First Bank a busted flush?'

Rankin was indignant. 'George, they create the accounting rules and, yes, we use those self-same rules to maximum effect . . .'

'Use them or abuse them?'

Rankin looked up at that but decided to let it pass. 'Nobody can unravel their bank's finances in forty-eight hours – it's ridiculous. I bought into your vision, George. I've backed your plan one hundred per cent from the get go. I've backed it and I continue to back it – I've delivered. I'm asking you to deliver for me.'

George washed his face with his hands. 'When they check the books tomorrow will they find a black hole?'

'No, not in a day, not tomorrow.'

'But *could* they find something?'

'Over the weekend, maybe.'

George threw his hands up. 'Maybe? You never told me about a "maybe".'

'Maybe – but once the second trade has taken place and all the contracts have settled we'll be fighting fit. Any black hole would be old news, it would be history. By Saturday we'll have the best balance sheet on the Street. They'll rap our knuckles for some accounting practices but that's it. I explained all this at the beginning.'

The Secret Service chief thought about what he was hearing. 'That's it?'

'That's it. But we need time to fight the Treasury – till Monday.'

'I can't stop the Treasury Secretary and the Fed doing what they believe needs doing. What else can we do to help you?'

Rankin racked his brains. 'You can keep the other banks off my back.'

'What do you mean?'

'They're asking for more money, collateral, before the close of business tomorrow. It'll break us.'

George spoke with a heavy heart. 'I'll see what can be done.' Telling Rankin with his look that that probably wouldn't amount to much.

The bank CEO dared to hope that he could, knowing that Carlton needed him as much as he needed Carlton. For the first time all day he felt slightly relaxed.

'Now, tell me what the fuck happened at the hotel this morning?'

Rankin had to take a moment to remember. 'Nothing. I mean, Byrne invited himself to breakfast.'

'And the shootings?'

'I don't know where that came from, honestly. I mean, I'd left by then. I didn't even know they were there. They must have followed me or Byrne.'

'Jerry, they were hired to do two trades. Can we just leave it at that? Can we? Shootouts in hotels for god's sake? Crimes mean evidence. Evidence means a trail. Trails lead somewhere. I will not allow anything to come back to me. Are we clear on that? Are we?'

'Me neither. We're aligned here, right?'

'Like all the best deals.' The ferry was halfway to Red Hook, Governor's Island slipping along to their right. 'What did Byrne want?'

'His parents' money back.'

'Are you going to give it to him?'

'Yeah, when the devil ice skates to work.'

Carlton gave a small smile. 'Anything else?'

'Wanted to know who would want to hurt me.'

'What did you tell him?'

'Aside from the Treasury Secretary, nobody.'

'What else did you talk about? Tell me everything.'

'There's nothing. He called my stock down –'

'He got that right.'

'And then . . . nothing.'

'Then what? You said "then"?'

Rankin shrugged. 'Well, he looked at my phone.'

Carlton held out his hand. 'Give it to me.'

'What do you mean?'

'I mean, *give it to me.*'

Rankin, confused, pulled out his phone and handed it over for the second time that day. 'What's up?'

Carlton held the phone up like an offending item. 'How long did he look at it for?'

'About a minute, maybe two, that's all.'

'Could you see what he was doing?'

'Yeah, he was sitting right opposite.'

'*Opposite?*' The deputy director looked out of the ferry window in disgust, sickened, glaring at the calm expanse of Upper Bay whilst he composed his thoughts. He turned back to face Rankin. 'It's bugged.'

'There's no way –'

'It's goddamn-well bugged. You . . .' Carlton looked heavenward for strength. 'Who have you spoken to, since then, on this phone? Think.'

'It's my personal phone, not many.'

'Who? Exactly?'

'Castle, my PA and – oh god . . .'

Carlton was shaking his head in near despair. 'Not our friend?'

'The Russ –'

'Shhhh. Don't say it. I don't want to hear it. I've got to keep clean hands here, OK. Don't *ever* tell me who you used. I don't want to know their names, their histories – I don't even want to know their goddamn nationality. Understand?' Carlton ran a hand through his white hair to compose himself, like this was all getting too close, too dangerous.

Rankin almost pleading now. 'We were careful, George. There is no way either of us said anything untoward. Guaranteed. No way.'

The Secret Service chief looked up, angry and determined. 'Text him on your work phone to tell him to disregard your next call, to take no action on it.' Rankin hesitated, unsure. 'Just do as I say.'

Rankin pulled out another cellphone, his Black-berry, and quickly sent the message. 'OK, done.'

Carlton handed the private phone back. 'Right, now call him on this one and tell him to meet you at the Brooklyn Docks, Pier 12, at four p.m. Then I want you to toss the phone over the side.'

The river taxi was pulling into dock. Carlton stood, the journey and meeting over. Rankin, out of sorts, nowhere near the top of his game, looked up at him.

'Then what happens?'

'If my guess is right, Michael Byrne will attend the meeting at Brooklyn Docks.'

'And then what?'

Carlton leaned down to Rankin. 'Then Mr Byrne will walk into a trap from which he won't return.'

Rankin felt better just hearing the words. Carlton righted himself and began to walk off.

'And the collateral, George? The extra money the banks are asking for?'

'Yeah, yeah. I'll see what I can do.' Not looking back.

24

I walked out of Gabriella's dark store into the bright sunshine of Little Italy. My mood was less than ecstatic. 'Well, that was helpful.'

Martinez was hard on my heels, the door slamming shut behind her. 'I didn't mean to offend her.'

I turned to face the detective, mustering what patience I could. 'She was just trying her best.'

'I've said I'm sorry. I just didn't think "ferry horn" was very helpful. Manhattan's an island, that's about forty, fifty miles of coastline – *if* the Russian is even *in* New York.' She was getting pissed now and that wasn't going to do either of us any good.

I looked off to one side, knowing how easily this argument could deteriorate and knowing there wasn't time. 'OK, fine, but Gabriella's gotta be handled with kid gloves and all that. That problem will torture Gabriella, haunt her, from now until she's located it and she won't locate it.'

'Why not?'

'Because, Martinez, there's forty or fifty miles of Manhattan coastline and that's if the Russian's even *in* New York.'

Martinez had a realization that put a wide smile on her face. 'So I was right?'

My phone trilled to tell me I had an email. I pulled it out and saw that a new audio file had arrived. I put it on speakerphone and leaned close to Martinez for her to hear. I hit PLAY.

Russian: Hello?
Rankin: Hi, it's me.
Russian: Yes?
Rankin: We need to meet.
Russian: OK.
Rankin: Remember the container port, next to Pier 12 in
*   Brooklyn?*
Russian: OK. What time?
Rankin: Four p.m.
Russian: OK.
Rankin: See you then.
Russian: OK.

The file ended and we looked up at each other. She spoke first. Excited.

'Pier 12? Could be our . . .'

'Ferry horn.'

But I wasn't happy. That phone call was bothering me.

'What's up, Byrne?'

'It's maybe nothing, but the speech patterns just then . . .'

She nodded – she was there already. 'Different, wasn't it? More direct, to the point.'

I could see her mind working, wanting to broach something. 'What is it?'

'Byrne, I've been thinking . . . We should call Ashby.'

'It's too early. What if Rankin and the Russians are planning a trap?'

'All the more reason to go in heavy.'

'Martinez, if there's a no show or any kind of screw up then I'm back in custody and whatever's going to happen tomorrow is still going to happen tomorrow. Who else is trying to stop it?'

'OK, so what if you're right – what if it is a trap?'

'We try not to fall into it.'

'How?' She had a slightly nervous look. But not for herself.

'Two ways. The first – and my preferred route – is to call Rankin and ask him if this is a trap.'

She pulled a face. 'And the less shit idea?'

'Go to Pier 12 and take a look.'

She pulled another face. The one that says 'I hope you know what you're getting us into'.

I didn't.

25

The crossroads were deserted. No houses, no people, no trees, no hedges. Just Pennsylvania farmland as far as the eye could see, the summer crops cut, the land stubbled, barren.

A black Lincoln Continental sat parked up on a grass verge. Sitting against the hood was Mr Bingo, a sports bag on the car roof beside him. An ear and one side of his face was bandaged, the result of his scalding at the hotel restaurant earlier that morning. He thought about his burns, thought about how he could feel his raw skin every time he moved his jaw. Thought about his twin brother, dead. Thought about what he must have gone through when he died. Thought about Byrne. Thought about hurting him. Killing him slowly, painfully, the Russian way.

The sound of an approaching car woke him from his reverie. He could see it a long way off, dipping in and out of sight as it made its way towards him along the dusty track ahead.

After a minute or so the car, a newish Toyota pick-up, slowed to a halt by the Russian. It had two occupants, a smartly dressed thirtysomething couple, maybe husband and wife, he didn't know, he didn't care. They left the car running but opened their doors together. The female paused by her open door whilst her tall male companion approached Mr Bingo.

'Yous don't mind if I just do the formalities.' Texan, confident, flashing an apologetic but winning smile below his reflective police-patrolman-style sunglasses.

The Russian held his arms out as Mr Texas patted him down. He was thorough and if there had been a weapon on Mr Bingo's person the Texan would have found it. It wasn't hard to find the Texan's weapon, his revolver was stuck down the back of his pants. *Goddamn amateurs*, Mr Bingo thought to himself.

Mr Texas stood up and the 'isn't this weather lovely' smile returned. He nodded at the sports bag on the hood of the Lincoln Continental. 'May I?'

Mr Bingo stepped to one side. 'Be my guest.'

Mr Texas took off his shades and hung them from his shirt pocket. He unzipped the bag and swallowed at what he saw. Money. An awful lot of money. The intermediary had said these foreign guys were prepared to pay top dollar and right now he had no reason not to believe it. He zipped up the bag and nodded brightly at his partner.

The small slightly jumpy woman pulled out a large black briefcase from the cabin of their pick-up and approached the Lincoln where she set it down on the hood. She stood, unsure what to do next.

'Go on, honey, show him.'

She cautiously clicked open the latches and lifted up the lid. Inside sat a dozen large, tightly wrapped packages of what might have been fresh bread dough.

'You be careful with this.' Her accent West Coast, ever so slightly dudish. 'This'll take out a square block.'

Mr Bingo gave a smile that was meant to charm but only added to the crackling nervousness of the meeting. 'I'm very thorough.'

Even the experienced Texan was getting jittery, keen to move now. 'Anything else or are we all done here?'

The Russian was looking at the briefcase. He closed the lid and the latches. His taciturn persona was making his counterparts edgy but they were relieved to see him pick up the sports bag and hand it to the Texan. He smiled again, more broadly. 'A pleasure doing business with you.'

'You too, sir. Any time.'

The Texan looked from the Russian to his girlfriend.

A quiet crack sounded in the distance.

A bullet tore through her face.

She fell away from them like a limp rag doll, lifeless.

The Texan spun to see where the bullet had come from. The Russian snatched the gun from the back of his pants and aimed it at his back. But his actions were superfluous as another bullet ripped into one side of the Texan salesman's head and out the other. He flopped to the ground. Mr Bingo stood over the bodies and put another bullet into each of them, into their heads. For good measure.

In a field three hundred yards away another Russian stood up and efficiently dismantled his rifle, placed the parts in a small sack then made his way towards his colleague.

26

The Brooklyn docks. I scanned the deserted container port. A sea of wide open spaces dotted about with the odd shipping container. Three piers, two with enormous warehouses bookending an unloading dock manned by two enormous cranes. Quiet and off the radar. A good place for a low-key meeting.

On the other hand, cranes, shipping containers and a wide open space with nowhere to hide. The perfect place for a trap.

'What do you think?'

I zoomed in and out with my binoculars. Searching the crane cabins, searching the warehouse rooftops, searching the container doors – searching everything. There was nothing out of the ordinary except the black Mercedes limousine with its blacked-out windows sitting in the middle of the empty car park, engine off.

'I can't see anything. Just the car.'

Martinez looked over the edge of the rooftop. She moved slowly, not wanting to catch anybody's eye. We were five storeys up, looking down from one corner of the port. 'So, do you think it's a set-up?'

'I can't tell.'

Nothing was moving down below, but I didn't know what to make of it.

'Do you think we should go down there, take a look at that car?' She was on edge.

'Not yet. If it is a set-up, they would have had their people arrive early. The car could be empty for all we know.' Which was my way of saying we didn't know much.

'Or it could have Rankin and whoever this Russian partner of his is.'

'That's true enough.' I drummed the binoculars with my fingers, thinking. The car was sitting by itself, nothing in any direction for over one hundred feet. 'Getting to that car will not be easy. Getting to it unseen will be impossible.'

Martinez turned to face me and slid back down against the low wall running round our rooftop position. 'What are you thinking?'

'I'm wondering what Jay-Z would do.'

She looked at me, uncomprehending. 'Don't you mean JC?'

I pulled out my smartphone. 'No, I mean the mayor of New York.'

Special Agent Diane Mason sat across from her boss in the back of the stretch Mercedes. She looked out through the tinted windows at the empty container port car park. She checked her watch.

'Sixteen thirty-seven. Are you sure he's going to show?'

Deputy Director George Carlton gazed lazily at her, his eyes narrow like a snake's. 'Are you hoping he won't?'

Agent Mason pushed her jacket sleeve over her watch, failing to hide her discomfort. 'You talk like we have different agendas.'

'Don't we?'

'Not if you want the president to have a safe visit to New York we don't.'

Carlton's cheek twitched. 'Rising up the ranks of the Secret Service is about taking the helicopter view, Diane. It's about seeing the world in satellite photographs.'

'Well, of course I want people like Byrne brought in. He's a known . . .' She wanted to choose the right word.

'Terrorist?'

'Of course he's not a terrorist.'

'Really?'

'No.' She was adamant, hating the lazy and cynical way the word had been tossed about since 9/11.

Carlton sat forward in his seat, exercising authority and familiarity. 'Let me tell you what a terrorist is, Diane. It's someone who wants to hurt not individuals but the United States itself.'

'I think perhaps you've read more into the Patriot Act than I have.'

The deputy director probed her face, looking for clues. 'You know, when you strip away all the analysis, all the directives, all the intelligence, it just boils down to patriotism, Diane.'

'I guess if you strip out all the intelligence that is where you get to.'

Carlton reacted to her remark with a crooked grin. 'America needs to tell the world that you are either its friend or its enemy. We are not fooled by the inbe-tweeners.'

Mason frowned. Spoke carefully. 'Didn't that president leave office?'

'Are you America's friend or its enemy? Are you patriotic or unpatriotic?'

Special Agent Mason was feeling an ugliness to this conversation. Feeling like Carlton was offering not a rhetorical flourish but was actually questioning her credentials.

'Because, Diane, Byrne didn't just kill people, he killed patriots – bankers – who are one of the pillars of our global standing in the world.'

Mason was almost leaning away from her excitable boss, finding his manner rather hectoring, like a polit-ician on the campaign trail. 'Some would argue that the bankers costing the United States over $2.8 trillion in federal support was just about the most unpatriotic thing anybody could do. That's the cost of a war, that's an untold number of schools and hospitals . . .'

Carlton lowered his head. Mason believed he was fighting a rage, controlling himself, but he lifted his head, laughing. More disconcerting still. He pointed a finger at her.

'You know, I checked the security footage of the time Byrne escaped from our custody. You seemed to be talking in the corridor, Diane. You seemed to be collaborating . . .'

His mouth was smiling. His eyes were accusing. His eyes were damning.

There was a burst of static from a comms device next to Agent Mason. 'Eagle One?'

Relieved by the diversion Mason quickly picked it up.

'Go ahead.'

A burst of static. 'Eagle One, we're not quite sure what's going on here but there's a large number of unidentified subjects – mainly young men – streaming into the car park.'

The Secret Service officers swapped a look of non-comprehension then looked out through the car's windows.

'Can you give us more information?'

Another burst of static. 'We're not sure, but there are carloads, busloads of unidentified young subjects just turning up, like –'

'Like what?'

'Like, well, like it's some kind of event . . .'

Mason went to speak further but Carlton grabbed the comms unit from her hand. 'This is Carlton – why the hell didn't you turn them away?'

More static. 'Sorry, sir, but there's just so many of them.'

Mason was looking out of the window. 'Jesus. Look.'

Carlton looked, but couldn't begin to understand. Mason didn't understand either, but she understood enough to think, *Christ, Byrne, what are you up to this time?*

We had descended from the rooftop position and were now standing at the corner of the dock car park watching hundreds of people stream in. Young, mostly black, mostly men, and all excited.

Martinez shook her head. 'Can't wait to see what happens when they find out Jay-Z *isn't* sitting inside that car about to make a new video and *doesn't* need one thousand extras at a hundred dollars a head.'

'Neither can I.'

'You'll be barred from those fan websites if you keep posting those rumours.'

I looked through my binoculars for the hundredth time that hour. 'It's not that I mind – it's people shooting at me and hitting a bunch of youngsters I mind.'

Martinez looked at me like I was slightly crazy. 'What about minding people shooting at *you*?'

'Yeah, that as well.' I gave her the binoculars and

started to zip up my hooded top. 'Be ready on the bike, Martinez. If it all kicks off, just get yourself the hell out of here.'

She took her phone out of her pocket and nodded at the phone in my hand. 'That thing got a good camera?'

I wasn't following her. 'Five megapixels, why?'

She gave her phone a little shake. 'Well, eight beats five. And nobody's set a trap for me out there. *You* be ready on the bike – but *you* be ready to take *me* the hell with you.'

She wandered towards the throng of young New Yorkers surrounding the Mercedes limousine. She was walking towards possible danger, a possible trap. Doing it for me. And as she walked away all I could think was, *What a great ass.*

The Mercedes was surrounded by hundreds of young people, fresh off the street and the projects and the surrounding tenements, whipped up like they had just gate-crashed a post-Grammies party.

'Jay-Z! Jay-Z! Jay-Z!'

Martinez struggled to make her way through the crowd, sharing excited looks with many, apologizing looks with those that felt they were being pushed in front of.

'Jay-Z! Jay-Z! Jay-Z!'

People were banging on the trunk and hood of the

blacked-out Mercedes, not aggressive, but needing to vent their excitement.

'Jay-Z! Jay-Z! Jay-Z!'

One of the rear doors began to open. A cheer erupted from the crowd, filled the air, ecstatic. A middle-aged white man in a suit stood before them. The kids didn't quite know what to make of it, the cheering continuing in pockets as half the crowd thought that maybe the man was an agent. They weren't far wrong.

'Jay-Z! Jay-Z! Jay-Z!'

Carlton lifted up a hand for calm. The noise subsided, the occasional whistle rising into the air. 'Why are you here?'

Too many people all explaining at the same time.

'For the Jay-Z video!'

'And a hundred dollars'

'Thass right!'

Cameras clicking, flashes going off, Martinez snapping him with her camera-phone, not knowing who he was, another banker? The Russian?

'There's been some misunderstanding. We're having a private meeting in this car.'

Cries of 'Bullshit', 'Where's Jay-Z?', 'Where's my money?'

Martinez tapped a message into her phone to go with the photo she was sending. 'Got him.'

*

I was watching the mob scene from three hundred yards away, in agony that I wasn't by Martinez's side. Somebody had gotten out of the car but the crowd was blocking my view. My phone beeped. I pulled up the text message. Oh shit, oh Jesus, oh no . . . A picture of my old boss, Deputy Director George Carlton, was staring me in the face.

I dialled a number, barked into the phone. 'Martinez, get out!'

Martinez, hand to her free ear, was struggling to hear. 'What?'

'I said get out. It's the Secret Service – it's a trap.'

Her eyes widened and she looked around furtively.

Agent Mason emerged beside Carlton. The crowd's cries fell away, a note of irritation entering their catcalls.

'Where the fuck is the mayor?'

'Where the hell is Jay-Z?'

Special Agent Mason held up her hands to the crowd, trying to placate them. 'I'm really sorry, but I think there's been some kind of mistake.'

On a shipping crane a Secret Service spotter was scanning the crowd with a powerful pair of binoculars. He roved his sight over the portion of the crowd where Martinez was. Returned his view to where she was standing. Watched her bob and weave, look around, worried, alert, turning briefly to show more than half of her face. That was all the spotter needed. He didn't know the face, but his training and experience told him it was the face of *somebody who shouldn't be there*.

Special Agent Mason ignored the waiting and unsure crowd and held the comms unit to her ear.

'What? Say that again . . . ?'

Special Agent Mason looked up and made eye contact with Martinez. And she knew in an instant that her spotter was right. She spoke into the comms unit as Martinez attempted to melt back into the crowd, attempted to make her way through and out.

On top of one of the massive warehouses nearby a sniper looked down the sight of his rifle, scanning calmly but quickly across the crowd. Agent Mason's voice was in his ear-piece.

'Latino, long dark hair, twenty-five to thirty years of age, wearing a dark biker's jacket. She is a suspected target, repeat *suspected* target. Do *not* fire until an association with our original target has been established. All ground units close in and apprehend the new target.'

Martinez appeared in the sniper's rifle sight. A clear view of her as she left the crowd behind, caught in the round telescopic lens.

He followed her, the deadly crosshairs centring on her head. Tracking her.

I didn't need my spy-glasses now. Baseball-capped heads were popping up on every vantage point – cranes, rooftops, high-rise windows. I yelled into my phone.

'Keep your head down and make your way towards me as quickly as possible. Do *not* run. You hear me, do *not* run.'

Martinez in view now. A hundred yards away. Almost home free.

Then it began.

Body-armoured Counter Assault Team agents burst out of the shipping containers, running round the outside of the Jay-Z crowd towards her. I knew their training and I knew their intentions: they were looking to make a grab.

I shoved away my phone, slammed my visorless helmet on and fired up the Ducati. 'Fuck.' Pointing it at Martinez, seventy-five yards away, agents closing, closing too fast.

Martinez looking up at me, hopeful, scared, the bike racing towards her, a furtive glance about her, the nightmare vision of balaclavered agents sprinting towards her, an involuntary cry. She started running as I slid the back wheel round in front of her, her leaping on the motorcycle, me wrenching back the accelerator –

*

A spotter in a window overlooking the car park had Byrne's face in his sights. He grabbed his comms. 'All agents, she has joined the target, repeat she has joined the original target.'

Carlton saw it just as the message came over the system. He squeezed the TALK button so tight he was in danger of crushing the device in his fist.

'This is Carlton: shoot on sight – I repeat – *shoot the targets on sight*. Shoot both the targets on sight – *now*.'

Agent Mason behind him involuntarily put a hand to her neck in distress.

I aimed the bike towards the exit of the car park, but the way was suddenly a collection of Secret Service sedans and jeeps, screeching to a halt, blocking the path, Counter Assault Team agents – head to toe black armoured suits, armoured helmets – piling out and aiming their Remington 870 shotguns from behind their open doors.

I veered back into the car park as bullets tore up the tarmac beside us, bullets raining at us from ground level and above. The crowd was affording some measure of restraint from the CAT agents but I could see them repositioning, CAT agents trying to take the crowd out of the equation, penning us in, back inside the car park. There was an easy exit close past the crowd of hip-hop fans, a hole in the fast-closing dragnet, a gap

I could just about squeeze through before they closed me down. Freedom was just a pull of the throttle away, right there in front of us. But what if the CAT agents got trigger happy as we passed the Jay-Z fans . . . ? What if, what if . . . ?

Oh damn it.

I fired the bike away from the young crowd towards a forest of shipping containers as more sedans and jeeps burst into the dock, all magnetically drawn towards their prey, approaching from all directions.

We had lost the cover of the crowd but gained the cover of the stacks of shipping containers. Secret Service cars were careening their way towards the nest of steel blocks, agents leaning out of windows, firing off rounds at our escaping motorcycle, me doing my utmost to lean the bike left and right, slamming it round corners, bullets flying off the rust-coloured boxes about us.

We emerged from the far side to see the thing I wanted to see – and not see. Another exit, but four crouching, helmeted CAT agents spread across it, spraying bullets at our bike, forcing me to describe a wide circle in the dock, surrendering to the Secret Services plan of hemming us in towards the far corner, towards the far warehouse, Secret Service cars bearing down on us.

Martinez tapped me on the shoulder and then stabbed a finger at a gap in the enormous warehouse door. *A way in – but was there a way out?* It was the least worst idea we had and I gunned the bike towards the opening, bullets sparking off the surrounding containers, peppering the parked up lorries, taking out their windows, this hail of bullets closing in on us, on our motorcycle, zeroing in, feet away, inches away then –

The bike cannoned into the vast space of the warehouse, three storeys high, the centre made up of walls of cargo waiting to find containers and shipping. The roar of the roadster's engine seemed to tear through the air itself, beating against the industrial walls. For now we were alone. For now.

The Mercedes limousine screeched to a halt by the dockside warehouse. Already there were a dozen Secret Service vehicles, including a Secret Service mobile-incident truck. Scores of agents formed a ragbag semicircle round the warehouse entrance, shielded for the most part by their vehicles, guns trained on the narrow entrance, the guns giving nobody inside the warehouse a chance of escape.

Deputy Director Carlton made his way round the first line of cars to Commander Becker of the Counter Assault Team.

'We have the targets in the building, sir.'

'Escape routes?'

'This is the only exit, sir.' Becker pointed at the massive warehouse door, partially open. 'Time is on our side.'

'Just what do you mean by that, Commander?'

Becker was surprised his stance had not pleased his superior. Even back in Afghanistan they didn't go in guns blazing where restraint could reduce casualties on their own side. 'I mean, we can wait the targets out, sir. Bring them in on our terms.'

'We have a presidential visit in under twenty-four hours, Becker. Are you telling me you plan to assign the entire Counter Assault Team away from protective duty in Wall Street to a siege in the Brooklyn Docks?'

'I didn't mean to suggest –'

'Bring this situation to a close – now.'

'Certainly, sir. Do you want the targets dead or alive, sir?'

Carlton leaned into his subordinate. 'Which one's quicker?'

We sat on the bike at the far end of the warehouse, in between two cages of goods, in the dark, facing the aircraft-hangar-sized door at the very far end.

Martinez pulled her helmet onto her head. 'How many do you think there are?'

My mind was racing faster than I'd just raced the bike. 'Enough.'

'Oh.'

She was breathing heavier than usual, like a cornered animal, like what she was. I was running through our options and concluding that we didn't have many. Boxed in with only one way out was a bad starting point for an escape.

'Let me call Ashby. There's no need to get killed here, Byrne.'

I nodded slightly. 'Strike you as the negotiating type, did they?'

But after a moment I regretted my words just as I regretted getting Martinez into this spot.

'Look, you do what you have to do, Martinez. It's not you they want – you could give yourself up. No need for us both to . . .' I didn't want to say it, didn't want to remind her of the danger she was in.

She spoke deadpan, unemotional, unconvincingly. 'Hell no, Byrne. Wouldn't miss this for the world.'

We stared intensely at the vertical bar of light at the end of the walls of cargo. Stared at it as we both ran ideas rational and irrational through our minds. Stared at it like a force of will might change what was on the other side of it. I couldn't believe what I'd done. Expected a trap, planned for a trap and walked right into a trap. But my fury at myself would have to wait.

'Byrne, what's that film where the two cowboys burst out of the barn and try to shoot it out with that South American army?'

'*Butch Cassidy and the Sundance Kid.* Big shootout with the Bolivians at the end. A classic.' My eyes fixed on the gap in the warehouse door at the end.

'Do they win?'

My eyes scanning the warehouse walls, looking for gaps, looking for hope, looking for the last thing that they would expect . . . 'Who?'

'The two cowboys?'

'Well, it's a freeze-frame. They come out firing but you never really know.'

Martinez nodded like she understood but chewed on her lip nonetheless. 'So, it's possible they got away?'

I chuckled mirthlessly. 'God no, they got creamed.'

'Oh.'

Martinez, breathing heavily in the dark.

Suddenly the warehouse doors parting, startling both of us for an instant, the light too bright at first, then our eyes adjusting, adjusting to the sight of a small army of CAT agents behind a wall of vehicles.

'Byrne?'

'What?'

But a small sob was all that came. When she didn't reply I turned round in my seat, took a good look at her, sitting cornered in the dark, saw the brave smile clinging to her lips, the eyes, wet now, eyes that didn't want to die. Heard the croak in the voice. 'Next time I say "Let's go to Bolivia . . ."' She tried to hold her smile, but she couldn't.

And even with the world closing in on us, all the sand draining from the timer, I found myself thinking, *This is as about as beautiful as a woman gets.*

I turned back.

Knowing that whatever else happened, that I was about to die trying.

Agents casting long shadows at the end of the afternoon started to creep forward, en masse. I leaned into the handlebars and pulled the throttle wide open, the bike bucking like a stallion under us as it hurtled towards the gap at the end, the agents at the end.

Seeing their targets' plan the CAT agents knelt down and assumed firing positions, none of them backing off from the approaching vehicle, none of them running for cover, every one trained to choose fight over flight, every one committed to executing the plan of executing the targets. Then, all as one – Becker's command ringing in their ears – they opened fire, a wave of bullets filling the warehouse alleyway as the bike screamed towards them.

Then –

Nothing.

The motorcycle had disappeared. The noise had cut in half – it was there, it was racing, but nobody could see it.

Then in their ears, one of the agents yelling, 'They're on the first floor – they've gone up a ramp, they're on the first floor!'

Becker. 'Go, go, go!'

No hand commands, no silent gestures, just CAT agents storming the building, seeing now the motorcycle sprinting down the far side of the warehouse, back on itself, towards the end of the warehouse. Gunfire sporadic now, agents taking their shots as they could, a cacophony of gunfire from the myriad weapons deployed – Heckler & Koch MP5 submachine guns, Remington 870 shotguns, FN P90 submachine guns – wood and metal spraying up as they were cut by bullets.

The agents spread out along the length of the warehouse, down each alleyway, ready to close down the targets. They held their fire as they scanned the floor up above. Searching with their eyes, searching with their guns.

Commander Becker pulled a rifle grenade from a clip on his armour. Very carefully he slotted it onto the adaptor of his MP5. Grenade in place, he raised the submachine to his shoulder and looked through the sight to the gangway up above. Finger on the trigger.

On the first floor, tucked away in a far corner, we waited on the bike. We'd risked our lives with that last dash and succeeded in rising exactly one floor in the warehouse. Not good, Byrne, not good. It was a dark corner but that would only afford us so much cover for so long, the purr of the motorcycle engine guaranteed that. The gunfire had abated whilst the CAT agents repositioned themselves. They moved quietly and I couldn't begin to second guess their next move and certainly didn't want to wait for it. I decided that smart, well-planned tactics were out, desperate measures were in.

I turned on my seat. 'Martinez?'

'What, Byrne?' Somewhere beyond fear, beyond hope. She had that look I'd seen before. The one where they hope that when the bullet comes it finishes everything in an instant. Because nothing mattered any more but *right now, this moment in time.* There was nothing Martinez wanted in the world, not a single material possession. Another chance at life was all she wanted, wanted it with all her being, every molecule in her body screaming to survive this dead end I'd driven her into. And even in this wretched moment not an iota of blame directed at me. If I had a team of her, hell . . .

I took a good look at her. Wanted to take it all in, every last feature of her sublime face. 'Martinez . . .'

That heart-breakingly brave smile again, only now a single tear trickling down from her eye, tracing her beautiful nose down to her waves-on-a-tropical-storm lips. 'Byrne?'

'Let's go to Bolivia.'

She reached forward and kissed my cheek.

'For luck. My luck, not yours.' She blinked her wet eyes, tears coming out of both now.

And I thought, *Not today – not like this.*

I turned back, got my head down and felt the

burning, screaming, thundering rage inside me. Not today – not like this. Not Martinez.

It was moving time.

I pulled the bike's trigger.

Martinez hugged my back for all she was worth.

We launched down the gangway. Below us twenty agents saw us – saw us flitting behind pallets of goods and all as one fired their guns at us, emptied their guns at us, pounded us with automatic rifles, machine guns, automatic revolvers, furiously peppering the world about us as we whipped along, the bullets tearing up and through the haphazard boxes and cargo, wood splinters showering about us, rendering a clear line of vision impossible, only the square of light of the window at the end, packaging and pallets exploding about us, the square of light getting larger, the bike approaching at sixty miles an hour, too late to change the plan, too late to change the course of events, too late for anything, just crashing through –

Becker saw his moment, tracked the accelerating Ducati up and above, and, anticipating the targets' next move, launched the grenade at the wall before the window.

Outside the warehouse the waiting Secret Service personnel all looked up as one, all without any time to react beyond witnessing the audacity of their suspects as the Ducati rocketed out of the first-floor window in a spray of glass – a fireball exploding behind them, flew across the sky and down onto the top of an eighteen-wheeler's trailer, dipping down before the rider seemed to straighten it through sheer force of will, before accelerating off again, down off the front of the truck, landing, almost bouncing off the car park deck as the rider and passenger righted themselves and streaked away and out of the dock. Out and gone before the Secret Service agents knew what had hit them, too fast for anyone.

The Counter Assault Team raced out of the warehouse in pursuit only to find themselves penned in by the very ring of vehicles intended to snare their prey. The disappearing roar of the targets' Ducati confirmed what they all suspected: that the entire operation was in tatters.

Carlton slammed a hand onto the roof of his Mercedes and shouted at everybody and anybody. 'That guy's fucking insane! How the hell did he pass the psych test for the Secret Service?'

Mason was not alone in thinking the same about Carlton.

The assembled crowd of hip-hop fans, hundreds of young Brooklynites and fellow New Yorkers, had watched, transfixed by the events that had just unfurled.

As they witnessed the motorcycle bursting out of the nearby warehouse window in an explosion of glass and flames, down onto the truck then off through the docks a cheer worthy of the arrival of Jay-Z on stage erupted. They stamped their feet, yelled, screamed and did everything they could to register their appreciation of what they had just seen.

A short street kid in low-slung baggy jeans and a Yankees baseball cap was nodding his approval as his two sidekicks whooped and applauded beside him.

'Now that's what I *call* a music video.'

27

The grand, oak-panelled conference room was filled with the great and the good of the United States regulatory community. At the centre of the long walnut table was inlayed a circle with the words 'The Federal Reserve Bank of New York'. Above the table were two ornate art deco chandeliers, hanging from the high, corniced ceiling. Around the table were a dozen officials, at the head of which sat Treasury Secretary Peterson. Almost everybody's jackets were on the backs of their chairs.

Peterson was keen to set the tone of a war room. 'OK, let's be absolutely clear here, we are not doing another Lehman's. We are not going to run out of options, but instead we are going to formulate a workable rescue plan for this bank. Where exactly are we? Clarissa?'

A middle-aged Hispanic woman halfway down the table held up a slew of notes. 'We've been contacted by the chiefs of more than thirty central banks demanding assurances that First Bank of America will not go under. A number of them are threatening to freeze First Bank's overseas assets without it.'

Peterson shook his head emphatically. 'Clarissa, we can*not* give out that kind of signal at this point. Let's not have the Far East tail wagging the American dog here.'

'Mr Secretary, there is a genuine risk that Asia will pull its money out of the United States. They do not have the appetite for more write-offs because of our bad banks.'

'OK, OK. What about the markets?'

A youngish man with an improbably neat demeanour coughed to clear his throat before speaking. 'The bears are shorting the hell out of First Bank – and right now everybody's a bear. First Bank is off ninety per cent since a week ago, now below three dollars. As a consequence all the banks are off, which is dragging down the entire market – as you all know, the S&P closed down four point three per cent today. It's carnage out there.'

Peterson nodded – he got it. 'Credit?'

An older African American gentleman with small shiny glasses and blue bow-tie referred to his notes. 'Mr Secretary, the overnight markets are drying up. It's Bear Stearns and Lehman's all over again. I believe it is fair to say that the fears concerning First Bank have not been contained and they have now bled into the wider system. Unless we act swiftly we will be putting every bank at risk.'

Peterson groaned inwardly. 'OK, the rescue plan. Where are we?'

A seasoned banker along the table was rolling up his shirt sleeves. 'Barclays are worried we're using them to bid up the Chinese.'

Peterson looked taken aback. 'Well, we are.'

There was silence before genuine laughter rippled around the room.

The seasoned banker continued. 'Before they allow Barclays or any other UK entity to bid, the Bank of England wants a guarantee from the Fed that it will underwrite all and any toxic assets on First Bank's books.'

Peterson scoffed. 'Jesus, those grin fuckers are at it again. What else we got?'

'Goldman's and JPMorgan want the same as the UK regulators.'

Peterson threw his hands up in despair. 'Christ, everybody wants the moon on a stick.' Then he smiled wearily, in resignation. 'Still, let's be honest, everything's on the table here. OK, what about the bond markets . . . ?'

The door opened and the Fed's communications director strode in. She was a well-presented Chinese American woman wearing a tight silver Ralph Lauren power suit. She looked distinctly anxious, not helped by the Treasury Secretary's scowl at her unannounced intrusion.

'I'm so sorry to barge in, but I think you need to see this.'

She clicked a remote control at a large television on

a tall stand in the corner. Everybody half rose or rose altogether to crowd around the set. CNN showed a crowd of reporters hustling a man trying to enter an office building. The strapline at the bottom read 'Live from New York: The Next Lehman's?'

On the television, 'Mr Rankin? Mr Rankin?'

Jeremiah Rankin, almost about to enter his bank's Madison Avenue offices, turned back from the security guard holding the entrance open for him.

'Mr Rankin, did you meet with the Treasury Secretary today?'

'Yes, we did meet earlier today.'

Peterson flung a wild hand at the screen. 'What the fuck is he doing? Go inside! Don't say another fucking word.'

Another reporter. 'And can you reveal the substance of those talks, Mr Rankin?'

'I will say no more than we had a frank exchange of views about the state of First Bank of America . . .'

Peterson again, angrier. 'This is deliberate. This is sabotage. What the fuck is he doing?'

'. . . the state of the banking industry . . .'

The seasoned banker stood with hands on hips, staring in disbelief. 'He's committing hara-kiri live on television, that's what he's doing.'

'. . . and the health of the wider United States economy.'

Peterson ran his hands over his bald head. Had to

turn away. 'Fucking fuck. He wants the stock down. He wants to destroy the share price. He's a financial suicide bomber, that's what he is.'

The communications director had a thought. 'Why is he using the front door to his office? He only goes in by his private elevator in the car park.'

Peterson turned, his mouth sealed with anger, but nodding, agreeing, pointing a finger from her to the screen. 'He's playing us. He's fucking with us. Unless he's got a royal fucking flush, he is about to cash out. Permanently.'

Everybody watched the cameras stay on Rankin as he disappeared inside First Bank's headquarters. Everybody angry and disbelieving, everybody gesticulating at the screen and exchanging angry expressions of disbelief.

Peterson looked from the television to the heated crowd in the room to the communications director. Looked at the sheen of her tights up her calves. Remembered his last visit to New York. And wondered if she were free again tonight.

28

'You're playing a dangerous game, my friend.'

Jeremiah Rankin's office was the largest office of any CEO in Manhattan. He had made a point of it. Apart from the portion dedicated to the generous Brazilian rosewood desk, there was also a sizeable conference table in its own space as well as a quadrangle of chesterfield buttoned-leather couches round a large, low table. It was in the latter that Rankin was presently sitting with Moffat Agron.

Agron was Russian, short, with a taut, hungry frame shaped more by a diet of cigarettes than exercise. His dark, intense eyes were topped by thick black hair slicked back and his tailor flew to wherever Agron was in the world to provide him with the very smart but very casual business suits he chose to wear.

Rankin poured them each a single malt whisky from a crystal decanter.

'"Game" is the right word, Agron. Cheers.'

They toasted each other as Rankin unbuttoned his shirt and loosened his tie from his neck. The Russian did not follow suit as his suit was never accompanied by a tie. One of the privileges of billionaire status. As was smoking in your bank's CEO's office.

'How are you enjoying life upon the yacht?'

His mouth working a cigar, Agron raised his eyebrows in appreciation. 'I must confess that when you said it was preferable to a hotel I had my doubts and yet . . .' A smile finishing the sentence. 'And your bank is OK with my staying on it?'

'Take as long as you need – it's at your disposal. You're a customer. Our best customer.'

'I think the only customer not shorting your stock right now.'

'I won't be offended if you do.'

'On the contrary, we are very long First Bank. We bought your shares all the way down. We hold one of the biggest private positions in the marketplace.'

Rankin tilted his cut glass tumbler at Agron. 'I'm flattered.'

They sipped their whiskies.

'But you must be careful, no? This second trade . . .'

'How is that trade going? Have you placed it yet?' Rankin wanting to seem cool, hoping the Russian could not see his intense interest.

Agron was nonchalant. 'No, not yet. Tomorrow morning I believe. Trust me, the less you know . . .'

'I understand, it's just that the markets have come off a lot more than we ever expected – than we ever had a *right* to expect.' Rankin sounding out his counterpart, talking just a little faster than usual, struggling to hide his discomfort. 'I mean, when we started talking about the second trade, I mean, the markets were a hell of a lot higher than they are now, a hell of a lot higher. I can't believe how *much* they've come off.'

Agron gave nothing away, but drew on his cigar, considering its flavour. 'Go on.'

'Well, after what I just said to the reporters outside, this second trade . . .'

Agron blew a long salubrious cloud of smoke out of his mouth. '*Da?*'

'Well, there's an outside chance we won't need it.'

The Russian smiled a sly smile. 'What was it you told me when we first spoke about the second trade . . . ?'

Rankin flashed a small smile of his own. '"I don't play dice."'

'You don't play dice, yes, that's it. I liked that. But now you are entertaining an element of chance, *da?*'

'Well . . .'

'Is my organization also playing dice when it buys First Bank stock?'

The Russian's eyes had a sleepy, soulless look that gave Rankin a momentary glimpse into the paths his client had walked and the deeds he had perhaps committed. Time slowed for the First Bank CEO as a heavy silence sat between them, growing in intensity. Rankin suddenly remembered that he had forgotten to breathe and did so as calmly as he could. He waved away his recent remarks, regretting having raised the issue. Kicked himself for thinking that this type of Russian, this type of man, was somebody playing by his rules. 'Go on, Agron, you were saying, about the second trade?'

The Eastern European billionaire allowed a beat to pass, a dance in the power game between all players. 'The second trade will be placed tomorrow morning. We will close the trade later the same day, as agreed. If we still agree?' An enquiring look at his host.

Rather than concede the point yet again Rankin sipped from his whisky. 'And now we need to talk about compensation for this trade.'

'*Da*. My associates are very keen to transfer the stock whilst your price is down here, better all round, no?'

Rankin gave an assenting nod but placed his glass down with some decisiveness. 'Yes, yes, that mechanism is in place. But can I raise an alternative at this hour?'

'This eleventh hour?'

Rankin wore a slippery grin. 'You see, instead of stock, what if I gave you something even better?'

'Cash?'

They both chuckled at the joke with differing degrees of sincerity. 'Something better than cash.'

The Russian didn't rush to react but pondered the

door that Rankin was pushing at. The billionaire gently swirled the ice in his whisky, stared into it, thoughtful. 'When money speaks the truth is silent. Tell me, my friend, what is better than cash?'

Rankin paused for effect, an antique clock at the far side of the room chiming gently six times as he did so. 'How about the keys to the kingdom?'

Agron eyed him with a mixture of suspicion and interest. They were sitting in near darkness, the late September afternoon bringing an early red dusk across Manhattan, flooding the room with an orange hue. 'Do I still get the yacht?'

'But of course.'

The Russian nodded gently. 'Go on.'

Rankin was in his element. Taking his time now. 'How much do you understand about the American sub-prime credit bubble at the beginning of this century . . . ?'

29

Martinez and I had ditched the bike for good. We had taken a cab down to Madison Avenue and were now watching the front and one side of the First Bank of America headquarters from the corner of the street opposite. By the main entrance was a swarm of camera crews, waiting for a story, the same way stray dogs hang around the back doors of restaurants.

Martinez had her back against the wall with me leaning into her, trying to be hard to find in a city that we felt was looking for us. We were trusting that the various agencies' idea of fugitives didn't include couples canoodling on street corners.

'Are you absolutely sure about that description?'

Martinez flicked a glance at the bank opposite. 'Definitely, I got a good look.'

'It must have been Mason in the car with Carlton.'

She gave me a sympathetic look. 'You seem bothered.'

I tried to brush it off, tried to allay her fears – and mine. 'I don't . . . If he ordered her along, he ordered her along.'

'Unless the whole set up at the docks was her idea? Face it, Byrne, it could have been. Don't rule it out.'

I stole a look at the bank. 'True. But Rankin set up the meeting which still begs the bigger question, how involved is the Secret Service with Rankin. I mean, is it just Carlton? Just Mason? Is it Carlton *and* Mason? Is it the entire *Service* . . . ?'

'Basically, how balls deep are they with this guy?'

I grunted a laugh. 'That's quite a mouth you've got on you.'

She parted her bee-stung lips. Ever so knowingly. 'It doesn't stop at the mouth . . .'

My attention was suddenly caught by a black Bentley Arnage gliding to a halt outside the front of the bank. Pulling up slightly too fast. The driver, chauffeur's cap in place, stepped out, his door opening onto the kerbside away from us. He pulled open the rear passenger door in readiness. There was something about the body language I recognized but had to put aside as I looked out for his employer.

A First Bank security guard pushed one of the tall entrance doors open and stood doorman-like, awaiting the exit of somebody important. The dozen camera crews perked up, each one's journalist reporting the possibly dramatic unfolding event urgently to camera. A short stocky man with dark features, slicked-back hair and an impeccable suit walked casually out of the bank like he was leaving a bar, brushing past every camera crew, making no attempt to hide himself. Our man? Our Russian puppet master? My gut screamed 'yes'.

He leaned down and into the back of the waiting Bentley and the driver carefully closed the door after him, turning to face our side of the street as he did so.

'I know him.'

Martinez turned her head as far round as she dared. 'The passenger?'

'No, the driver. It's the guy I tangled with at the hotel this morning. The one that got away.'

She saw him, bandages taped down the right side of his face, covering his burns. 'Looks like you're off his Christmas card list.'

'There's something else, Martinez . . .'

The driver – Mr Bingo – undid a button on his jacket in preparation for getting into the car, looked about himself. I studied him, with the cap, imagining him without it, with it, without it, with it, without it, not here, not here but somewhere else, somewhere I'd been, recently . . . That was it, oh my god, that was *it* . . .

'Martinez, I know where I've seen . . .'

Suddenly Mr Bingo looked up, saw me looking. I turned to Martinez.

'Kiss me.'

And thrust my face into hers.

I spied Mr Bingo out of the corner of my eye, saw him halting, bothered, scrutinizing us . . . then letting it go. Which is more than I could say for Martinez, who was getting into the role-play very successfully, one

302

hand running up the back of my head, grabbing a handful of hair. I didn't doubt anyone watching it would believe her performance – I did.

The Bentley eased away. I let it pass then grabbed Martinez's hand and pulled her after me. 'Taxi!'

We piled into the back of a yellow cab, the driver waiting for my instructions in the mirror.

'Follow that black Bentley.'

He pulled out to follow like this was what every passenger asked. 'Where's your boxes?' His Bronx accent thicker than a bad impersonation of Tony Curtis.

'Boxes? What boxes?'

'The boxes with all your belongings? I thought you might work for First Bank – sounds like they won't see out the weekend.'

I gave him a quizzical look in his mirror. 'No, no we don't. What makes you say that about First Bank?'

'S'not me, s'all over the news. The next Lehman's. Brudder, I'm taking all my money out of my bank tomorrow. I want it where I can see it. Yeah, but not where my wife can see it. Am I right?'

I gave him a smile in his rear-view mirror that was meant to signal the end of our conversation. I watched out for the Bentley, and was satisfied we were keeping it in sight.

'Martinez, the Bentley's driver . . .'

'Yeah?'

'I've seen him before.'

'At the hotel, you said.'

'No, no. At the First Bank headquarters – the *new* headquarters in Lower Manhattan.'

'The night the four bank executives were murdered . . . ?'

'Yeah, that night.'

'Was he in the meeting?'

'No, he's the one who signed me in *downstairs*. He's the security guard the police haven't been able to find.'

She thought about this and realized just how many dots needed connecting. 'Why would the Russians be killing First Bank executives?'

I didn't know. 'A deal with Rankin?'

'OK, why would Rankin be killing four of his execu– The SEC! The four executives went to the SEC the week before they died. They knew something about First Bank that was worth killing them for.'

I nodded. She was right. That had to be it, but Martinez was ahead of me.

'Why would the Secret Service help Rankin . . . ?'

I wracked my brains, but nothing was coming up, nothing rational. 'I really don't know.'

'Could the Secret Service be so worried about another bank going under that they're murdering anybody who might say anything bad about their bank?'

I gave it some thought. 'Jesus, they'd need to poison the nation's water supply. No, it's rotten.'

'This situation?'

'No.' I took my eyes off the Bentley for a moment, looked at her. 'First Bank. It's rotten to the core.'

We sat in silence for a while, watching the Bentley as it headed south-west. After a while I gave Martinez a sideways look.

She turned, pulled one leg under the other. 'What?'

'You know, when you pretend to kiss someone you don't *have* to put your tongue in their mouth.'

She smiled to herself. 'Yeah, I know.'

Nice. And yet somehow still like a girl playing at being a woman, somehow –

The abrupt stopping of the cab wrenched us back to the job at hand.

'This is as far as I go, folks.'

We both looked up. We were near the south-western tip of Manhattan. The Russian's Bentley had stopped in Battery Park City, on the corner of Pumphouse Park. Our taxi had stopped fifty yards past. We watched as Mr Bingo held the door open for his boss. They exchanged some words and the boss was joined by two heavy-set men in dark suits who I immediately took to be his bodyguards. The three of them then walked away as Mr Bingo returned to the limousine. We waited whilst he drove off past us.

I pushed a couple of notes into the waiting hand of the cabbie and we got out.

'Where do you think they're going?'

I looked about us, feeling the heat of the police presence, raised for the president's visit tomorrow. A cop on every corner, so many you would think they could pass a message from one end of Manhattan to the other just by shouting it to each other. 'I think I know where.'

We followed on foot through the patch of green that was Pumphouse Park and, as I expected, the Russian we were tailing made for North Cove Marina.

Martinez stood next to me. Close next to me. 'And where would that be?'

The marina boasted a couple of dozen berths, but only a couple suitable for mega-yachts. I was in no doubt it was the 120-footer they were making their way towards. I was keen to get my binoculars out of my pockets, but was conscious that it was just the kind of behaviour that would grab the attention of the nearby NYPD.

We waited until they'd reached the far end of the marina and made their way up a gangplank past two more bodyguards and out of sight.

In the Hudson River a ferry's horn sounded as it chugged away towards New Jersey. A long, mournful note, crying out across the waters.

I looked at Martinez. I said it before she could. 'Ferry horn.'

'All right, point taken – I'll send your gadget geek some flowers. Should we get a closer look?'

I watched, thinking. 'No, I think we need to do a bit of digging.'

'You got a friend who might know something about the owner of that boat?'

I made a mental note of the boat's name, *Eagle Rev*. 'Yeah. He's called Google.'

She pulled a playful face. 'Let's get back to the apartment then.'

She made to go but I held her arm, gently. 'We can't go back there, Martinez.'

'Why not?'

I waited. I wanted her mind to slow down a bit. I wanted her to listen. 'They made you at the docks. They'll know everything about you by now – including where you live.'

She wasn't comprehending, not initially.

'Martinez, they don't want me any more . . .'

'What do you mean?'

I said it slowly, as gently as I could. 'They want us.'

A moment passed then it began to sink in. And I saw that look they get. When the ground beneath their feet falls away. When everything they've built their world on is taken from them. Like a person sentenced to life for a crime they never committed.

Her phone was ringing. She pulled it out slowly, numb. The name flashing up, 'Ashby'. She watched her fellow detective's name blinking at her, telling her to hit the green phone icon.

'I can't take this, can I?'

I wanted to find the right words then realized there weren't any. 'No. They're tracking it. Even if he doesn't know it, they're tracking him to track you.'

She looked up at me, all the playfulness and sexiness gone now. Not scared, just broken, just empty.

'All I wanted was my gun and my badge back. I didn't want this. I . . . Byrne . . . I want my life back.'

30

We were standing in the lobby of the Greenwich Hotel in the Tribeca district, a fusion of modern and Japanese tastes. It shouldn't have worked, but it did. Martinez was unconsciously hugging herself against cold weather that didn't exist, standing next to me with a thousand-yard stare. I was dealing with checking in. With Lower Manhattan in virtual lock-down for tomorrow's presidential visit we had to be prepared for extra security everywhere we went. I hoped my trip to my favourite store in Little Italy earlier in the day had done the trick.

The receptionist looked from us to our passports with their very old and doctored-just-enough photos of us, with their fake names and fake dates of birth. He was satisfied and smiled in recognition of this fact. Fact is, it wasn't the receptionist I was worried about. Every passport of every customer in every hotel in New York City was going to be scanned and those pictures sent immediately to the Washington D.C. headquarters of the Secret Service. As our details popped up on an intelligence analyst's screen I didn't want them – or their data-crunching software – to put two and two together.

The receptionist placed a credit-card-sized door-swipe on the counter. 'Your room is the Greenwich Suite. I'll have somebody take up your bags.'

'We don't have any. Just this.'

I held up Martinez's laptop.

The receptionist didn't skip a beat. 'Would you like help carrying that?'

'No, we'll manage. Do you sell swim gear?'

He looked from Martinez to myself. 'We'll have a selection sent up.'

The bellboy left our room with the kind of smile a twenty-dollar tip for not carrying bags puts on your face. Martinez began to take in her surroundings and roused slightly from her quasi-catatonic state.

'What is this place?'

She was commenting on the duplex suite we'd booked into with its thirty-foot-high windows, sitting room, dining room, kitchen, office, two bedrooms and roaring fireplaces.

'I was trying to be inconspicuous.'

She looked around her – gawped around her. 'How is living like a couple of Hollywood celebrities being inconspicuous?'

'Because they're not looking for a couple of Holly-wood celebrities.' I walked off.

'Where are you going?'

'We need to find out about that yacht.'

Martinez padded after me as I made for the office. 'Wow. This office is bigger than my apartment.'

I dropped my jacket over the back of a chair and booted up the laptop at the desk. 'Stay here a hundred nights and you could buy your apartment.'

She perched on an ornate chair, uncomfortable with her surroundings, uncomfortable with her situation. 'What's the plan, Byrne?'

'Find out who owns this boat.'

I was trying to strike a balance between being gentle with her and pushing on. I suspected I was failing. I turned the laptop to face her. It had a page listing what yachts were berthed at the North Cove Marina. I was pointing at berth N1, *Eagle Rev*.

'I mean about us? What's going to happen to us?'

'What do you mean?'

'I don't want to be a fugitive, I don't want to be wanted, Byrne.'

'Everybody wants to be wanted . . .'

I looked at her, hoping for a break in the clouds.

'No, I'm serious.'

I steeled myself and turned my chair to face hers. 'OK, we have three options.'

She stared at me, out of ideas and out of steam. Waiting to hear what I had to say, nothing suggesting she believed I actually had anything to say.

'We could run.'

She shook her head.

'We could hand ourselves in and hope that a group involving the Secret Service, the Russian mob and a very wealthy and crooked banker go lightly on us – oh, as well as not killing the president tomorrow whilst we're in custody.'

She shook her head.

'Or we do the only thing that you know in your heart is ever the right thing to do.'

She looked at me enquiringly.

'We do our best.'

She turned it over in her mind. 'And if our best isn't good enough?'

'Then we'll take down as many bad guys as we can on our way out.'

She sat in silence, reconciling herself to the inevitable.

'Byrne?'

'What?'

'Could you ever love a woman who'd taken such a beating from some bad guys that she had to eat through a straw for the rest of her life?'

I reached out for her hand, held it between mine. I looked into her eyes, my brow creased, knowing that she needed to know that what I was about to say came from the bottom of my heart. 'No, Martinez. No, I couldn't.'

She pushed my hands away with half a scowl and half a smile. 'Fuck you, Byrne. Fuck you very much.' She nodded at the laptop. 'So – what's so special about *Eagle Rev*?'

'Think about the name, does it mean anything . . . ? Look closely. Does it suggest anything at all?'

'Don't tell me you're getting all *Da Vinci Code* on me. What next, you're gonna tell me Bernard Madoff is descended from Jesus? Was the credit crunch caused by the Illuminati? What?'

OK, she won there. '*Eagle Rev*. It's an anagram.'

She stared at me. Profoundly unimpressed and having fun letting me know it.

I took her point. '*Eagle Rev* is an anagram of "leverage".'

Finally she was interested. 'That's that thing banks do.'

'Banks, hedge funds, corporate raiders . . . Anybody with society's best interests at heart.'

'OK, so we find out who owns the yacht the Russian is staying on and that should lead us to who he is?'

I turned to the laptop and began to do just that. 'Well, let's hope so. Right, it's a Bermuda-based company, Vega Corporation.'

'Have you heard of them?'

'Well, "Vega" is a word associated with options trading, but I don't think that's what it means here . . .'

'Why not?'

I was tapping my way through the names. 'Because the Vega Corporation is owned by another company in Bermuda, Proxima Centauri Limited and that's owned by Wolf Three Five Nine Limited . . .'

'Are they also terms to do with options trading?'

'No. They're constellations, well, stars. And, if I'm right, Wolf Three Five Nine Limited will be owned by Lalande something . . .' I hit ENTER and a new search result came up. 'There we are: Lalande Two One One Eight Five Limited.'

Martinez leaned down next to me to look at the laptop. 'How did you know that?'

'They're the names of stars in increasing distance from the planet Earth. Haven't you ever watched Carl Sagan talk about the cosmos?'

She gave me a look that confirmed the negative of that. 'Whoever is doing this seems keen to put a lot of distance between the yacht and its ultimate owner.'

I checked her face, there was a small smirk on it. She put a hand on my shoulder as she watched the screen. I had to make a mental effort to not think about it. She leaned her head down next to mine, possibly closer than it needed to be. *The job at hand, the job at hand . . .*

'So, Byrne, how long is it going to take you to get to the end of this?'

'No idea. I've got an application that runs a spider over all this data, collates the information for me.'

'When will that be finished?'

'Right about . . .'

A window opened automatically onto the screen. It showed software built to my own specifications by my good friend Gabriella the gadget expert. It was a mind-mapping programme – bubbles linked to various bubbles, showing the connections between entities. The software crawled the web and showed, where possible, connections according to my parameters. The links could be anything, NFL teams, movie stars, even the sexual indiscretions of politicians – if the computer's memory could take it. Today I was looking for any corporate entity linked directly or indirectly to *Eagle Rev.*

On the laptop screen the animation grew in real-time, one bubble labelled 'Vega Corporation' linking to another labelled 'Proxima Centauri Limited', then another bubble 'Wolf Three Five Nine Limited', and another 'Lalande Two One One Eight Five Limited'. Then another and another and then dozens and then scores, multiplying like lightning-fast single-cell organisms . . . The screen scaling down the graphics as it did to accommodate them all, showing at first a messy spider's web of linked bubbles, but soon the picture began to form into a tall triangle as bubbles were added to and added to at a seemingly endless rate, until I knew that we were looking at thousands of bubbles.

'Now *that's* interesting.'

Martinez looked uncomprehendingly at it, fascinated. 'What is it?'

'It's a matrix of special purpose vehicles.'

'What's a special purpose vehicle?'

'It's a very clever ruse for moving your profits about. It's a type of offshore company. Enron had them, Lehman's had them. You set up an SPV in somewhere like the Caymans or, in this case, Bermuda. You "sell it" your bad debt, or whatever, and suddenly your balance sheet looks a whole lot healthier.'

Martinez was confused and slightly appalled. 'But you still *own* the SPV, *that* would show up with the bad debt on your balance sheet.'

'Not under US accountancy laws it doesn't have to.'

'But that's – that's helping crooked banks to hide their losses.'

'Tell it to the SEC.'

'I don't believe it.'

'Neither do I – I have never seen this many SPVs in one company.'

Martinez stared at the matrix of dots, mesmerized by the implications. 'Think of the accounting, think of all the extra admin and cost. Who would do such a thing?'

'Somebody with something to hide.'

On the right hand side of the laptop's touchscreen was a button called '3D'. I tapped it with my finger. The tall triangle of companies now formed a virtual cone. I dragged my finger across the bottom of it – the cone spun, bubbles and their labels spinning with it.

'Jesus, Byrne. It's a pyramid.'

I looked at her. 'Isn't it just.'

'But who owns it? Who's at the top of the pyramid?'

I dragged the image down with my fingers then squeezed apart the details of the bubble at the very tip of the cone. It read, 'First Bank of America.'

I thought Martinez was going to fall off her chair. 'Oh my god. First Bank is hiding losses in all those SPVs?'

I squeezed my eyes and stood up. 'Actually, they might not be.'

'But look, look at all those SPVs . . .'

I shrugged. 'That could be any bank on Wall Street.'

'What do you mean?'

'I mean, they all do that. Play the system to maximize profits. You'd be amazed how many banks have SPVs that look like that. Really. Tax avoidance, they all do it. All we know – for certain – is that our Russian is staying on First Bank's yacht.'

'What do we do now?'

I was tired. It had been a long day. 'I need to think.'

I stood in a shower big enough to wash an A-list celeb and his entourage all at the same time. Its rain showerhead dropped a storm of hot water onto my shoulders as I leaned against the wall trying to piece together a way ahead.

What would we find in those Bermudan SPVs? Everything or nothing? Was the Russian mobster and his First Bank association enough to call this in to Diane? Was anything enough? She'd been there with Carlton today at the Brooklyn docks, at the heart of the trap. Was she even on my side? Was she even on the Service's side? Was the Service even on *America's* side? Oh shit. Who the hell could I tell that would get this plot against the president stopped without getting myself arrested? I was no good to anyone arrested. Especially myself. OK, I had a plan, but it was a long shot, a very long shot, and . . .

That's when I felt Martinez's body press up against mine. Close. Legs, stomach, breasts, all pushing up against my back, an arm tentatively sliding round my side. But a certain tension betrayed her shyness, the need for me to not see her body completely yet. She laid her cheek just below the back of my neck. Stood there. Holding me. The rain of the shower splashing relentlessly onto us.

I turned but kept her close. My hands on her hips now. I looked down into her face.

'I said I needed to think.'

She looked up at me, her hair almost wet through, water droplets hanging off her long eyelashes, her bright brown eyes sparkling as they looked into mine.

'I thought we could practise pretend kissing again and this time I'd try to keep my tongue out of it.'

I slowly ran my right hand up her spine to the back of her head where I gently took a handful of hair. 'Do you think you could do that?'

She looked at me like she was trying to take in every last contour on my face. 'No, Byrne. No, I don't think I could . . .'

31

The Citation X. The executive jet of Rankin's choice. By adding this to his bank's Challenger 300, Falcon 2000, Gulfstream G200 and Hawker 1000, he felt he had completed the set – of their smaller business jets. The aircraft sat eight, but this evening's flight was just for the bank's CEO. He was slouched in a wide beige leather seat halfway down the plane, pondering the events of the day, of the week – of tomorrow.

A catwalk-quality stewardess hired as much for her gymnastic qualities as her skill at air hostessing arrived. She half crouched and placed a whisky on the table before him. The Chanel No. 5 perfume she had applied – just for his pleasure – drifted towards the CEO.

'Will that be everything, sir?'

Rankin hardly registered her. 'Yeah, thanks, Kate.'

She rose and walked back towards the cockpit. Not bothering to correct him for getting her name wrong. Not bothering to remind him how many nights they had spent together around the country during overnight stays.

Rankin's Blackberry buzzed on the table before him. He watched it, wondering whether to answer it. Looked at it. Saw the name of the JPMorgan CEO and knew he had to.

'Bob –'

'Save it, Jerry.'

Rankin sat up slightly, alerted by the aggressive tone. 'What is it?'

'I don't know whose cock you've been sucking over at Treasury but I've been told to give you till Monday to come up with the eight billion.'

'Oh.' Rankin didn't want to show his relief. 'Well, I appreciate your understanding.'

'No, Jerry, I don't understand – that's just how it is.'

'OK.'

'Are you going to make it to Monday, Jerry?'

'Sure.' Rankin stretching his neck, the street-fighter within still with a few rounds left in him. 'Sure we are.'

'Good. Because we want our money.'

'You'll get your –'

The line went dead.

'– money.'

Rankin looked at his phone. Saw his reflection in it. Tight. Drawn. Worried. Older. Old.

'Shit. The goddam Treasury's carving us up already.'

If the Treasury was giving First Bank more time he figured it was because they wanted it to reach the weekend for their own purposes. Had he left it too late? Could he turn things round by the end of tomorrow? He knocked back his whisky in one.

'Hey, Kate. Kate, can I get another one of these?'

32

We collapsed onto the king-sized bed, exhausted. Both hot, both sweaty, both disorientated – both exhilarated. We stared at the ceiling, panting, thinking our own thoughts, both certain that if we'd had any inhibitions about each other before that they were now well and truly consigned to history.

'That . . .'

She needed oxygen to speak. I needed it to listen.

'. . .That is the second best fuck I have *ever* had.'

I turned my head on the pillow to look at her. 'What about the earlier orgasms?'

'All faked.'

I looked back at the ceiling. She rolled onto her side, facing me, a perspiration-covered arm and leg sliding across me, one dark golden breast resting on my bicep. We lay there, enjoying the moment, enjoying the feeling of each other.

'Byrne?'

'Yeah?'

'There's something I'd like to know.'

'One hundred and twenty-six – but I would put you in the top ten, no question.'

She slapped my chest in reprimand. 'Bernard Mad-off . . .'

I gave her a sideways look. 'If this is your idea of talking dirty I'm not sure it's gonna work.'

'Bernard Madoff . . .'

'Yeah?'

'How much did he steal in his pyramid thingy, his Ponzi scheme?'

I had to gather my thoughts for the new direction the evening was taking. 'Well, the headline figure is $65 billion of client monies, but when you think that a lot of them got in early, made a profit even, well, the actual *cost* to the clients was around about $18 billion. Give or take a billion.'

'And how much did the banks lose, in the credit crunch?'

'Do you mean lose or cost?'

She perked her head up to look at me. 'What's the difference?'

'Well, what they actually posted as losses was a fraction of what they cost the tax payer. And they were only able to *post* losses because the tax payer propped up their industry. Most of them should have gone bust.'

'OK, so how much did the banks cost the taxpayer?'

'Last count? Over three trillion dollars.'

She propped herself up on one elbow to look at me. 'Madoff went to jail for what he did. Why didn't the bankers do time?'

'They said what they were doing was just a legal enterprise gone wrong.'

'Was it?' She was really ticked off about it. 'What about responsibility? Accountability? Isn't that like Greyhound telling all their drivers to floor it everywhere and then when all the buses crash just saying "sorry, we were trying to maximize profits"? Isn't it?'

I chuckled. 'That's as good a summary of the credit crunch as I've heard.'

She sat with her head on my chest, fuming such that I could feel the breaths coming out of her nose. 'I mean, just what the hell *were* they doing? I've never understood the credit crunch.'

I considered her, considered what I wanted to say, wondering whether I wanted to get down to brass tacks.

'Let me think.'

I looked about me for something to use. On a nearby occasional table I saw a coffee set with two bowls of sugar cubes, one white, one brown. I picked the bowls up and brought them to the bed where Martinez was sitting up against some pillows, a sheet pulled to her chest.

'The credit crunch was two very different things. Mortgages and insurance. But not in the everyday sense. Joe Schmoe on the street didn't cause the credit crunch – we couldn't have if we'd tried. Only banks can do that – and the way they do that is leverage, or gearing.'

'Leverage? That's like debt, right?'

'Yeah, you borrow against something, like your house, you're leveraging it. You see, banks hate a dollar. Because a dollar is worth . . . ?'

'A dollar.'

'Exactly. You can't pay yourself a $10 million bonus by sitting on a dollar. But lend that dollar out twenty, thirty, forty, fifty times, well, then you're making money. And the best way to do that is derivatives.'

'Are those the things Warren Buffet called "financial weapons of mass-destruction"?'

'That old communist? Yeah.'

She screwed up her very pretty nose. 'What is a derivative?'

'It's very simple. It's just something derived from something else. So gold and oil and shares aren't derivatives because they're real things. But a contract that referred to gold or oil or shares, whose value depended on their movements in the markets, would be called a derivative.'

'OK, that's simple enough. So are all derivatives bad then?'

'No. But Warren Buffet wasn't suggesting they were. He was suggesting that certain types of derivatives were becoming too dominant, too dangerous.'

'OK. So, how did mortgages and insurance screw up the economy?'

'The mortgages first. Around the turn of the

century some very clever mortgage brokers decided that instead of arranging mortgages between home-owners and banks they would lend directly to the homeowners themselves.'

'What, you mean they became banks?'

'No. They became *shadow* banks.'

She squinted at me.

'They wanted to retain as much control of the money – and therefore profit – as possible so they extended these loans to homeowners but then sold them, as a bundle, to a Wall Street bank. The mortgage brokers got their – bigger – commission then passed on all the risk.'

'So the Wall Street bank just sat back and collected the interest?'

'What? Sit there collecting interest on a perfectly good loan? Where's the fun in that?' I held up a white sugar cube. 'No, the Wall Street bank packaged all the little loans together – all those little grains – compacted them together and made one big loan out of them.'

'How can they do that?'

'Remember derivatives? Contracts that are really about something else?'

'Yeah.'

'The bank made derivatives out of the bundle of mortgages, packed them all together and called them a CDO.'

'Do I need to know what a CDO is?'

'No, no you don't. It's a collateralized debt obligation. It just means a bundle of debts with something as collateral. It's the name they gave the mortgages that were bundled up and sold on.'

'All those different mortgages sold on? Just like that?'

'Oh no, not until the ratings agencies, people like Moody's, and Standard and Poor's, had approved them.'

'Which they did reluctantly . . . ?' She sounded sceptical.

'Which they did with relish. Helped devise them even. They'd been doing it with corporate loans for years but home loans? That was something altogether new. And thus the first mortgage-backed security was sold. The mortgage brokers made their commission selling on the loans and then so did the Wall Street bank.'

I placed the white cube on the sheet, between her legs.

Martinez looked at the single square of sugar. 'Is that when it all went wrong?'

'God no. Pure as the driven snow those mortgages. But there is *nothing* Wall Street likes more in all this world than a new product – a new way to make money. And when they saw there was an appetite for these bundled mortgages they asked the mortgage brokers for more.'

'And?'

'They gave them to the Wall Street bank as fast as they could.'

I placed two more white cubes on the sheet between Martinez's legs, beneath the original one.

'And when the other Wall Street banks saw that another bank was making money a new way *they* wanted bundles of mortgages to sell on, and suddenly virtually all the Wall Street banks were taking as many as they could get.'

I placed three more white cubes beneath the last two, a triangle of sugar blocks forming.

She looked at the cubes, she looked at me. 'But surely there's only so many mortgages the brokers could supply . . . ?'

'You've just reached a conclusion in ten seconds that the regulators didn't reach in ten years. When the mortgage brokers realized the appetite for these mortgages on Wall Street, well, they started to drop their standards a bit, take on a bit more risk, less credit-worthy homeowners . . .'

I place four sugar cubes beneath the last, but this time three white and one brown.

'Would they be the sub . . . ?'

'. . . Prime mortgages. Careful – nobody likes a brainiac. Sub-prime, meaning "below the best". Well, when the mortgage brokers realized that Wall Street was lapping these up, that the ratings agencies were giving them their stamp of approval, Jesus, they dropped their standards just a little bit more, then a bit more, then they dropped them . . . ?

'Completely.'

I laid out longer and longer lines of sugar cubes, now the brown increasingly outnumbering the white.

'Suddenly we had Easy Money mortgages where you could get a hundred and ten per cent of the value of the house – effectively *getting paid* to take out a mortgage. No Doc mortgages where you didn't have to show any proof of what you were saying on the application. Ninja mortgages where homeowners had No Income and No Job –'

'Who the hell was Wall Street selling these to?'

'Anybody and everybody. All over the globe. These CDOs, these bundles of mortgages, were being mixed with baskets of assets that weaved them into the entire global economic system. If people defaulted on these mortgages, the effects would be felt around the world. Retirees in Scandinavia could lose their pensions because of defaults by home owners in Colorado.'

She looked at the shape the sugar cubes had described between her legs. Wide at the base, narrowing to a point at the top. 'Call me crazy, Byrne, but that's a pyramid.'

'Oh, you're crazy.'

'And everybody involved must have *known* these sub-prime mortgages weren't going to be repaid.

I mean, how did the mortgage brokers, the banks, and the ratings agencies allow all this to happen?'

'Because everybody was making so much money. As long as the music's playing on Wall Street everybody gets up to dance.'

'But they *knew* this scheme couldn't pay out ultimately. How – I mean – this is *unbelievable*.' She shook her head, as much in sadness as disgust. 'So what happened?' She pointed at the beginning of the pyramid between her legs. 'I mean, the ultimate buyers of these things, the people at the top, needed interest paying on their loans. What happened?'

'Simple, the mortgage brokers and Wall Street banks just kept recruiting more and more homeowners to take out more and more mortgages . . .'

I laid the last brown sugar cube.

She looked from my empty hand to me. 'We've run out of sugar.'

I nodded in agreement. 'That's just what the bankers said right before the system imploded. Because the whole thing was . . .'

'. . . A Ponzi.'

Martinez seemed genuinely depressed by this realization. She looked at the pyramid of sugar cubes between her legs, starting all white, ending brown.

'What about AIG? That's not a bank?' Her mood dark now.

'You're right, that's insurance.'

'I never understood that either.'

'Oh, that one's even simpler. You see, about the same time mortgage brokers were looking to become shadow banks some people approached AIG in London. These people had some exposure to a company and they asked AIG if they would insure them against the risk of that exposure.'

'Hang on, I thought shares *were* their exposure to the company.'

I shook my head like the disappointed schoolteacher. 'God, Martinez, you'll never cut it in finance. It's not about what's straightforward or reasonable or right, it's about what's profitable. Now, AIG and other insurance companies liked the risk profile of this new wheeze so much that they offered this insurance to other people. It was a new product, a *new* revenue stream . . .'

'And there's nothing Wall Street likes more than a new product, a new way of making money?'

'Right.'

Martinez whistled as it sank in. 'So pretty soon AIG and the others, they were on the hook for entire companies going bust?'

I shook my head. 'It was *much* worse than that. You see, derivatives are pretty much unregulated, and so AIG and others started offering insurance to people who didn't even *have* exposure to the companies they wanted insurance on.'

She started back at that. 'But that's — that's just plain gambling!'

'Tell it to the regulators.' I pointed my way down the pyramid of sugar, from the first white sugar cube at the tip of the existing pyramid between her legs and down along the lines. 'So what began with a fairly small exposure for the insurance companies soon involved them accepting bets massively out of proportion to events . . .'

'Bets they couldn't possibly pay out on.'

'You got it.'

She was glaring at me now. 'And the only way to make that work was to keep getting in more and more insurance premiums . . . ?'

'You got it squared.'

Suddenly Martinez flipped the sheet up sending the sugar cubes flying about the bedroom where they clattered off walls, mirrors and furniture.

'It's another fucking Ponzi, Byrne! The banks and the insurance companies were running Ponzis! They ran Ponzis and got bailed out with tax payers' dollars! We gave Bernard Madoff a hundred and fifty years without parole and we gave the banks and insurance companies hundreds of billions and a pat on the back.'

'So? Run for Office.'

She slammed her fists down on the bed beside her, looked about the bedclothes, her thinking dancing before her eyes, rearranging ideas that had built up in this room tonight, coming to a conclusion.

'I want two things, Byrne.' Fuming.

'What?'

'I want to take down one of these legalised Ponzi schemes. I want at least one bank to have to admit that it's running a pyramid scheme that it knows will never pay out. I want everybody to learn that banks that do this are no better than the Bernard Madoffs of this world. I want to get Rankin and First Bank of America.'

'OK. And what's the second thing?'

'I want to know . . .' Her hard look melted and she looked poutingly, admonishingly at me, slid her hands onto my shoulders, up round my neck. '. . . Since when was a little bit of brown sugar such a bad thing?'

I let her pull me down onto the bed, let her pull my face up to hers, let her pull my face down till my mouth sank into her luscious soft lips.

'Byrne, do you have the energy for another ride around the block?'

There was a knock at the door.

'Energy, yes . . .'

I wrapped a towel round me as an annoyed and confused Martinez covered herself with first the sheet then some bedding, not knowing where to put herself. I opened the door and accepted what was given to me. I closed the door and got a look from Martinez that was pure mistrust, unsure why I was holding a coat hanger bearing a dozen bikinis.

'. . . Time, no.'

Martinez looked from the bikinis to me like she already didn't like what she was about to hear.

'Why did you choose this particular hotel, Byrne?'

'Because it's got a swimming pool.'

'Are we going swimming?'

'No we're not.' Her eyes narrowed. 'You are.'

33

As Martinez rose and fell in the water with her unhurried stroke the soft lights of the hotel pool gave witness to her naturally bronzed body, its curves highlighted by the near-fluorescent yellow bikini she wore. On her back there was only string, the suspended detective wanting to give men the best possible view of the goods on display. A couple of hotel employees discreetly spied her athletic yet curvy form as she leisurely turned to begin another lap. But one man made no such attempt to hide his interest. One man stood and stared.

Martinez had already observed him and resolved to stop at the end of the next length, hoping he might approach her. As she reached out to touch the side she heard the splash of the man behind her as he dived into the water at the far end. It was a small hotel pool. He would soon be next to her. And stop he did.

'Nice pool.'

Martinez looked at the Treasury Secretary like she hadn't noticed he was there. 'I guess so.'

She turned away and he knew he would have to work a bit. 'Japanese, you know.'

She looked at him, wiped her hair back with both hands, her breasts rising as she did so, Martinez a hundred per cent alive to the effect this had on men in general, and not disappointed by the effect it had on this man in particular. 'Really? I would have had you pegged as an American.'

His face formed a grin. 'The pool house. The hotel had it shipped over from Japan. It's two hundred and fifty years old.' Martinez went to comment, but he cut her off in good humour. 'The pool house, that is.'

Martinez was playing it cool as instructed. She addressed the Treasury Secretary with an air of boredom. 'You here on business?'

'Yeah, just for the night. I always stay here. It's got everything I need.' He gave her a suggestive look. 'What about you?'

'Oh, a few days. My husband had to fly back to Miami. He's a producer.'

'Brave man.'

'Why's that?'

'Leaving his beautiful wife behind like that.'

She twitched her lips. 'Yeah, who knows what dog'll come sniffing around.' She saw Peterson was pleased his intentions were understood. 'Still, he knows I gotta be discreet. I play around with anybody in this town the paps'll have it on the front page before I'm back in my hotel room.'

The Treasury Secretary couldn't place her implied

celebrity status, but was delighted she had something to lose. The last thing he needed was some mercenary broad doing a kiss and sell. He'd always made a point of banging somebody with as much as him to lose, but, these days, who was that?

Peterson held her stare longer than he should have, long enough to telegraph his intentions. 'Then don't leave your hotel room. Beats swimming all night.'

Martinez drew a finger along her lips, just in case he'd forgotten to look at them, forgotten to see their moist full shape. 'Maybe this is as wet as I want to get.'

'And maybe you're the Queen of Sheba.'

Martinez turned to the side of the pool and pulled herself half out of the water so that she was resting on her taut arms, her breasts squeezed between them, challenging the security of the skimpy yellow bikini and Peterson's control of himself. 'Well, the Queen of Sheba's staying in the Greenwich Suite all by her little bitty self, and she's got an hour to kill before dinner.'

Before Peterson, heart racing, could find the words he was struggling with, she had finished getting out, grabbed her robe from a lounger and made for the door, with every male set of eyes watching her unapologetically exposed buttocks rise and fall as beautifully as her breaststroke.

34

There was a soft knock at the hotel door. Martinez, still in her pool robe, steeled herself and opened it. The Treasury Secretary stepped in, holding a bottle of champagne. He handed it to her, chilled, ready to share.

Martinez's eyes glistened at the sight of it. 'Well, aren't we the Casanova?' She closed the door after him. 'Mind if I double lock it?'

Peterson looked her up and down as she did so, registering her bare legs, savouring what was about to come. 'Why? Worried your husband might try to break in?'

I paused before I spoke. 'Worried you might try to break out.'

Peterson spun round startled. 'What the fuck is going on?'

But he saw the gun in my hand and the uncompromising look in my eye.

'Is this some kind of shakedown? Do you know who I am? Do you realize the kind of trouble you're getting into here?'

I took in the scene and had to admire his manner.

Strong without being belligerent, tough without being nasty.

'The married United States Treasury Secretary is held up at gunpoint in a young single lady's room and *we're* in trouble.'

I allowed this observation to sink in. Peterson didn't need any more prompting to see how this could play out and his tough demeanour quickly readjusted under the heat.

'What is it you want? Money?'

I nodded. Peterson wanted to swing a punch at me but knew it was a seller's market.

'How much?'

I jiggled the gun like I was weighing the figure up on the spot. 'Make me an offer.'

Peterson sneered at us both in turn, suspecting that we knew that as an ex-Goldman's man he was worth a cool quarter of a billion. 'Are we talking millions?' Letting us know it was risible.

I slowly turned my head from side to side. 'Billions.'

The Treasury Secretary went to protest at the ludicrousness of the demand, but I cut him off.

'Not *your* money. Take a look at that laptop.'

Peterson, utterly at a loss now, looked around until his eyes alighted on a laptop by the kitchen counter. Suddenly the shakedown was taking a darker turn for him, suggesting a perverse level of preplanning that ran ahead of his imagined possibilities for the trap he had walked into. He cautiously approached the desk and sat before the portable computer with its picture of the three dimensional cone of dots on it. He looked at the screen but . . .

'I don't understand. What am I meant to be looking at?'

I put down my weapon on the kitchen worktop. 'It's the network of special purpose vehicles First Bank of America has offshore in Bermuda.'

Peterson was all at sea, looking from the laptop to us, his captors. 'Hey, what's going on here? What's this all about?'

'It's about First Bank's network of special purpose vehicles in Bermuda.'

Peterson almost forgot he was being held under duress and looked again at the model. He reached inside his pocket and pulled out his reading glasses, which he slipped on. Martinez leaned in next to him and pulled two fingers apart on the touch screen to increase a detail. She looked at Peterson, older in his reading glasses, self-conscious of this fact now.

'Don't worry, you still got it.'

He gave a noncommittal smile, but was not-so-secretly pleased by the remark. He leaned towards the laptop. 'But there have to be hundreds here.'

I shook my head. 'Try thousands. All holding monies off the balance sheet.'

Peterson looked again at the model then back to me. 'Losses?'

'Presumably.'

'And you felt you had to tell me this at gunpoint?'

Martinez and I exchanged resigned looks and sat on the arms of the armchairs we were standing by. She spoke now.

'We're sorry to do this, Mr Secretary, but we're kind of wanted by the police.'

He looked from Martinez to me, suddenly realizing who we were. 'God in heaven, I got briefed by Homeland Security about you two earlier today . . . Detective Martinez and former Special Agent Byrne.' He was suddenly concerned for his safety, back on edge.

I held up my hands. 'Sir, we just want to be heard out. The fact of the matter is First Bank has got a black hole at the centre of its finances . . .'

Peterson was back on familiar territory with the confidence and irritation that came with it. 'You think we don't know that? You think we're not dealing with that?'

Martinez could not contain herself. 'We think he's going to assassinate the president.'

'Who?'

'Rankin.'

'Black holes? Assassinations? What the hell is going on here?'

I was suddenly profoundly self-conscious of the fact that we must look and sound like a couple of conspiracy nuts and knew we had to communicate complete reasonableness. 'Mr Secretary, we believe *something* is going to happen tomorrow.'

'Yes, a ground-breaking with the Chinese premier for the offices of Bank of China.'

Martinez now. 'No, something terrible. We can't prove it yet, but Rankin was behind the murder of his senior executives.'

'Murder? Because of losses at the bank?'

I was frustrated that I didn't have anything firmer. 'Because of something worse.'

'Worse? What? What is it that's worse?'

I stood and walked off to the kitchenette, frustrated with myself. 'We don't know. But it's bad enough to kill for and to possibly kill for again tomorrow.'

'OK.' Peterson pointed at the computer screen. 'And what do you want me to do about all this?'

I was matter of fact now. 'You've got to give First Bank a backstop.'

'A backstop? What kind of backstop?'

'Well, if you want my advice, a perfect solution would be to sell it to the Chinese.'

'You're holding me at gunpoint to tell me to get the Chinese government to buy First Bank? Have you any idea how the real world works?'

My patience was being tested, but I was more annoyed at myself than anybody else. 'Sir, with all due respect, letting Lehman Brothers go bust was the worst decision of the credit crunch – we all know that. Propping up the banks and insurance companies has stretched our credit-worthiness to breaking point. Can the United States government really underwrite another major bank right now?'

'Yes. If it's just about these offshore losses.'

'What if it's something worse?'

'Worse than losses?' Peterson knew in his own gut that we might have a point, but also felt his own frustrations rising. 'Byrne, give me something with meat. I mean, if you're so sure Rankin's killing people, why not get him arrested, let the authorities deal with it?'

I couldn't contain a sigh. 'Because tomorrow's triple witching.'

Martinez almost gave me a double-take. 'Did you say witching?'

I nodded, knowing that away from the markets it sounded a bit goofy. 'Triple witching.'

Peterson stepped in. 'At the end of every month lots of contracts settle, finish, in the marketplace. Because of the extra volatility this produces near the closing bell some wiseguy back in the day dubbed it "The Witching Hour". Then every *quarter* a whole bunch of stuff expires on the *same* day – index futures, index options and stock options. Suddenly you got all this volatility making the markets whip around and as a result it's known as –'

'Triple witching.' Martinez with her best 'pick me, please, sir' smile.

Peterson grinned, clearly helpless in the face of her charms. 'You're quick. Ever thought of a job in Treasury?'

I hated to break up the party but – 'Sir, if Rankin is taken into custody there'd be havoc in the markets and the US government wouldn't be able to orchestrate a summer camp concert, let alone the orderly winding down of a major investment bank.'

Peterson thought the solution was staring us in the face. 'So – we take Rankin into custody on Saturday.'

Martinez shook her head. 'Even if he hasn't flown the country by then Potus could be dead. I mean, the president. Sorry.'

'I know who Potus is. I watch *24*.'

The three of us stood in silence, mulling over our options. Peterson's agitated face told me he wasn't about to disagree with me for the simple reason that he agreed with me. He shucked his shoulders, trying to loosen himself up a little.

'What? What else do you know about these SPVs?'

I leaned on the kitchen worktop. Dropped my head slightly, feeling the fatigue now. 'Nothing.'

He didn't react critically, but instead sat in thought, trying to formulate a plan, but we hadn't given him enough. Everybody in the room knew it.

'Byrne, you dug up this offshore web of SPVs – fine, you're as smart as they say you are. But I am not going to ask the president to have our country stand behind First Bank because two fugitives have a hunch that there is something bad in that nest of offshore companies. I'll level with you, this is new information – this is *worrying* information – but bring me something I can work with. I move against Rankin and First Bank on the back of these – and it turns out these SPVs were just an overzealous tax-efficiency move? My grandchildren will still be paying off that lawsuit in their old age.'

Martinez looked from Peterson to me, bemused that nobody was pointing out the obvious. 'Why don't we just lift the lid on the SPVs, see what's in them?'

The Treasury Secretary almost laughed but wasn't quite in the mood. 'We don't have the authority. Bermuda's a sovereign state. First Bank could tell us, but if they haven't volunteered this stuff so far I can't see them doing so in a meaningful timeframe.'

I lined up three champagne flutes along the kitchen work surface and decided we had nothing much to lose by pushing this, pushing the Treasury Secretary. 'You're going to ask the other banks to bail out First Bank at the weekend, aren't you?'

Peterson went to deny it but then thought, *What the hell.* 'Yeah. You say Rankin's killing people because of what's in those SPVs? Well . . .' He trailed off.

Martinez finished it for him. 'You'd kill to know what's in them?'

He flashed a bleak smile at her. 'Yeah, yeah I would.

Otherwise the bail-out of First Bank this weekend is going to be nothing more than a crapshoot.'

They both looked up at the sound of the cork I'd just popped. I poured three glasses of the Treasury Secretary's generously donated Kristal. I leaned across and handed the other two a glass each then saluted them with my own flute.

'Mr Secretary?'

'Yes?'

'Do you think your people can get access to these SPVs within a "meaningful timeframe"?'

Peterson deflated, defeated. 'No. No I don't. Rankin's stonewalling us and there's only one day left to the weekend. And it's not exactly a state secret to accept that you're right – the US cannot withstand another Lehman Brothers, not right now. The bond markets alone would slaughter us. Rankin thinks he can pull some kind of rabbit out of the hat, but you're telling me the rabbit is some kind of attack on the president. The whole thing is a clusterfuck.' He glumly sipped his champagne.

I had moved round to stand next to Martinez. 'Sir?'

'Go on?'

'Would you have a plane we could borrow?'

The Treasury Secretary half chuckled at the unlikeliness of the line of enquiry. 'Why? Want me to help you flee abroad?'

'Yeah. To Bermuda.'

35

Walk down a flight of stairs halfway along 15th Street NW, north of Pennsylvania Avenue, and you will find the Sleeping Dragon. It has poor decor, poor furniture and poor lighting. The mismatching chairs and tables were well-worn when the owners bought them and had only gone downhill since. The wallpaper was out of fashion when it was put up and that was before anybody could remember. The place is tatty. Clean but tatty. It only has one thing going for it. One little thing that is also everything: the best Cantonese food in Washington D.C. This best-kept-secret quality suited the family who ran the restaurant as they preferred to serve familiar faces with familiar food and were more than pleased for a private party to close down the store for the night. Tonight was such a night.

Around the basic table with its basic plates and basic cutlery sat eleven men who hoped to change the course of history. They were the kingmakers of American politics. Men whose backing almost guaranteed electoral success. Men whose knowledge, influence and connections could take any worthwhile candidate to within grasping distance of the very White House itself.

The only missing ingredient, the magic ingredient, was financial backing – but Rankin was here to supply that. Opposite the First Bank CEO, across the large round table, sat Deputy Director George Carlton of the United States Secret Service. It was for his benefit that Rankin was introducing the shaded group that sat below the feeble lamp suspended above the table.

'. . . We have Jim Steiner, the one and only lobbyist you'll ever need . . .'

A large gentleman in a white suit with accompanying white waistcoat nodded to George.

'Rupert Humber who ran the Morrison campaign in Tennessee last year . . .'

A tall thin man full of nervous energy nodded vigorously. 'Overturned a twelve point lead in the last eight days of campaigning.'

Rankin smiled charmingly. 'And ain't he proud of it.'

The table laughed politely.

'And last – but by no means least – there's Senator Brown. Mr Senator.'

A small serious man with about as little hair as he had morals gave a practised smile from behind thick black glasses.

Rankin clapped his hands together. 'Now, all that's missing is the money.'

Everybody laughed as one, laughed as generously as they hoped Rankin would prove once campaigning got underway.

Rankin let them settle, enjoying the glow that holding the purse strings brought, enjoying being a player. 'But seriously, gentlemen, we all know that our great country is being buffeted by the winds of terrorism, the rise of Asia, a government obsessed with subsidies for their – if I may say – socialist interests . . .' Nods from the group around the table. '. . . The lunacy of the environmental movement whose fingerprints are on every decision made here in D.C. And it is this good fight that we must battle if we are to steer this country towards its destiny. And I can recommend no greater warrior, no greater defender of the American faith, no greater captain on this voyage than my good friend George Carlton.'

There was a smattering of supportive applause from the group, the men suffused with the glow of people about to receive a lot of money for some very clever, very underhand, but very routine work.

Deputy Director Carlton cleared his throat and adopted a statesman-like poise. Not now the angry agency operative, but the smooth political operative, the other side of his career coin, a side he had been quietly shining over the years till he hoped it would dazzle, dazzle on a night like this.

'Gentleman, firstly may I thank you for coming out on such a cold September night to discuss my candidacy. Jeremiah has spoken of each and every one of you in the most glowing terms, but even better than that – you all passed the Secret Service background checks.'

Again more laughter, loud and hearty, though to a man alarm bells rang at such a real prospect. But George Carlton was pleased to have cracked the ice with the joke he had practised so much on the plane on the way up. Now, though, he furrowed his brow, wanted them to know he was a thinker who had thought on something. A man of responsibility.

'But cold though tonight may be, maybe I can warm you with the thought that perhaps history will trace a finger back to the events of this evening and say, "Then – then did a group of men say, 'No more will the United States sacrifice its security interests for the sake of the fanciful notion of world peace.'"'

'Tonight we are all on a timetable, gentlemen. Of course we are. We are busy men in a busy world. Well, let me, if I may, tell you about another timetable. A timetable I have warned the empty suits here in Washington of for too many years. This timetable is the terrorists' timetable. And it has a cross on it. But this cross is not on a particular day or month or year . . . This cross is on America.'

He looked about the table, for effect mostly, but knowing that such a look after such a remark pulled the listener in even further.

'Because mark my words, gentlemen – and judge me by this if you will – there is a terrible reckoning coming for those that have chosen so-called tolerance and so-called human rights over the vital interests of our nation. Because the same nation – the Nation of Terror – that attacked on 9/11 is about to strike again.

'Gentlemen, I will not divulge that which has been entrusted to me, but I will say this. They are here, they are vengeful and they are ready.'

And now he looked at them again, looked at them to let them know that this was not some fanciful hypothesis but something he knew to be fact and was divulging – in confidence – to them. The group hung on his every word, excited by the revelation and excited that they were now part of such a trusted circle. To be at the *centre of things* – the very meaning of Washington D.C. itself – was happening right before their eyes. *We matter.* They felt it and believed it. And for the right fee they were prepared to do something about it.

'But I come not to spread doom and gloom – I'll leave that to the Democrats . . .'

Some pointed laughter, laughter that turned serious at Carlton's now sober look.

'The right administration, with the right agenda, with the right resolve can not only defeat these suicidal extremists but can use that very victory as the event that turns the tide against the rising powers of the East, that guarantees American supremacy for centuries to come. Refuse to act and the decline of this great nation is inevitable. Act now and our security and prosperity is assured.'

Rankin surreptitiously looked for the reaction of the men around the table. It was nervous. It was excited. It was perfect. For the first time all evening his confidence in the plan had returned. The bigger picture, his role in events – at the *heart of events* – was thrilling once again. *Forget what had to happen for the plan to work. Focus on the prize, Jerry. Focus on the second trade.*

It was going to prove to be OK. Even if a lot of people would have to die to prove it.

36

New Jersey. We sat outside a small square mock-colonial home from the roof of which I didn't doubt you could see the nearby Passaic River. It was the address of the hospice finance director I'd been investigating until recently. Him and his pregnant girlfriend.

'I think they're decorating . . .' Martinez was craning her neck through the top of the windscreen of our rented Toyota Camry. 'At this time of night?'

This time of night was almost midnight. And I had a feeling I knew what room they were decorating, though I was fifty-fifty on whether they were going for pink or blue. 'Well, at least we won't have to wake them up.'

Martinez looked at me, doubtful. 'Are you sure we need somebody else?'

'I can't do this by myself – there's not enough time.'

'But are you sure he's the guy we want? I mean, Peterson did offer us some of his.'

'His guys are not allowed to do what we're about to do.'

She stopped looking out of the window and gave me her full attention instead. 'Byrne, *we're* not allowed to do what we're about to do.'

'Yeah, but we're going to do it anyway. We're going after a thief and you know what they say.'

Martinez shrugged. 'Never wear red and green . . . Unless you're an elf.'

I saw the outline of our man up the ladder, struggling to get his paint-roller to the ceiling. I imagined that stakeouts for Detective Ashby must have just flown by with this wise-acre beside him. Still, I could imagine worse ways of spending my time.

'Martinez. Lesson one of Entrapment 101: set a thief to catch a thief.'

The door was opened cautiously by a very tall middle-aged man in paint-covered gym clothes and a toupee that he was unaware was sitting slightly awry. From behind him squawked a voice that was as nasally Brooklynite as it was nebbish.

'Who is it, Larry?' He shushed her but she was insistent. 'We shouldn't be opening the door at this time of night.'

Larry turned his tall frame towards her with a slightly stately gait. 'Will you let me deal with this?' He returned to Martinez and myself on his front porch. He spoke guardedly. 'Yes? What is it?'

'Larry Betts?'

He looked at each of us in turn, weighing up the situation, weighing up how much trouble we'd brought with us. 'Yes?'

'Can we come in and talk?'

He tried to hide behind decorum. 'Can't this wait till morning? We were in bed.'

I let the obvious pass. 'You tell me, Mr Betts. Can the financial affairs of the Notre Dame Children's Hospice wait till the morning?'

I thought he was about to be sick. Whatever trouble he'd been expecting, it hadn't been anything this bad.

Larry Betts sat on the large leather couch, its plastic wrapping still on, being hugged by his Russian-doll-shaped partner. She was as fussy as she was neurotic, as needy as she was pregnant, which was very.

'Aw, Larry, this, this is Gawd's way of punishing us.'

He patted her hand. 'Nonsense, Imelda. You mustn't say that kind of thing.'

'But a Roman Catholic and a Jew, one of us has to be wrong.'

Larry rubbed his brow like he was trying to remove an ink stain. 'How did you find out?'

I sat in a plastic-wrapped armchair of my own, Martinez standing by the front door. 'Father O'Shea approached my company a few months back. I was investigating you for W. P. Johnson. I was actually quite impressed by the way you constructed the books. You should work in a bank.'

Imelda hugged Larry's arm and looked heavenward.

'Oh, our little baby's gonna be an orphan. He'll never see his lovely nursery.'

Larry squeezed her hand with infinite patience. 'Melly, he won't be an orphan – you'll be here.'

Martinez was leaning casually against the front door. 'After aiding and abetting? I can't see the prison authorities letting you take the baby in with you.'

Imelda looked at Martinez like she'd just grown another head. 'Argh! Larry! What have we done? What have we done?'

Larry there-there'd her with a rub of his hand. He faced me stoically. 'So, what now?'

I sat forward in my armchair, getting down to business. 'You have two choices, Larry. You can hand yourself in and throw yourself on the mercy of the courts –'

'And Gawd, Larry, don't forget Gawd's mercy.'

'Or you can come with us to Bermuda right now, help us unravel a set of crooked books and I'll find a way to make your situation right.'

Larry looked like he'd misheard me, wasn't sure what to make of what I'd just said, but he was a smart guy and began to grasp what was going on.

'You're . . . You're not here as a representative of W. P. Johnson, are you?'

I shook my head slowly from side to side.

'And if I called them up they would tell me you didn't work for them any more, wouldn't they?'

I nodded slowly.

Hope sprang into Imelda's eyes and she grabbed Larry's arms like they only had one number to go in the state lottery. 'He needs your help, Larry – don't settle for less than you need to.'

Larry's measured manner told me that he never allowed any of her extremism to influence his decision making. 'But I've borrowed . . . that is, taken quite a bit of money from the hospice. You can't make that money right.'

I clasped my hands together. 'What if I gave you a stock tip which, if used the right way, could fix your situation with the hospice by the end of business tomorrow?'

Larry took fright. 'Oh, no, I couldn't gamble with the hospice's money, that would be unethical.'

I frowned as I thought about that last remark. 'Really? Well, remember those American Electric convertible bonds you put the hospice into for two years?'

'With the six point twenty-five per cent return, yes?'

'AE is going to go bust within four months and you'll be losing every last cent of it. How's that for gambling with their money?'

Larry rubbed the fingers of one hand over the knuckles of his other like they were worry beads. Then he came to a decision. The right decision. 'Do I need to bring anything with me?'

'Just that mind of yours.'

Imelda began to wail. 'Don't go with these people,

Larry. Who knows who they are or what they're up to? That's it – I'm turning us in. I'm going to the police. If you leave me alone with our baby, I'll turn us all in, I swear.'

Imelda snatched up the phone and held her finger over the number pad as if it had the power to electrocute us all. Bluffing though she was, she had us over a barrel. If Larry wanted to tell us to whistle Dixie, the only question I had was what key? I hadn't banked on the crazy girlfriend. And I didn't have a plan for her.

But maybe I'd been over-thinking it.

The phone flew out of Imelda's hands as Martinez yanked it on a cable none of us had noticed she'd picked up. The phone smashed into the wall behind her, fracturing into four or five parts before scattering about the floor. Then Martinez took it up a notch.

'I *am* the fucking police, lady, and either your guy comes with us or you'll be giving birth manacled to a prison hospital bed in a room full of crack whores.' Martinez pulled the phone cord between her two hands like her next bright idea was to strangle her. 'Your fucking choice. OK?'

When Imelda just stared, frozen with terror, the detective found a new gear that even I didn't know she had.

'I SAID . . .'

We drove the Camry towards Teterboro Airport where we were to pick up our flight. Imelda was stroking and pawing at her man like it was the last time she'd get to feel him. Larry, so tall his head was bumping against the car's roof, was slightly abashed at such a public show of affection, but clearly some large part of him depended upon it as well.

Imelda spoke in a subdued, buttoned-up fashion. 'Now, Larry, you do as the nice couple say, OK. If there's anything they want you to do, you just do it, OK. Don't start any trouble.'

Like Larry needed telling. 'I won't, Melly, I won't.'

I swapped a look with Martinez. Her face said it all. *Mess with me, Byrne, and you're getting a slice of that yourself.*

Bring it on.

37

The elderly man's eyes snapped open at the sensation of cold steel against his cheek. He tried to move his head off the pillow, but the barrel of the revolver had him pinned down.

'We don't keep any cash or jewels in the house.'

'We're not looking for cash or jewels in your house.'

He was straining to look round but between the darkness of the room and the proximity of the gun he saw nothing. 'I am to tell you that the bank has numerous anti-kidnapping measures in place, many of which I'm not even allowed to know the details of myself. Taking me hostage will not achieve anything. I'm sorry but it won't, honestly.'

'I'm afraid you're not listening. We don't want cash, we don't want you – we just want your passwords.'

The whites of the old man's eyes flickered as they darted about, as he tried to out-think his intruders. 'None of my passwords allow the movement of any monies or assets whatsoever. You'd be restricted to looking at read-only files. That's the truth. I swear to god that's the truth.'

I turned on the bedside light. The old man in the

bed was momentarily blinded, hooding his eyes with a hand.

'Then I've definitely come to the right place.'

We were in the substantial family room – or one of the substantial family rooms – of a substantial Bermudan mansion. Larry was sitting obediently on one of the many Louis XIV couches. In most houses I would have suspected reproductions. In this house I wasn't so sure. Sitting in what must have been at least three acres of cliff-top grounds, it boasted enough bedrooms to host a banking convention – but then maybe that was the idea.

Martinez had the Bermudan bank CEO and his more-irritated-than-scared middle-aged wife sitting back to back on dining chairs she had brought through from another room. She bent over the pair solicitously.

'Now, do either of you need to go to the toilet?'

Neither said a word in their various states of anger at the situation. They had read it well. We were not sociopathic robbers – but we were on a mission. They had cooperated fully and seemed to just want us gone and the ordeal over. That worked for us.

Martinez held up a length of rope. 'OK, tell me if I tie you up too tight.'

I surveyed the scene. All was in order. 'Larry?'

Larry and I entered the study. Its corner view boasted a vista that stopped us both in our tracks. An uninterrupted aspect across the bay to the dots of lights and life beyond. But despite the proximity to the cliffs there wasn't a single sound coming from the sea. The mansion of cedar and glass had triple-paned windows throughout. Everything about the place was rock solid. Dependable. Like the banker.

Larry took the Bermudan bank CEO's computer at the central antique desk and I placed my laptop on a bamboo table between two couches in a similar design. I was pleased to see there was a flat-screen television hanging inset in the book shelves of one wall and switched it to Bloomberg. The Asian markets were down. A lot. The European markets had just opened and were heading south at a rate of knots. There was red all over the screen. And when New York opened in less than five hours it would be the same there.

'The passwords worked, Byrne.'

Larry was already off and running, working feverishly, for me, for Imelda, for absolution. It was a relief to have him on board. We could get in there, but what would we find? What would we have time to find?

38

The young man sitting at the low rent kitchen table was unshaven and unkempt. His face had seen too little light, his body too few good meals and his thinning hair better days. Round his head he had a leather strap, wrapping a magnifying glass to his left eye. The effect was to make him look like a crazed Victoriana jeweller, somebody who might have stepped out of a steampunk graphic novel. It conferred on him the status of either genius or lunatic. Or perhaps a little bit of both.

The subterranean criminal sat in a small unloved Formica kitchen doing an unloved job. A rolled-up cigarette between his teeth was there more as a nervous habit than appetite as it had long since gone out. But his nerves stopped there. Everything else about him was as calm as the Dalai Lama. He moved slowly and he moved deliberately. He moved his gigantically enlarged eye fastidiously across every detail of the work at hand. He moved the way a bomb-maker should.

The young man had a cellphone opened before him, its guts modified beyond repair by his adaptation of the device for his own explosive purposes. He was employing a small soldering iron to weld a wire into the innards of the cellphone that ran to a slightly larger brick-shaped object. The detonator.

Mr Bingo watched this from across the table, a chipped mug in his hand holding some vodka to see him through the night. His view of the work was blocked by the lid of a briefcase that was opened towards him, the Thin-haired Russian applying his skills inside, his Mad Max monocled head only occasionally rising into view.

Mr Bingo spoke in their mother tongue to his colleague.

'How long before it's ready?'

'You don't have to stay.'

'You think I want to stay in the room with this thing? The boss wants a call, wants to know it's done. Come on.'

The Thin-haired Russian was hunched over his work. 'Would you rush Chekhov? Would you rush Tolstoy? Would you rush Rachmaninoff?' He sat up, stretched his shoulders, rolling them, rolling his neck with them, doing it all at leisure. He saw the impatient but somewhat impotent stare of his associate opposite and sniggered. He pushed the magnified eyepiece up and onto the top of his head and reached for the bottle of samogon, the milky brew he preferred over the traditional vodka. But Mr Bingo seized the drink, held it fast against the Thin-haired Russian's attempt to take it.

'Not whilst you're working.'

The Thin-haired Russian's lips spread into the approximation of a smile, displaying two rows of yellowed teeth. With a single finger he rotated the briefcase so that it was facing Mr Bingo.

'That's why I waited until I had finished.'

Mr Bingo looked down at the wraps of dough-like explosives packed into the briefcase, at their heart, side by side, a coverless cellphone with numerous wires linking it to a detonator. He released the bottle, which was taken and opened by the bomb-maker, who poured the samogon into his own mug. 'I don't understand why you had to use a Mont Blanc briefcase. What a waste.'

The Thin-haired Russian knocked back the fiery brew in one, enthralled by the warmth that erupted in his neck and chest. 'You seem to be forgetting, we're bankers now.' He refilled his mug and lifted it to Mr Bingo. '*Budem zdorovy*. Let's stay healthy.'

39

The television told it all. The build-up to the ground-breaking site visit by the American and Chinese leaders that afternoon, the ongoing hunt for the as-yet-unnamed Madoff Murderer, the perilous health of First Bank as well as the bloodbath in the Asian and European markets. What a shit-storm.

But the bit I liked the least was the display ticking away in the corner of the screen: 'Friday 09:03 EST'.

The sun had long since risen over Bermuda, but as every waterfront house and cove and beach came into view I just felt the sands of time slipping through our fingers. This was such a long shot. I was fighting self-doubt, that we should have used our time more wisely. Maybe I should have taken Martinez's advice, maybe I should have put a gun in Rankin's ear and told him to spill the beans or I'd spill his brains. But a confession would blow the plot's cover. They'd just as likely move it somewhere else, somewhere earlier, even. Lose the trail we had and we'd probably lose the trail altogether. As I'd been telling myself all night, what a shit-storm.

There was a tap at the open door. I was sitting on

the couch in front of my laptop. Martinez stood in the doorway looking like she might have grabbed some shut-eye.

'You guys want some coffee? Breakfast?'

'Both please, angel.'

She waited a moment, as nervous as I was. 'How's it going?'

I pulled a face that told her the news wasn't good.

But she was here to try to lift our spirits. 'Larry?'

The tall, professorial middle-aged man, his toupee long since removed, didn't even look up, raking through the internet files as if his life depended on it. 'Not good. There are just too many damn companies. I can't find a dollar that is just a dollar. Everything's so leveraged, sold on, lodged against another trade – it's like a hall of mirrors where every number merges into the next. I don't know where assets begin and liabilities end. And I think the reason First Bank has named all its SPVs after star systems is because there are so goddamn many of them. Too many of them. Then there's this 13.7 billion figure that the option trades keep referencing. Is it a deferred loss? An exposure? A profit? It's impenetrable. I've tried adding it to every line of the balance sheet and I can't get it to work. If it's a loss, they are up a galactic-sized creek without an interstellar paddle, I can tell you that much.'

I got to my feet, walked over to a window and

opened it. I needed some air. I needed to clear my head. Trying to think of everything meant I was starting to think of nothing. My eye wandered over the view. The path from the cliffs meandered down to the beach where a small jetty stood. Tethered at its end was a stunning wooden speedboat. I couldn't tell from here but it looked like a Riva Aquarama, the Ferrari of the boat world. The Riva Aquarama was a twin-engine luxury runabout with a beautifully varnished mahogany hull and convertible roof. Real *La Dolce Vita* stuff. Given the quality and opulence of the mansion we were standing in I suspected it really was an Italian original. Nice work if you could get it.

Larry leaned back, his body begging for a break. He dropped his head back on the chair, stared at the rotating fan on the ceiling, his mind as devoid of ideas and inspiration as mine was. He'd thrown himself heart and soul into running those numbers but there wasn't the time, there just wasn't the time.

Martinez wasn't following Larry. 'Is it the loss we've been looking for?'

Larry and I didn't say anything. We were too damned tired. The only sound was the soft wafting of the ceiling fan broken by the occasional wave crashing down below outside the open window. Larry and I were in danger of slipping into a torpor.

Martinez lingered with the guilty air of an able

person desperate to pitch in but aware that this was the wrong territory. But more than that she hated to leave us so despondent.

'Don't lose heart, guys. Maybe the 13.7 billion is the size of the black hole you keep talking about.'

I looked from the sea to Martinez. In the far reaches of my mind the weak flame of an idea had just flickered into life. But it was so weak, so easily snuffed out, that I felt that if I even turned my head too fast it might be extinguished.

'What did you just say?'

She pushed herself off the door frame. 'Sorry, I'll leave you guys.'

'Say it!'

She jumped at the bark in my voice. 'I said, maybe it's a $13.7 billion loss.'

'No, Martinez – say it *the way you just said it.*' The whisper of an idea so fragile in my mind that anything could make it disappear.

She gave me a look that told me I was unnerving her. 'I said . . . Maybe the 13.7 billion is the size of the black hole you keep talking about.'

I took a step towards her, clenching my fist in excitement. She tried to back away, but bumped into the door frame. I slammed the desk with my hand.

'What's up, Byrne, what?'

'The . . . 13.7 billion isn't a number. I mean, it isn't a financial number –'

Larry clicked his fingers. 'Oh god, it was right in front of us . . .'

Martinez was none the wiser from when we'd been talking finances. 'What are you guys going on about?'

Larry suddenly burst with energy, sitting up and tapping furiously into the computer. I ran round to watch over his shoulder. This would be quick now. This would be instant. Lines of financial data were streaming down the screen, pouring down like a waterfall of digits – but order was coming to the matrix, the computer crunching the account details together. Larry was alive. He had rediscovered why he got into this game, the numbers balancing, the numbers telling the truth, the numbers never lying . . .

I could have kissed Martinez I was so excited. Hell, I could have kissed Larry. 'Martinez, the Big Bang occurred – the universe came into existence – 13.7 billion years ago. The number isn't a profit or loss, *it's a goddam account*. We kept thinking it was a number on the balance sheet – that's why we couldn't get anything to add up. *We'd* skewed the numbers by 13.7 billion. But it was the actual name of one of the offshore accounts. An account that if we tally up will tell us the combined exposure of all these opposing options tra–'

What I saw stopped me.

Dead.

Larry covered his mouth with a hand, horrified. 'Holy Mary Mother of Jesus.'

We stood staring stupidly at the number on the screen.

Martinez looked from one of us to the other, our shock infecting her. 'What is it, Byrne? Larry?'

We still couldn't speak.

'Come on, guys, say something.'

I spoke but it was as if the voice belonged to somebody else. 'Today is Triple Witching, the biggest options settlement of the quarter. If the market closes down five hundred points from where we are, First Bank stands to make $20 billion.'

Martinez was unnerved by us now. 'And if it doesn't?'

Larry spoke with the same numbness that had possessed me. 'They'll lose over $100 billion. It's AIG all over again.'

I slumped my back against the wall.

'But First Bank can't possibly survive this kind of loss, can it?'

I looked at her. 'The system can't survive this kind of loss. The real loss – after the knock-on effects – would run into hundreds of billions, maybe over a trillion dollars. Even if the government had the money America's credibility would be used up.'

Martinez got it in an instant. 'Which means Rankin is going to make sure the markets close right where he needs them to.'

I just stared at the numbers whilst she played out everybody's thinking.

'Which means he's going to do something terrible.' She looked at me, sickened by the irrefutable logic. '. . . Like killing the president.'

40

'I thought we did very well last night.'

Rankin stood in a corridor, keen to keep the conversation from the occasional passing person.

Carlton's voice on the phone had a slight edge of impatience. 'Yes, yes we did. Are your friends satisfied that the candidacy has legs?'

Rankin was Mr Congeniality itself. 'George, they loved you. Couldn't believe you hadn't made this move earlier, said you were a natural. My phone's been ringing red hot this morning. You are about to sit at a very big table, my friend.'

Carlton couldn't hide a small degree of pleasure revealing itself in his voice. 'Yes, well, that's why we went.'

'Yeah, that's right.' Rankin pinching his lips together before continuing. 'Look, George . . .'

'Yes?'

'Have you been following the markets?'

'Yes, they've had a rough ride.'

'I mean, overnight?'

'Not overnight, no.'

'Well, I think some of that Asian bird flu might still be doing the rounds. Asia, Europe, everything's off.'

'OK. And?'

'Well, it's just that . . . we're at an interesting point here, George.'

'What do you mean?'

'Well, you know, with the right form of words, with the right corporate action by First Bank, well, I believe we could achieve everything we wanted to *without* the second trade.'

Carlton was titanium-like in slapping it down. 'Now, Jerry . . .'

'Just hear me out. When we started, you know, the planning, well, we never in our wildest dreams thought the markets would be so far down at this point . . .'

'The second trade stands.'

'But I can get us where we need to be *without* the second trade. The money's nailed on now, George. The market's just about where we need it . . .'

'Jerry, for the last time, the second trade stands.'

'But we can achieve everything we need to achieve without, George, *without* . . .'

'You say a fucking word and I will personally see to it that it is the last time you ever speak again.'

Rankin was torn between fear and the need to stand up to him. 'Is that a threat? Is that a threat, George?'

'Of course it's a fucking threat. And what the fuck do you think you're doing having this conversation on the phone? We had the whole ride from D.C. to the airport to discuss this –'

'I didn't know Asia was going to be on its fucking deathbed this morning.'

'It won't be just Asia that's on its deathbed if this conversation continues. There is the bigger picture here, Jerry. This isn't just about you, understand? This is about the future of our country. Now, see this thing through to the end. Do I need to explain myself any further?'

'I thought we were partners on this.'

'Don't be a prick, Jerry. This thing is bigger than you will ever begin to understand.'

'What? What did you say, George? George . . . ?'

Rankin looked at his phone. Deputy Director Carlton had gone.

The First Bank CEO held his head like he was battling a migraine, like he was being tormented by thoughts he wanted rid of. How did he ever let Carlton talk him into this? How did he allow his ego to be flattered into playing a role 'at the heart of America's future'? Carlton's plan made sense – it worked – when the markets were riding high. It worked for Carlton and it worked for Rankin. God knows Rankin's situation had been desperate back then. But to not change the plan now the markets were down here, when people didn't need to die to get the result he needed? And not even people in a distant country that he might see on the news, but real people, people he worked with here in New York City, in Wall Street. Maybe even people from First Bank. What have you done, Rankin? So what if it aroused suspicion, couldn't he at least have gotten a heads-up from Agron so that he could shepherd his own employees away from danger? Wasn't that his job? Wasn't that his *responsibility*? Nobody *had* to die now – the markets were in the sweet spot. Why kill people if they didn't *have* to? How could Carlton not see that the situation was different now, that it was time to cut the trade . . . ?

And then a penny fell into the slot and Rankin's mind whirred into action like some sad little Coney Island arcade machine. Because finally Rankin realized the terrible truth: that Carlton wanted a catastrophe not to make Rankin's part of the plan work but *for its own sake*. The deputy director needed an agenda-defining event to launch his pursuit of Office. That First Bank's problems were never *ever* the issue . . . That he, Rankin, CEO of Wall Street's oldest investment bank, had been played. Rankin a puppet to Carlton's diabolical puppet-master. It was never about the money.

He slumped against a wall. 'Oh Christ, what have I done?'

Rankin speaking to no one now, having to articulate his horror, wishing it wasn't true. But this wasn't a dream. This was reality. And he knew the nightmare was just beginning.

A bell, not unlike a school bell, began to clang and

clang and clang and Rankin remembered why he was there.

The bell continued to ring.

On the floor of the New York Stock Exchange pit traders of every age and ethnic make-up watched with varying degrees of interest the group on the Bell Platform. Every day the honour of ringing the opening bell was handed to a company launching a new product, an individual who warranted recognition or, best of all, a company launching on the exchange itself. It was the last that had its people crammed into the Bell Platform today.

At the back of the modest balcony hung a large wall-sized banner proclaiming 'Omega Bank – Dual Listing – New York/Moscow'. Standing before it was the usual crowd of publicity-awkward suits drawn from the various executive roles at the bank. However, unbeknownst to most, a little colour had been added by the presence of the bandaged Mr Bingo, the Thin-haired Russian and, at the centre, Moffat Agron, Omega Bank's CEO, ringing the bell like a kid ringing the bell on an old steam train.

The banner at the back of the Bell Platform ruffled as Rankin, trying and failing to hide a sense of profound nausea, emerged onto the platform, late for the very listing his bank had engineered. Forty million dollars in fees that would quickly be making their way to a Swiss bank account of Moffat Agron's choosing.

Rankin looked out at the sea of New York Stock Exchange workers milling feverishly about like worker ants below the platform. People. Real people. *His* people. The talk and planning and plotting giving way to action and Rankin realizing that he couldn't pull the trigger – that he didn't want *anyone* to pull the trigger. But if he tried to stop things now the consequences would be terrible – for him. What had he done? Just what had he done?

The First Bank CEO half-heartedly applauded the Omega Bank staff as they applauded themselves. Then he saw something that made him catch his breath, made him want to steady himself. Rankin saw something he instantly knew to be the second trade, knew to be a bomb. A skinny young man with thinning hair and an ill-fitting suit had a Mont Blanc briefcase on the ground next to him and was discreetly sliding it behind a panel with his foot. Sliding it out of view. Sliding it with the intention of leaving it behind.

On the television in the CEO's study in Bermuda we were packing up. I was wrapping the power lead round the laptop, Larry sending the last of some emails.

But Martinez wanted our attention. 'Guys, look – on the TV!'

We looked up to see Bloomberg showing the

Opening Bell live from the New York Stock Exchange. We looked up to see Jeremiah Rankin applauding the CEO of Omega Bank right there on the television.

Martinez touched my shoulder. 'It's him, Byrne. The guy at the marina.'

'That's our Russian.'

I took a step towards the television, taking in the face of the man I had seen leave First Bank's offices the day before. I read the scrolling news bar at the bottom of the screen. 'Moffat Agron, CEO of Omega Bank.'

I looked at Larry. 'We need to send one more email.'

Rankin, standing amongst the Omega Bank executives, was on autopilot. He was still clapping but his eyes were looking from the now-hidden briefcase to the young wiry man.

'Excuse me.'

It was a small plump Russian man waiting for Rankin to make way. The bell had stopped ringing and the group had turned to leave. Rankin was blocking the exit and had no choice but to clear their path by leaving the platform himself.

The First Bank CEO figured he would wait in the corridor, wait till everybody had gone, get the briefcase, get rid of it. He could achieve his goal without the second trade – he could achieve this without the bomb, without the bloodshed and destruction and fallout that it would cause. Couldn't they see it was simpler this way? Couldn't they see it was —

But somebody grabbed his arm. Friendly but firm. Rankin looked round with ill-hidden fear, like he was convinced it was a police officer, as if his very thoughts had betrayed him. Instead he met the beaming face of Moffat Agron.

'Well, I thought that was a huge success.'

Rankin could feel the Omega Bank CEO guiding him away along with the departing crowd. Behind them stood Mr Bingo and the Thin-haired Russian, waiting impassively for them to leave.

Rankin threw one last glance at the Bell Platform door as the group swept him away, along with his hopes of stopping the calamity.

41

Martinez gunned the sleek Italian speedboat across the bay towards the tiny Bermudan island occupied by L. F. Wade International Airport. Larry sat in the back, exhausted from his night's work. Martinez and I rode up front, the wind blasting her hair backwards, both doing our best to not fall out of the boat as it bounced across every wave large and small.

I had the phone glued to my ear. 'Mr Secretary, we've sent it all over to you to look at – it's there in black and white.'

The Treasury Secretary stood leaning his head against a window of the New York Federal Reserve, Liberty Street below empty of traffic in the run-up to the presidential visit.

'Byrne, you stole that stuff, it's inadmissible – in fact, for god's sake, don't even tell me how you did it.' But more angry at the law's limits than our behaviour.

I was standing, gripping the top of the boat's windshield. 'Sir, this isn't a court case – this is about what's going to happen. At four o'clock this afternoon when it's discovered that First Bank has a $100 billion liability hanging over it the US economy is going to fall off the edge of the world.'

Peterson rubbed a hand back and forth over his hairless head, a head devoid of ideas. 'Christ, Byrne. If what you say is true, we're screwed either way. If the markets don't collapse, First Bank implodes, taking everybody with it. And if the markets *do* go down the bail-out of First Bank will prove unnecessary and Rankin gets to walk away with a healthy balance sheet and billionaire status.' He slammed the window. 'Goddammit.'

The boat lifted out of the water after topping a wave, landing with a thump.

'Sir, we're talking the lesser of two evils here. You can deal with Rankin another day.'

'Can we, Byrne? The way the rules are written we might even find that son of a bitch hasn't broken the law with these goddamn trades. Don't forget, everybody walked away from AIG.'

The Treasury Secretary turned and sat against the tall window.

'Byrne, I can't manipulate the markets here – we're a democracy, for god's sake. The repercussions alone, Jesus, it doesn't bear thinking about . . . Look, I've got to make some calls, I've gotta go. I'll get my guys to look at what you've sent – thanks. I appreciate it.' He paused before his next remark. 'I owe you, Byrne.'

As the long wooden speedboat neared the airport island, Martinez turned towards the western corner where a small cluster of aircraft hangars stood in the Bermudan sunshine.

She gave me a concerned look. 'What do you think?'

'I think his hands are tied. I think we're on our own.'

Martinez took in the news slowly. She shook her head at it then focused on the job of piloting the boat up to the shoreline. 'Do you still want Ashby to meet us when we land?'

'Can we trust him?'

'I trust him with my life.'

'But do you trust him with mine? Hell, it's the only way we can get there in time. Larry, did you charter the new plane?'

Larry nodded earnestly. 'Sure, it's all arranged.'

42

Special Agent Diane Mason sat at her desk in the New York field office. She was closing down her computer, readying herself to join the presidential party arriving at Battery Park in the Marine One helicopter. Potus's actual approach to the edge of Manhattan was the single biggest logistical nightmare she had faced in heading up the Advanced Party for his visit today. The various vantage points for attacking Marine One in and around Manhattan were a terrorist's dream come true. Tall buildings, low buildings, parks, waterways, bridges, thousands of cars, millions of people, every kind of cover a budding fanatic could ask for. But Special Agent Mason had repeatedly walked hundreds of Secret Service personnel and local law enforcement officers through the route Potus would be taking, including emergency exit routes in the events of an attack or incident, and she was satisfied that every inch, every angle, every opportunity had been secured and locked down. The Secret Service sticker tape was on the doors that would remain sealed for the duration of the visit, on the streets that would remain closed off, on the manhole covers that would remain in place now the sewers had been checked and OK'd.

The presidential limousine was in place and under armed protection. The car, unofficially nicknamed 'The Beast', was a black one-off stretched Cadillac. So big was it that its underpinnings came not from a car but from a truck. Its military-grade armour was over five inches thick and the bullet-proof glass so deep the car needed artificial lighting inside to give any semblance of normality for the passengers. Were the wheels taken out by any kind of small-arms attack the run-flat tyres would get the president to the nearest airfield and beyond. The motorcade surrounding The Beast, even on this short trip, would consist of thirty-five cars. People knew when the president was in town.

It had finally been agreed that five Kestrel helicopters in presidential livery would arrive in Manhattan. These were the helicopters used by the Secret Service to transport the president throughout the United States and the rest of the world. Whilst presented as stately carriages of the twenty-first century, they were in fact heavily fortified airships packed with anti-missile weapons as well as numerous other countermeasure devices. Four of the Kestrels would act as decoys, landing at different points around the city, with the fifth carrying Potus and his family to Battery Park on the southern tip of the island. Here they would join the cavalcade up a closed-down Water Street before arriving at the building site and the ground-breaking in Wall Street itself at 1500 hours.

In addition to all this Special Agent Mason had had to countenance the requests of the Chinese Embassy and their desire for a processional arrival at the ground-breaking. Their head of state was arriving from their consulate on 12th Avenue and it had taken a lot of explaining to get them to understand that Special Agent Mason would not be closing down the whole of Lower Manhattan to accommodate his journey. In the end they agreed on an extensive police escort via FDR Drive. She quite liked the symbolism of the presidents arriving at Wall Street from their respective East and West directions (give or take a bit of north and south) but decided it was one to tell her mother at the weekend.

Special Agent Mason took a moment at her desk, running through the checklist that had haunted her every waking and sleeping hour for the past month one last time. The job had been a serious test. She was more than capable of running the teams, but the learning curve and interdepartmental coordination had stretched her to breaking point. Deputy Director Carlton had entrusted the entire exercise to her and had stayed true to his word of not interfering with the arrangements for Potus himself. His present preoccupation, as far as she could see, was catching Byrne. But since his escape from the warehouse in the Brooklyn docks the trail had gone cold and even she was

beginning to suspect that he may have fled the city limits. She wouldn't relax now until Potus had gotten back
on that Kestrel and waved the Big Apple goodbye.
She'd even put a bottle of red out for her return home
tonight. She would have earned a very big drink.

Her thoughts were interrupted when her phone
rang with a number she didn't recognize.

I stepped through a door in the rear of the aircraft to
a cabin that boasted a double bed. On my phone was
the picture of the Secret Service's five-pointed gold
star, my icon of choice for this particular number.
Chosen in happier times. I saw the contact had picked
up and I put the phone to my ear. 'Diane, it's me.'

'My god, are you OK? I mean, what are y– Where
are you? You've got to give yourselves up. You've got
to, please.'

She had already answered one question. She had
studiously avoided saying my name. This told me that
possibly as high as the NSA my name was on a watch
list and any mention of it would get the attention of an
Information Analyst. Every time the names 'Mike',
'Michael' or 'Byrne' got mentioned in a phone call anywhere in the United States right now somebody got
another file on their desk. If somebody said my full
name a SWAT team would probably be headed for
their location before they'd even put the phone down.

I was sitting on the edge of the aircraft bed undoing

my shoes. I hadn't slept in almost thirty hours and sleep was the only thing on my mind. I could hear the engines of the Gulfstream revving higher as it began its taxi along the runway.

The next thing I said for posterity and Diane would know it. I said it explicitly because if I didn't see this day through I wanted this conversation to hit every senior desk in every Security Agency.

'Diane, there's going to be an attack in Lower Manhattan – probably on Potus – at approximately 1545 hours.'

Diane sat up sharp behind her desk, got to her feet. 'How – how do you know this?'

'Don't worry how I know it, but we're certain something's going to happen to make the markets come off and we're certain it's happening in New York today.'

'OK, and why 15.45?'

I had taken my jacket off and was pacing in the tight space of the double-bed cabin. 'Because the markets need enough time to react, but not enough time to correct themselves. You know how quickly they bounced back after the 2004 Madrid train bombings, well, even if Potus survives the attack, the markets won't be able to factor that in before they close at 1600 hours.'

'Who's behind this?'

'There are three key players. Jeremiah Rankin – the

First Bank CEO – as well as some Russian mobsters who we believe are being run by the owner of Omega Bank, a guy called Moffat Agron. Check him out. He was a minor player in the Moscow mafia in the early nineties, disappeared presumed dead, only to re-emerge as the majority shareholder of Omega Bank during Yeltsin's big sell-off of Soviet assets.'

Special Agent Mason was checking Moffat Agron on her database before Byrne had finished speaking. On her computer screen the Omega Bank CEO's profile picture came up as well as case notes linking him to suspected money-laundering in the early 1990s. She nodded, knowing this suspect was consistent with what she was hearing.

'OK, you said there were three key players. Who's the third?'

There was a pause. A pause Mason didn't like.

'Who's the third?'

'You tell me, Diane.'

'I don't understand – what do you mean?'

'The third person or persons are whoever arranged the surprise party for me at Brooklyn Pier.'

Diane bent at her desk almost as if she'd been winded. 'Carlton organized it, said he had some intelligence . . . Carlton? Look, is this . . . Is this personal?'

'No, Diane . . .'

*

'. . . This is happening.' I sat on the edge of the cabin bed, exhausted. 'Diane, I know you were at the Brooklyn docks, I know you were part of the trap . . .'

I figured her mind must be dizzy with scenarios and possibilities: Was I playing her? Was I trying to out-manoeuvre Carlton? Turn the tables?

'Mi – . . . About the docks, I had no choice. I promise you that.'

I was surprised at how much I wanted that to be true. 'OK, Diane, we're landing at La Guardia at approximately 1400 hours.'

'Do you want me to send a car?'

'No, it's all arranged. I'll contact you when we get close.'

'You have to come in. You have to let me bring you in.'

She needed her back covered. We knew this call would be crawled over a thousand times and every nuance squeezed to within an inch of its life. Diane was talking to a known fugitive. Some would try to argue that she was consorting with a known fugitive. She could be in a lot of trouble, and I never wanted that for her.

'Diane, I'll come in. When it's over, I'll come in.'

'But . . .'

I switched off my phone and looked at it for a long moment.

Hoping to god we could put a stop to all this.

*

On a lower floor of the Secret Service New York field office a lone communications officer sat in a small darkened room decked out on three sides with banks of screens and computer panels all dedicated to one thing: monitoring the Secret Service itself. Powerful data-analysis software red-flagged those conversations that touched on any keywords, phrases or even conversation types that could or did give any cause for concern. Cause for concern meant the betrayal of secrets, the non-authorized discussion of USSS affairs or anything else Deputy Director Carlton chose to be concerned about. And right now the deputy director was concerned about Special Agent Mason.

The communications officer moved a pointer on a screen back in a recording and clicked on her mouse.

Mason: *Mi* – . . . *I had no choice. I promise you that.*
Byrne: *OK, Diane, we're landing at La Guardia at approximately 1400 hours.*

The CO hit a PAUSE icon on her computer screen and the telephone conversation stopped. She picked up a desk phone of her own and tapped a pre-programmed number.

'Deputy Director? I think there's something you ought to hear.'

*

The Gulfstream was airborne and ascending steeply into the clear blue Bermudan sky.

Martinez backed into the sleeping cabin and closed the door after her, locking it for good measure. She stood with her rear to the room and unbuttoned her shirt.

'Well, Mr Byrne, I do believe the Mile High Club would be a fitting addition to our list of bedroom achievements . . .'

She turned with a mischievous but confident look on her face, her top wide open, her full bronzed breasts sitting up in a low-cut purple silk bra.

Then her face fell.

Because lying on the bed, comatose, was Byrne.

Martinez sighed and considered him and considered her options. And it was an easy decision to make to crawl onto the bed next to him, wrap herself around him and resign herself to a two-hour siesta.

43

Deputy Director Carlton was loading the rear of his maroon-coloured Chrysler 300 in the basement car park below the New York field office.

'Go on, go on.'

The communications officer stood to one side, uncomfortable with the news she was breaking.

'As I said on the phone, the male individual then told Special Agent Mason that it was a conspiracy between the CEO of a bank, some Russians and . . .'

Carlton was busy putting the last of his bags and papers into the boot of his sedan. 'And?'

'Well, and, as I said, you were mentioned.'

Carlton stood, completely unphased by the development. 'You did the right thing coming to me about this. Byrne has been trying to turn Mason for a prolonged period now and I fear he is prepared to go to terrible lengths to achieve his aims. Now, what I'm about to tell you is in the strictest confidence . . . Do I have your confidence?'

Uncertain as she was, a noticeable thrill ran through the young CO as she realized her importance in the game that was afoot. 'Yes, sir, you most certainly do, sir.'

'Good, good.' Carlton started to look around himself somewhat helplessly. 'Oh, where's my briefcase? I've left it upstairs.'

'No, it's just here, sir. Do you want it?'

She was pointing inside the trunk.

Absent-mindedly Carlton waved at the briefcase, closer as it was to the CO than himself. 'Yes, yes, would you?'

She leaned into the trunk of the car to where the briefcase was wedged in the far corner. She didn't feel the five-inch serrated blade enter her side, didn't feel it penetrating her kidneys, just felt the searing pain, petrifying her body in a rapture of agony, paralysed, unable to do more than gag in life-consuming torture as the knife was ripped out, her body pushed against the lid of the trunk, the knife thrust repeatedly into her chest, her heart, her lungs. She had no sensation left to feel the man bundling her body into the trunk, no receptors sending out the sound of the slamming trunk, no awareness of the darkness that enveloped her, consumed as she was by an infinite darkness of her own.

44

Special Agent Diane Mason looked about her desk to make sure she had forgotten nothing. Satisfied that she hadn't, she hooked her handbag over her shoulder and made for her office door. But she was forced to step back in surprise as the door swept open rapidly before her.

'Carlton.'

The deputy director entered, backing her into the room before closing the door after himself. 'Going somewhere, Diane?'

'To Battery Park, of course.'

The walls dividing Mason's office from the large, busy open-plan office beyond were floor to ceiling double-paned with slat blinds inside. Carlton moved about the office twisting the blinds to a closed position.

'May I ask what's going on?'

Carlton considered her with an arch look. 'No, Diane, may *I* ask what is going on? I believe you have vital information about the Service's most wanted fugitive and you have said nothing about it.'

Mason was wrong-footed by his knowledge of her

conversation but instantly decided to stand firm. 'I was just about to make arrangements concerning that.'

'Oh, just about to, were you?' He gestured to the chair behind her desk. 'Take a seat, please.'

She warily returned to her seat, placing the handbag on the desk next to her. 'I have to be in Battery Park, sir.'

Carlton stood across the desk from her. 'You are also in possession of information concerning a clear and present threat to Potus and yet you have not reported it to anybody.'

'What were you expecting me to do, run up and say, "I hear you want to kill the president"?'

'You could have gone over my head, if you believed Byrne's conjectures, if you had followed procedure, if you didn't put Byrne before the Service.'

Mason resolved to confront the situation head on. 'You wanted this to happen on my watch, didn't you, Carlton? You wanted an attack on Potus whilst I was in charge of Protective Duty. You wanted to ship me out of the Service once and for all.'

'I wanted you to follow procedure. I wanted you to do your job. You think I give a damn if a fugitive makes wild claims about me? Let him – that's why we do investigations, Diane. And maybe – just maybe – at the end of this you would have understood that Byrne is a subversive maverick hell-bent on settling old scores whatever the price.'

'I did not –'

He began to walk round to behind her desk, Mason wanting to watch him but not admit her fears. He leaned over her now.

'You should have gone to the director of Homeland Security, you should have reported this, you should have arranged a welcoming committee for Byrne at La Guardia. I suggest you get the director on the phone right now so we can not only make this incident a matter of record but decide between us – as a *team*, Mason – whether we need to call off the president's ground-breaking visit immediately.'

Mason was at a loss. Everything he was saying was . . . right. This is exactly what they should do. The man she had suspected two minutes earlier was behaving like a real deputy director of the Secret Service with the welfare of Potus and a visiting head of state as his number one priority. Which meant Byrne was playing her, which meant the protection of Potus was compromised.

'Come on,' he prompted at her inaction.

She hated having him standing right behind her but couldn't argue with the logic of logging Byrne's accusations with their ultimate boss and thrashing out a strategy. She was confused about Carlton, utterly confused. He was in her office *doing the right thing*, but if it was a bluff there was a mighty trail of evidence building up against him. Bewildered, she hit the button for the speaker-phone which purred into life. Which was when she was hit by the smell . . . a strange kind of smell. Oh Jesus –

Before she had even started to rise, to turn, to fight, the cloth was over her face, Carlton's large hand gripping it over her nose and mouth. She knew to hold her breath and if she had had a moment more could have braced herself, leapt backwards, fought. But by being one beat behind him she had allowed herself a small gulp of air from the sodden cloth, its fumes burning her throat, scorching her lungs, evaporating her mind.

The deputy director held her from behind until he felt the unmistakeable slump of unconsciousness. Then he lowered her forward in her chair where she lay across her desk. He tipped her handbag over onto the desk and amongst the female paraphernalia that fell out was her service revolver. He picked it up.

The plan was changing fast, becoming compromised. Carlton knew he couldn't do more with Mason right there and then. He'd have to come back, leave her here and come back after the second trade, tonight. How much did she know? Who else knew? Did *anybody* know? He would need to ask her these questions. But how to get her out of the building? Unseen?

Carlton looked down at his latest problem, lying still across the desk. What could he do? He glanced up at the blinds blocking the windows. Were there cracks?

Could people see in? He sighed heavily, resenting the details he was having to attend to. He lifted Mason from her chair then, holding her in position, kicked it away where it rolled to one side. Carefully – fearing noise, not her welfare – he lowered her to the ground behind the desk. He crouched to satisfy himself that she could not be seen from the other side. She couldn't.

He stood up and considered the prone body. Had he used enough chloroform? How much was enough? Was it even the right approach? Keeping her alive, giving himself a chance to ask questions. Would she break under questioning? Ah, hell, everybody broke under questioning. He remembered the revolver hanging at his side. He'd almost forgotten it was there. He raised it like an alien object, like he had to remind himself what it did, what it was for. Carlton pointed the gun at her head. Again he looked at the doorway. Now considering its usefulness at muffling sound. He looked down at Mason and weighed it up. Risking her waking before his return versus somebody hearing the shot. How long did chloroform keep you asleep? Minutes? Hours? Days? He flexed his trigger finger. Had to tie up the loose ends. Had to cover his tracks. Had to *take control.* Then he saw her face. A human face. A real victim. A whole life he'd have to take. And killing her became . . . harder. Too hard right now.

Christ, she was out cold. Dead to the world. Maybe even dead. A problem for another time.

He pocketed Special Agent Mason's gun and hit '0' on the phone.

'United States Secret Service?'

'Get me Commander Becker, Counter Assault.'

He sat on the edge of the desk.

'Becker.' The CAT agent spoke his own name with a hint of menace.

'Commander, Carlton. Get a team together immediately. The fugitive Michael Byrne is on a plane bound for New York.'

45

New York's La Guardia airport was awash in a bright September sky as the executive jet taxied towards a hangar, sparkling in the sun.

The plane's interior was wood-panelled with private sleeping quarters at the rear. Amongst the plush leather seats was a two-seat couch running along the side. It was here that Larry was perched on the edge of his seat.

The stewardess, a very neat and very tidy fortysomething Puerto Rican, approached him. 'Just to let you know, sir, we have been asked to clear the runway and we will be disembarking in one of the hangars.'

Larry mumbled a thank you.

The stewardess gave a professionally warm smile and made her way forward and waited by the door they would be exiting from. The cabin dimmed as they entered the hangar. Larry, scared, had to fight shivering nerves. Had to remember what he'd been told. Mustn't think about Imelda or their unborn child. Mustn't think of the things he craved most in the world because he would fold under the fear. Just remember what will happen.

The aircraft came to a halt. The note of its engines fell from their high pitch to the lower rumble of motors slowing, motors closing down. The stewardess worked the controls of the plane's exit. She lowered the plane door and descended the steps out of the aircraft.

Larry wished with all his being that Imelda was there. That he could hug her one more time. Desperately wanted to tell the woman who finally loved him the way he had always wanted to be loved that he loved her too. Instead he slid back in his seat, picked his corduroy jacket up from beside him and hid his face in it, breathing through the cloth. Doing his best. Doing his very best to protect himself from what was happening. From the tear gas canister that he had been told would be lobbed into the cabin. From the black-armoured storm troopers raging into the plane. From the beams of lights sighted down the barrels of automatic weapons.

'Nobody move! This is the United States Secret Service!'

The gas-masked Counter Assault Team agent swept the beam of his laser-sighted submachine gun through the smoke and across the cowering, coughing figure of Larry and knew immediately that this was not a person he was targeting. He moved towards the private cabin in the rear, approaching with gun at shoulder height, with gun at the ready. Knowing that despite assurances that no guns had been brought aboard he should be ready for any eventuality. The CAT agent, now joined by three others, moving up the aisle, approaching the back of the plane. The CAT agent pausing by the door to the private cabin at the rear. Facing his colleagues. Silent hand signals. *I will kick it open and drop to my knees. You will take a position behind me. You cover the suspect on the couch.*

Fingers counting down. *Three. Two. One.*

The door kicked open, the roar of commands, 'Hands where I can see them, face down, now! Now! Now!'

46

Martinez and I stepped carefully down the steps of the Falcon executive jet. It stood inside a small aircraft hangar. On a wall opposite hung a sign that read TETERBORO AIRPORT.

Standing on the tarmac, leaning with his back against a green two-tone seventies muscle car, was Detective Ashby of the NYPD. Martinez put out a hand and they exchanged a war-buddy handshake, more like the beginning of a mid-air arm-wrestle than anything else.

'Marti.'

'Ashby.'

Martinez stepped back to make space for me, self-conscious, almost like a girl introducing a new boyfriend to her parents.

'You know Michael Byrne.'

I could see from his body language that we weren't about to hug or anything.

I looked at his motor. A car bought with the heart not the head. 'Nice wheels.'

He nodded in a small way a few times. Slowly. On his time. '1970 Dodge Challenger. The same one they used in *Vanishing Point*, the Barry Newman flick. That scene at the end, when he drives into those bull-dozers and it explodes? Bam. I knew then that I just had to have one. Driven it every day since.'

Martinez coughed as she spoke. 'Yeah, great for undercover work.'

Detective Ashby stood up off the side of the car with a frosty air that was doing nothing to break the subzero mood. Martinez tried to find a break in the ice.

'Look, Ashby, thanks for doing this. We have to get to Rankin and we don't have much time.'

'Yeah, I got Johansson on it, he's solid. They've been trailing him since you called. Rankin's currently at the First Bank offices on Madison Avenue.' Never taking his eyes off me.

Martinez looked at us both urgently. 'Unless you have any better ideas I say we go to his offices and find out what the hell's going down – even if we have to beat it out of him.'

Ashby stroked his chin. 'Yeah, well, I got a better idea. A much better idea.'

Before anybody could react Ashby – moving with the speed of a hummingbird – had his gun in his hand and pointed at my gut.

Martinez couldn't believe her eyes. 'Ashby, what the fuck are you doing?'

His eyes still on me. 'I'm doing what you should have done days ago – I'm arresting his crackerjack ass.'

'Ashby!'

'There's some plastic handcuffs on the passenger seat, Martinez, get 'em. We're not having David Blaine doing any more TV specials.'

'Ashby, we haven't got time for this.'

'Yes we have.'

'There is a group of people conspiring to attack Potus, Ashby, what the fuck?'

'Potus? Who the fuck is Potus?'

Martinez couldn't believe it. 'The President of the United States. Don't you watch *24*?'

'You know I don't. I'm a *CSI* and *Wire* guy. And if somebody's planning an attack on "Potus" then tell it to the Secret Service.'

Martinez was almost pulling her hair out. 'Ashby, the conspiracy *involves* the Secret Service.'

I saw the flicker of doubt in his eye, the flicker of hope for us.

'What the fuck you on about?'

'The head of the Secret Service is wrapped up in this. If we don't try to stop this, nobody will. I'm telling you the truth, Ashby, please.'

I could see the hand holding the gun gripping and re-gripping. Uncertainty. Hesitancy. A gap for us to escape through. Could she turn him or should I disarm him? *Could* I disarm him? Should I swipe his gun to the side, knock him out, allowing us to get away? But could I do that and still carry Martinez with me . . . ? I doubted it.

Ashby threw her a quick glance. 'It's not just Rankin and the Russians?'

'No, Ashby, it centres around First Bank, but it goes all the way to the top.'

'Look . . .'

They both looked at me.

'If it's any consolation, Ashby, I'm happy for you to arrest me once this is all over. But first we have to deal with whatever is about to happen during the president's visit.'

Martinez threw me a filthy look. 'You said *I* could arrest you. I'm the one without the badge and a gun here.'

Ashby kept his gun on me but was looking directly at her now. 'What do you think's going to happen to me when they find out I smuggled you guys back to Manhattan in the middle of a manhunt?'

Martinez was hands on hips now. 'Do you realize the shit I have been through in the last few days? I've lost my badge, my gun, been shot at —'

'*You've* been through —'

I put my hands up. 'Guys, can we continue this in the car?'

I was already in the back when they moodily slammed their respective car doors shut.

'He's my arrest, Marti.' Ashby turned on the ignition.

'He's mine.'

'No, he's *mine*.'

I interjected. 'Ashby, you're wrong.'

He turned in his seat, a threatening look on his face, wanting to stare me down. 'Oh – you certain about that?' Still undecided about me.

'This isn't the car they used in *Vanishing Point*.'

'You what? I think I know the car they used. It was a 1970 Dodge Challenger R/T with a 440 cubic-inch V8 engine. You're sitting in the *exact same* model, my friend.'

I did my best sympathetic face. 'Yeah, but the car that actually exploded at the end – the one you fell in love with? – it was the stand-in car, a 1967 Camaro. If you look carefully you can see the name on the fender at the end of the shot.'

Ashby stared at me. Speechless.

Martinez exploded with laughter. 'You freak, Ashby! You bought the wrong fucking car! You freak! Oh, Byrne, you've made my fucking day!'

Ashby levelled a fuming stare that went from me to his laughing partner. He placed his police light on top of the car. 'One more word from anybody and I'm driving this heap of shit into the Hudson.'

Ashby pulled away with a screech of tyres, the car's siren screaming as the car raced towards New York City.

47

Jeremiah Rankin's PA stood at the door of his office. Looking towards the bank CEO behind his desk, at the end of the long room, he suddenly looked small to her. Not the man whose ferocity had built the bank into the investment powerhouse of the late 1990s and beginning of the twenty-first century. Not the man whose prowess and wealth and drive had captivated her, thrilled her, bedded her. Instead he was looking like a broken figure, as broken as the bank.

'Jerry?'

Rankin took a moment to look up. Took a moment to register. 'Zoe. Yeah. What is it?'

'The team from the SEC would like you to join them in the board room.'

'OK.'

'Are you going to?'

'No.'

'They kind of . . .' She tailed off, her nerves shot.

He waited. 'They kind of what, Zoe?'

'They kind of insisted.'

'The answer's no. Have you managed to get Charlie on the line?'

'He's still not taking your calls, Jerry.'

Rankin nodded. Like he understood.

'Jerry?'

Very slowly he looked at her. 'What is it, Zoe?'

She was waiting by the door for she didn't know what. Wanting to ask if there was anything else, if there was anything she could do – if there was anything anyone could do.

'So, we're all moving out.'

'No, Zoe, don't listen to that bullshit. It's all going to be OK.'

She had to fight back the tears. 'I was talking about the office move. They're moving everybody at executive level this weekend. To the new building.'

'Oh. Yeah. Are they? Oh. Yeah, sorry, they are, yeah. I misunderstood. Um, get me a coffee, Zoe, would you.'

'No problem, Jerry.'

She left, spooked by the otherworldliness of her boss, wiping the tears from her face.

After Zoe had left Rankin stared at his phone. Trance-like. Tired now, tired and cornered. After a minute of this he snapped out of it, galvanized himself. Had to make the call. Hoped to god it would work. He dialled a number. Then –

'Hi. Look, we need to change things.'

*

Moffat Agron stood leaning against a low rail at the bow of the motor cruiser yacht in the North Cove Marina. Across the river from the marina stood New Jersey, its modest high-rise buildings feeling almost half-hearted against the bombastic statement that was the cluster of buildings scraping the skies of Lower Manhattan. But the Omega Bank CEO wasn't appreciating either view, even though both shorelines were backed by a powder blue September sky. He was preoccupied by his phone call. Worried by his phone call.

'Change things? I don't understand why you're introducing problems here.'

Rankin stood at the panoramic window in his office on Madison Avenue, Manhattan down below.

'I didn't say there was a problem. In fact, it's an opportunity. You'd still get paid, but I'm telling you, we can achieve *everything* we want to achieve without the fallout from the second trade. If I announce we are considering going into liquidation – a Chapter 7 filing – at 3.45, the market will drop like a stone. Then tomorrow I just reverse my decision and the fall out will be nobody's problem but mine. Because the fallout from the second trade – I mean, that's as serious a heap of shit you could ever get into. Why would you not want to do this?'

An NYPD Harbour Patrol boat skimmed along the river, at the rear a spotter with telescopic binoculars scanning the shoreline. Agron ignored it, concentrating on his phone. Talking into it at arm's length, receiving Rankin on the speakerphone.

'But I thought you had other parties to consider here, *nyet?*'

'Don't worry about that end of it, that's my problem.'

Rankin leaned his forehead against the window at the soul-sapping nature of his predicament. 'I'm willing to live with the consequences here. Please, I don't want to do the second trade.'

'But you are forgetting, a trade was entered into, you cannot back out of a trade, you cannot break your word – the dice are rolled.'

Rankin clenched a fist against the window. 'No, no, I don't want to roll – I want to *un*-roll the dice, they're *my* fucking dice. This is *my* operation, my trade, my decision. I'm telling you to undo it.'

Moffat Agron looked out across the Hudson, thinking, calculating. 'You have to consider my situation here.'

'What situation?' Rankin's rising desperation evident over the speaker.

'My hands are clean of this. I don't even know the details of how the second trade is going to be placed.'

Rankin's eyes searched the city below as if the truth lay hidden down between the buildings. He didn't believe his Russian counterpart now, didn't know what game was being played, didn't know if *he* was being played. 'Well, I have some good news. I know about the second trade. And I'll deal with it.'

413

Agron stood, speaking *at* the phone now. 'No, no, this is not what we agreed. I must insist that you do *not* proceed with –' But he saw that the call had been ended. He screwed his eyes up in anger. '*Pizdets.*' He leaned against the railing and shook his head at the fuck-up rolling out before him.

'Do you think he's bluffing?' The question coming from behind him.

The Omega Bank executive stood and turned round to face Deputy Director Carlton, standing against the bridge of the boat. Unobtrusive, like a shadow.

'I don't know. I mean, he was on the Bell Platform with us, he may have seen it.'

Carlton gritted his teeth, biting his tongue on the remonstrations he wanted to deliver. 'Fucking gutless bankers. They don't mind raping millions of people – but ask them to kill a few hundred and Jesus . . .'

'We could always trigger the bomb early . . . ?'

Carlton eyed him, almost suspiciously. 'Do you have the number?'

'Me?' Agron was disbelieving. 'Have you lost your mind? I want nothing to do with it. Dimitriov has it.'

Carlton wrestled with some options but, agonizingly, had to discard them. 'No, no. It wouldn't work. Rankin's right, any earlier and the markets will correct themselves. We need this to be chaos until close of business. If First Bank goes under, shit, the dominoes that will knock over will undo all our good work.'

Agron sat against the railings. 'What do you want to do?'

Carlton faced the river and took in a deep breath. He felt nauseous. The wheels were coming off his juggernaut. It had been gold dust getting Diane Mason to run this detail, keeping the whole Protection operation at arm's length from himself. It was a masterstroke turning a desperate investment bank CEO to his agenda, bending Rankin to his will. A bank willing to launder all the money for the black ops that lay ahead? It was priceless. It opened the way for the funding of all the proxy battles Carlton wanted kept off the Washington radar, it was beyond perfect, it was the freedom to fight dirtier than anybody had ever dreamt the United States was capable of: the freedom to *take the fight to the enemy*. Carlton was on the cusp of creating the shadow agency the nation had always needed. Let others fight over the White House – he just wanted to head up the AAA: the Anti-American Agency with its global reach and domestic dominance. He wanted to be its J. Edgar Hoover, its legend. Get to the Senate, drive through the legislation – then reshape America and change the world.

But Rankin was doing his utmost to fuck it all up.

Now he, the Deputy Director of the United States Secret Service, was being sucked into the terrible events about to befall his country on the eve of announcing his candidacy for the Senate. And the only

415

way to fix it, the only way to see the plan through, was to take direct control of the operation immediately.

'I want to stop Rankin before he stops the bomb. Agron, get some men together. Now.'

Overhead a huge Kestrel helicopter in presidential livery was flying low along the shoreline. Coming in to land.

48

The approach to the Holland Tunnel was chaos, vehicles backing up all the way to the Pulaski Skyway. I immediately concluded that it was Mason's protection plan that was causing the major rerouting of traffic flow. We had had an OK journey from Teterboro so far but now we were inching along as the merging of the New Jersey Turnpike with our skyway doubled the number of vehicles and then some. We had slowed to nothing.

I checked my watch. 2.46. Time ticking away. Getting a helicopter to one of the Downtown helipads had proved impossible with the no-fly-zone surrounding the president's visit. So we were stuck in traffic. As I had feared.

I looked past Ashby at the sea of cars snaking up ahead. 'What's going on?'

'They've limited all the traffic to the west-bound tunnel.'

Martinez and I both exclaimed as one at the prospect of being jammed in there for the next two hours. It just wasn't an option. Martinez smacked her forehead in frustration.

'Jesus, Ashby, I *told* you to take the Lincoln Tunnel. What were you thinking?'

Ashby barely raised an eyebrow. 'You finished?'

'Don't, Ashby, just don't. Not today, OK?' Each knowing how to rile and get riled by the other.

To our surprise her partner was all smiles.

'Don't stress it, Marti. They're allowing emergency services through the east-bound tunnel – our journey just got quicker.'

Confronted by the log-jam of vehicles ahead Ashby booted up his lights and sirens and, after the typical initial difficulty, the crawling lines of cars pulled to the right creating a space for us to travel down. I swapped a small, relieved look with Martinez. Finally, a break.

Impatiently I looked up ahead and was gratified to see the top of the multi-lane-wide sign above the Holland Tunnel. We were picking up speed and I dared to hope the worst of the journey was about to be behind us.

Except then something caught my eye.

A helicopter. A black helicopter with tinted windows, tilted forward, keeping abreast of us, a few hundred yards across the turnpike.

I pointed at it. 'Hey, guys, what's that?'

At that moment both Martinez and myself slid to the right as Ashby over-cautiously steered round some traffic.

Martinez strained to see through the cars we were tearing by. 'What's what, Byrne?'

'What's *that?*' And a break in the skyline as we headed for the Holland Tunnel suddenly revealed it. Closer now. Closer to our vehicle because *it* had been worried about losing *us*.

Martinez was peering up through the windscreen and was alarmed by how obviously it was tracking us, veering away now. 'What the fuck? Ashby, what's going on?'

All the city traffic was being filtered north up Jersey Avenue. We emerged from this into an empty space. The entrance to the Holland Tunnel was wide open, nothing between us and it. Suddenly we had a dozen lanes to ourselves as we pelted towards the entrance.

'I haven't got a clue. I didn't speak to a soul. Not a soul.'

Ashby flicked a look at me in the rear-view mirror and the eyes matched the voice. They were *wrong*.

We were in the tunnel before I could make my next move. Martinez cried out.

'Byrne . . . ?'

I had thrown an arm round the front of Ashby, not to attack but to get the gun from inside his jacket. I succeeded, escaping a flailing hand that he clawed at me, but reality made me reassess the progress I had made.

Ashby slammed the brakes on – hard – until we halted, came to a standstill with the screeching of burning rubber, throwing up a cloud of smoke. A cloud that slowly caught up with us then drifted over and past us. Towards the pair of bulldozers blocking our path and the two dozen Counter Assault Team members positioned behind the massive shovels, pointing their guns at us.

Martinez cried out again, aghast at this turn of events. '*Ashby?*'

He eyed us both carefully, backed against his door as he was. He spoke with a scintilla of remorse, but no more. 'Oh, come on, Martinez. Orders is orders.'

Martinez looked from her partner to the deadly line of CAT agents.

I shoved the gun at Ashby's face. 'Back it up now.'

He shook his head. 'I think it's a bit late for that, Byrne.'

I misunderstood him for a moment then the sounds behind us told their own story. I turned and looked out of the back of the car. The entrance to the tunnel, two hundred and fifty or so yards away, had been sealed off by a phalanx of armoured anti-riot vehicles. There was no way the car was smashing its way out in that direction. Either direction, in fact.

Martinez looked at Ashby like she didn't recognize him, like she couldn't bear to be near him. 'But why? Why?'

'Come on, Martinez . . .'

He carefully reached out to her, inviting her to join him. She screamed a scream that was pure anger, pure fury, causing Ashby to whip his hand away like he'd burnt it.

'Don't touch me! Don't you *dare* touch me!'

I put my anger with Ashby – and myself – to one side. I pointed the gun at him. 'Now what happens?'

Commander Becker stood behind the barricade afforded by the bulldozers' front-shovels. About him twenty of his team pointed their weapons at the occupants of the car fifty yards away, the Dodge Challenger parked slightly askew due to its emergency stop. The Counter Assault Agents were body-armoured up, including helmets and balaclavas, somehow resembling a South American government death squad.

The car's police lights on top and in the front grille were still flashing, its sirens still whup-whup-whupping.

Beside Becker stood a subordinate holding a loudhailer and microphone on an extendable cable. Becker held out his hand and the CAT agent passed him the mic. He put the comms unit to his mouth, his eyes never leaving the targets.

'Please turn off your lights and sirens.' His voice boomed mechanically off the tunnel walls, echoing eerily about them.

None of us reacted initially, the completeness of the trap self-evident.

Ashby turned his head to me. 'Mind if I turn them off?'

I stole a glance behind us, nobody moving, nobody

needing to. I looked at the CAT agents positioned behind their makeshift and very effective bulldozer barricade.

'Yeah I do mind. If he wants them off then I want them on.'

Ashby sighed like this was petty behaviour that wasn't going to get us far. Martinez watched everything, both of us at the end of the road.

Commander Becker watched the occupants failing to react to his instructions. It irked him. And grimly amused him. He wanted to control the environment. It wasn't yet under control.

He spoke to the assembled CAT agents. 'On my command turn off their lights and sirens.'

His team pulled their MP5s into their shoulders and slid one finger over a trigger each.

'. . . Now!'

With calm and methodical deadliness the two dozen agents began to pour bullets towards the Dodge Challenger, a hail of metal obliterating its rooftop siren, shredding the front grille, then the lights, reducing to debris everything they touched.

Inside the car we were out of sight after the first bullet, all hiding behind the limited cover the car afforded, as the tunnel was filled with gunfire that I could hear tearing the car to pieces about us, the infinite hellish hammers banging so loud that even though all three of us were shouting at the others to 'Get down' not one of us could make ourselves heard above the cacophonous noise.

Beyond the din I could feel the car rocking. I knew it wasn't from any movement on our part but the ruthless plugging of bullet after bullet into the vehicle.

We were powerless to stop it, without any means to resist, to –

It stopped.

It stopped as suddenly as it had started.

Martinez spoke at the same time as me. 'Are you OK?'

But the fact of asking told us we were both OK. For now.

Ashby was whimpering such that I thought he was wounded until I realized it was the beginning of a scream. He sat upright and looked at the Secret Service agents through his windscreen, untouched but for parts of the car that had exploded and landed all about.

'What the fuck? What the fuck Jesus fuck is going on?' He slammed his steering wheel with both hands. Livid. Beyond comprehending what had just gone down.

Martinez spoke slowly and deliberately. 'I repeat, Ashby: we think the conspiracy involves the Secret Service.'

Ashby wasn't buying it. Wasn't having it. He threw his door open.

'We had a goddam deal –'

A fresh tornado of bullets exploded from the CAT agents causing us all to drop out of view again, the mechanical thunderstorm pounding our ears. I peered up to look at the open driver's door, seeing the wing mirror explode into a thousand pieces, the window shattered into splinters of nothingness, the door pierced by such a concentration of bullets that it began to swing down, off its hinges, down until – a butchered skeleton of its former shape – it fell to the ground, sweeping behind us in a shower of bullets.

Again the assault stopped. The first wave of silence almost as oppressive as the gunfire until we adjusted to the new calm.

We rose up again, this time sitting in silence, watching the CAT agents through the settling dust. Knowing their game plan now. I felt Martinez's hand slip back through the front seats, find mine, squeeze mine.

After an effort she managed to speak. 'I think the deal has changed, Ashby.'

He looked at her, his face a picture of regret. 'I'm so sorry, Martinez. Guys, I'm so . . .'

She looked for a moment like she was going to spit in his face. Then the sourness disappeared. 'Oh, what the hell. You could always slam the car into those bulldozers, fulfil your bullshit *Vanishing Point* fantasy. Oh, sorry, forgot, wrong car.'

She gave Ashby a defiant stare – a Fuck You stare.

But she softened when she saw the look of remorse and affection he was wearing for his loose-mouthed partner. They both gave a soft almost-laugh.

'I was thinking of changing it anyway.'

She nodded as she stared ahead. 'Yeah, I hear the 67 Camaro's quite good.'

They both tried to laugh, but couldn't quite get there, their throats too dry.

Martinez turned and for the second time in as many days gave me the brave smile. The look of love. 'So, Byrne, what would Jay-Z do?'

I looked from one to the other with my best and last shot. 'He'd want to know if Ashby's wife packed him a lunch today.'

They both looked at me like it needed repeating.

Commander Becker had stepped away from his line of men, beyond the SUVs they had parked behind the bulldozers and walked a further twenty-five yards away down the deserted tunnel. He had his helmet off, balaclava pushed up onto the top of his head, a cell-phone-like comms unit held to his ear.

'Sir, those weren't our original instructions.'

Deputy Director Carlton stood in Battery Park, at the southern end of Manhattan Island. Before him, approaching across the water, was the one of five Kestrel helicopters bearing the seals of the office of the

President of the United States of America. The helicopter bearing Potus himself.

Like Becker, Carlton had also separated himself from the team he was working with, scores of Secret Service agents forming a ring about the wide expanse of green.

'Becker, a change of plans is not uncommon. All three targets are considered grave threats to the safety of the commander-in-chief.'

Becker looked past his men to the trashed Dodge Challenger and its three trapped occupants.

'Not from here they're not. Sir, if you will . . .'

'. . . I will not, Becker. There is a trail of evidence connecting these people to the deaths of four bank executives, at least six Russian known criminals and the kidnapping of a leading Bermudan banker.'

'But, sir . . .'

Carlton was spitting venom into his phone now, raising his voice to make himself heard over the descending Kestrel helicopter.

'I am *your* commanding officer, Commander Becker, and I *order you* to eliminate those targets. Is that understood? . . . What? . . . What?' The helicopter whipping up the air about him.

'I said, message received and understood, sir.'

The call was over and Becker slowly slipped the comms unit into a front pocket without enthusiasm.

He looked again at the wretched car, its two tones blurred by the blanket of dust that had settled on it from the chaos rained down by their gunfire.

Refusing orders had gotten him court-martialled – with honours – in Afghanistan and he knew from experience there was no upside to fighting them.

He grimaced at the task at hand.

I nestled my cellphone in the bowl I had fashioned out of the tinfoil from Ashby's ham roll. He stared on in a cross between hope and wonder.

'If this works, Byrne, I'm gonna buy my wife a pink Cadillac. Shit, I'll even drive it sometimes.'

Martinez, too, was holding her breath, knowing how slight our chances were. 'Ashby, if this works Mila's gonna spend from now to eternity whooping your behind for what you done to me.'

He pulled a face that was all concession. 'Yeah, you got that right . . . How's it looking, Byrne?'

I shook my head. 'Still no bars. This tinfoil boosts any cellphone signal but we're too far down the tunnel.'

Martinez doubted her next idea before she'd even said it. 'How about we stick it out the window?' She saw the look we started to give her and threw up her hands. 'OK, OK, I forgot about the Bolivian army out there.'

Ashby's face clouded over. 'Right, I've got an idea.

I'm not saying it's any good or nothing, so don't shoot me . . .'

Becker rejoined his men. He had no relish for the task ahead, but knew the only way to deal with such duties was quickly. He turned to deliver his instructions when –

'Sir, they're on the move!'

Becker peered across the barricade to see the battered car struggling to reverse, its engine crippled by their earlier attacks. Nevertheless the vehicle was creeping backwards, crunching over glass, its pained engine wailing pitifully as it did so.

The commander shook his head at their desperation. His shoulder-mounted comms unit broke statically into life.

'Commander, the targets are on the move and heading in our direction.'

Becker nodded to himself, knowing a wounded beast when he saw one. He spoke into the comms unit almost regretfully. 'Take out their rear tyres, would you.'

A burst of static then, 'Affirmative.'

From down the tunnel a short burst of automatic rifle barked out.

The car dropped slightly at the back as its tyres partially rode off the wheels. The Dodge Challenger stopped reversing. Everybody silent, watching the muscle car with a morbid fascination – the death of something unusual, the way one might watch a beached whale dying on the shore.

There was a sudden screaming whine from the car's engine as it was revved to its maximum output, its battered body wrenching itself backwards at an even slower pace, every rotation of the wheels a desperate last gasp.

Becker screwed up his eyes, pained at the pitifulness of their display, pained by what he was about to engineer.

'Somebody stop that car.'

Twenty sub-machine guns raged into life as the CAT agents sprayed 9mm bullets into the front wheels, the rubber tearing off, flying about the car until only the hubs were left, the car settling lower, grinding to a halt.

The gunfire stopped.

Becker took a deep breath. Then his mood changed, darkened. He remembered Byrne escaping from the Secret Service field office in Brooklyn. Remembered Byrne giving him the run-around at the docks and thought, *Stop being such a sentimental prick, Becker.*

Momentarily angry at himself, Becker pulled down his balaclava and retrieved his helmet.

'On my command . . .'

I looked at my phone. One bar and the message 'Sent' on my text app.

Martinez was looking from me to the phone and back again. 'Do you think it worked?'

I closed my eyes for a moment. 'I think it went. I wouldn't bet my life on it.'

Ashby grunted. 'We just did.'

We all shared a hard stare that said 'we gave it our best shot' as well as any words could.

They turned to face the front in time to see what I had just noticed. Two pairs of Counter Assault guys peeling off either side and shuffling their way down their respective walls towards us.

Martinez whipped a look from one pair to another. 'Do you think they're coming to apprehend us?'

Ashby grunted again. 'They've had plenty of opportunity to do that. I think they're moving in for the kill.'

'Byrne, how many bullets you got in that gun?'

'Ashby?' It was his gun I'd taken, after all.

He cast a grim look across the approaching men. 'Less bullets than there are people out there, that's for sure.'

Martinez eyeing with growing alarm. 'Byrne, you know what I said about not killing any law enforcement agents during this investigation? Well, I changed my mind.'

I ordered both of them, 'Get down.'

They both went to ask 'Why' then saw why. They ducked down out of sight and I pointed the revolver through the windscreen and at the nearest CAT agent, just under a hundred yards away. Hoping Diane would understand, I squeezed the trigger.

All four CAT agents froze before one screamed out in agony as his leg buckled from beneath him, his body falling against the tunnel wall then away to the ground.

'Man down!'

'I'm hit!'

'MAN DOWN!'

'Oh fuck, fuck!'

A sudden flurry of gunfire smashed into our car, but it stopped almost immediately, my guess being that they didn't want to hit their own in the crossfire. I could hear a scurrying of feet and a quick glimpse above the dashboard confirmed my prediction that they were getting back behind the makeshift barricade.

Even out of sight, I could hear the injured CAT agent yelling and fighting his yells, his pain echoing off the tunnel walls.

The wounded agent was carried by two of the team to a waiting SUV. Commander Becker was fuming. He couldn't believe he'd taken a casualty. Of all the things . . . Becker had privately cursed Carlton's suggestion of liquidating the targets in the Holland Tunnel. You couldn't use explosives down here, you couldn't get a clear sniper shot. Getting close meant risking *exactly* what had just happened – on *his fucking watch*. An injury meant twice the enquiry afterwards. It was a fuck-up and it hadn't even ended yet.

Furious at Byrne, Carlton and the whole sorry mess, Becker gripped the loudhailer mic in his hand. 'Men, on my command . . .'

We were huddled down in our seats. I felt sick that they were at the front, that they would be the first to go. Martinez grabbed my hand and I received a look that loved life.

She spoke one more time to her partner. 'Ashby, what you thinking about?'

He started to speak, but she never heard the answer. From outside. '. . . Fire!'

Then it began. Waves of bullets, crashing into the car like a hailstorm, buckling the car, bouncing it up an inch or two off the ground, the sound of a million drums banged by the devil himself. The booming, pounding, endless noise. The last we would ever hear.

The windscreen burst in on us as a hurricane of bullets punched pockets of glass out of it, scattering tiny shards about the car. I could feel the front wings of the car ripping as the gunfire ate its way towards us. The engine was being reduced to junk that was atomizing with the relentless spew of semi-automatic fire, the attacks penetrating the car deeper every time, until there was nothing, no car, no protection, between us and the inevitable. The dashboard shaking now, a bullet tearing into one of the seats – the driver's? Dials on the dashboard popping as bullets destroyed them from behind.

The tunnel echoed infernally with every round, every bullet, every hit. Till the noise blurred into one unending metallic roar. A roaring waterfall of gunfire.

And then I saw her, in a garden. Wearing her favourite dress. Wearing the only dress I ever remembered her owning back then. My favourite dress in all the world. She was smelling a single rose. A crimson Paul's Scarlet that she had self-consciously clipped from the climber she had been admiring. Letting its perfume fill her nose. Living in the moment. And for that brief instant I knew she didn't have a care in the world. For that brief second she wasn't married to my dad, she didn't live in a cramped apartment that would soon be condemned, she hadn't missed out on love and laughter. For that brief moment she was anyone and anywhere, but choosing to spend that moment with me. And giving me a smile that was mine and mine alone. And me knowing that all I wanted to do was protect her the way Dad hadn't. Then Mom somewhere else, somewhere that was nowhere, somewhere saying, 'It's not the money, Michael. It's not the money.' And me suddenly understanding, understanding too late. And me wanting to stand in just one more rose garden. Hers. And then . . .

Silence. The world as I knew it had become noiseless, perfectly and utterly still.

I had to remember where I was.

The first thing I sensed was glass and plastic covering my back. Then I remembered . . .

'Jenni –'

Martinez lifted up her own glass-and-plastic-covered head and looked at me strangely, her heart melting. 'You called me Jenni.'

Then a yell outside. 'Jesus H. Fucking Christ!'

I looked up and saw a large man who I assumed to be their commanding officer marching towards us.

Martinez squeezed Ashby's arm. 'You OK?'

Her partner brushed some debris off his head and looked around, dazed and confused. 'What's happening?'

The Counter Assault Team officer was almost with us. I didn't worry about shooting him, somehow I didn't think I'd need to. He watched us as he approached, seeming to seek somebody out. Me. He came to the rear passenger door, opened it and shoved a phone at me.

'It's for you.'

I put it tentatively to my ear. 'Yes?'

'So we're quits now, right?' I recognized the voice. It was the voice of the man I'd texted god knows how many minutes ago. It was Treasury Secretary Peterson.

I was sliding myself out of the car. 'Yeah, well, for now.'

'Great. But next time don't leave it so late. I haven't always got this much pull.'

I took a moment to get my bearings. 'The information we sent, have you been able to do anything?'

Peterson went quiet for a moment. 'No. Not yet. On which note, I gotta go.'

'OK.'

He'd gone and I was looking at a pretty pissed CAT commander. But I didn't care. I was thinking about getting after Rankin and Carlton –

– and then Commander Becker punched me in the jaw, slamming me back against the colander of a car.

I righted myself, waiting for another attack, but realized nothing was coming.

'*That's* for shooting one of my boys.' He stood taller, honour restored. 'Now – where can I give you a ride to?'

49

The Beast, the presidential limousine, was nestled at the centre of a thirty-five-strong escort made up of motorcycle outriders, blacked-out Secret Service Protection SUVs as well as a couple of regular limousines for some city dignitaries. This was not a slow, crowd-pleasing public procession and despite the absence of Special Agent Diane Mason the Secret Service was sticking to its plan of a swift delivery of Potus to the ground-breaking site at the east end of Wall Street. It was a sizeable escort, but between Mason fretting over the myriad vantage points for launching an attack in downtown Manhattan and the White House's chief of staff insisting that the Commander-in-Chief not be upstaged by the rumoured grand arrival of the Chinese premier it was quickly decided that such a large number of vehicles was appropriate.

The presidential convoy was heading down State Street and into Water Street. Every road closed to all traffic but the president's with the sole intention of minimizing any external threats to his safety.

Deputy Director George Carlton sat in the back of a black Secret Service sedan at the very rear of the motorcade. Behind the ambulance carrying the president's blood. He looked up and around himself, seeing with his practised eye the Secret Service agents dotted along the rooftops, allowed himself a humourless smile and thought to himself, *Every external threat planned for.*

Officer Johansson rode his NYPD motorcycle in a deliberately understated fashion, keeping right behind the same taxi he had followed all the way down Madison Avenue. He wasn't interested in the cab in front of him. It was the cab three cars in front that he cared about. That he wasn't going to let out of his sight.

Ashby's voice came out of the walkie talkie on the motorcycle officer's coat lapel, a siren wailing in the background. 'Where are you now, Johansson?'

Officer Johansson didn't take his eyes off the taxi ahead of him. Didn't take his eyes off Rankin in the back seat, looking around nervously, left, right and behind.

'We're south on Broadway and Liberty. Looks like he's heading for Wall Street.'

'Keep on him, Johansson.'

'No problem, sir.'

The officer clicked off his walkie-talkie with a gloved hand, and rode and watched.

*

Another smaller convoy was also heading towards Wall Street. Three colossal, black Chevy Suburbans. They were not attempting to deliver their passengers to their destination in a courtly fashion. They were attempting to deliver them as fast as possible. An exercise they were succeeding in, courtesy of their no-nonsense grille-positioned police lights, blaring sirens and the fact that everybody who saw the black behemoths racing towards them in their rear-view mirrors didn't *need* telling to get the hell out the way.

Ashby, Martinez and I were on the back two benches, Commander Becker – as I had learnt he was called – was up front with a driver.

Ashby was shaking his head. 'I don't get it. He'll never reach the ground-breaking site. There's a ring of steel round that end of Wall Street.'

I hit the call button on my phone, waiting for Diane to answer. 'Come on.'

Martinez looked at me anxiously. 'Is she picking up?'

A cellphone rang repeatedly, unanswered. The phone lying on the desk along with the strewn contents of Special Agent Mason's bag. The agent lay slumped next to it.

Her eyes opened weakly as the ringing stopped.

Then closed again.

*

The yellow cab pulled to a halt on Broadway at a security cordon by the pedestrianized entrance to Wall Street. Rankin jumped out and headed straight for the security barriers where he was stopped by a female Korean NYPD officer.

'I'm afraid you won't be able to get beyond Broad Street, sir, not until the presidential visit is over.'

Rankin's heart was in his mouth. He rubbed his hands in front of his face, as if cold, to hide what he feared were obvious nerves. 'That's OK, I have a meeting closer than that.'

'OK.'

The officer allowed him through, comfortable that he wouldn't be able to get through the inner cordon.

A little distance away Officer Johansson was dismounting his motorcycle, talking into his walkie-talkie as he did. 'Sir, he's just entered Wall Street from Broadway.'

The three black Suburbans, sirens off now, were racing down Broadway.

Ashby spoke into his comms unit. 'We're right behind you.'

The Suburbans pulled up sharp fifty yards from the entrance to Wall Street. Johansson was running towards us before we'd even gotten out of the doors.

'Sir,' speaking to Ashby, 'he didn't go down Wall Street but went into the Stock Exchange.'

Commander Becker spoke like the man tasked with countering any planned or actual assault on the president – impatiently. 'Is that where the attack is happening? Potus is two blocks from there.'

The New York Stock Exchange? Two blocks from the president. Was the bomb *that* powerful? Was the attack going to happen *from* the NYSE? Was I missing something? A sniper attack? What? *Think Byrne, think.*

The Stock Exchange, the New York Stock Exchange, the New York goddamn *Stock Exchange*!

Of course.

I wasn't just missing something, I was missing *everything*. The NYSE. Oh, Byrne, right there in front of your nose, plain as day . . .

Rankin's plan was cascading into place in my mind, starting to make sense . . .

I ran a hand down my face, the totality of what Rankin was planning – so clear I felt overcome, everybody and everything a blur as my mind raced over the events of the week, reinterpreting them, realizing I'd come at this whole thing from the wrong angle, that I'd been barking up the wrong tree the whole time. Martinez saw the turmoil I was in.

'What is it, Byrne? What's up?'

I shook my head. 'Idiot.'

Martinez shaking her head now. 'Who? Who's an idiot?'

I looked at her. I looked at all of them. 'I'm an idiot. There *is* no attack on the president.'

Becker was more confused by the day's events than ever. 'What do you mean, no attack?'

I wanted to stand and berate myself but there wasn't the time. 'Rankin just wants the markets to come off –'

Ashby said it. 'He's going to attack the Stock Exchange.'

Martinez looked from one of us to the other. 'But Potus . . . ?'

'He doesn't need to attack the president. He just has to carry out an attack *near* the president. Imagine how it will look on the news for the first hour. An attack near Potus? The markets will assume the worst, there'll be pandemonium. That's all Rankin wants – more chaos in the witching hour.'

Martinez wasted no time. 'What sort of attack, Byrne?'

I pulled a face that told her I didn't know. 'Could be anything from an outage to razing the NYSE to the ground. Either way, we need to get in there and stop whatever he's planning.'

Martinez shook her head.

'What?'

She looked at me like something was missing for her. 'There's plenty of ways to go about this. But actually killing people? In Wall Street? Don't you think . . . ?'

I finished it for her. 'There's more.'

We looked at each other as we ran it through our minds, neither of us nailing it.

Becker wasn't in the mood for our conjectures. 'What should we do? Is this an attack on Potus or not?'

I was still distracted by what the hell Rankin had planned. 'What did Special Agent Mason tell you to do?'

'Nobody can get hold of Mason.'

My head snapped up at him. 'What do you mean?'

He was matter of fact. 'Nobody's been able to get hold of her since you landed at Teterboro.'

I thought about the chances of Diane ever going AWOL on duty. I thought about the chances of Diane going AWOL on duty on the day she was overseeing protection for Potus. The number zero came back twice in a millisecond.

I returned my gaze to the commander. 'Your job's to protect the president. But get somebody to find Mason and tell her what's happening. We'll take Rankin from here.'

But Ashby wasn't happy. 'Hang on just a minute.' He turned to the CAT commander. 'Becker, can we get a couple of guns here?'

That made the large CAT agent's chest heave with laughter. Contempt and humour all at once. 'Detective, the Treasury Secretary can stop me from shooting you but even he can't get me to give you a gun. That's

442

not about chain of command – that's about rules and regs.'

He bounded into his Suburban, slammed the door and was off. Job done.

Ashby looked after him, mortally offended. 'Son of a bitch kills my car then won't give me a gun.'

I held out his detective-issue revolver. He took it sulkily.

'Damn right, taking my gun off me . . .'

We made our way towards the Stock Exchange and to whatever the hell it was Rankin and Carlton had planned.

A maroon-coloured Chrysler 300 paused on the far side of Broadway. Through the passenger window Byrne, Martinez and Ashby could be seen passing through the police cordon and down towards the NYSE.

'Oh Christ.'

Deputy Director George Carlton watched them with compounded gloom. He sucked in some air, fighting exasperation. He reached inside his jacket and pulled Special Agent Mason's Sig Sauer P229 automatic revolver into his lap. *Who knows, maybe I can pin some of this on Diane yet?* And the thought gave him the first moment of cheer all day. The thought of using the gun. Using it on Michael Byrne.

*

443

A black Lincoln Continental cruised slowly past the scene. Inside, the Thin-haired Russian and three Russian bodyguards looked at the police cordon at the top of Wall Street. The car did not stop but cruised on down Broadway.

50

I followed Martinez and Ashby through security at the New York Stock Exchange. Ashby flashed his detective's badge at a security guard and pushed through a large plain door. I joined them only to be hit by a cacophony of voices yelling, crying, shouting, hollering, ordering, demanding, offering, pleading, cajoling. We had been hit by the unmistakeable din of the New York Stock Exchange trading pit.

The room was enormous, a cathedral to money. The neoclassical design of pillars and high ceilings made the room instantly recognizable as one of the great landmarks of the city. Its vaulted seventy-two-foot-high ceiling and warehouse-size dimensions were truly appropriate for the world's largest stock exchange.

Dotted around the room were kiosks, round counters with a wrap of screens above each of them detailing market information. Like some feverish Exposition there were terminals squeezed in everywhere and somehow the hundreds of brokers, floor traders, specialists and runners here, in their coloured jackets and headsets, made sense and order out of the relentless deluge of financial information.

All these people saw here was information, but all I could see was cover, distraction, places to hide. People to mingle with, people to blend with. Too many exits, too much cover, too many opportunities to hide yourself – or to hide something devastating.

Martinez didn't even try to conceal her frustration at the milling swarm of people. 'Damn it, it's like Grand Central in here.'

We made our way through the throng of stock exchange workers, moved together, looking about, but seeing nothing, hemmed in by the relentless activity. We circled a few kiosks, making no attempt to stay unseen, discretion the last thing on our minds. Startling Rankin might be the best way to flush him out. Wherever the hell he was.

Ashby was despairing. 'Byrne, there must be, like, a million places to hide a fucking bomb down here.'

Martinez cut in. 'But there's only one place to hide it up there.'

We followed her finger, pointed directly at the first floor Bell Platform jutting into the room. Jeremiah Rankin was on the platform, searching around his feet for something.

Ashby instinctively checked for his gun. 'Let's go!'

Rankin peeked out of the Bell Platform exit, the Mont Blanc briefcase clutched to his chest, and checked the corridor both ways. Convinced nobody was around he stepped out, closing the door behind him.

'Hold it right there!'

Rankin froze, not daring to look to see who had spoken. His mind so guilt-ridden that images of SWAT teams throwing him to the ground had almost paralysed him since entering the building.

Ashby walked towards him, gun held out in front of him, aiming at the bank CEO. 'Don't move a mother-fucking inch, motherfucker. You are under arrest for the attempted bombing of the people of New York. You have the right to remain silent and all that shit, but for now let me tell you that you so much as breathe wrong and I will put a bullet in you. Because I have no fucking idea how that fucking thing is triggered so any move is the wrong motherfucking move. Do you motherfucking understand?' Ashby's alarm real, Ashby's concern for our well-being putting him on a pretty short fuse himself. 'A small nod will do. A very fucking small fucking nod.'

Rankin was hunched around the briefcase, holding it tighter than ever, his mind melting down under the implications of an actual arrest. He nodded pathetically.

We had stopped halfway along the corridor. Ashby's eyes were almost twitching as he watched for any movement from Rankin, any suicidal act that might take us all together.

'OK, Rankin. Now I want you to do *exactly* as I s –'

Without warning gunfire peppered the walls about us. We dived aside as plaster and ceiling tiles showered all around. Ashby returned gunfire, once, twice . . .

Rankin's heart leapt uncontrollably at this new injection of chaos. I saw him spin to see what we could see: a small group of armed men in suits. He looked around in desperation and spotting a door leading to a stairwell opposite leapt at it, barging his way through and out of sight.

We beat a quick retreat back towards where we had just come from. Martinez was incandescent.

'Motherfucking Becker and his rules and regs!'

I pointed back the way we had come. 'We need to find a way after him.'

We looked up to see the Russians piling through the stairwell door Rankin had taken a moment earlier, but not before one fired a warning shot back up at us.

Martinez looked through another door. 'Guys, this way.'

The First Bank CEO ran along a basement corridor trying every door handle he found, but each and every one was securely locked. He heard a door crash open behind him.

'Rankin!'

It was a voice he recognized. It was George Carlton's. Not in sight but round a corner. Close – and closing in.

Frantically, looking back as he did so, the terrified First Bank CEO tried another basement door handle not believing it would open. When it did he almost fell into the room, nearly dropping the briefcase in his surprise. Fighting a palpable terror he closed the door as quietly and as quickly as he could then backed into the darkness.

The four Russians tried every door between them, Carlton following at the rear, Special Agent Diane Mason's revolver in his hand, pointing down along his leg. He was in the mood to put a bullet in Rankin. He was in the mood to externalize the feral anger that had overtaken him at having to jeopardize everything he had worked so hard to achieve, had planned so meticulously, all under threat because of a prickless bank CEO.

'Come out, come out wherever you fucking are . . .'

A bald stocky Russian stopped as a door handle he turned surrendered up a room. He looked at everybody and raised a finger to his lips. They all fell in quietly by the door, ready to enter the dark room.

Rankin sat crouched in the dark. About him was the pounding mechanical *thum thum thum* of thousands upon thousands of machines whirring relentlessly away, added to by the sound of hundreds of air-conditioning units. Warm and cold currents of air swirled about him.

His breathing was fast, the breathing of the doomed quarry.

The strip lights came on above.

Rankin flinched, almost squealing. A primal urge surged up inside him. He wanted to beg for mercy, hope to god an ounce of compassion would see him through, but that was his terrified mind speaking. His rational mind clawed its way back. Told him that he could only fight his way out of here. How many men had he seen? Three? Four? Plus Carlton. He'd *heard* Carlton. No, no, *no*. How did he fight his way out of this?

At the entrance to the room stood Deputy Director Carlton, the Thin-haired Russian and three Russian bodyguards – one bald and stocky, one with a buzz cut and one with blond hair slicked back into a pony tail.

They took their time, taking in the room. It was the communications room that served the New York Stock Exchange, a mammoth space with rack upon rack upon rack holding all the computers, servers, telephonic equipment and power units that supported the operation above. The room was laid out like a library with partition after partition of whirring equipment. There was a route down the middle and each side. Carlton nodded at a pair to search down a flank each whilst he walked down the middle.

They walked in tandem, emerging from each row

of servers together, walking slowly, cautiously, determinedly. Around them millions of dollars' worth of bonds, equities and options from every corner of the globe were changing hands every second. Traders in Tokyo, London, Hong Kong, San Francisco, Frankfurt and beyond were buying and selling from each other at a relentless pace, the servers blinking as they processed the torrent of trades, travelling at the speed of money. All working their way through the servers in this room. And were the server they depended on to fail, within a second the trade would be rerouted to another server within the self-same room. And were the room itself to fail, the power to cut, the telephone lines to drop, the very room itself wiped out by accident or design, every last trade would be rerouted to the disaster-recovery site in New Jersey. A back-up facility costing tens of millions of dollars, that had never been used, and – everybody upstairs hoped – would never be used ... But a back-up facility that Carlton fervently hoped would be used before the working day was through.

'Mr Carlton.' It was the bald, stocky Russian who had spoken, but they all saw it together. Rankin, crouched on the floor of a half-empty server cabinet, the briefcase open before him, a hand hovering inside.

'Come any closer and I will take us all together, so help me god.'

The Russians stood their ground, but each became

decidedly wary of this new development. Carlton laughed it off menacingly. He looked down at Rankin.

'What? And not become a billionaire? Not stick a rigid middle finger up at every big swinging dick on the Street? Not have the pleasure of phoning up that prick Peterson and telling him that you'll be suing the Treasury and the SEC and the Fed into the next century for butchering the good name of First Bank? We pull this off, Jerry, the whole game changes. We both get what we want, we both get what we agreed.' His warm commanding tone tempered by his private need to get the bomb back in place, get the plan back on track.

Rankin, almost pleading now. 'But why complicate things, why attract all this heat – why murder . . . I mean, people don't have to die . . .'

'Yes they do, Jerry, they always do. Every great advance in human history was achieved through *blood*, sweat and tears. It's nature, Jerry, red in tooth and claw. More people died in Africa yesterday than are about to die here today. Did you do anything about it? . . . Do you really care about people *that* much? Of course you don't. But if we don't do this, Jerry, if we let America continue to bend its knee to every yellow fucking imperialist from across the Pacific the streets of this great country will flow with blood. This isn't about you and it isn't about me – it's about the destiny of the United States.'

Rankin bent over the briefcase, his face creased up, tears rolling down his cheeks. 'But why take the risk, George . . . ?'

'You're a banker, Jerry, you love risk – that's where the money's made. And, anyway, you don't get your billion without my deaths. What's it gonna be?'

Rankin wiped the back of his hand across his nose, partially clearing the mucus and tears away. Carlton leaned in towards him, sensing, correctly, that the fight had gone out of the bank CEO. Gently, he took the briefcase.

'It's OK, Jerry. It's OK, I understand . . .'

And Carlton had the case away from the bank CEO, Rankin rocking quietly, almost delirious in his torment and conflict.

Carlton righted himself, closing the briefcase as he did. 'There, now we can get on with our day?'

Then he shot Rankin through the leg.

Rankin's howls filled the room, screaming in pain and surprise, disbelieving, angry, confused. 'What the fuck, George, what the fuck did you do –?'

Carlton's face contorted with hate. 'Why? Why? You fucking cunt, fucking my plans up because of your belated attack of conscience. You cunt, you stupid fucking cunt . . .'

Carlton in his fury stamped on Rankin's wound, causing the bank CEO to scream like a snared beast, agonized and helpless. Carlton stamped again and again, kicking Rankin now, just wanting to hurt him, until the Thin-haired Russian stepped in and pulled Carlton back.

'Mr Carlton, please, we need to go . . .'

And that was when the lights went out.

51

For a moment it was pitch black, then everybody's eyes adjusted. The walls of loudly humming servers were now clearly visible and the effect of their rows and columns of red and green and yellow and blue square lights was to suggest some technopolis-Manhattan skyline at night. A soft ghostly glow gave everybody enough form to make each other out, but not enough to see more than ten feet ahead.

Rankin lay moaning.

Carlton bent down to him and spoke in a threatening whisper. 'What noise does a dead banker make?'

Rankin took his moaning to a whimper and then some hard breathing, desperate to quash his own noises. Carlton nodded at the Russians to return the way they had come. They fanned out, but now it was hard to see each other walking along the rows of servers, so low was the light.

Walking was precarious. The soft neon glow of the servers was not enough to light the aisles that had fallen into darkness. The five men walked carefully back in the direction of the exit, this time more uncertain, each with their gun ready, aimed ahead of them, ready to fire at a moment's provocation, the slightest threat. They walked in near silence. Waiting for the interlopers, the trespassers, to give themselves away. But, despite themselves, they each found that as they moved through the dark room they were unsure of their footing, as if the ground not being there was a possibility.

They progressed through their respective aisles like shimmering ghosts, not trusting the shadows. Each of them agitated, hating the silence, hating the vulnerability of the darkness, hating that the rules had changed, wanting to break the tension by firing off their weapon. It was worst for the Thin-haired Russian. He ran his bony fingers through his hair, a bundle of nerves at having to be in a situation of gunplay, of stealth, of possible hand-to-hand combat. He made bombs – he was meant to be a hundred miles away from his victims. Too far away for them to hurt him.

On one side of the room there was a crash, some cries, the falling of a body, gunshots, everybody suddenly shooting, the Russians, Carlton, their jangling nerves finding relief in their desperate attacks, firing wildly. Then all at once each of them collecting themselves, sensing their loss of control. Regaining it.

Then nothing.

Everybody stock still.

Everybody trying to gauge what the fuck was going on.

Somebody lay on the floor making low semi-conscious sobbing sounds. Carlton carefully edged towards the sound, knowing it to be one of his own, when his foot hit something. He looked down. The buzz-cut bodyguard was disabled, on his back, wanting to move but unable to. A cylinder, a fire extinguisher, which Carlton quickly concluded had done the damage, lay beside him.

The sound of activity elsewhere in the server room had all four standing alert, wired.

Carlton hissed at the others. 'Go and get them.'

The three remaining Russians carefully continued down the aisles. Carlton edged his way back to the middle of the server room, stood his ground, wanting the fight over before he got further involved.

I watched the bald bodyguard step nervously through the electronic gloom. I could see that he was way out of his comfort zone, probably willing the lights to come on so he could thrash it out with his antagonists. Thrash it out with me. He wasn't one to hide in the dark – he was used to seeing the whites of people's eyes, smelling their sweat as they exchanged blows. Even in the dark I could sense that cloak and dagger unsettled him, needled him, meaning that his anger and nerves were presently vying for his attention, overwhelming him. Which made him careless, careless when the network cable slipped round his neck and

I pulled it tight about his throat, cutting off the oxygen, the blood, the life. He reached behind him, over his shoulders, grabbing at the air, wanting to grab any part of me. But I was low, pulling tight, pulling with all my strength, a flailing foot kicking off my shin uselessly, me fiercely pulling the stocky bodyguard until he was lifted off his feet.

A useless shot of the revolver into the ground was his last act.

I lowered him gently to the floor and took the gun.

Along the central aisle Martinez, armed only with a small chemical fire extinguisher, crept along, hunting for any sign of life, watching for a person to engulf in a suffocating cloud of CO_2. But no one lay in wait. Instead she felt the muzzle of a gun on the side of her head. Fuck.

'One move and you're dead.'

She didn't doubt that Carlton meant every word he had just said. She stood rooted to the spot.

'Put that down.'

Very slowly she lowered the canister to the floor.

Carlton raised his voice for all to hear. 'Either you give yourselves up or I shoot the girl.'

I froze, a rush of different emotions pumping through me, concern for Martinez, doubt at the veracity of his words . . . Bluff? Forcing a mistake? I needed to stay alert, to be alive to every deadly development. The room had gone still, everybody waiting for another to make a move.

Martinez broke the silence. 'Fuck him, guys – kill these fuckers.'

She wasn't sure if she heard the sound first or felt the explosion of pain in her shoulder as she slammed off a server and onto the floor.

'Oh *Jesus*!'

Martinez reached a hand up helplessly to the hole in her shoulder, the air connecting with the wound, a searing lava-hot poker of pain penetrating her, overwhelming her.

I tried to place Carlton. Was he to my left? My right? The dark had gone from being my friend to my enemy.

Then Carlton speaking to the room. 'Shall I finish her off?'

Martinez, through her pain, shouted to us. 'Fuck you, you motherfucker. Kill him. Finish the job!'

'Spunky little thing, it might take three bullets, maybe four. Here, let me try . . .'

'OK, OK, all right.' It was Ashby, flicking on the lights, seeing Carlton at the same time as me, in a space at the centre of the room. Martinez moaning angrily with pain somewhere out of my line of sight.

Ashby and I stood waiting for Carlton to make the

next move. He waved us closer with his gun, too edgy himself to speak at first. I carefully stepped out into the centre with my hands up. I gave Ashby a look of What The Fuck Have You Done? before seeing Martinez propping herself up against a server, a bloody wound in her shoulder rendering her incapacitated on the floor. Seeing her gasping, hurting, I felt a sudden rage at Carlton, a desire to hurt him, rip his jaw off in my hands, anything to punish him. But a small thin-haired Russian relieved me of my newly acquired gun and held me at gunpoint, and a ponytailed bodyguard had his gun trained on Ashby. Martinez looked at me and tried to pull a brave, reassuring face. Only Martinez.

Carlton looked at the scene with something approaching repulsion and put the Mont Blanc briefcase down between two rows of servers. 'What the hell am I supposed to do now? This is not how this fucking thing was meant to happen.'

Ashby spoke almost politely. 'Sir, if I may . . .'

Carlton gave Ashby a quizzical look. Ashby took that as invitation enough to continue and stepped gingerly into the central clearing like he was walking on eggshells. Holding his revolver with his fingertips, he carefully reholstered it for everybody to see.

'Now, Deputy Director, sir, I do believe there is a win-win situation to be had here.'

Carlton looked at him with a profound sense of

incredulous curiosity. 'What deal could you possibly believe I would enter into with you?'

Ashby cautiously picked his way towards me, making sure everybody could see what he was doing so as not to set off any panic. Very slowly he lifted the side of his jacket and delicately unhooked some handcuffs off his belt.

'If I may be allowed . . . ?'

Carlton had enough interest to see this partway through at least. 'Go on.'

Ashby went round the back of me and to my dismay cuffed me – in clear view of the Thin-haired Russian – to a rack of servers. Ashby mindful of not making any sudden movements, of not causing any alarm.

Now Ashby was wearing his best Denzel Washington smile, where no bird in any tree was safe from his charms. 'You see, you want Byrne and I want Martinez. You want the bomb – I want to get the fuck outta here. Afterwards it's your word against ours and you've got the bigger cojones so it all works out.'

Carlton seemed genuinely taken with the proposition. 'Fascinating. It all makes perfect sense. You take your little girlfriend here up to safety and I stay here to kill Byrne – and assorted others.'

Ashby smiled winningly, like he'd finally met a man on his own wavelength. 'Exactly.'

Carlton put his gun to his mouth as if giving due consideration to the proposition. 'Yeah, in fact, I could see myself going for it – if I was as dumb as you clearly think I am.'

The deputy director pointed his gun at Ashby. I knew enough about the body language of gunmen to know what was coming next. So did the detective. On the floor Martinez defied her pain with a reflexive cry of alarm.

Time stood still. The very sound of the servers themselves seeming to slow in the moment.

We all knew what he was about to do and couldn't do anything about it before it was done.

He pulled the trigger –

All the oxygen seemed to vanish from the room –

Ashby's eyes widened –

The gun clicked. Empty.

Oh fuck, oh god in heaven, we breathed again . . .

Carlton threw up his hands, despairing of nothing going right, as if it were everybody else's fault. 'Mary wept!' He turned to Ponytail. 'Well, kill him, then, kill him.'

Ponytail turned his gun on Ashby. But Ashby wasn't waiting a second time. Before he could get off a bullet Ashby had his gun out of his shoulder holster and in his hand. He fired at the Russian, but not before the Russian had fired at him.

Both of them flew across the room, launched away from each other by the other's shot. The Russian hit in the chest, Ashby hit in the stomach, both down and out, out of the game.

Carlton looked about himself startled. Somehow, even in the gunfight, his attention had switched to something else. 'I don't believe this . . . Where's the briefcase?' Frantic now, looking around. 'Where's the fucking briefcase? Where *is it*?'

We all looked round as the door to the server room slammed shut at the far end. Carlton checked everybody, trying to see who was missing. Martinez on the floor, me handcuffed to the server rack, the Thin-haired Russian pointing his gun at me, Ponytail and Ashby bleeding to death if they weren't already dead. Then he realized what had happened.

'That fuck Rankin. That . . .' He slammed a fist through the air, his patience stretched to breaking. He spun round to the Thin-haired Russian. 'That does it – detonate the bomb.'

The small nervous man was shocked. 'But we'll be buried in rubble.'

An anger that would not be brooked was rising in Carlton. 'Good, it'll provide the first fucking alibi I've had all day. He'll be in the street by the time you call him – just make the call.'

Carlton leaned down and impatiently pulled the revolver from Ponytail's hand. The bodyguard, his chest blown open, was dribbling blood, mumbling into the afterlife.

The Thin-haired Russian pulled out his cellphone. I was standing next to him, surreptitiously feeling the server behind me with my fingers. I knew what Ashby's plan had been — to pull my little Houdini stunt — but Ashby didn't realize I needed a pin of some sort to do my part, he hadn't stopped to think how it was actually done . . . *Right now I was as handcuffed as the next guy.*

The Thin-haired Russian scrolled down his phone, presumably looking for the number to the briefcase's detonator. I was pulling at different switches with my fingers frenetically behind me, desperate to pull one out. I was appalled at what was about to happen, at what I couldn't stop. Rankin would be running past people, innocent people, maybe towards the president, maybe away, but this was New York, a living, breathing city. People were everywhere: the carnage, the bloodletting would be immense . . .

The small man found the number he was looking for. He looked up at his employer, concerned. 'You want I should call now?'

A switch from one of the server covers pulled away in my fingers. I turned it in my hands, the back a perfect pin. A perfect pin for what I had to do but there wasn't time —

Carlton waved his gun at the Thin-haired Russian dismissively. 'Just do it. *Please.*'

Me digging away with the pin. Watching the Russian's thumb hover over the green CALL button of his phone. The Thin-haired Russian shaking his head like this was one dumb fucking idea, but hitting the button anyway.

Me levering the pin inside the handcuff lock.

Carlton impatient. '*Well?*'

Me straining, the pin insufficient, straining to unlock the cuffs. Had I bent it into the right shape? Was it strong enough to lever open the catch? Needing more time, not going to make it . . .

The Thin-haired Russian watching the cellphone, me exchanging a look of desperate concern with the struggling Martinez, both of us knowing that this was an attack we couldn't stop. Both of us watching the Thin-haired Russian watching his cellphone then looking up at Carlton.

'No signal.'

Had I heard right? No signal . . . ? Jesus. I sagged against the rack behind me, heaving a sigh of relief. 'Oh, you mother.'

The Thin-haired Russian considered me indifferently. So wasn't expecting the fist that I swung round and into his face.

The small skinny man bounced off the server behind him in time for me to grab his head and twist it with a loud crack. As his body dropped I grabbed the phone and gun from the dying man's hands and rolled out of sight round the wall of servers as a bullet sparked off the wall next to me.

'Goddamn you, Byrne!'

I waited behind the cover of a server wall, listening for Carlton's next move. I didn't have to wait long. There was a scuffling sound.

'Get off, you fuck.' Martinez, weak but defiant.

Carlton now. 'I'll swap the phone for the girl.'

Crap. I stood against the server, thinking, thinking fast.

'Don't do it, Byrne. Run! Take the phone and run! I fucking mean it! Go! Run!'

'Will you shut up.'

A cry from Martinez. The cry of somebody who'd been struck.

I was struggling now. New York City versus the life of Martinez. Shit. Was this the time to compromise . . . ? There was never a time to compromise. I said something, anything, to buy myself some valuable seconds. 'How do I know you won't shoot me?'

'I promise not to.'

We both knew this conversation was about buying time, thinking time. I popped out the revolver's magazine and checked for bullets. 'How do I know you won't break your promise?'

'You don't. But I've got a gun at the base of her skull and I'm ready to bet her brains that you'll give me that phone.'

I slammed the magazine back into the gun with the palm of my hand. *Think, Byrne, Think.*

I looked at the Russian bomber's phone in my hand

then pulled out my own. In the reflection of a glass server rack door I could see the warped image of Carlton watching, waiting for me to reappear, to break cover. He wasn't looking at the reflection, was unsure about my next move, his head whipping from one aisle to another, twitchy. I looked back down at the dead man's phone and realized what I had to do.

'Tell you what, Byrne. I'll make it interesting. I'll count to three shall I. One, two . . .'

'OK.'

I stepped out, my gun pointing at Carlton. The deputy director stood almost completely screened by the injured Martinez, looking ever so carefully round her.

The detective, standing awkwardly from the grip on her hair, spat out the words. 'Shoot him, Byrne, don't mind me, fucking shoot the fucker.' So scared but so brave. They definitely broke the mould.

I aimed the gun at the slither of head revealed by Carlton.

'Do it, Byrne.' And then Martinez allowing a moan of pain to escape her, the day so hard. Then just as quickly using anger to control herself. Looking at me like all she wanted in the world was for me to kill the mother standing behind her, whatever the cost to her. Willing me to do it, urging me. Doing her damndest to make it easy for me, should I ever have to look back and recount the scene, account for my actions to others, to myself.

The deputy director laughed scornfully. 'Oh, I don't think he'll shoot, precious. It's not his gun, you see. He's not familiar with the weight, doesn't understand the flight of the bullets. There's too much doubt in his mind, look at him.'

Me not saying a word, refusing to let hate get hold of me, clouding my thinking. Holding the gun with two hands, my best aim on Carlton, but knowing Carlton had a point, a good point. It was a tough shot.

'Now give me the phone, Byrne. I'm going to back out of the room and you can have your little bird with her broken wing at the door. OK?'

Me not saying a word.

'The phone, Byrne.'

Still with the gun on Carlton, I put the phone on the floor and skidded it across to him. Carlton eyed the phone hungrily. Knowing that he was at his most vulnerable when he went down to it.

'OK, lady, gently does it . . . I want you to pass me the phone.'

Carlton lowered himself and carefully dragged Martinez down with him. She looked at me for my blessing. I gave a small nod in assent, in resignation. She felt for the phone and handed it back behind herself. Her captor took it off her.

'That's right. Now, get back up. Good girl.'

I kept the gun on him as best I could. Waiting for that fraction of a second, that uncovered moment.

Carlton examined the phone, looked through it then put it away, switching looks between myself and the task in hand.

I looked down the barrel of my gun, through the sight, at Carlton. Not enough there. Not enough target.

'Tell me, Carlton, is all this worth it?'

Carlton, getting out another phone, working his way through it. 'Is what worth it, Byrne?'

'The innocent lives lost, the fear you'll make people feel in their homes with this pointless attack?'

'One man's attack is another man's wake-up call. This is about waking up America, Byrne. This is about equipping the security services with the powers they need to deal with external threats. No more waiting like good little Puritans for the crazies of this world to attack us but getting in there first, every time, with our own attacks.'

Me edging my way round, microscopically, trying to find an angle. 'And what about the internal threats? Who protects them from people like you?'

Carlton looked up and smiled. 'Spare the rod and you spare the child, Byrne. This one bomb will save the people of the United States from countless bombs to come. We're talking about the greater good here.'

'So you found a greedy banker in Jeremiah Rankin to be your financial powerhouse then you found a gangster banker in Moffat Agron to be your thug for hire. And now all he has to do is blow up the New York Stock Exchange and Deputy Director George Carlton's plan is complete.'

Carlton thought about it with mock interest. 'You know, I couldn't have put it much better myself.'

Me almost with a shot now, Martinez almost safe. I held my own cellphone up in my free hand. 'Did you get that, Mr Secretary?'

Over my phone's speaker Treasury Secretary Peterson's voice came loud and clear. 'Every word of it. Carlton, on behalf of the United States government, you're fired.'

Carlton flinched. His face betraying the all-encompassing horror filling his mind, the sickening realization coursing through his body: that he was undone. Condemned with his own words, his own testimony. Raging at the implosion of his grand design he pointed his gun at me, me standing exposed. I dived behind another server as two bullets followed me from the deputy director's gun.

In the glass of a server door I could see Carlton looking wildly about, like he was seeking inspiration in the fixtures of the room. He smiled bitterly to himself, at the situation. And I saw an unmistakeable look of resignation.

'Fine, Byrne. Bravo. But, like I said, it's about the bigger picture. And if our lives are what it costs to make America wake up and start protecting itself then so be it.'

I had my back against the end of a server, trying to figure out Carlton's meaning when the deputy director spoke again.

'You see, Byrne, maybe it was the crappy Russian cellphone he was using . . .'

I could see Carlton hitting a button on his own device.

'. . . But our good old American phones both seem to have a perfectly good signal down here.'

My eyes stretched open in terror at the thought of what Carlton was about to do. I raced into action, no choice, no options left. As I tore round the corner Martinez fell limp, damning the consequences. Carlton ignored her and trained his gun on me, fully exposed now, me waiting for Martinez to clear, Carlton getting the first real chance, a clear shot, Martinez blocking my line of fire, Carlton's gun on me, the gun ringing out –

Not mine.

Martinez hitting the deck. Me watching Carlton hover. Teeter. Then fall away to one side, his phone dropping from his hand.

Then I saw her. Behind Carlton, Special Agent Diane Mason, standing, breathing heavily, lowering her gun. Stricken at what she had just done.

But that was an instant, a moment, then Martinez and I waited for nothing and dived for Carlton's phone, reaching it together, stabbing the red phone symbol in competition, me thumping it madly with my thumb. The call ended here – but out there? On the network? Were we too late?

All three of us waiting.

Waiting for the explosion.

The chaos and the terror and the death.

Would we feel it down here, hear it even, the servers with their rhythmic hum seeming to rise in volume as the seconds ticked by?

One

Two

Three

Four

The explosion that never came.

The realization coming slowly to all of us . . .

. . . that we had succeeded.

Me reaching over to Martinez, hugging her close, her wanting me, wanting my protection, wanting the agony to stop, sobbing into my chest, a lifetime of pain turned into tears. Then remembering herself, remembering her partner.

'Ashby. Ashby! Oh my god, Ashby . . . !'

52

I mounted the basement stairs two at a time and noticed blood every few steps. Rankin was bleeding bad. I sprinted through the lobby of the New York Stock Exchange, out through the front door, and made for the cordon at the top of Wall Street and Broadway. The same female Korean NYPD officer was standing with Officer Johansson.

'Rankin?'

'He went that way, sir.' Pointing down Rector Street, opposite. 'He was carrying a briefcase. I'm sorry, sir, I didn't know if Detective Ashby still wanted him tailed.'

But it didn't matter. I had a pretty good idea where he was going.

'Johansson, I need your bike.'

I pulled up two blocks from the NYSE. I had left the intensity of Wall Street and the presidential visit behind, which, like any visit from Potus, created a concentration of people about him and left the surrounding area typically quieter than usual. Right now there was nobody about. The streets as abandoned as

473

the skyscraper I sat outside. The building that was soon to be the new home of First Bank of America.

On the glass entrance to the building was the smear of a bloody red handprint.

He was here. Which meant the bomb was here.

My phone beeped. I pulled it out of my pocket and saw that a text message had arrived. I clicked on it and saw the name of Treasury Secretary Peterson.

I entered the immaculate but desolate lobby. Its arched ceiling was at least three floors high. As for the walls and floor, I hadn't seen so much marble since visiting a real Roman palace in Italy. Pride before a fall.

Apart from me the only other person was a security guard, seated behind a long, curving wooden, reception desk. He stood as I entered. Six foot six, overweight, handlebar moustache, his hand palm-out towards me with his best Don't Fuck With Me manner. He reminded me of a mildly reformed Hell's Angel. A mildly reformed Hell's Angel who'd been given strict instructions, which I could see he enjoyed enforcing.

He saw I was intent on walking straight in and skipped to the end of the reception desk to cut me off.

'Stop right there, sir. Nobody is allowed to enter here . . .'

He had puffed out his chest, a lifetime of being the biggest guy in the room giving him an uncompromising air. I didn't have the time or the inclination. I grabbed his hand, twisted it and slammed his head down onto the end of the desk. As he fell away I jabbed a nerve ending in the side of his neck, buying myself a good hour of peace from him. I left him where he lay bleeding on the pristine marble floor and made my way to the elevators.

One of the cars had just reached the forty-sixth floor of this forty-six-floor building. I had to figure that was my man and that was where he had gone. I pressed the button to call my ride. I felt something on my fingers. I looked at the tips which now had traces of blood on them. Rankin's? The security guard's? The Russians'? It was that kind of day.

I was riding up these floors for a second time, only this time I really had come armed. I readied my gun, an FN Five-seven given to me by Diane before leaving the NYSE. This was the second Service revolver I'd held in as many days. This was no time to walk in unarmed. *Hope for the best – plan for an assault with deadly weapon.*

I remembered the remark the now-dead compliance officer had made on the video-conference footage I had been shown in the police interview room three days earlier. The expensively fitted elevator really was like something out of *Star Trek*, decelerating exquisitely, with a satisfying *whoosh*, a sudden slowing that did nothing to unsettle the passenger. All dedicated to getting bankers from one floor to another without a hair out of place. I was in the wrong job.

I stood flat against the wall as the doors opened. A quick glimpse round the edge suggested nothing threatening. Just a reception area with a glass door beyond it, bloody where it had been pushed open, blood on the carpet leading up to it. I looked both ways and stepped out cautiously, gun before me. I checked my watch. 15.52. If anybody was going to trigger the bomb they would be doing it now. No time left.

I crossed the reception area and looked through the door, taking in the scene inside the room. At the far end of the room was a lone desk. On the desk I could see an open briefcase and what looked like a small stack of papers. Behind the desk, looking out of a window the size of the far wall itself, his back to me, was Rankin. I stood still, watching him, trying to figure out his next move, trying to figure out if he *had* a next move. He was motionless and I couldn't tell from here whether he was alive or dead.

The door opened silently and I stepped into the capacious room. The distance across the office was too far to attempt any kind of surprise dash so I was left with no choice but to move carefully across the carpet towards the seated figure at the other end. The evidence of the planned office relocation was all about. The occasional box was stacked against the wall. A long conference table with chairs – each piece of furniture in its own bubble wrapping – took up a space of its own. On the other side of the room sat a row of four double leather couches, yet to be arranged in another space of their own. The room was ridiculously large. Indefensibly large.

On a flat-screen television mounted on the wall near the desk, CNBC was on air, the sound off. An excited reporter was gesticulating outside the New York Federal Reserve, below her the strapline 'Markets Tumble On Chinese Concerns'. I was fully aware that Rankin would see my reflection in the window as I approached him and kept my gun trained on the back of his head.

Leaning against the wall near his desk was a frame containing – I assumed from its slightly worn condition – an original theatrical poster for the 1933 movie of *King Kong*. An illustration of the colossal gorilla standing atop the Empire State Building, Fay Wray in one hand, antiquated bi-plane in the other, other bi-planes rat-a-tat-tatting him as they flew by like wasps. Rankin was King Kong all right, right down to the bitter end.

I looked down at the open briefcase on the desk. It showed what I had feared – package after package of explosives with an improvised detonation device in the middle. Next to the briefcase was a small pile of documents.

I looked at his reflection in the window. I nodded at the open briefcase between us. 'Who's got the number to this?'

Rankin didn't turn to face me. He took his time in answering. 'I don't know. Carlton? Agron?'

Keeping the gun in one hand I used the other to take out my own phone. I placed it next to the detonator and tapped into one of the applications. On the screen of my phone a green bar moved left and right, the word 'Scanning' fading in and out above it. Not an application I believed you could buy at the online Apple App store, breaking, as it did, the Communications Act. Still, I figured the possible $11,000 fine and one year in prison was better than the alternative. The software was attempting to jam the cellphone's signals, seeking out the phone's frequency and, essentially, screaming it down. The bar on my smartphone stopped moving and turned red. Across the graphic the word 'Jammed' popped up. I breathed a bit easier. Hope for the best . . .

The First Bank CEO had not made any attempt to stop me. Now was a good time to get some answers.

'Why me, Rankin?' The bank CEO staring away from me, over Manhattan.

'Why anybody, Byrne?' The trace of a grim smile formed on his lips in the window. 'It was Carlton's idea. We needed somebody to draw fire and he came to me with your name a few years back. Told me to get a salesman to call your father. Talk him into a bad investment, anything to suck you in. We all knew Madoff was crooked – nobody pays those kinds of commissions if they're not. Remember those reports that whistle-blower guy was firing off? Mark something.' He made a noise that was somewhere between a snigger and a death rattle. 'Hell, I knew he was right – everybody on the Street knew he was right. So we called your father and put him into the Madoff fund. The rest was clockwork. Madoff blew up, your father, mother, whatever, they lost their money. Enter Michael Byrne, financial investigator. Pretty soon you were kicking up a stink and we figured enough people would believe you were motivated to hurt us. Carlton thought his ship had come in.' Again the wheezing chuckle. 'Christ that guy hates you.'

'Hated me,' I corrected.

It took a moment, then, 'Oh,' and he started to laugh, except that it turned into a cough instead. 'The Russians did a good job on that security footage, but a rather lousy job of kidnapping you, don't you think?'

I nodded as I thought about it. 'But why bother to kidnap me? Why not just get rid of me, be done with it?'

His mouth creased into a mean little smile. 'Carlton wanted your reputation destroyed. That's all he said. Seemed to me like the guy knew how to carry a grudge.'

I got it. He wanted people to believe that the man

who had publicly humiliated him all those years ago was anti-American, my fall from grace reflecting in his ascendency. Nice idea. Nice try.

Instinctively, I glanced around the room for any other assailants. 'I think you're insane, Rankin. Did you really think you could pull it off?'

He slowly swivelled round in his chair, unable to hide his grotesque smile, trails of blood wiped down his shirt.

'I did pull it off. Look where the markets are closing.'

He pointed a limp finger at a chart on the silent television screen. They had come off the 500 points he needed – 653 in fact – and there was one minute till close of business.

'After all we went through, some Chink at their central bank has said the Chinese government is divesting itself of a chunk of its US T-bonds. The markets are pissing themselves. And First Bank didn't even have to threaten to go into liquidation.' He looked at his watch weakly, coughed again. 'It's four p.m., Byrne – you know what that means.'

'All those options held by all those Bermudan SPVs have just settled in the money.'

'You're looking at a goddamn billionaire. And when my lawyers explain how Carlton coerced me into helping him I think it'll be business as usual.' The words were defiant but the bank CEO was sweating, struggling.

'What about Moffat Agron? How will you square that one?'

'The guy's got diplomatic immunity. They do things properly over there.'

I didn't disagree with him, but instead picked up my phone and went to my text messages. 'I got this from Peterson. It's private but I think he would have wanted you to hear it. "Byrne, told you a democracy couldn't do anything but thankfully China isn't one. They will be scaring the markets today – will retract later – but in meantime have agreed to buy FB" . . . That must be First Bank, right? . . . "agreed to buy FB this evening – for a dollar."'

Rankin took a moment to take it in, to grasp it. I watched the idea work its way through his mind like a marble dropping down through a child's clumsily constructed toy maze. He gasped, the full magnitude of Peterson's plan suddenly crystal clear to him. And in that one moment his world fell in like a house of cards and he began mouthing silently like a traumatized goldfish. 'But . . . but he can't do that.'

'Oh, I think history and the law will be on his side with this one.'

The bank CEO seemed cleft down the middle. He seemed destroyed. He couldn't get a handle on the carousel of thoughts running around in his mind.

'But our balance sheet, my stock . . .'

'Will be worth shit when the other banks dump your collateral on the market at the same time. There's fifty ways Peterson can engineer this and if he ever runs out of ideas I've got fifty other ways of doing it. After what you tried to do today I can't see the president hesitating for a second before signing any piece of legislation that forces the sale of First Bank.'

He began to understand the army of antagonists lined up against him, that he had been so focused on winning the battle that he had lost the war.

'Rankin, if we don't get you to a hospital, you're going to bleed to death.'

He looked up at me, an old man now, the colour gone from him. Working his mouth like it would create words for him. 'I . . . Not yet.'

The failed bomb-plotter wasn't going to get any argument from me. I watched him for a moment then figured I better get some answers whilst I could.

'Tell me about Omega Bank, Rankin. What was the plan with the Russians?'

I wasn't sure if he could see now, so remote was his stare, like he was gazing into a different dimension that I wasn't privy to. His eyes slowly came round to me. 'That was, that was – that would have been,' a funereal smile, 'Omega Bank would have been my greatest ever achievement. I was proud – oh, I *am* proud of that. You see Agron understood. That was vital, you understand. But he did, he *got* it. He totally got the sub-prime bubble. He understood how we set it all up. He understood all about the impossible mortgages. He understood how they were passed to us. He loved the way we sold them on to the municipal pension funds and the like. He knew, like us, that it was all going to blow up. And I sketched out my vision for him, my dream. The sub-prime bubble over here . . . ? It was a template, you see, it was the perfect template for any kind of bubble.' He smiled the kind of smile an arsonist smiles when he's admiring his work. 'But we couldn't do it here for a while, the United States had been burnt. Yes. Russia, though, oh, brave new world . . .'

The full scale of it crashed down on me like a six-foot wave. The animal. Fucking animal. 'You were going to reproduce the sub-prime bubble in the East, set them up the way you set the American people up?'

Rankin smiled, almost deliriously proud. 'Russia, China, South-East Asia. We were going to teach them to love risk.' He attempted to pick up the pile of papers on his desk. I looked down at them, the top sheet showing an engineer's drawing of a boat. 'I even gave Agron the bank's yacht into the bargain.' He laughed before coughing again.

'All so you could blow up their economies to make a quick buck.'

He smiled a secret smile to himself. He knew he didn't need to tell me that I was right. But I was still lost on one thing.

'And your role in this new sub-prime bubble was what?'

Rankin's smile broadened but he said nothing.

'What were you going to do? Buy all the repackaged mortgages off Omega Bank?' *Then I understood.* Son of a bitch. *Sons* of bitches. '. . . By the time it all came crashing down and First Bank's balance sheet imploded you'd be . . .'

His smile got wider still. '. . . Long gone.'

I shook my head, revolted, understanding him now, understanding the whole last ten years. 'It would be the next CEO's problem.'

He waved a tired hand at the room. 'That's why we get paid so much, Byrne, to clean up all these messes we keep inheriting.' He dry heaved a laugh that never came, his body not up to it.

'You're just a pedlar of Ponzis, Rankin. You're just a con man, a huckster.'

'Me? Why just me?'

'I wasn't just talking about you. I was talking about your type.'

Rankin laughed, coughed. Some bloody spittle appeared at his mouth. He dabbed a hand at it. The sight of it sobered him slightly. 'You know, Bernard Madoff went to Sing-Sing for his pyramid scheme, but when us banks got together and created a Ponzi the government bailed us out. He should have been a bank, Byrne. That's where the money is. Shit, the bigger our fuck-ups the more they give us.'

'Money without responsibility.'

The fading bank CEO smiled at me, revealing his teeth, red from blood. 'Sorry about your mother's Mad-off investment, Byrne.' He coughed, blood spattering the paperwork for the yacht. 'If you hadn't helped to ass-fuck First Bank I could have written you a cheque for the money.' He gesticulated at some imaginary cheque-book which perhaps, in his state, he really thought he could see.

'It's OK, Rankin, I made the money back shorting your stock.'

He gave me an enquiring look.

'Oh, I always short a bank when it starts killing its employees. It's a rule of mine.'

Rankin half coughed, half vomited blood over his hands.

'I will – I will have that doctor, after all.'

I closed the briefcase and collected the bloody paperwork for the yacht. I knew it was too late. 'Sorry, Rankin. Nobody's bailing you out this time.'

The phone rang.

He lifted his tired eyes towards me. 'What about you, Byrne?'

Me about to leave. 'What about me?'

'Why didn't you just head for the hills? Why did you hit back at us so hard? Why?'

It was chewing him up. Even as he was about to

cash out for good he wanted to know, was burning to know. I looked into his fading eyes and told him the simple truth. 'I wanted my mom's money back.'

His face clouded over, his brain turning over my reply at an ever-decreasing speed. The phone still ringing. 'I don't . . . understand.'

I nodded. 'I know.'

I looked at the ringing phone. Rankin couldn't have picked it up if he'd tried. I leaned over and hit the speakerphone. A young woman spoke. Zoe, his PA. Her voice faltering, a mixture of anger and uncertainty.

'Jerry?'

'Yeah.' His breath rattling in his throat now.

'I've been looking all over for you. Jerry?'

Rankin getting his breath first. 'Yeah . . . ?'

'Your personal banker called again. He said the value of the stock you lodged with his bank is so worthless that he's going to have to foreclose on your properties. All of them.'

The bank CEO's eyes tried to express something – surprise? mirth? – but failed, not physically up to the task.

'Jerry, is this going to affect my bonus? Are we even going to get a bonus? . . . Jerry? Jerry . . . ?'

Jeremiah Rankin silenced the phone with a weak finger which slid off onto the desk, the life force gone out of him. Ever so slowly the First Bank CEO eased back in his chair. The breaths slow now, difficult to come by. And with what seemed a great effort he turned his bloodshot eyes towards the poster of King Kong and breathed a long, last breath.

53

When I got to the North Cove Marina in the Battery City district of New York Diane was already there with a half dozen NYPD cars and the same number of black unmarked Secret Service vehicles. They had formed an impromptu car lot round one side of the water, effectively blocking off the berths along one edge. At the end was the 120-foot motorized yacht, *Eagle Rev.*

Special Agent Diane Mason, Captain Novak of the NYPD and a large number of law enforcement officers were assembled by the straggly line of parked cars. I eased my borrowed motorcycle to the side of the group where Diane and Captain Novak stood. She didn't give my lack of a crash helmet a second glance. I readjusted a brown leather satchel I'd thrown over my shoulder before leaving Rankin's office.

Diane looked up at me almost remorsefully. 'Agron's got diplomatic immunity. We can't touch him.'

I didn't speak but looked down towards the gangplank running up to the super-yacht. Standing beside it on the dock was Mr Bingo. Smoking a cigarette.

'Michael, we've served Agron with Undesirable

Alien papers. He's got to be gone by tomorrow. He won't be back.'

I looked from the Russian to her. I put a hand on the leather satchel. 'I've got something from Rankin. Something of Agron's.'

I gently pulled away on the bike and down the grass verge towards the docks.

'Michael . . . Michael . . . !'

As I started along the towpath of the marina Mr Bingo spotted me. His head twitched with curiosity, surprise almost. Then a nasty smile crawled across his face.

I approached nice and easy on the bike. As I did so he flicked the half-consumed cigarette over and out to the Hudson River. With something approaching the anticipation of pleasure he slowly peeled his jacket from his shoulders and let it slide off before dropping it at the foot of the boat's gangplank. With one hand he eased his tie off and added it to his jacket. I kept rolling forward. Then he did something that could only mean one thing. Business. He slipped off his shoes, put them next to his jacket and tie. Then, finally, pulled off his socks and tossed them into the shoes. He adopted the strong, centred pose of the Spetsnaz fighter. Judo, karate and wrestling all rolled into one. All coming my way.

I paused five yards from where he stood. I flicked a look in my wing mirror. The law enforcement officers had followed me down and formed a line behind me, stopping behind Diane Mason's outstretched arms.

I considered Mr Bingo. The bandage down the side of his face did not completely cover the burns from the day before, the skin around it lobster pink, smarting. Almost sensing that I was recollecting the scalding he'd received in the hotel, his face contorted into a nasty grimace. As I sat on the idling bike he proceeded to show me what I had coming, performing a series of deft, fluid, lighting-fast chops, punches, kicks low, kicks high, finishing with what would surely have been a deadly round-house. He landed low then commandingly rose up, filling his lungs with air through his nose. Then, with his leading hand, he twitched his fingers. Beckoning me into the fight.

So he wanted to tango. And there was me with a bad case of disco fever.

I cranked the motorcycle's throttle right back, causing it to fly out from under me. It reared into a wheelie, crashing its quarter ton of metal smack into Mr Bingo, carrying him with it over the edge and into the dock below. Job done.

I hitched my leather satchel up on my shoulder and headed for the gangplank.

Captain Novak stepped forward. 'Jesus, Byrne, don't do anything else. However unpalatable, we have a duty to protect him – and we will.'

'It's OK, officer.'

We all looked up. At the entrance to the yacht stood Moffat Agron and Nadia, Rankin's Russian girlfriend. Agron stood dressed in a blazer, a man who had made his money, cocooned from the criminality spreading out from under him like a slick from a damaged oil well. Rising above it all.

The Omega Bank CEO was a study in nonchalance. 'What is it you want, Mr Byrne?'

I looked at Nadia. Femme fatale or no femme fatale, she looked stunning in her light white dress. But she was also looking sheepish. And in that instant I understood how Rankin had been played by Agron's female agent. The fastest way to a banker's heart is through his ego. She was the honey trap that snared Rankin back at the beginning. By 'happy coincidence' she had known Agron. Introducing them. Nurturing their relationship. It all added up so nicely. It was clear to me how the Russian's tentacles had reached out and pulled Rankin in: Carlton and Agron playing the First Bank CEO all along. Nicely done, I had to admit.

I took a few slow measured steps up the gangplank. Twenty police guns came out of their holsters. I could almost feel them pointing at me, but I didn't look round. Just opened the leather satchel.

'Don't do anything, Michael.' Diane worried now.

But not as worried as Agron. Wondering what the

lunatic in front of him might be giving back to him. Wondering whether I just didn't give enough of a damn to take us all sky high. I tipped the bag over into the yacht.

Nadia gave a tiny yelp of terror, Agron's eyes did a poor job of hiding his own fear as the contents hit the deck.

Papers.

Messily dumped in a pile, blowing about the boat.

The Russian banker's relief was palpable.

I cast a hand over them. 'It's from Jeremiah Rankin, Mr Agron.'

The Russian waited, collecting himself, regrouping so that he could carry himself like a billionaire again. He waited for me to say more.

'It's the title deeds to this boat. His last act as CEO of First Bank of America. He wanted you to have them.' I shoved the empty satchel at him. 'And, by the way, congratulations. I see you're taking more than the boat home.' I looked from Agron to Nadia. The young woman decided she didn't want to see any more and stepped away, out of sight.

In his own time the Omega Bank CEO looked from the pile of papers to me. 'That's right, Mr Byrne. I'm taking home an understanding of your great banking system. I look forward to reproducing its success in my mother country.'

I looked slowly about the boat, taking my time, then back to him. 'Knock yourself out, Agron.'

'I intend to, Mr Byrne.'

Diane and I walked past the cars, marked and un-marked, into Pumphouse Park. The sun was setting over New Jersey, turning to burnt orange everything under its glow.

'Look, Diane, about the film of me shooting the four bank executives . . .'

'Oh, it's a fake.'

I stopped. Rooted to the spot. I hadn't expected her to say that.

'You knew?'

She was doing a poor job of suppressing her mild amusement. 'I always knew.'

'But . . . But you said Park had checked it, told you it was real, said it was "a keeper".'

'Oh, yeah . . . That. That was a lie.'

'You *lied* to me? Why would you do that?'

Her amusement giving way to a worried frown, apologetic. 'Because I was in a bind, Michael, and I fig-ured you were the only person who could help me.'

'You weren't in a bind – *I* was in a bind.'

'Before all this, I knew Carlton was planning some kind of move.'

'Why didn't you report him?'

'Carlton? He was totally wired in. An internal investigation into him? He would have walked away from any schemes and we most probably would never have caught him. I'd been trying to get close to him for months, but was getting nowhere. But if anybody could get to the bottom of this it was you, Michael.'

'Why not just come out and say it? I'd have helped you – why play me?'

'Because it was the only way I could get you to come back to work for me at the Service.'

'Come back? Now hang on, Diane . . .'

'Head of the Markets Abuse Taskforce.' Saying it like it was a done deal.

'I didn't say I was coming back.'

She waited but I didn't say more.

'OK, Michael, if that's what you want. You get back to your desk at W. P. Johnson.' She patted my arm. 'But you be careful with those pencils. You sharpen one of those too much, hell, you could have an eye out.'

She held her hand out. I glanced down at it then up at her.

'What?'

'The gun I lent you.'

I reached round my back, pulled it from my pants and gave it to her. Maybe more reluctantly than I would have liked to have admitted to myself and certainly to her.

I stood wondering if there was much more to say.

Then she did something that told me there wasn't. She pulled a new gun out of her holster. Only it was more than a new gun, and it was more than just standard issue. She held it out by the barrel, inviting me to take it. I didn't need any persuading. Feeling that shape and weight in my hands. Believing I would know it in the dark. Because that's how you feel about your old service revolver. Thinking it felt . . . just right.

I studied the gun, turning it over in my hand, turning the memories over in my mind.

'Do I still get to be . . . proactive?'

She raised an eyebrow, saying it like she might regret it: 'As proactive as you need to be. No more.'

I looked at my old gun for the longest time then slowly made to give it back – to her genuine surprise.

'Michael?'

'Diane, I worked for Treasury. The whole reorganization, working for the Department of Homeland Security, it's not me.'

But she didn't take the gun, just smiled. It was my turn to ask the question.

'What?'

'I didn't say you'd be working for the DHS. The Markets Abuse Task Force is a Treasury department with Secret Service protocols. You'll be answering to me and Peterson and nobody else.'

'Peterson?'

We stood staring at each other. I was out of objections

and she knew it. She didn't ask for the gun back, but just turned, began to walk off through the trees.

When she was halfway across the park I called after her. 'Do I get to shoot bankers?'

'Only the bad ones.' Not looking back.

I spoke to myself. 'Better get me an Uzi . . .'

'I heard that.'

54

An attractive African American nurse opened the window of the private room at the New York Downtown Hospital. From my visitor's chair I watched her move about the room in that ergonomic way medical staff do, the minimum of fuss. She gave me a warm smile that might have crossed the professional threshold and I was watching her leave the room when my panning gaze landed upon Detective Jenni Martinez.

She stood in the doorway wearing her arm in a sling and an accusing expression on her face.

'Get a good look?'

My face broke into a smile. 'I was just thinking how much she reminded me of you.'

She did not reciprocate. 'Yeah, or something like that.'

'Martinez, if you need a witness I saw everything.'

It was Detective Ashby, propped up in bed by a mountain of pillows, no shortage of tubes feeding in and out of him. Martinez went to his bedside and they swapped a gentle version of their war-buddy greeting.

'Don't worry' – she threw me a half-dirty look – 'he's the one who's going to wish he had witnesses when I'm finished with him.'

Ashby considered us both. 'Well?'

Martinez was baffled. 'Well what?'

'Well, who gets to arrest Byrne?'

Martinez was amazed it needed discussing. 'I had to put up with his shit for *three* days.'

Incredulity from Ashby. 'I got shot in the gut because David Copperfield here suddenly forgot his party trick.'

I raised my hands, the peace maker. 'Look, don't I get one phone call?'

Ashby was feeling magnanimous. 'Who you calling, your stockbroker again?'

'On a Saturday?' I shook my head, as if disappointed by his schoolboy error, and dialled a number. 'I'm calling Boom.'

They shared a confused look. I showed them the phone's screen. It showed the message 'Dialling Boom'.

They were even more perplexed by that.

'Boom?'

'Boom?'

Eagle Rev was cruising out of New York harbour. Behind it Manhattan rose up into the bright blue sky. To one side the Statue of Liberty held her torch aloft, its message of hope and welcome forever irrelevant to the passengers of the departing yacht.

On a rear sundeck Moffat Agron and Nadia sat on

plush outdoor loungers. They were sharing a midday cocktail, both dressed light and luxuriously, like they were about to head off to an English summer garden party.

A phone rang, breaking into the cut-glass comfort of the moment. It persisted.

Agron waved a hand. 'Do get that, Nadia.'

She dismissed his suggestion with a shake of the head. 'It's not mine, and your phone's switched off in our cabin.'

Agron looked about himself. 'Then where is it coming . . . ?'

His gaze fell upon something under one of the benches running along the side of the deck. A black briefcase. His eyes exploded open just before the boat did.

The yacht tore apart in every direction, flames carrying wood and metal and plastic out every which way. A plume of black smoke rose into the air as the sonic boom of the explosives bounced off every shore before the debris of the boat floated down all around where it had sat just one moment before.

In the private hospital room all three of us looked out of the window at the explosion that had just made itself heard throughout three boroughs. We watched the plume of smoke rise out above the buildings and disappear into the sky above.

I looked at my phone and then their What The Hell? faces. I shrugged. 'Damn . . . the line's dead.'

Martinez went to speak but was beaten to it by my phone ringing.

I looked down, surprised to see the gold, five-pointed star of the United States Secret Service flashing at me. Special Agent Mason's number. I took the call.

'Diane?'

'Nice fireworks, Byrne. Now get to JFK. We're on the next flight to Columbia.'

I went to acknowledge her request but she had one last thing to say.

'Oh, and, Byrne?'

'Yeah?'

'Bring your gun.'

I caught my reflection in my phone, in the gold star. She was gone.

And I was back.

Acknowledgements

Firstly, the readers: Alistair R. for being the first and the most surprised. Barney M. for being my target. Susannah M. for being critical. Emma R. for doing her job of liking it. And, most importantly, The Reader . . . you're the point.

My agent, Jonathan Lloyd at Curtis Brown, for being upstanding and outstanding.

Team MJ: Alex C. for his syncopated, phlegmatic style. Nick L. for his detail and monk-like patience. And Sam M. for her eagle eye and manner.

Richard W. for telling me what I should have already known.

Regulators, for following the elephants down the street with their shovels.

Bankers, without whose tireless efforts to find new ways of making money for themselves the events of this novel would not have been possible.

And, finally, taxpayers for bailing out the banks without any strings attached. You shouldn't have. No, really, you shouldn't have.